The
Cobra
Conspiracy

iUniverse, Inc.
New York   Bloomington

The Cobra Conspiracy

iUniverse books may be ordered through booksellers or by contacting:

iUniverse
1663 Liberty Drive
Bloomington, IN 47403
www.iuniverse.com
1-800-Authors (1-800-288-4677)

ISBN: 978-1-4401-6280-0 (pbk)
ISBN: 978-1-4401-6279-4 (ebk)

Printed in the United States of America

iUniverse rev. date: 8/26/2009

The
Cobra
Conspiracy

by

Roger A. Naylor

Other Titles by Roger A. Naylor

A PAPER STATUE – Historical Fiction: WW II – Air war over New Guinea

BLACK ROCK BAY – A northwoods terrorist thriller

CALIFORNIA TRIVIA – (with Lucy Poshek) – Trivia about the Golden State

For more information about the author and his books, including sample chapters, visit www.rogeranaylor.com.

Dedication

To the noble minority—those government, business, and social leaders who factor morality into their decisions.

Epigraph

After a momentary silence spake
Some Vessel of a more ungainly make:
"They sneer at me for leaning all awry:
What! Did the Hand then of the Potter shake?"

The Rubaiyat of Omar Khayyam, LXXXVI

Acknowledgements

A creator of fiction works like a funnel, a device to collect life's experiences, focus them, and direct them to a conclusion that is meaningful to the reader. On this project, one who fed valuable contributions through this aperture was son-in-law Dick Roche, a long-time chief engineer on supertankers. Dick introduced me to incinerator ships and arranged for Jeanne and me to spend time aboard *Apollo I,* the first of the phenomenal pair of ships referred to in the story. As always I am grateful to my Jeanne, the indispensable fountain of encouragement and ever reliable proofer who finds those things my tired, old eyes miss. And, of course, every writer needs those faithful readers who propel him onward!

Prologue

He flew face down, arms outstretched, with that eerie feeling of weight-lessness. He knew he ought to fall. Men can't fly.

Beneath him stretched an endless, black void. He tried to climb up away from it, but he couldn't. He tried to turn left, then right—no success. He twisted his body to one side, then the other, but the threatening blackness was everywhere. A terrible world, one nobody should ever see. The balloon of panic swelled in his belly. Miraculously, he was still flying, but what was the point? No buildings, no meadows, rivers, or mountains, and no *people.* If he flew forever it might still be like this.

He could taste the blackness—*taste* it. He ran his tongue over its coarse surface. It tasted like blood. No, more like asphalt—like asphalt and blood. He withdrew his tongue, then tried again. The same. Bitter asphalt and blood.

From somewhere out in the blackness he heard sounds, sounds like voices, but there were no words. He looked for the people but saw only the blackness. The voices grew louder.

"-kay, urn -im ove- gent- -ow."

Strong hands grasped his flying body, slowing him. He was turn-ing, slowing and turning. And then, he crashed. It was not a hard crash, but he knew he was no longer flying. The thrill of suspension was gone, and something cold and hard pressed rigidly, unforgiving against his back. The black faded to dark gray. Have my eyes shut? he wondered. Open—got to open!

The darkness remained, but the voices grew louder, more distinct. He felt hands touching and probing about his body, some gentle, some firm, some almost rough. Something had a tight grip on his leg, his left one, squeezing, tightening, as though to pinch it off. He kicked at the enemy with his other leg.

"Hey, man! Stop that!" a deep voice thundered. "He's coming around—almost got me."

"Vitals look good," a female voice said. "Got that bleeding stopped?"

1

"Okay here, Angie. If he doesn't kick my teeth out."

Who are they? What are they doing to me? he asked himself. Got to open eyes. Got to—

A bright star appeared close to one eye, the left. It hovered, moved about briefly, then flew off into outer space. Suddenly it glowed again before his other eye, hovered, moved about, and just as abruptly disappeared again.

"We're paramedics," the female voice said close to his face.

What is that? he wondered. That nice voice smells of garlic?

"You've had a bad time of it," came the voice again, but you're going to make it. What's your name, mister? Your name?"

"Buck. You—"

"A little louder, mister? Your name?"

"Buck. You—"

"What'd he say, Angie?"

"He said, 'Fuck you.' Nice guy, huh?"

"I guess, if I took the kind of beating this dude took, that's probably what I'd say, too," the man's voice replied.

What? What'd he say? Got to open. Open!

"Hisa name'sa Buck," came another voice. "He's a customer. Name'sa Buck."

That voice, that's—I know that voice, he thought. That's—that's Dante! Help me, Dante!

"You know him, Dante?" the garlic voice said. "What's his last name?"

"I dunno. Don'ta really know him. Justa Buck."

Dante! You know me, damn it. Help me, Dante! He screamed, but nobody seemed to hear him. The dark gray began to slip back into blackness. His body felt light. Oh, no, he thought—not again!

* * *

Time had simply vanished, totally lost, until he felt one arm being moved. He waited, expecting the other to follow suit. It didn't. Why not? he wondered. His head—it hurt, hurt badly, like someone was pushing a red hot spike into the back of his skull. Why? With a determined effort, he finally willed his eyes to open, only to be blinded by vicious white light. Blinking rapidly, he tried to adjust. A pretty Filipino nurse gradually came into focus. Holding his arm and checking his pulse, she smiled at him, her dark eyes flashing.

"Good morning, Mr. Barnum," she said. "Welcome back. You have headache?"

"No damn words," Buck said, "—describe—headache I have. Who you?"

"Very good sign, Mr. Barnum."

"What—worst damned headache of my life?"

"No, 'course not. But it good you so alert, able speak so good. Very good sign, Mr. Barnum."

"Very good sign, very good sign. What about my headache?"

"My, you spunky, too. Dr. Norman be in—check you. Then you probably get something for pain."

"What day is it? What time is it? How long have I been here? What—"

"What happened you?" She finished her count, gave his hand a squeeze, and stepped back. "Thursday, seven o'clock in morning. You brought in Long Beach Memorial 'bout eight last night. You 'member what happened?"

"I—" Buck paused. His attempt to trace events backward hit a wall. He tried to reach back for something he remembered, anything to grab onto, but it was all a jumble.

"Don't worry much. It come back to you," the nurse said.

"What's—wrong with me?"

"Have serious concussion, bruised ribs, and stab wound in calf of left leg, about four inch long, but not too deep." She laughed, a warm, friendly laugh. "How you do that, Mr. Barnum? We get stab wounds alla time, but in leg? How you do that?"

That explains the pain down there, Buck thought, but it's nothing compared to this headache. "Don't know how I do that," he snapped. "Anyone know I'm here?"

"Oh, yes. A young man, and a beautiful, young lady waiting down the hall. Your son and daughter?"

"Son and daughter?" Slowly, a vision of Bob and Sunny filtered through the pounding in his head. "Oh, oh, he groaned, "uh, do me favor?"

"If I can," she replied.

"Don't tell them I'm—yet. Need time to—head straightened out. Okay?"

"Hokay," she echoed, starting for the door. "I tell them you not wake up, need little more time. Oh," she stopped in the doorway, "a Detective Bercovich wants us call. Wants see you—soon as possible."

The name, Detective Bercovich, roared out of his muddled memory like a rocket.

"Tell you what," he said, "don't call 'til kids leave? I—uh—don't want family upset—the police around."

"Hokay," came the chipper answer. The door closed behind her.

Detective Bercovich, Buck thought. Yeah, seems like I *really* need to see Detective Bercovich. But right now, I need to fight my way past this pain. Got to think. Got to remember who did this. Think—think! He clenched his fists, tightened every muscle in his body, and put all of the strength he had into the effort. Somehow, he managed to relegate the pain to a secondary level, but nothing came to him. After several minutes of the fruitless struggle, he was exhausted. He sighed and momentarily gave it up. Then something within him demanded yet another effort.

"Damn," he muttered. "What did I *do?* How did I *get* here?"

Still, the questions found no answers, and the effort pulled him steadily down until fatigue took over. Closing his eyes, he felt himself drifting again. But this time he drifted quickly through the blackness into a scene so clear, so vivid, it startled him. He saw himself seated in an office waiting room, seated next to a fat lady. The luxurious office decor impressed him because he was there for a job interview. A place this nice, it would be a good place to work.

Chapter 1

"Ms. Barnum?" She paused, then turned a cold, mechanical smile toward the fat lady next to him and repeated, "Ms. Beverly Barnum?"

"I—think you must mean me," he said, rising from his chair and turning on a smile he hoped was more genuine than hers. "The name is Buck, B-U-C-K, Buck Barnum."

In that moment the suppressed anger toward his mother flared again. Damn it, he thought. After forty-one years I *still* get upset by this? He strode toward the woman with his stomach in, chest out, and shoulders as broad as he could make them. His teeth were clenched behind the frozen smile.

The sour-faced secretary appeared to be in her late fifties. She peered over her half-moon glasses with a penetration that did nothing to ease his anger.

"I'm sorry, Mr. Barnum," she said coldly. "*I*—am Ms. Erichs. This way. Mr. Roland will see you now."

As Buck followed the prim figure down the hallway, he struggled to recover from the shaky start. You need this job, he thought. Don't blow it, Buck. But this old biddy?

He smoothed his freshly trimmed, brown hair as he walked, his fingertips feeling the streaks of gray. "Distinguished," it had been called, but the word meant something else to him. They approached a glass hallway divider. A sturdy, almost handsome six-footer in a subdued charcoal plaid suit mirrored his every step. "Some dude, Dad," he could hear his daughter Sunny saying. The thought turned the encroaching lines around his eyes and mouth into a slight smile.

They passed an office on the left, apparently Ms. Erichs's domain. The name-plates on the open door indicated that somewhere behind her desk were the offices of Charles H. Hudson, CEO, and Garland Grigsby, CFO. Just beyond the suite, they passed through another hallway door. Buck felt as if he had been beamed to an underworld, for where there had been the plush, red carpet, he saw worn and chipped gray tiles. And where there had been freshly painted white walls with frequent hangings, there were now faded, smudged beige walls with nothing to break the planes but the doors up ahead. With but a few more clicks of Ms. Erichs's sharp heels on the hard surface, Buck followed her into an office marked: EDWARD ROLAND – V.P. ENVIRONMENTAL CONCERNS.

"Mr. Roland, this is Beverly—*Buck* Barnum." With an icy glance at Buck, she brushed past him and was gone.

"Well, Buck Barnum! How are you?" The figure bolted from behind the desk and vigorously shook Buck's hand. He was, perhaps, a few years younger and several inches shorter than Buck. His pastel blue shirt was open at the neck, and his tie hung loosely. While he appeared to be rather soft, he was quite trim. His reddish complexion was topped by strawberry blond hair, neatly parted in the middle, and the combination of his warm, blue eyes and radiant smile provided a startling contrast with Buck's guide of seconds before. "Did you have any trouble finding us?"

"No, a piece of cake, almost."

Buck felt the coat of ice he had worn down the hallway begin to melt. He sank deeply into the chair that was offered, and then, remembering the articles he had read on interview techniques, he lurched to an upright posture. Nearly twenty years since I've interviewed for a job, he thought.

Roland chattered on about the warm, dry weather and the dust from nearby construction.

"I feel like I already know you, Buck. Your good friend Peter speaks very highly of you, and I have nothing but confidence in Peter's judgment. Glad you're interested in the job. How much do you know about it?"

"Well," Buck stalled. Should he relax and follow Roland's lead, or should he stick to his outline? Would Roland use those trap questions? "As I understand it, you're looking for a P.R. man for this new project involving sea-going incinerator ships. My investigative experience, the years of newspaper work, and my freelance writing should qualify me quite well." The statement slid forth as he had rehearsed it. Good start, he thought.

"Are you up on the hazardous waste threat our country faces?"

"I, ahh, I know we have a problem, but to be honest with you, I'm anything but an expert on the matter. I'm good on research, though, and in no time I'll *be* an expert." He tried for a modest smile as he said it.

"Ho-Ho-o-o! I like that! Just what Peter predicted. Tell you what. Here," he paused, handing Buck a glossy red, white, and blue folder that was stuffed with a packet of papers. "Materials on our project that you can take with you. In fact, I'll have a ton of reading for you."

Buck caught the positive implication, but the cautious part of him resisted assumptions. He studied the cover, a very professional job. In the upper left corner was a logo done in black letters: SEA-GOING INCINERATION, INC., a Subsidiary of Southern California Boatbuilding Company. Centered on a sea of blue was an artist's rendition of a ship that was strange and yet beautiful. In the lower right corner was a table:

ARK II

Overall length - 381 feet
Beam - 62 feet
Gross tonnage - 4,940 tons
Liquid cargo capacity - 1.33 million gallons
Number of cargo tanks - 12
Sustained sea speed - 15.5 knots
Range/full load - 6,670 nautical miles

The name, Buck thought, interesting choice. Noah saved us with the *Ark*. Now they'll do it again with *Ark II?*

The ship appeared from the side view to be quite large. Its brilliant white hull rose from the black water line to a red main deck. Near the bow was an immense, white superstructure that rose five levels upward, topped by what was obviously the bridge. Projecting upward from the bridge stood an antennae cluster including various heights and shapes.

Two enclosed lifeboats hung from stanchions on the boat deck, just aft of the superstructure. Their small windows gave them the appearance of miniature houseboats. The low main deck that swept aft for a full two-thirds of the ship's length was all but covered by a red maze of large pipes and steel framework. A white, railed catwalk was centered above the network of pipes, and it threaded its way the length of the main deck from the front superstructure toward the stern.

"Wow!" Buck exclaimed. "An incredible piece of engineering, isn't it?" Pointing to the other raised structure near the stern, he asked, "And I suppose this part, with the two huge stacks is the incinerator section?"

"Uh huh! That's the meat and potatoes."

"And you're going to *build* this thing?"

"It's already built. Tied to the dock right out there," Ed replied, motioning back over his shoulder. "Been through her sea trials already and passed with flying colors. Right now, we're making some crew changes and minor adjustments while we wait for the Environmental Protection Agency's approval to take her out on the all-important test burn."

Buck scanned the picture again. She was surprisingly streamlined, considering the towering superstructures fore and aft and the gaping void between. A unique vessel, unlike any he had ever seen. He looked up to catch Ed Roland studying him intently.

"I'm not quite sure how I—I'd fit into all this," Buck said, thumbing through the papers. "It seems that someone has already done the necessary writing."

"Would seem so, wouldn't it? Let me explain our roles. Your friend, Peter Hamlin, is the Project Manager. He's in charge of the whole show. He reports to C.H., that's Hudson. And me? I'm the Vice President for Environmental Concerns, and I report to Peter."

Buck raised one eyebrow. He didn't mean to—an old habit.

"You're confused by our chain of command?" Roland asked, the grin returning to his face. "I came into Essee Beecee two years ago. My background is chemical engineering with some commercial communications experience. I'm the guy who writes all that stuff, does the press releases, the presentations for the bigheads from Washington, and runs around speaking to citizens' groups. So far, I've done a pretty good job. The title? They just tacked the V.P. on. More credence, more pizzazz."

"And if you were just the P.R. man, your audiences would tend to say, 'Just more B.S.?'"

"You've got it! Of course, when we get into the chemicals involved, I *am* the expert, and when our adversaries begin to spout their home-brew wisdom on the subject, I'm the guy who throws water on their acid," Roland said, grinning and thumping the desk with a fist.

I like him, Buck thought, but there's something— "Mr. Roland?"

"Ed."

"Ed, I don't quite understand. With your expertise in chemistry and your communications skills, where would *I* fit in?"

"Good point, Buck, good. Say, would you like a cup of terrible coffee?"

"Is there any other kind? Sure, I'd like that—black, please."

"Oh, it'll be black all right. Back in a second," Roland said as he popped from his chair and left the room.

Buck took the moment to scan the room, aware that Ed Roland's magnetism, along with his own apprehension, had kept his focus to the front the whole time. The small office was not simply drab. It was dingy. From the ceiling that had probably once been white dangled a four-foot, hooded, fluorescent light, similar to the one he had mounted over the workbench in his garage. The dirty walls were partially hidden by old chemistry structure charts and tables, yellowed press releases, and a myriad of printed materials, all carelessly mounted with thumbtacks or tape. The old metal desk was light gray, and the scarred linoleum top had been covered with a sheet of plate glass. Only the personal computer and the hinged pair of gold-framed photographs on Roland's desk suggested that the occupant was indeed of the twenty-first century. Buck was resisting the urge to turn the photos, to learn who was most important to this man, when he sensed the movement at the door.

"Here we are," Roland said, slipping behind his desk and carelessly plopping Buck's chipped mug on the glass desk top before him. "Good luck! Now, back to Essee Beecee and you."

"Excuse me, Ed. Essee Beecee?"

"Oh, I'm sorry! It's S - C - B - C, Southern California Boat-building Company, Essee Beecee," Roland laughed. "Now, the situation here. You're right. It *would* seem that the writing must be about done. The submissions to the Washington agencies, the specs, marketing materials, and press releases are just about all wrapped up. The ship is nearly ready. We're entering the final phase now. We're working on getting final approvals for the test burn site at sea and the temporary cargo loading station out there on the vacant lot. Then there's the construction of our permanent terminal on the East Coast, and we're in business—a very necessary and lucrative business. You know, Buck, we're doing a very good thing here, a *tremendous* thing! Our stock doubled in nine months, got up into the high thirties."

"That's impressive."

"But our incineration program means much more than mere profits. Did you realize that nearly every firm that manufactures or alters the structure or shape of a product generates hazardous wastes, often toxic chemicals? Most of these wastes are being released into surface waters or buried in the ground where they will inevitably get into the water tables. Incineration is the answer, and sea-going incineration is far cheaper and safer than land-based incineration! I can't begin to fully describe the situation in the time we have, but I'll put you onto the necessary books and printed matter to educate you."

"I read about Love Canal and Times Beach." Buck noticed that, while Roland's eyes continued to sparkle, the smile was gone. The pace had quickened.

"Just the tip, Buck, the tip of an underground iceberg so large— it's terrifying! And nearly seventy percent of our industrial hazardous wastes is being disposed in unsafe and often illegal ways."

"It sounds like we've created a monster!"

"Exactly. Right on. And it's everywhere, all over the country—the world! You know, this was a serious problem all the way back to the industrial revolution, only we didn't know it. And now we're into the twenty-first century and we've begun to acknowledge the situation for what it is. But really, things haven't improved very much at all. We have a long way to go.

"Buck, at this stage, I need help. I'm spending much of my time in meetings, meetings in Washington to keep things moving there, and local meetings to try to educate people who don't understand sea-going incineration. Peter and I need someone working with us so that, when we're tied up or gone, there's still someone to handle the unforeseen, ahh, things that come up. What do you think, Buck? Interested?"

Buck hesitated as long as he dared. "Well, yes. Yes, I am." He could see Roland's eyes watching him over the rim of the coffee mug. The mug came down, and there was the broad grin back again.

"Good—good!"

Buck was uncomfortable with his own answer. He still wasn't sure what the job was, but he had to keep it alive until the blanks were filled in.

"I think you'll do well with us, Buck," Roland continued. "We need your communications skills, and we *really* need your determination. His expression suddenly turned serious, almost grave, and it unnerved Buck. "And we'll work well together!" Just as suddenly, the infectious grin was back.

"What's next?" Buck asked.

Roland looked at his watch and sat forward in his chair. "Damn! The time! I lost all track." The serious face returned. The end was coming. "Tell you what. I know nothing about the money thing, but your old friend Peter tells me he knows what it will take to get you aboard. That's between you two. We'll cram a worktable and a computer into the office here. After a week of study, you'll probably be on the ship for a while."

"That sounds interest—"

"Here," Ed Roland tossed three books across the desk, "here's some reading to get you started." Roland was out of his chair, extending a hand across the desk, pronouncing the end of the interview.

Buck thanked Roland and shook the hand firmly. He bundled up the reading materials, stepped into the stark hallway, and headed up front. When he reached the dividing line, he marveled again at the abrupt change in decor. From the old to the new? From the unimportant to the important? Or was it a change from the real heart of this creature called Essee Beecee, the part that makes it all happen, to a mask painted on a head that was disproportionately large? He wondered about the two men, Hudson and Grigsby, who were so safely, luxuriously sequestered behind Ms. Erichs.

He walked briskly to his little red pickup, climbed in, and tossed the folder and books onto the right-side bucket seat. As he stopped at the front gate and waited for the portly guard, he glanced back over his shoulder. The curving, blacktop drive cut through the heart of the immense vacant lot back to the drab office building. Not a tree, shrub, or blade of grass in sight. Behind the office building, he could see two large, gray corrugated metal structures that extended perhaps a hundred yards to the left and right. A line of cars, pickups, and motorcycles sat nuzzled against them like nursing animals.

Buck surrendered the plastic VISITOR badge.

"Thank *you!*" the stubby, little guard said, pushing his glasses up with his bird finger. Buck wondered how the pompous security man would do in a crisis. He reminded Buck of Jackie Gleason's sheriff in the Smokey movies.

Pausing at the stop sign, he collected his bearings in order to retrace his route out of the drab neighborhood, with its clusters of the familiar grasshopper-like oil wells, and back to Ocean Boulevard. He made his way up the high Vincent Thomas suspension bridge over the main north-south channel of the Los Angeles Harbor. Soon he was turning past the Los Angeles Maritime Museum into the Ports O' Call Village area of San Pedro.

Buck had always been fascinated by the quaint strip of tourist shops and its winding brick walks, its shrubs and trees. The Village was constructed to resemble an old New England seaport, and the buildings ranged from rusty, corrugated sheet metal to Cape Cods with weathered shingles and white trim. Unfortunately, many were vacant. At the Rum Barrel, he found a seat at an outside table on a redwood deck overlooking the main channel.

"Ah, thank you, dear," he said to the attractive and pleasant blonde who set the large Margarita before him. Friday—Margarita day. For a number of years it had been a ritual for Buck and Roberta to eat at Juan Jose's, their favorite Mexican restaurant, and the event included one or two Margaritas before dinner. The memory dulled the pleasant edge of Buck's mood.

"Guess I might as well join you, since we're both waiting for people," a voice said.

"Huh?" Buck looked up into smiling eyes that were set in an older, pockmarked face behind a handlebar mustache.

Without invitation, the intruder with the shiny, clean-shaven head slid gracefully into the chair opposite Buck. His white T-shirt revealed a weightlifter's frame that was but half the age of his face. He plunked an orange-colored drink on the table.

"Rob McNair," the stranger said, extending an enormous right hand. The corners of his mustache curled upward when he grinned. "And you are?"

"Buck Barnum," he replied, somewhat surprised at the polite firmness of the man's grip. "Glad to have you aboard."

"Oh, a tourist, eh?" McNair laughed.

"No, not a tourist," Buck countered. "As a matter of fact, I work for a shipyard over there," he motioned. "What made you think—"

"Your clothes, the way you stare at all the passing boats, and your welcoming me aboard," McNair said, laughing again.

Buck was fascinated by the personable man with the awesome physique. Their conversation drifted along quite naturally, and Buck quickly learned that McNair was an engineer from the *Kimberly Canyon,* a large supertanker that was presently unloading Alaskan crude oil on the opposite side of the peninsula. Buck explained that his own project was the new incinerator ship, *Ark II.*

"Sure, everybody's heard about the burner," McNair said. "She's a helluva piece of engineering—got the latest of everything. Kind of too bad, though. . . ."

"What do you mean, too bad?"

"Well, let's put it this way. If I had millions to gamble, I'd be on the first plane to Vegas. Better odds. Oh, there's my friend. Nice to meet you, Buck. Maybe I'll see you around."

With that, McNair sprang to his feet, shook Buck's hand, swept up his glass of carrot juice in the other massive paw, and swaggered across the deck to another table.

Chapter 2

While ships and boats of all sizes plied the channel past The Rum Barrel, new arrivals filed noisily into the bar. But Buck's mind was elsewhere. A part of him wanted to jump up on the table and shout, "I've got a job! Buck Barnum's got a *real* job!" But his body felt heavy on the chair. Just what *is* this job, he wondered? No doubt about it, good old Peter had greased him into this thing, but into *what*?

A burst of laughter nearby interrupted his thoughts. Happy hour was underway. The Rum Barrel had somehow filled with people who seemed determined to exorcise the demons of the workweek and lubricate the gears of weekend relaxation before hitting the packed freeways for home.

Peter, ol' bud, Peter. Over two decades had passed since he and Peter became good friends. Peter, the brilliant quarterback, and Buck, the linebacker, the defensive leader who covered any lack of finesse with hard-hitting aggressiveness. At Bartholomew College, they had discovered the chemistry among opposites that sometimes develops from mutual respect. Some friendships couldn't survive the stresses of a workplace relationship, but Buck knew this one could.

Even though Buck and Roberta were already married and had little Bob and Sunny while at college, Peter had remained close, often spending an evening with them playing Scrabble, cards, or even Monopoly. And when Buck had been tempted to join Peter and the lively crowd of singles, it was his friend who had said, "Get your butt home where it belongs before I kick it."

Buck got up and stretched. He edged his way through the crowd and located the peanut barrel in a far corner. Taking the last basket from the shelf, he scooped it full and started for his table. Neat idea, he thought as he crunched his way through the layer of peanut shells that covered the floor. Wonder who thought of it? Back at the table, he tossed the first two peanuts into his mouth and recklessly flipped the shells to the floor, amused at the don't-give-a-damn feeling that the trivial, wanton act inspired.

"What are you, some kind of pig?" A hand gripped his shoulder. He knew the voice and the grip.

"Damn! If it isn't Peter Jennings Hamlin! You're going to be late for the network news," he quipped as his old friend slipped into the chair across from him. The tall man, meticulously dressed in a blue pin-striped suit, his slender, handsome face framed by neatly combed black hair, would always remind Buck of the famous news anchorman.

"How are you doing?" Peter asked. "Get along all right with Roland?"

"Nice guy, really nice guy. I like him."

"What's your feeling about the job? You going to take it? Or are you going through life disguised as a freelance writer?"

"What's the money?"

"Right to the point. Why am I not surprised by that question?"

"Because you know how tough it's been since I left the *Chronicle*. You know what a flop my venture as a travel writer was. Is that valuable knowledge going to cost me now?"

"And you know better than that, Buck. How does six thou a month, with full insurance benefits, sound—with a review and raise in six if the job goes beyond?"

"What do you mean, *if?*" Buck popped a couple of peanuts into his mouth.

"Because of the nature of this endeavor, we simply can't project any farther than that. But you can count on six months wages, and I promise, I'll do everything I can to keep you on after that. Okay?"

"*Six thou* for a P.R. writer? A writer who doesn't have anything left to write about?"

"Oh, you'll earn it," Peter said, his eyes continually sweeping over their fellow patrons on the deck. "I'll make sure of that."

"Doing what?"

"We've just created this position. We don't even have a job description on it yet. You'll write the incredible, success story after the burn. Until then, I need you to learn as much as you can about *Ark II* and the process so you can be ready to help us as things come up."

"Problems?" Buck asked, raising one eyebrow. "I'd think most of them should be behind you by this time." He sipped his Margarita and licked his lips.

"Most of them *are* behind us, but this is crunch time. Everything has to come together," Peter replied.

"Don't you think it will work?"

"No doubt at all. We *know* it will work. If we get her into operation, she'll be the first operating incinerator ship specifically designed and built for the job. We'll be able to incinerate over fifty of the most toxic chemicals with ninety-nine and ninety-nine hundredths percent efficiency! That's not quite perfect, but it's light years ahead of where the industry has been."

"What happens to the other hundredth of a percent?"

"One of the neatest things about this project. The incinerators burn at twenty-three hundred degrees Fahrenheit. That's hot, Buck, really hot. But despite the high temperature, there are two undesirables left from the burn. The first, the effluent from the stacks contains a small amount of hydrogen chloride. By conducting the burns far out to sea and allowing for the prevailing winds, the hydrogen chloride settles into the sea where it is neutralized by the alkaline in the water and, I might add, with no harm to marine life."

"And thereby averting the matter of acid rain?"

"Right. The second? A couple barrels of contaminated ash that are returned to shore and carefully buried in approved sites."

"That's it?"

"That's it."

The blond waitress served their drinks, and Peter went on to describe the double-hulled construction, the computerized monitoring devices, and the safety features of *Ark II,* including the unique bow thruster steering engine that enables the ship to make sharp, evasive maneuvers if necessary.

"And there will be explanations of all of this magic in my materials?" Buck asked, sipping his Margarita and savoring the sequence of salt to bittersweet slush.

"It's all there, and after you've read up on it, you'll see it firsthand. What we have here is such a failsafe setup of systems and alarms that once a burn begins, you can't even fart or the alarms sound, the rotating beacons flash, and the incinerator shuts down."

"They'd better not allow any beer or beans aboard!" laughed Buck. "Can't you just see the captain, interviewing a prospective crewman? 'Well, Seaman Smith, I'm not allowed to ask your age, but do you ever pass gas?'"

Peter exploded in laughter, rocked back on his chair, and nearly went over, his customary dignity left dangling near the rafters.

"You're saying that *Ark II* is so safe," Buck said. "Safer for whom, the crew?"

"Crew, environment, *everyone*. It's complex, Buck, but two weeks from now, you'll be a believer."

"What happens, Peter, if this overloaded tank of toxics catches fire? I have my talents, but given a choice between torch swallowing and swimming, I'm in trouble."

"A catastrophic fire is about one inch from impossible," Peter replied.

"Buddy, this is interesting, exciting, but right now, I'm hungry!" Buck announced. "What about you?"

"Me too, Buck. I told Diana this morning that we'd probably continue this session over dinner, so she's not expecting me."

Buck moved quickly to take care of the tab. When they reached his little, red Chevy S-10 pickup, there was Peter's silver Porsche parked beside it. Buck smiled at the strange pair, somehow such a reflection of their own relationship. When with Peter, Buck occasionally felt like a Chevy truck, but Peter had never treated him as anything but an equal.

"The Catamaran, in Naples Plaza?" Buck repeated. "I'll follow you if I can." The Porsche accelerated rapidly but controlled, as though it knew exactly the pace the pickup could match. As they swung into the lane that would take them back across the Vincent Thomas bridge into Long Beach, Buck was poring over all he had learned, trying to capsulize, to organize, so he could develop a shopping list of the things he still needed to know.

Sure, he thought, I'm going to take the job. After the pitiful money he'd made in the last year, it was like winning the lottery. In fact, it was more money than he'd *ever* made. But there was something about it. He wondered just what Peter was up to. Would his ol' bud create a paper position just to help him out? Yes, he *would*. But *could* he? Buck doubted it.

The rush hour traffic thickened as the mismatched tandem headed eastward through Long Beach. Buck grimaced at the misnomer, *rush hour*. "From three o'clock to seven," he mumbled to himself, "should be rush *hours*." And most of the rushing, it seemed, was simply to change lanes, with very little ground actually gained.

A gentle sea breeze filtered through his open windows, perking him up as they paralleled the shoreline of the harbor. He followed Peter into the Naples Plaza area, and soon they were parked in a lot behind the Catamaran Cafe. A small, lighted plastic sign over the rear door said simply, THE CAT.

Inside, Peter led the way up front through a narrow, dark corridor, the kind of tunnel usually reserved for the hired help and service people. The pungent odor of disinfectant hung in the hallway as they passed the rest rooms, but it gave way to beer and garlic when they reached the bar area.

A short, husky man in black trousers and a white shirt and carrying several plastic-coated menus hustled to meet them. He was in his mid-forties, with a dark complexion, bushy, black eyebrows, and a head that was bald but for the few strands carefully combed over the top.

"Ah, Peter!" The man shook hands warmly with Peter, his smile and large, brown eyes energizing the greeting. "Peter Hamlinio! How gooda to see you again, Peter."

"Hello, Dante. How are you?" Peter said. "Dante, this is my good friend Buck Barnumini."

Buck matched the shorter man's powerful grip, but his own smile gave way to a look of confusion. "Good to meet you," he said, "but, *Hamlinio?Barnumini?*"

"Oh, oh! A compliment! A compliment, eh, Peter?"

"What he means," Peter interjected, "is that all the *best* people are Italian, so when you are accepted by the master here, you are given an Italian handle."

"And I thought I was in a Greek place!" Buck said.

Their host sobered, blinked his big eyes, and then broke into a wide, toothy grin.

"Ahh, Peter! Another troublemaker! I'ma not sure the place handle two troublemakers atta once, but we try. Welcome, Buck Barnumini! Welcome!"

He led them to a secluded corner booth, took their orders for drinks, and hurried away.

"Peter, how do you *find* these places?" Buck asked, surveying the crowded, dimly lighted restaurant.

The wood of the old booths and tables was dark, nearly black and worn to a sheen that had replaced its long gone varnish. The red and white checkered tablecloth appeared clean, if faded. Up front, along the left side, was the bar, and behind the bar was an immense mural, perhaps twenty feet long and reaching from the back bar to the ceiling. It was an ocean scene, with a variety of catamarans sailing this direction and that. Lights were focused on the painting, causing the bright colors of the boats and their sails to nearly leap from the wall into the darkened room. While some of the craft were really quite good, the painter had occasionally lost perspective.

"Ahhh! You lika my painting?" the owner asked as he served their drinks. "Costa me much, but itsa so nice, don't you think?"

"Why—yes. Yes, nice, Dante." Buck replied, forcing his answer past his conscience. They placed their orders, and their host scampered off to the kitchen.

"Now that you've been accepted here, I'll let you in on something," Peter said softly, leaning forward. "He's no more Italian than you are. He's from Afghanistan."

"Afghanistan! What about my veal parmigiana?"

"Relax, Buck. Our veal will be quite good. I'd bet on it. But, I'd also bet that the recipe came from *Betty Crocker*."

"Why does he do it? What's the point?"

"Just for the hell of it. It's a standing joke among the regulars, and the others really think they've been to Italy."

"So, what does he do when some Italians come in?"

"He strings it out, to see how long he can make it last. Then, when they've nailed him, he turns it into good fun and discounts their dinner. They go away laughing with him."

Buck shook his head.

"But, make no mistake, Buck, he's a *lot* smarter than he seems. There isn't much that goes on in the business and political arenas between here and the harbor that escapes Dante. He's passed some valuable tidbits to me through recent years."

"Ohhh, it makes more sense now. It just didn't seem like you, Peter, wasting a lot of fuss on some buffoon." He looked Peter in the eye. "You really do respect him, don't you?"

"Treat him well," Peter said. "You never know when you might need him."

As their food was served, Buck made a special effort to join in the charade, and Dante seemed pleased.

"Now, where did we leave off?" Peter asked. "Oh, yes. Get this, it's very important. Once the chemicals are in *Ark II's* twelve big tanks, there are only two ways they can be removed. They must be burned in the incinerators, in which case the computers monitor, record, and transmit all the data directly back to shore, or they *can* be pumped back into the shore-side terminal by shore-based pumps.

There is absolutely *no* plumbing aboard *Ark II* that would accommodate off-loading anywhere but at the terminal. In other words, it is physically impossible for *Ark II* to dump one drop of the stuff at sea. It's either burned or it stays on the boat until she's back at the terminal."

"I think I understand, Peter. But why the emphasis?"

"Because some of the earlier European burners were accused of simply dumping the stuff at sea. It's possible. After all, they were only converted tankers."

"So the accusation, whether true or not, casts a shadow on the process, right?"

"More than that. Greenpeace pushed that one all the way to the London Convention. Result? The Convention has issued a ban on at-sea disposal—including incineration."

Buck's eyebrow went up. "But—"

"With support from some Washington agencies, we've appealed for a one-shot test burn. We should have clearance in a few days, and then we can prove our system is effective and safe."

"Now, wait a minute, Peter," Buck said, jabbing the tabletop with an index finger, "you've told me how well the system incinerates the chemicals. But a shipload of this stuff bopping around the ocean sounds dangerous as hell to me. Just why is she so safe?"

"She has all of the latest radar, satellite communication, collision avoidance gear, along with GPS. She can detect another ship headed for the burn area far in advance and alert the other to the situation. In addition to all the electronics, she has the bowthruster."

"Collisions happen, and the only shark *I'm* comfortable with is the one on my plate."

"This is the most collision-proof civilian vessel ever built, but *if* a collision occurred, remember she's double-hulled and double-bottomed. The tanks are well-separated with double bulkheads between them."

"Ah, Gentlemen," Dante interrupted, "your after dinner drinks. Your brandy, Peter," he announced, placing the drinks before them, "and you, Buck, I thinka you lika Kahlua, on the rocks." Touching his temple with a forefinger and smiling triumphantly, Dante turned and was gone.

"Now, how did he know that?" Buck asked. "Did you set this up?"

"No, but I told you not to underestimate Dante, didn't I? Buck, I can't give you the whole story tonight on the pollution threat and Essee Beecee's capabilities to reduce it. But, one thing you can be sure of right now, we *need* you." Peter's face took on an expression Buck hadn't seen often, the warm facial features seeming to plead, while the dark, brown eyes commanded.

"I appreciate that—no, I'm grateful for that." This is it, Buck thought. Two choices—got bad vibes about both. He wished he knew how to be subtle.

"Peter," Buck said, "I can't blow it again. Now, you don't really need another writer. Just what *do* you want?" He watched Peter's face for the reaction. His friend took a drink, glanced around the room, and then fixed his gaze once more on Buck.

"I guess I'm asking you to be my middle linebacker."

"Now that's the strongest hint you've given so far. What you mean is, you've got some difficulties, some people raising hell with your game plan, right?"

"Nothing obvious yet, but there are some who *might* raise hell. I need you to figure them out and keep us one jump ahead."

"I take that as a real compliment, Peter. But, did you happen to notice that sailor back at The Rum Barrel? The one with the shaved head and the Schwarzenegger build?"

"Couldn't help but notice. What about him?"

"Sharp guy. He says you've got a loser. Says he'd take the money to Vegas—better odds. What does *he* know that *I* don't?"

"Buck, hand a few million to any lifer of his vintage, and what will he do with it? Invest it? Of course not. How about it? Come in with me on this?"

Buck looked past Peter, at nothing in particular. As always, Peter's appeal was powerful. He had a way of reaching inside Buck, twisting things around, and pulling something out that Buck hadn't known was there. And, defying all logic, Peter was a perpetual winner. Buck tried to organize the onslaught of information the day had brought forth. But the facts refused to separate, to fall into pigeonholes. The answer didn't come. Well, he thought, I need the job. Peter needs *me*. And that money? Wow!

"You're on, ol' bud!" he said. The broadest smile he had felt in months took command of his face. He couldn't erase it, couldn't control it. It felt good.

"Thanks," Peter said, reaching across the table and giving Buck's forearm a squeeze. "It'll be great, working together again." Peter grabbed the check, and in no time, they were outside in the parking lot unlocking their vehicles.

"Peter!" Buck called over. "Do I have a title?"

"Let's say you're a—special assistant."

This time, the Porsche was not considerate. By the time Buck cleared the humpback bridge over the San Gabriel River, the silver bullet was out of sight. The sun had set, and dusk was leading quickly to night as he made his right turn onto the Pacific Coast Highway and headed south.

"What a day this has been. Damn, I've got a job!" he muttered aloud, thumping the steering wheel with his fist. Don't really know what it is, he mused, but I've got a job, it's important, and I like the pay! Boy, will *that* give me a boost. With what I give Sunny at Long Beach State and with what I've done to the credit cards, I *guess* it'll help.

No more gambling the expenses of those travel-writing trips against the potential income. How many times had he taken off on a trip with an editor's encouragement only to find out too late that someone had already done that article? So, why had he tried it?

Buck glanced at the rear-view mirror and moved over to the right-hand lane. A black Cadillac flashed past him and cut quickly in front of him The New Jersey vanity plate read: *D Cobra.*

Normally amused by license plate humor, Buck tensed slightly as he read this one, for it reminded him of the "snake" label he had once attached to a man, NFL superstar quarterback Casey Nester, the man who had tipped Buck's quest for a freelance writing career into a downward tailspin.

After getting dumped on the Nester project, Buck had been desperate. Man—to think he had been fired after four months on the project! Buck could feel his emotional high threatening once again to slide into the quaggy morass of anger. He had been there so many times. Nester had given him the job of ghost writing his autobiography. But then the football player took Buck's concepts, groundwork, and outline and handed them to an old friend. And Buck had been so enamored with the bum he had signed a contract as flimsy as toilet paper. And to think he had tried so hard to make Nester look good!

He loosened his tie and unbuttoned his collar with his free hand. Be honest, Buck thought. It was the fame, the recognition that you were after, wasn't it? After all those years as a small time sportswriter, you saw a chance to go big with national exposure. Wasn't that really it? And you didn't have to quit the *Chronicle* when they went weekly. You quit because you were tired of the job and too damned stubborn to cover things other than sports.

His thoughts went to Roberta. Three years after their divorce, it shouldn't matter any more. But it still hurt to know that she was talking to Bob and Sunny about his male menopause, as though he was some adolescent who had flushed his brain down the stool. He hoped this job with its good pay would change that.

As though on command, the competition on the Pacific Coast Highway thinned, and he was allowed an occasional glance across the dunes. He always found it fascinating to look out to where the brightly lighted oil-pumping platforms hovered over the black sea like gigantic extraterrestrial creatures. Big things would be happening out there, and he was destined to be a part of them.

Minutes later, he had passed through Huntington Beach and Newport Beach. Once in Corona del Mar, he turned left on Marguerite and began ascending the coastal range hill. Halfway up the incline he turned right on Sandcastle and then made a left into Palm Cove. It was but a short distance to the cul de sac at the end, and his headlights reflected, as always, from the front window of the neighboring Lee home. Turning left into his own drive, he noticed a black car parked at their curb. *That's unusual*, he thought. *The Lees almost never have company.*

Buck entered the kitchen and flipped on the light. The phone rang as though triggered by the switch.

"Buck Barnum here," he said, sorting through the day's mail with his free hand.

"Barnum," a high-pitched, almost squeaky nasal male voice said, "that fuckin' incinerator barge is doomed."

"What? Who is thi—"

"You better abandon ship right now, or yer gonna go down with it. An' that's *after* we break both yer legs. You been warned." *Click.*

Buck slowly replaced the phone. A swarm of bees buzzed through his mind. He couldn't separate the questions, let alone answer any of them. But he could feel the heat of the smoldering Barnum fuse.

Chapter 3

Buck guided his Chevy pickup through thick layers of Pacific fog that wafted out of the Monday morning darkness to hide the Coast Highway. His mind was a cauldron of conflicts. Small bits of confidence and chunks of determination stirred against the large lump of apprehension that churned within him as he headed for his first day on the new job.

The entire weekend had been spent buried in the thick volumes Ed Roland had given him. While he'd had difficulty staying with the portions on chemistry, he had found himself fascinated by the history on the disposal of toxic wastes. It was clear that the threat to the nation's drinking water was a giant shadow compared to the isolated incidents of direct contact with toxics in the Love Canal and Times Beach episodes. Terrible as they were, they might turn out to be just the beginning.

He thought about the new job. Today, this week, he would not worry about *producing* for Essee Beecee, he resolved. He would concentrate on finding out what's going on, what needs to be done, and then prepare himself to do it. If they don't like his approach, it's *their* problem! He was counting on Peter to buy him enough time to get his feet on the ground. After that he could take care of himself.

There were signs of light filtering through the fog as Buck wheeled into the parking lot behind Dante's Catamaran. He took the booth he and Peter had shared, and in no time, a bright, young man, dressed in jeans and a T-shirt, had taken his order. A college student, Buck mused, probably right between Bob and Sunny in age.

He sipped at his juice, passing the waiting time thinking about his family. He had long been aware of the close link, almost telepathic at times, between Sunny and himself. But Bob? He must have been blind not to see that Bob wasn't—and would never be—the father's son. Funny, after twenty-two years, he found he was not as close to his son as he had thought. And after all of the things they had done together, the time they spent together. What was he, blinded by ego?

That Sunny! He could see the pixie face and long, sunstroked blond hair that belonged on a magazine cover. But no magazine cover could do justice to that personality, a blend of aggressiveness, intelligence, poise, and compassion. Sunny's positives, however, went far beyond his. She never seemed to have problems. He wasn't sure how it happened, but he was sure that girl would always be in control of her life.

And then, there's still Roberta. For the last three years, Buck had drilled himself, had practiced at shutting her out of his life. But she was the kids' mother and she lived in the wealthiest section of neighboring Newport Beach, much too close for Buck. He was still trying to accept the fact that, despite the pain it caused him, the divorce had not totally removed her from his life. She acted as though they were still close friends, but to Buck she was a non-healing sore.

Buck and Bobbie, as she was known in college, fell in love in the spring of their freshman year. It was the typical football player-cheerleader romance until she became pregnant. She dropped out of school, and by the time Buck graduated their family included Bob and Sunny.

Those were tough times, Buck thought, shaking his head. Tough times, but we faced them together. Anyway, he was glad she got the chance to finish college that he had promised her.

The young waiter served Buck's scrambled eggs, bacon, and toast. Absorbed in his thoughts, Buck mumbled aloud, "The thing I don't understand—"

"Something else, sir?" the young waiter asked.

"Huh? Oh, no, thank you."

The rumination continued as he ate. After a thousand examinations of the events, he still didn't understand how he had missed it. Looking back on it, the signs were there, as bold and bright as a fast food menu. The delightful, little blonde had become a beautiful woman. At her insistence, the "Bobbie" was exorcised from Buck's brain and replaced by her given name, Roberta.

After finishing her college business major six years before, she had taken a job with well-known and high-priced Howard's Boutique in Newport Beach. Even then at age thirty-five she was still energetic, especially on the tennis court, but she had become ever more concerned with her looks and sex appeal. For years Buck had drawn satisfaction and pride from her mild flaunting and flirting. He had reveled in the confidence that the petite beauty who stirred interest in the men and jealousy in the women belonged to him.

But when she announced that she was leaving him to move in with, and eventually marry her boss, Howard Corson, Buck found himself swamped in disbelief, shock, and humiliation. Buck should have seen it coming, because it had been coming for twenty years. He took her for granted. They seemed to share love and sex; he didn't know there was anything missing.

Yeah, Howard, he thought. Howard Corson, a handsome, suave Hollywood type with his great pride in associating with some of the "dimmer" stars of the entertainment world. That provides the perfect stage for Roberta. Most of the women in their circles would gladly trade physical attributes with her.

Fortunately, Buck was saved from total destruction by the anger that boiled over when he learned that Roberta had been carrying on the affair with Howard for more than two years.

"You haven't done anything particularly wrong," Roberta had said the night she played her cards. "I just found a man and a life I love more."

He had been allowed to keep their Corona Del Mar home, the home the kids had grown up in. Buck was glad for that. He had willingly accepted the pay-off for her guilt. Considering his losses, he was grateful to be able to keep his home.

The kids, however, had moved with their mother to the palatial home in Newport Beach. He followed Bob's athletics and made every attempt to be part of his son's life, but the relationship had become strained. It seemed clear that Bob preferred his mother, but while it hadn't yet come out, Buck had the feeling that Roberta was fueling the strain.

Sunny, on the other hand, had made every effort to spend time with Buck. That generated some resentment in Roberta which, in turn, had kept the sore festering.

The split had shocked Buck, left him demoralized and stripped of his confidence. He tried to deny the manhood issues, but they were there. A year later, he quit his job as a sports reporter and began the search for a whole new life.

The waiter returned to top off Buck's coffee.

"I don't suppose Dante ever comes in this early?" Buck asked.

"Oh, sure. He's been here for hours. He's cooking this morning. The regular morning cook didn't show."

"He cooked this? You tell him that Buck Barnumini is impressed by his talent. Tell him that, would you?" After a few minutes, Buck paid the young man and left.

It was just before eight o'clock when Buck strode down the hall beyond the demarcation line and into Ed Roland's office. Ed wasn't there. Buck looked around the office. His work table had not yet been installed. He decided it would be presumptuous to take Ed's place behind the desk, so he dropped into the other chair and pulled a book from his attaché case.

"Heyyy, good morning, Buck!" The smartly dressed man with the broad smile strode in and shook Buck's hand. "Set to go at it?" he asked with a wink.

"Sure am, Ed. But before I go at it, I need to get a clearer picture of what *it* is."

"We'll start on that immediately. Here's a note pad. Come with me. We have a meeting with the big muckamucks."

Buck followed Ed Roland down the hall, past the barrier, and into the executive suite. He tripped on the edge of the thick, plush carpet but quickly righted himself. Ms. Erichs was at her desk. She looked up at them. If her face communicated anything, it was not good.

"Good morning, Viola! How's my favorite girl this morning?" Ed's bubbly greeting reeked of insincerity.

"The meeting is about to begin," she said. "Go right in."

"Bitch," Ed said under his breath as they moved away.

Following Ed's lead, Buck stepped into the large, plush office. It was a bright room, completely furnished in elegant cherry wood. Behind a massive desk sat an immense executive chair and a large, matching credenza. A long conference table stood off to the right. A coffee server, a stack of china mugs bearing the S.C.B.C. logo, and a tray of rolls and doughnuts topped a second credenza on the left side of the office.

Roland took Buck toward the group of four men dressed in expensive business suits who had gathered near the coffee dispenser.

"Gentlemen, I'd like you to meet Buck Barnum, our new, ahh, special consultant."

Buck was puzzled by the title, but in the tension of the moment he let it pass. "Buck, this is Captain Charles Hudson, U.S.N. retired, our CEO."

"Glad to have you aboard, Barnum," Hudson said.

The CEO was in his fifties, short and solid. Everything about him suggested strength. Hudson's mixed gray-black hair was only slightly longer than a crewcut, and his angular, chiseled face combined with squinting gray eyes to intimidate. When Buck was victimized by the bone-crushing handshake, he knew he was meeting yet another of the little-big men. Napoleon, he thought, Napoleon Hudson.

"Buck, this is Dale Craws, our V.P. of Production."

"Good morning. Nice meeting you." Craws was in his late forties, average height, with a nearly handsome, smiling face and wavy brown hair. Buck sensed that his grip was a determined effort at firmness, but he knew instantly that the man was weak.

"I believe you've met Peter Hamlin."

"Good to see you again, Barnum," Peter said, showing briefly his onstage smile while his eyes looked right past Buck.

"And this," Ed said, leading Buck to an extremely tall, wiry, bald-headed man, "is our bean counter, our CFO, Garland Grigsby." Grigsby had a tense, noncommital face with probing, blue eyes that peered over the half-glasses perched on his nose. "Garland has been with the company longer than all of us collectively," Ed went on, confirming Buck's estimate of Grigsby's age at something in the sixties.

"Hello." The handshake was so brief that Buck wasn't sure it had happened.

"Gentlemen!" Hudson called out. "It's time." Following Ed Roland's lead, Buck helped himself to a doughnut and coffee before moving to the large table.

"Here," Ed pointed, "we sit at the low end."

Buck looked across and toward the high end. Peter was looking at him. His face was blank, but his eyes gleamed. Buck read the message, *I think you'll find this interesting.*

The office door closed with a thump, and Viola Erichs, her notepad clutched primly to her breast, strutted to the chair on Hudson's right. When she had completed her ceremonial settling in, she placed the dangling glasses on her nose and leaned forward to the writing position. Buck's attention moved from Ms. Erichs across the table to Grigsby and back again. Their small reading glasses were identical! Even the cords by which the glasses could dangle matched. He shifted his gaze to Peter, who smiled.

Charles Hudson began the meeting by calling for the weekly reports. His organizational talents showed quickly, and the concise, dynamic manner in which he spoke left no doubt about who was in charge.

"Craws, you're first."

"Sir, final adjustments and preparations are coming along nicely. The four crew replacements report this morning. The bugs in the warning strobe lights have been worked out. We've upgraded the communications radios, and the latest GPS navigational equipment should be here in a day or two."

Buck happened to look at Grigsby in time to catch a slight shake of his head.

"The company from which we've leased the tank trucks," Craws continued, "has agreed to our modifications of the trucks. Dr. Keene, head of the incineration crew, has his plan for the blending and loading ready." Craws went on in a soft, pleasant, but nervous voice. While his presentation was explanatory, the upturn at the end of each statement suggested a question, as though asking, "Is this all right, sir? Is that all right, sir?" His face reddened, and he stammered occasionally as he responded to questions from Hudson. Shorthand flowed from the pen of Ms. Erichs.

"Anything to add here, Peter?" the CEO asked.

"No, sir," Peter said.

"Roland, what do you have?"

"The drafts for the marketing packet are finished. When Peter has signed off, I'll get them right to you." Ed then outlined a planned piece of additional material. Buck was impressed with Ed's positive and expressive delivery. His eloquence could turn the most trivial accomplishment into a profound achievement.

"I believe, sir," Ed continued, "you have the finished copies of the materials for our presentation to the EPA on Wednesday?" Hudson shuffled some papers and nodded. "I met with two more environmental groups last week."

"How did that go?"

"As well as could be expected, sir, " Ed answered with a smile.

"What the hell does *that* mean?"

"It's always difficult to overcome emotions with facts. But I think—"

"You do that with *dramatic* facts."

"Yes, sir. That's what they got," Ed Roland replied. His complexion changed color, but the smile was still pasted on his face. Grigsby shifted in his chair and shook his head again.

"You've got to approach those sons-of-bitches with real strength," Hudson said. Ms. Erichs quickly scratched out some symbols and paused, waiting for her next entry. "Don't show any weakness, or they'll be all over you! Peter? Anything to add?"

"No, sir. Keep up the good work, Ed."

Buck tightened and watched for the reaction. To his surprise, the leader simply looked directly at Peter and nodded affirmation. Grigsby cleared his throat.

"Peter, what's the status with EPA and coast guard?"

"As you know, Ed and I meet with EPA on Wednesday in Washington. We've offered to move the test burn site farther out to sea, to a point over two hundred miles from the coast and well between the Los Angeles and San Francisco shipping lanes. That should ease any fears of acid fallout reaching the coast. Our previous margin already was more than safe, but this nearly doubles it.

"The EPA people are with us," Peter went on, "but to say we have their *official* approval for the burn would be premature. They're still nursing wounds from the last round. The question is whether they have the political balls to try it again."

The secretary made another hurried alteration.

"Coast guard is satisfied with the changes we've made to the ship. They're ready to endorse the burn proposal when they're satisfied with our temporary blending and loading plan. They'll be represented at this meeting, and I've been assured of their support."

"What about the London Convention?" Hudson asked. "Do you have anything new on getting the ban lifted?"

"My sources at EPA tell me that if they approve our test burn, it could possibly lead to clearance from London Convention for the test burn within a week. But EPA is really being cautious. The monkey's on *their* backs on this one. They're very, very apprehensive about asking the London Convention to change its permanent stance on burning." Peter paused, took a sip of coffee and glanced around the table.

"Obviously," Peter continued, smiling slightly, "I can't sit here today and tell you the ban will be lifted. Whether or not our earlier European friends actually dumped their loads in the ocean, the *perception* that they did is what brought about the ban. I doubt that the Convention will lift the ban after our successful test and then let the Germans and the others go on with business as usual. So, to get a lobby effort strong enough to even hope for a permanent lifting of the ban, we have to convince our competitors to raise their operations up to our standards. I have established some rapport, I believe, with two of them. In principle, they agree with me. I think they can swing the renovations financially. But I also think they're going to ask us to share our technology."

"Christ Almighty," came a low voice. It was Grigsby.

"Anything else, Peter?" Charles Hudson asked, directing a scowl at the CFO. Peter declined and sat back in his chair.

"Financial report, Grigsby?"

Garland Grigsby said nothing. He leaned forward, directing an expressionless stare at Hudson. One by one, he shifted his gaze to each of the men around the table. The silence was stifling. Buck realized that he himself was barely breathing. He felt some relief when Grigsby passed him by. Then—*whack!* Grigsby smacked the table with the palm of his hand. Buck flinched with the others.

"Just what in the God-damned hell would be the point of a report?" Grigsby shouted.

Hudson flicked a hand toward Ms. Erichs who again scratched something out.

"This is no *business!* This is nothing but a God-damned *lemonade stand!*" the bald man continued.

Another flick of Hudson's hand. Buck couldn't help but notice the pattern as Grigsby continued the outburst. The angry face looked at Peter, back to Hudson, looked at Craws, back to Hudson, looked at Roland, back to Hudson. Boy, I'm glad I have nothing to do with any of this, Buck thought. This old guy is ready for a white coat with straps on it.

"What in the hell is the matter with you people? We were doing well in the yacht market, with a few missile frigates tossed in. Then we abandon all that, buy this God-damned white elephant from up the coast, and go into the glorified garbage business!"

Sheesh, thought Buck, observing Grigsby's pulsing temples. What have I gotten into? This old dude is really boiled! And what's this 'white elephant' business?

"Strike all that!" Hudson directed Ms. Erichs. "That's irrelevant opinion," he continued, pointing a finger at Grigsby, "and it's out of order here! We've been all through this before!" Hudson bellowed. "The board determines policy, and the board chose to go with *Ark II*! Now," Hudson's voice was suddenly calm, "do you have a report for us?" It seemed to Buck that Hudson's eyes were bouncing sparks off the older man's armor.

Grigsby rolled his eyes, sat back, and took a deep breath. When he leaned forward again, he had developed surprising composure.

"On one point, the matter of board policy, you're right." His tone became conversational, except for a cumbersome emphasis on diction that gave his words a halting rhythm. "Gentlemen, what is the point of my weekly report on the budget, when you completely ignore it? I told you last week that we were close to a million over budget, even before the costs associated with the terminal. And today? Today we bought new radios and hired a man—for *what?* Hell, I'm not even sure *why* we hired him," he said, flinging a gesture in Buck's direction.

Buck stiffened. His hands clenched into fists, and his face felt hot. He was about to react when he saw Peter gesture with the palm of his hand. What's *with* this guy? What's going on here? He glared across the table and then scanned the group. All but Grigsby were studying the tabletop.

"And then, as if we can't throw money away fast enough," Grigsby continued, "I think I'm hearing a proposal that we give our technology to our competitors? This is a *business?*" He swept up the papers before him and jammed them carelessly into his case. "Mr. Chairman, I conclude my report by stating more than anyone present cares to hear. We're farther over budget than we were a week ago." With that, the big man rose, snapped his briefcase shut, and stalked out.

"I regret this unfortunate display and waste of our valuable time," Hudson said coldly. "The matter will be dealt with. You all know what you must do. All ahead full. Meeting adjourned."

The subordinates vacated the inner office like a sudden burst of steam from a tea kettle. Quietly, just one *poof,* and they were gone—with Buck leading the way.

Chapter 4

"At first I thought Grigsby was crazy!" Buck shouted. "Crazier than hell! Then I began to see it. It's the *rest* of you who are crazy! He's the *sane* one!"

Peter sat quietly tilted back in his chair behind his large desk, his arms folded across his chest and his head bowed.

"And when he said he didn't know what I was here for," Buck went on, "I was hurt—angry and hurt. Then it hit me. Grigsby doesn't know what I'm here for—and he's *sane*. If I don't know what I'm doing here then I'm probably *sane*, too! Damn it, Hamlin, you could have clued me in. I might have been a little better prepared for this goose grunge if you'd handed me a gun—or a clown suit!"

As Buck finished his first round, he kicked at a chair leg for emphasis. Had he not been focused on the chair he might have seen the smile in Peter's eyes.

"You know, Peter, I asked several times. The only thing you really told me about this job was that you might have some opposition out there," Buck said with a wild sweep of his arm. "Out there? Man, with what you've got in here, you'd better not have too many out *there*!"

Anger and embarrassment sizzled through him like a lightning bolt chasing an icicle. The lightning bolt won. He knew he was out of control. The words spewed out before he could think of them. Yet, they seemed to be making sense. As he reached a peak, he realized that, strangely, the rage felt good. Then, his pace slowed. The pauses between sentences became longer, and his brain seemed to kick in with thoughts like, What am I *doing?* What have I *said?* Am I really this angry with Peter? Or am I just angry? God, I'm so tired. He looked at Peter. His friend simply sat there, his gaze fixed on the ceiling above Buck, his face expressionless. Buck stopped. The anger tank was empty.

"Tell you what," Peter said softly. "Just put yourself in that chair, and I'll be right back. He got up, circled the desk and left the office.

Buck dropped into the chair, took a deep breath, and exhaled. For the first time, he noticed the freshly painted walls, the large color photographs of ships, the new brown carpeting, and the attractive oak furniture in Peter's office. Damn, Buck thought, what have I done? Was all that really called for? Can't answer that. Can't remember what I said.

"Here," Peter said, returning and setting a fresh cup of coffee and a glazed doughnut before Buck. Peter rounded the desk with his own coffee and settled into his chair.

Buck snapped a big bite of the doughnut and followed it with coffee. Peter said nothing. He simply tilted back in his chair, sipping his coffee. Buck looked about the office. He felt silly doing it. Occasionally, his eyes swept past Peter, but no contact was made. As Buck finished the doughnut, Peter got up, closed the office door, and returned to his chair.

"Sorry, ol' bud, really sorry," Peter said.

"No need." As he spoke the words, Buck realized that he really meant them. He had come down the hall, furious with Grigsby, Hudson, Erichs, Roland, and Peter—everything to do with Essee Beecee! Sure, Peter had let him down, but it was the first time—*ever*. This is Peter, he thought, the friend who has always given to the relationship and seldom taken from it.

"I mean it, Buck, I'm sorry. I apologize for my deception and for not preparing you in advance. I always know what's best for others, but sometimes I'm just, just wrong."

"I'm sorry, too," Buck said, "for blowing my stack like that. But why didn't you level with me up front?"

Peter smiled. "With your self-confidence as low as it was, would you have taken the job? But," he hurried on, "I knew that, once committed and involved, you'd never quit. I promise, no more holding out on you."

"Okay, you hired me as a writer, although there were some vague implications attached. Today, I heard myself called 'special consultant' and 'a waste of company money.' Now, Peter, if you still want me, you'd better cut the garbage and give it to me straight."

"I think," Peter began slowly, "when we've finished this discussion, you'll understand it much better. I called you my linebacker the other day, but that suggests purely a defensive strategy. It might develop that to defend ourselves we have to go on the offensive. It might be better to call you our *point man.* We'll come back to that. The company leaders—what do you see there?"

Buck thought for a moment. "I see Hudson as a little Napoleon who rules with an iron hand. He might be tough. He might be all bluff. But I suspect it's going to be *his* way."

"Pretty good." Peter smiled. "He was hired about two years ago, at the same time the company decided to switch from commercial boat building to incineration-at-sea. He was selected, by a simple majority of the board, over Garland Grigsby, who had been with Essee Beecee for over thirty years. Of course, you picked up on Grigsby's feelings as to what our goals should be."

"Man, that explains a lot," Buck said, "But, with Napoleon at the helm, can Grigsby get away with crap like he pulled today?"

"Grigsby's pretty well-entrenched through longevity, support from two board members, and the amount of stock he holds. Hudson would like to get rid of him, and it may yet come to a showdown. But up to now, Garland's one thorn in the captain's butt that he hasn't found a way to remove."

"Who's right?" Buck asked.

"They're both right. Essee Beecee was one of the companies that recognized the course for survival, back when the American shipbuilding industry began to lose out to the Europeans, Japanese, and Koreans. Some of us cut back to small military ships and the profitable luxury yachts. The outfits that didn't adjust went belly up."

Peter paused to take a phone call, cut it short, and continued. "The *Ark II* project involves considerably more risk, but it also offers potential profits far beyond the old format. So, it remains to be seen. How do you read the other people?"

"Well, I have a lot of respect for Ed Roland, of course. I have to believe he does his thing as well as it can be done. Craws? He strikes me as a complete phony, the kind who tosses the buzz words around. You know, bottom line, cost efficient, management style. In fact, I'd bet that he *loves* to talk about his management style."

"You sure you've never met him before?" Peter laughed. "Just remember one thing, he's a sneaky devil. Don't ever say anything in front of him that you wouldn't say to Hudson and the world."

"Peter, you seem to stand well with Hudson. True?"

"Yes. I guess I'd say that I stand well with him—carefully."

"Then how about Grigsby? How do you manage that?"

"The same way. I think Grigsby respects me from the old days. Of course, he enjoys it when I do take a stand against Hudson. But I'll say this for Garland. He'll fight like a cornered lion on matters of principle, but the only one he truly hates is Hudson. Don't take today's remarks personally. He's really uptight about this new venture. If we fail, it could sink the company, at best maybe a chapter eleven. So here's a man who has been with Essee Beecee almost from the beginning. He's guided the company to steady profits, and now he's having trouble dealing with our game of roulette. I find his position understandable—even commendable."

"What about Ms. Erichs?" Buck asked. "She's either a very bitter lady, or she's anal retentive."

Peter laughed. "Could be both. She's been with Garland, and I do mean *with* Garland, ever since the rest of the dinosaurs went over the hill, so I think that tells you where she stands on things."

"You're kidding!" Buck choked. "Do you mean—"

"Mmm-hmmm," Peter nodded with a smirk. "I have to add, I've never seen anything to corroborate the rumor, but that's been the story for years."

"Incredible! Do they live together?"

"No, he's married."

"He's married?" Buck repeated, shaking his head. "What can he possibly see in Viola? Then again, they both seem sour to me. Boy, with her around for inspiration, I can't see how you ever got a ship's mast to stand up straight." He wondered about Mrs. Grigsby.

"Ahh, but you see how much experience we've had with toxics?" After a pause, Peter continued, "Now, Viola you *can* take personally. But I can't see her having any effect on *you*."

"What did Grigsby mean, 'bought that white elephant?' He lost me there."

"Sorry, that's one of those things I should have explained to you. Originally she was *Apollo II.* and we didn't really build her. *Ark II* is her second name. We bought her and did some modifications."

"What?" Buck flinched, spilling coffee on his trousers. He pulled out his handkerchief.

"She's the second of two sister ships, designed and built by a yard up the coast. Cost them over thirty-seven million each back in the early eighties. The bulk of it was insured by MarAd—that's the federal Maritime Administration."

"What happened?" Buck asked, blotting the coffee stains.

"Quite a story," Peter said. "This yard went into the development and construction of the boats with strong encouragement from the Feds. The EPA examined their specs and implementation plan and got all excited. They endorsed them, and supported their application to MarAd for loan insurance back in the eighties. The company went right into production. They planned to operate one out of New Jersey with an EPA-designated burn area about a hundred and fifty miles offshore and out of the shipping lanes. The other was to operate out of Louisiana and burn a couple of hundred miles out in the Gulf."

"They didn't finish building them?"

"Oh, they finished."

"Why haven't I heard about this?"

"They got a lot of press near the shipyard and in the proposed staging areas, but for some reason, the national media let it slip through the cracks."

"Misguided PR strategy by the builders?"

"Possibly, but here's the zinger. Parts of New Jersey and Louisiana are practically floating in chemical waste. But the NIMBYs, the Not In My Back Yard organizations, we think with support from certain competitors in the waste management field—you know who I mean—got emotions worked up to fever pitch. And eventually, the bureaucrats and politicians caved in. Result? No staging areas. The company kept fighting for the right to run test burns to prove the system was effective and ecologically safe, but the Feds crawled under the rug and left them high and dry."

"And the shipyard?"

"Forced to default on their loans. The bonding company went out of business. The two ships were sold for about five million each. *Apollo*

I was converted, of all things, into a fish cannery ship." Peter shook his head sadly.

"That's sickening!" exclaimed Buck, "even though it *was* good for Essee Beecee. Why didn't someone else outbid you and try what we're doing, take another shot at it?"

"Too risky. About the same time that the environmentalists blew these two ships out of the water, they got the London Convention—that's the international organization that regulates maritime activities—to put a ban on sea-going incineration."

"*That's* what Hudson was talking about! So we have to get EPA approval for the test burn, prove the system is effective and safe, get the London Convention to reverse their decision, and get the terminal built?" Buck whistled and sagged back in his chair. "My God, Peter, you were always a scrambler, but I never thought of you as a gambler. You only got cute when you were sure it would work. But *this* thing!"

"Strange, isn't it?" Peter said wistfully. "We never know quite what's waiting for us around the bend, do we?"

"Assuming we jump the first three hurdles, why go back to New Jersey for the terminal?" Buck asked. "That's where the first company got a butt-kicking. Why not operate right here?"

"Good question, Buck. There are several reasons to focus on the East Coast. First, there are millions of drums of chemicals waiting in warehouses, vacant lots, and on the docks in New Jersey, Pennsylvania, and New York. Most of these drums are the old steel variety with limited time before they start leaking. Second, off the east coast the prevailing west to east winds will take the stack effluent farther out to sea, where it will inevitably settle into the ocean and be neutralized. The *Ark* costs big bucks to operate. With the west winds out here, we'd have to go twice as far out to sea, and that would cut the profits dramatically. And a west coast terminal would necessitate hauling some of the chemicals as much as two thousand miles overland."

"But the east coast resistance—they *won* the first round."

"That was several years ago. They were sitting on an explosive toxic chemical dump *then*. Can you imagine what their situation is by *now?*"

"But—"

"And remember," Peter continued, "*Ark II* was only under construction then, not tested and approved. And," he gestured palms up, "we've learned from the first battle. Our political and public relations campaign is much better organized because of it."

Buck wiped a hand over the damp spot on his trousers. Man, he thought, it just keeps getting deeper. And why did he have the feeling that what he'd heard—was the *good* news? Buck got up, stretched, and walked over to the photo wall. He was attracted to the one in the middle, a large blowup of *Ark II*. Despite all of the negatives he had just heard, he was fascinated by the brilliant white ship with its deck full of red pipes and related paraphernalia.

"Well, *Ark II*," Buck said to the photograph, "I guess that brings it back to me. What can *I* possibly do for *you*?" He turned toward Peter and waited. Peter sipped his coffee, set the mug on the desktop, and leaned forward. His expression said nothing.

"We expect heavy opposition," he finally said.

"Who's the opponent?" Buck asked.

"That's plural, my friend—opponents. We know some of them, but unfortunately, not all. Those we're familiar with are primarily citizens' green groups. They're into lobbying and pumping out negative propaganda."

"Like Greenpeace?"

"Strangely enough," Peter replied, "we're not hearing much from Greenpeace. Our network tells us they're busy elsewhere and are just lending guidance to a local group called ASH, that's the Alliance to Save the Harbor. And, we're told there's one group that's a spin-off from Greenpeace—tougher, more radical, *real* monkeywrenchers. So far, we've yet to get a handle on them."

"Wait a minute. There's something wrong with this. The company and the green groups should be on the same side."

"That's the irony of the situation," Peter said. "To the Greenies, we're saying, 'There's a big batch of poison out there that's going to get you.' They're saying, 'No, there isn't, but you're not going to haul it out to sea and burn it.' The Nimby reply is, 'No, there isn't, and don't try hauling it through *our* neighborhood.'"

"Excuse me, you said something about your network?" Buck asked.

"Buck, here comes your first test in lip zipping." Peter said, lowering his voice to barely more than a whisper. "No one else knows what I'm about to tell you, not even Ed."

The look on Peter's face told Buck it was to stay that way.

"Dante hears a lot at the Cat, and he has friends all over the harbor area who have excellent hearing and vision. You follow?"

Buck whistled softly. "Now I'm really beginning to understand your relationship with that phony Italiano. So, if I read you right, you want me to do what I can to shut down those two green groups, especially the group of radicals. Right?"

"Yes and no. Ed's handling ASH. In fact, he's booked a speaking engagement with them. I *am* concerned about the wrenchers. But there's another group out there, a *big* and *powerful* group, that concerns us even more. The professionals—the *big* boys."

"Meaning?"

"Organized crime."

Buck swallowed. "You mean—" He shuffled back to his chair, plopped down hard, and stared at Peter's stonelike face. "like the *Mafia?*"

"Who's to say these days," Peter shrugged, "whether they're called Mafia or something else? They're spread out so well in so many legitimate businesses that they don't stand out like they used to. But we do believe this. Organized crime controls much of the waste disposal business in the country. It follows then that they have a lot to lose if we succeed."

"So you want me to what—go bare knuckles with a couple hundred hoods?"

Peter laughed. "Never come to that, Buck. But with your temper, I'd bet on you."

"Come on, Peter, don't toss the old dog a bone. This could get hairy."

"Not if we play it right. You see, we have some advantages over them. They don't know we're even looking their way. They don't know you. And we'll have Dante, his people, and someone else he's bringing in to help. What we want to do is identify them, and if we can, set them up for the law enforcement agencies—get them before they can get us."

"Peter! I've got a family to think of. You're trying to get me killed. Is that why you picked me for this job?"

"I picked you because you're smart, analytical, and if necessary you're tougher than anyone I know—in that order," Peter replied. "If you handle this right, we'll have them in a box before they even know about you. That is, if you can keep your temper in check and keep a low profile. And, Buck," Peter's tempo slowed, "if they decide to eliminate someone, don't you think *I'd* be their first choice?"

"I—I guess that makes sense," Buck said. "But why don't you hire a P.I., someone who knows how to handle these things?"

"As soon as they spot a detective hanging around, the big money moves, and *our* man is now *their* man. We've got to have someone we can trust. Now, if you don't think you're up to it, you're free to back out—no effect on our friendship, I promise. It's your call."

Buck's mind quickly retraced the issues, then Peter's needs. A new element had been added. But Peter was right. If a crime group decided on drastic actions, *he* would be their logical choice. He's the driving force behind this project, the key figure. Buck didn't know whether it was concern for Peter's welfare, the compulsion to do the right thing, the magnetic challenge of a task that seemed impossible, or . . . the money.

"Okay, Peter." The voice that spoke the words sounded strange, like a loud whisper in a distant barrel. "You stay on the level with me, and I'm in for the ride."

"You just got your first raise," Peter said, a broad smile breaking on his handsome face.

"I'm not sure that makes me feel any better." Buck tried to laugh, but only a choked "Hmph" came out. "Okay, set me up. What do I do first? Hit the books?"

"No," Peter said thoughtfully, "I'd focus on the things closer to home. Start with the press clippings and our notes on the New Jersey fiasco. Look at their methods, faces and names, anything that might connect with local people or groups. Ed will give you everything we have."

"Should I," Buck lowered his voice, "get in touch with Dante?"

"Soon. He's already lining up a meeting for you. I'll let you know as soon as I get the word."

"Were you that sure of yourself?" Buck asked, scowling.

"No, that sure of you," Peter said softly. "He'll be setting you up with some detective from Long Beach P.D." Peter rummaged through some notes on his desk, finally handing Buck a yellow Post-It note.

"Detective's name is Lenny Bercovich. Oh, I've authorized Ed to give you copies of the crew personnel files. Start getting acquainted with the ship *and* the crew."

"The crew? You think—"

"How," Peter cut in, "would you go about it if *you* wanted to stop this project?"

Buck hesitated. The surprises were still coming. Well, get used to it, he thought, and get out of here before he comes up with any more. Buck started for the door, then hesitated. "Oh, one other thing, Peter. I got a threatening phone call, a nasty one, the other night." He went on to explain.

Peter smiled. "We get those all the time. That's about as aggressive as most of these Greenies get," he shrugged.

The conference ended with that. A confusing conglomeration of thoughts and emotions sloshed about as Buck trudged heavily down the hallway toward Ed's office.

"Well, you asked for it, dummy," he mumbled to himself, "and now you know." First off, he'd have to dig around, see if he could find the *old* Buck Barnum. He was going to need him. But after all, for that kind of money he had to give it a—wait a minute! He jerked to a stop. He took the job Friday evening and within an *hour* he was already being threatened?

Chapter 5

"Good lunch?" Ed asked cheerily. He shoved the rear door of the office building open and headed between the two shop buildings toward the dock. Roland walked briskly, enthusiastically, the way he did everything. Buck struggled with the adjustable band on his white hardhat. "Soak up much of that reading material I gave you? I suppose you're an expert by now?" Buck smiled at Roland's habit of conspicuously placing his tongue in his cheek to accentuate his banter. His reddish complexion was even more vivid beneath the white helmet.

"The drawings of the ship are fascinating," Buck said, "and the history was interesting, too. Those cases of the midnight dumping in the East read like detective stories. It sounds to me like New Jersey is sitting on a toxic swamp. And some of the sneaky techniques they've used to get rid of the stuff—like dumping it down abandoned mine shafts."

They emerged from the shadows between the shops, and Buck bent over to follow Ed under the lowered boom of a mobile crane.

Clunk! Buck blinked as his hardhat thumped against steel.

"Watch your head! How about Pittston, Pennsylvania, where truck after truck pulled in behind that truck stop and dumped their loads down a hole? It ran right into the river!"

They straightened and paused in the bright sunlight. There she was! Not fifty feet away floated *Ark II* tied to the pier with thick hawsers. She rode high in the water, the hull rising far above the pier. Her tall, brilliant white superstructures fore and aft glistened in the afternoon sun.

"Wow! She's beautiful, and much bigger than I had visualized!" Buck exclaimed.

"Never been aboard a ship?"

"A couple of ferry boats. And I've done the harbor tour."

Buck felt the excitement swelling within him as they began their climb up the springy steel ramp that rose steeply from the pier to an opening in the ship's railing. His favorite digital camera, an old Canon, swung from his neck and bumped about as he moved. Once on deck, he clicked off several shots from fore to aft and back again. Through all the reading and discussions, he had thought she seemed real. But now, with the length and width, the massive red pipes and associated apparatus, the size and height of the forward superstructure that towered above their position on the forecastle deck, he was awestruck.

"If you'll follow me, we'll take the tour," Ed said.

"Lead on," Buck replied, hurriedly surveying the panorama. Docked portside, *Ark II* faced west toward the turning basin from which the main channel ran southward past Ports O' Call to the Pacific.

The forecastle deck extended back from the bow, splitting to wrap around the forward superstructure. Then the two sections called boat decks continued back along the port and starboard rails for another thirty feet, like balconies overlooking the pipe-covered main deck. On each boat deck was an enclosed lifeboat and a fire monitor station that resembled the water cannon on a large fire truck.

"I'm sorry," Ed said, as he stepped up and through the watertight door into the narrow passageway that ran the width of the forward house. "This tour will have to be a quickie, but then you can come aboard on your own and pick up more from the crew."

Buck followed Ed along the beige floor tiles of the passageway that split the forecastle level. In the center of the structure, just aft of the passageway, was a compact staircase that began three levels below them and ascended three levels upward. The passageways and staircases had walnut-grained, wainscot panels, with off-white panels above. Buck was glad for the study time he had put in. Things were where he anticipated they would be, and each room had a small, plastic sign above the door. In addition to the medical treatment room, the forecastle deck held six staterooms to accommodate two seamen each. The remainder of the seamen were housed one level below.

"How's this for class?" Ed laughed, opening a door. Though small, the stateroom was attractive, with its forest green commercial carpeting, its walnut paneling, double bunk bed, and matching furniture. The porthole even had a curtain that could be drawn. Behind a diagonal partition in one corner were the toilet, shower, and tiny lavatory.

"Crowded, but nice," Buck said, noting the small writing desk and accompanying chair. They ascended to A-deck, the officers' level, and Buck recalled that it held private quarters for the second mate, the radio officer, and the second and third assistant engineers. Their cabins, as Buck preferred to think of them, were the same size as the crew cabins below, but the officers had the advantage of privacy, along with extra furnishings, not the least of which was a tiny refrigerator. The observers' cabin was of the standard size, but it contained a double berth, a single berth, the writing desk, three lockers, and what Buck estimated to be four square feet of empty floor space.

"Wow, sardine time!" Buck said. "Is *this* where I'll bunk?"

"Not sure yet. We think we'll have three EPA observers aboard, each to cover two four-hour watches. If so, we'll add a berth somewhere else for you."

"Let's hope so," Buck said as he followed Ed up the staircase toward B-deck. Ed reached a landing midway up and disappeared around the corner. Then, a loud clattering resonated through the chamber.

"Hi, Chief!" came Roland's voice.

"Hey, ya lost? Later—" a second voice answered from somewhere up ahead. Around the turn came a huge, middle-aged man in white coveralls and a white hardhat, his boots thumping on each step only long enough to keep his gigantic frame upright. Buck flattened against the wall, and somehow the monster made it past him.

"What was *that?*" Buck shouted around the corner to Ed.

"That—was our chief engineer, Cliff Johnson. Neat guy, you'll like him. But stay out of his way when he's in a hurry! Six-foot-seven, two-sixty, and it's all muscle."

Aft of the B-deck passageway they found the private quarters for the first mate and the first assistant engineer, separated by a fan room. The large area ahead of the passageway was divided into two units, the captain's dayroom and stateroom and the chief engineer's matching facility. Each dayroom contained a computer terminal and was equipped with office furniture. They seemed like small apartments and were bright and cheery, with three forward-facing windows and one to the side. Good visibility, Buck thought. If anyone needs to know what's going on out there, the captain and the chief certainly do.

At the top level, the navigation and bridge deck, Ed allowed Buck a quick look at the radio room and then led him to the bridge. Buck stepped to the left, past the coffee stand and the public address system, to the windows on the port side. He paused just inside the door that led out to the port bridge wing. Turning slowly, he marveled at the view of ships, loading cranes, docks, and buildings. The perimeter of the bridge was enclosed almost entirely with glass—nearly 360-degree vision.

"Let's move on," Ed directed. He led the way through a small door at the rear of the bridge. Before Buck knew it, he was standing on a narrow steel grating high above the main deck. He wobbled briefly and grabbed for the railing. Far below, he could see two groups of small men gathered on the main deck. The blue jeans and silver hardhats of the seamen contrasted with the white coveralls and white hardhats of the officers.

"Up there," Ed motioned toward the housetop, "are the radar, radio, and SAT-COM antennas. Take the shortcut?" he asked. Without waiting for an answer, he started down the narrow steel gratings that served as steps.

Buck fought the panic that mushroomed within. With the see-through steps, it seemed there was nothing between himself and the main deck fifty feet below. He was determined to keep pace, by concentrating on each step, but he knew that his nervousness had not escaped Roland. Just when he was gaining some comfort on the treacherous steps, he bumped into Ed, who had suddenly stopped again at the boat deck level.

"I want to hold up here and tell you something about her design, a safety feature that makes her unique," Ed began, "something you wouldn't pick up from the drawings. From bow to stern, below main deck level, she's built in twelve separate compartments. The *only* way to get from one of those sections to another is to come up to main deck level, cross over, and go back down. Each compartment, whether a work station or a chemical storage tank, is literally sealed off from all others. Because of gravity, fluids seek a constant level. But they can't climb steps or ladders." Roland's cheek bulged again. "So, they stay where they belong."

"That's really impressive—"

"I'm going to have to cut the tour here," Ed said, glancing at his watch. "I think, whenever you're ready, you can see the rest of it on your own."

"Ed, do I understand we'll have a crew of twenty-two, plus three observers and myself?" Buck asked as they started down the shaky ramp.

"You got it," Ed said without breaking stride. He chattered nonstop as they walked back to the office. Buck vowed to exchange his notepad for the more convenient micro-recorder.

They had just reached the office when the phone rang. Ed answered it. He listened, looked up at Buck, and then replaced the phone.

"What's up?" Buck asked.

"Viola. You're wanted in Grigsby's office."

Buck raised one eyebrow, shrugged, and started up front. He entered the suite and approached Viola Erichs.

"Good afternoon, Mr. Barnum," she said without looking up. Buck was somewhat startled by her tone of voice. It wasn't friendly, but it didn't carry the hostility he expected. "You may go in. Mr. Grigsby is waiting."

She held out a manila file folder toward Buck, but her eyes remained fixed on the work before her. He took the folder and entered Grigsby's office.

"Close the door," said Grigsby.

"Certainly, sir," Buck replied. He followed Grigsby's gesture to the chair before the desk. The tall man wore an expensive gray suit. When he leaned forward and looked over his tiny glasses, the sharp nose, the steel face, and the penetrating eyes reminded Buck of a bald eagle. Buck wondered how a Californian could keep such a pale color. He decided that Grigsby must carry an umbrella to and from the parking lot.

"Won't take much of your time," Grigsby said curtly. "I want to apologize for that scene in the meeting." His voice warmed. It was almost pleasant. "Of course," Grigsby went on, "you really had no business *at* that meeting. But since you *were* there, you're aware that we do have some internal differences."

Buck nodded, meeting the other man's eyes with an unyielding gaze.

"And since you were privy to matters beyond your concern, you will be expected to maintain professional confidentiality. Can you do that?"

"Of course."

"Do you understand the issue?"

"Yes, I understand it quite well, and I understand and respect your concern for the company. That's your job."

The older man blinked. His head twitched, a jerky motion, as though shaking off a fly that had landed on his cheek.

"Good, Barnum, good."

"Mr. Grigsby, I have nothing but respect for a man faced with the responsibilities of your position. It's heavy duty, and I'll work with you the best I can. But, I'll be able to contribute more to a working relationship when I feel it's built on mutual respect." Damn! Where did that come from? Buck thought. But a part of him was relieved to have taken the offensive. He forced a slight grin and waited.

"How do you stand on the issue, Barnum? With me? Or against me."

The question caught Buck by surprise. Grigsby's face showed nothing.

"Mr. Grigsby, I was hired to do a job, and I'll do the best I can at that job. But I can do that better if I stay out of company politics."

"That's a political answer. Do you *really* think you can do that?"

"Try me." Buck felt the blood of the old Buck Barnum warming his veins.

"Sometimes," Grigsby began slowly, "life just isn't that simple, and sometimes people who refuse to take a stand are bigger losers than those who take the wrong stand. Now, the smart people position themselves for the long-range benefit of the company as opposed to short-term goals. It's too soon to know if there could be a future for you here at Essee Beecee, but when this is all over, we might be looking for a new public relations man. You give that some thought, will you?"

"Is there an explanation to go with this folder?" Buck asked, waving the folder Viola had given him as he entered the office.

"That's a list I compiled, a list of organizations who would have reasons to oppose the *Ark II* project." He almost smiled. "You might say it's a list of the reasons I don't believe the incineration program can succeed. Thought you might find it helpful . . . Buck."

"I'm sure this will be very helpful. Thank you very much." With that, Buck rose, reached across the desk to shake Grigsby's hand, and left. He took control of the strange session by ending it.

As he circled Ms. Erichs' desk, he glanced through the open door of the other office. Charles Hudson looked up from behind his desk, rose to a half-standing position, and waved for Buck to come in. Buck hesitated, drew a deep breath, and walked in.

"Close the door," Hudson ordered.

Oh, brother, Buck thought. Here we go again! But this one's not going to last long. He didn't offer me a chair.

"Well, how's it going?" the CEO began, a warm, wide smile on his face.

"I'm certainly learning a lot, sir."

"I'm sure." The smile disappeared, and the intensity of Hudson's eyes increased as he focused on Buck. "So, what have you come up with?"

"I—ahh—I don't really have much yet. I'm just—"

"You *haven't?* What the hell are you doing?"

Before Buck could answer, Hudson fired another volley, "Don't you think you'd better get started pretty soon? I was told you were a man who gets results. I certainly hope I wasn't misinformed."

Buck felt the heat rising. He struggled to contain it. "I have to understand who and what *we* are before I can begin to identify and understand our opponents and then anticipate their—"

"Sure, sure. We have a meeting on Friday. Certainly you'll have something to report by then." With a wave, he dismissed Buck as brusquely as he had begun the confrontation.

Buck was steaming as he left Hudson's office. He wanted to charge back into battle, do it over so he could come out the winner. But as he walked, he was surprised to feel the pressure giving way to pride. He had stood up for himself in one confrontation and controlled himself in the other. Maybe it was all the practice he'd had lately. Did Hudson *really* expect results so soon? Or was it the closed-door conference with Grigsby that set him off? On impulse, Buck turned and headed for Peter's office. He couldn't be running to Daddy Peter forever, he thought, but one more session was in order. He knocked on the frame beside the open door and walked in.

Peter looked up at Buck and studied him for a moment.

"I'd offer you a penny for your thoughts, but if I wait, I'll get them for free," Peter said, with a smirk. "One might think you're just a little pissed."

"One might be right." Buck told Peter about the two strange meetings.

"You said *that* to Grigsby?"

"Afraid I did. Wasn't too smart, but it felt good."

"Did you react to Hudson the same way?"

"No, I ate crow the whole time," Buck said.

"Good decision, Buck. If you had mouthed off to Hudson, you'd be history. He manages people through intimidation. He's like a rattle-snake. He'd rather use his rattles to keep you where you belong, but he'll bite you if you persist."

"It seems to me that our Grigsby wants me to help make the project fail."

"I think not," Peter said. "I think he wants you to help convince *us* that it's going to fail."

"Is it going to fail?"

Peter lowered his voice, "Just between us, Buck, we've got a fifty-fifty chance. The outcome depends largely on two people."

"Are you saying? . . . Man, that's heavy!" Buck said. "Back to foot-ball days, huh?"

"Striking parallel, isn't it? But, just like the old days, we won't do well if you spend your energy fighting the big C," Peter admonished.

"The coach?"

"The captain—Hudson. Now, let's have a look at Grigsby's lists."

"You think they're any good?" Buck asked.

"Grigsby is, among other things, a very thorough, methodical man. I don't think he'd just throw together a bunch of names. I'm betting it's a good, if not complete, list."

Huddling over Peter's desk, they discussed the list of commercial competitors first. Peter was confident that Grigsby had acquired the names through the state agency responsible for licensing companies engaged in the transportation or disposal of hazardous wastes. The list was composed of over thirty companies located in Los Angeles and Orange Counties, and it included addresses, chief executives, and data on services they were licensed to provide.

"Here," said Peter, "scratch these two. I know them well. They've done work for us. And some of the others are too small to be dangerous. Save you some time. You'd have to research that to know."

"What can you tell me about this list of environmentalists?" Buck asked. "Thank God, it's much shorter." They studied the list:

GREEN GROUPS
ASH (Alliance to Save the Harbor)
Friends of the Earth
Greenpeace
Groundswell
Izaak Walton League
National Audubon Society
National Wildlife Federation
Sierra Club
Society for the Preservation of Marine Life
Wilderness Society

"Well, we know of ASH, of course," Peter said. "Ed's on that one. A local group, started small but seems to be growing. If they ever latch on to some funding, they could become dangerous—at least politically."

"These are all enemies?" Buck asked. " A friend belonged to Audubon for years, and I've been close to Izaak Walton. I don't think they're the kind to zero in on us."

"Probably not. I'd put the established organizations, those with class, at the bottom of the list. If they become active, they'll use the media, and we'll know it immediately. If they do get involved, it'll be with press releases, lobbying, and, at the worst, picketing."

"Okay," Buck said, sliding the papers into the folder. "Any suggestions on how I proceed?"

"Think about it, Buck."

Buck hesitated, taking in the devious smile on Peter's face. "Oh, snoop around, make some phone calls, ask questions, and lie like hell about who I am and why I'm asking,"

Peter simply shrugged. "You take it from here, Buck. I'll be in Washington for a day or two, and—oh, you have a meeting set up for tonight at six—Dante's."

"A meeting? Tonight? Who—"

"That officer from the Long Beach Police Department, Detective Bercovich."

Chapter 6

It was almost six when Dante ushered Buck to a booth. Weird, Buck thought, Dante was uncharacteristically quiet—treated me like a stranger—no names, Italian or otherwise. The booth was one of the two that shared an isolated cubicle in the farthest corner of the Catamaran. He sat, wondering about Dante's strange behavior and what this meeting might bring.

Suddenly, a face peeked around the high back of the bench seat opposite Buck, startling him. The oval face was attractive, one that smiled—even without smiling. She had a California tan that was unsullied by makeup. Her brown eyes beamed through narrow openings beneath straight bangs that reached halfway to her eyebrows. A slightly disheveled mop of short, brown hair revealed a pair of elfin ears from which dangled large, gold loops. Buck was caught up in a magnetic field that stopped his brain and left him speechless.

"Mr. Barnumini?" she asked, her wide, sensuous lips breaking slightly into a cautious, dimpled smile. Her tiny, up-turned nose crinkled when she smiled. She stepped into full view where Buck's eyes quickly took in a shapely figure of average height. She wore tobacco brown, suede jeans and a tan, well-filled blouse with large, brown buttons that matched her jeans. Over her shoulder was slung a matching brown suede purse.

Buck sprang upward, but he found himself caught by the table, stuck in an awkward position, tongue-tied and perplexed by the attractive intruder.

"May I sit down?" The smile blossomed into a wide grin revealing perfect white teeth. Her eyes never left Buck's. They seemed to be enjoying his embarrassment.

"Oh—of course!" he stammered. As she slid into the booth across from him, he let his body sink back to the wooden bench.

"Lenny Bercovichio," she said in an alto voice that had the rich warmth of velour. She extended her right hand, and with her left she flipped open a small, black leather-covered folder showing an L.B.P.D.

badge. His confusion was complete. "Actually, it's Leonora Bercovich, but everyone calls me Lenny," she added.

The irony brought Buck's first smile. Man, he thought, I spend my life trying to duck the name Beverly, and this cute, cute girl, what is she, probably early thirties? She willingly tags herself, "Lenny."

"Am I under arrest? If I am, I'll go willingly." he said.

"That's what some of them say," she laughed. "Others get a little—difficult."

A busy waiter took their orders for drinks. Buck's bourbon and water followed her request for iced tea.

"Dante asked me to meet with you." She cast a quick look over her shoulder and another at the empty booth. "I owe him one, and he thinks I can help you with your project." Her explanation bumped Buck back to reality, although he didn't need the guilt that came with it.

"I'm sorry for being such a klutz," Buck said. I was sitting here, wondering why I'm sitting here, and suddenly—you took me by surprise."

"It's okay, Buck." Lenny smiled and continued, "You're the first one in a long time who didn't come right out and ask if I really am a cop. I've been with the department for twelve years now, made detective in seven."

The waiter brought their drinks and took their orders.

"I know a little about your incinerator ship, but I confess, only a little," Lenny said. "It sounds like something we've needed for a long time. Will it really do everything they say?"

"I'm not an expert myself, but I think it will," Buck replied. He went on to summarize the hazardous waste problem and stress the gravity of it. Then, after a brief discourse on the previous fiasco in New Jersey, he described the ship to her. Lenny Bercovich listened intently, her face sober but for the smiling eyes.

"Why haven't we heard more about this through the media?" she asked.

"My words exactly when I was brought into this. I don't know." My God, he thought, she's beautiful, warm, and intelligent.

"If you can eliminate toxic chemicals with ninety-nine percent efficiency, why put the incinerators on ships? Why not just build them on land?"

"There *are* a number of land-based incinerators in the country. As I understand it, our advantage over the land-based incinerators is that our acidic stack effluent falls into the ocean where it is neutralized by the salt water. The land-based have to add stack scrubbers to prevent acid rain, and they are *very* expensive. We can do the job more safely and a lot cheaper."

"Makes sense."

"Actually, the master plan that I hear bandied about includes both land and sea-based incinerators. It would add elements of risk and cost to truck wastes from mid-western cities like St. Louis to one of the coasts, so there is a need for the land-based units, too. But, a greater portion of the petrochemical industry is located on or near the coasts. That's where we come in.

"To ever hope to catch up with the stockpile of wastes and the daily production," he continued, "it'll take both types and new technology for recycling. No one of these approaches can handle the issue alone. If we keep burying everything in the ground, we're in real trouble!" Buck was surprised to hear himself carrying on with such authority and enthusiasm.

"I'm sold," Lenny said. Leaning toward Buck, her warm eyes focused on his, she asked, "How can I help?"

"There are outfits out there who are making a bundle by hauling and disposing the stuff. Some are doing it within the law, hauling it to certified dump sites, although even *that* simply postpones the day of reckoning. Got to be others who are dumping the stuff illegally. Then there are the green groups who oppose us. Some of them will do that legally, and—"

The waiter appeared with their dinner. The conversation lagged to occasional small talk for a time as they ate. Buck's mind was occupied with his attraction to Lenny Bercovich. Is it the face? The body? No, it's more than that. She's warm, concerned about me, or at least the project. And she's *comfortable.* When was the last time he felt so comfortable with a woman? Roberta—any woman? He could see now how a middle-aged man can give it all up for a younger woman. It's like choosing between comfort and cyanide. He glanced at her left hand. No ring. Twelve years with the department? She's not *that* much younger.

It was Lenny who brought them back to business. "And you want me to help identify the bad guys?"

"Right with me, aren't you?" Buck laughed.

Lenny's face became more serious than Buck had seen it. Her eyes still glowed, but with an added intensity. "You have to understand that there is organized cri—"

"Where the hell'sshh the men's room?" A small man, with a short ponytail showing beneath an old-style fedora, was standing there facing the blank wall across the aisle from their booth. He turned their way and then back to the wall, apparently searching for a door that wasn't there.

"Back that way," Buck said, motioning toward the main dining room.

The little man wheeled and marched unsteadily away. Buck rolled his eyes, looked at Lenny, and laughed.

"There—there is organized *crime*," Lenny began again, her eyes momentarily looking past Buck, "and there are *criminals* who are organized. Not all are part of the Cosa Nostra. The organized criminals are often harder to identify, but they're usually easier to prosecute. I've had some experience with both. More important, I can pick up scuttlebutt on the streets and at headquarters that you wouldn't have access to."

Buck explained his role, that of the neophyte trouble-shooter. At the same time, he tried to show something of his aggressiveness, realizing suddenly that he was more intent on impressing this fascinating woman than enlightening her.

"Here are some lists that we've put together for starters," he said, handing her copies.

"Before we go any farther," she cautioned, "I have to be sure you understand some things. I'm all for your cause," Lenny continued, "but we have to be careful here. Investigating suspected criminal activities is one thing. Getting dragged into legal, competitive business strategies is something else."

"Understood," Buck agreed.

"You also have to understand a couple of other things. One: juris-diction – the city of Long Beach is my territory. The Port of Los Angeles, where your ship is docked, is the domain of the L.A. Port Police.

We work together, and I have a close contact in the L.A.P.P. For whatever reason, Dante thought you ought to start with me. If we find things that spill over, belong to the harbor guys, that's where I'll send you.

The other matter: the department has some very strict rules on what I can and cannot share with a private citizen. That means, you tell me *everything*. I tell you *only* what I'm allowed. I run off at the mouth—I get my butt in a sling. You follow?"

"Got it," Buck replied. His imagination ran with the pleasurable image.

"You pretty tough?" Lenny asked.

"Well, I uh—"

"Football player?"

"Well, yes.

"If this involves the kind of people it might involve, you've got to remember, they make their own rules—no striped shirts, no zebras on the field. You leave the touchy stuff to us. Okay?"

Buck was embarrassed. It was like turning the trench warfare of a football game over to—he drew a quick vision of Lenny Bercovich dressed as a cheerleader. Man, she looked good! But he needed her help, wanted to please her. Back off, he thought. Don't chase her away.

"Okay," he conceded. "I'd say you're the boss, only I already have so many I can't count them."

Lenny laughed. "Well, my good man, you just picked up another," she said. Her eyes warmed. Engaging crinkles appeared at the corners. Buck felt the pull of the magnetism. "Now then," She scanned the commercial list. "Umm-hmmm," she repeated several times, making check marks as she proceeded down the list. Buck watched, wonder-ing what her checks represented. "I'll see what I can find on some of these."

She switched to the second list on which Buck had underlined three names: Greenpeace, Groundswell, and ASH. "I'd agree with your choices," she said. "Wouldn't expect any covert shit from Audubon or Walton."

Normally, Buck would have been slightly shocked to hear a four-letter word coming from a classy woman like this, especially to a near stranger. But she slid the word into context so smoothly, it wasn't offensive. After all, he reasoned, that's probably nothing compared to the vocabulary of her world. And it made him feel like he could say just about anything to her. He liked that.

"I've never heard of this Groundswell," Lenny continued. Of course, you know about Greenpeace. Typically, they use what they call passive interference. Don't know what's passive about trespassing and tying yourself to a ship's anchor."

"I'm sure these lists aren't complete," Buck offered. "If you think of others, add them."

"Of course," she agreed, folding the papers and jamming them into her purse. "I'll get back to you in a day or two. Do you have a card?"

She handed Buck her card and waited while he wrote his name, office phone number, and his home number on a slip of paper. He paused and found himself looking at Lenny's left hand, the bare ring finger. She abruptly changed posture, placing her elbows on the table with her forearms upright, lacing the fingers of both hands together, and resting her chin on the interlocked hands.

Buck looked up. She was smiling at him. He nonchalantly tossed the paper her way. As he pocketed her card he noticed the words, *four to midnight*, written on the back.

"Enough business," Buck said as their dishes were removed and coffee was served. "Tell me about yourself."

"Not much to tell," Lenny began, "native Californian, UCLA degree in law enforcement, married at twenty-two, mother at twenty-three, divorced at twenty-four."

"And still single after how many years?"

"Subtle as a brick, aren't you?" she laughed. With that, she slid gracefully from the booth and announced that she had to leave. Buck's watch said eight o'clock.

"Stayed too long, as it is," she said. "I *am* on duty, you know." Buck started from the booth, but she placed a hand on his shoulder, pushing him back. "No, please. I leave alone. You stay here for a few minutes. Finish your coffee." A quick smile, and she was gone.

Leaning over, he watched the trim, graceful figure swish around a corner and disappear. He sat back and sipped his coffee, aware of the conflict between disappointment and excitement that was raging deep inside of him.

"Oh, man," he said softly, "and I thought I was about dead."

Chapter 7

Long before the Thursday morning sun could creep above the eastern coast range of hills behind his house, Buck sat in the large, leather office chair in his favorite room, his oak-paneled den. Two days had passed since his meeting with Lenny Bercovich. He had yet to hear from her, but he had certainly thought of her many times.

Once again, he forced her from his consciousness by focusing on the job. Since the meeting, he had spent two days researching, developing his list of competitors in the waste disposal business. But his efforts seemed to be working against him. When he should be narrowing the list to the most likely prospects, he found it mushrooming in size. Maybe Lenny would call today and point him in the right direction. Yeah, maybe Lenny would call.

He heard the coffee maker finish its cycle, so he headed for the kitchen. With his cup filled, he started past the kitchen table to return to the den. Strange, he thought, as he stopped and looked down at the table and chairs. For so many years, that had been the family gathering spot. Most of their non-working, non-sleeping hours had been spent at that table. Now, he almost lived in the den with his computer.

Thirty minutes later he turned and headed up the Pacific Coast Highway. While driving through Long Beach, he decided that he would spend a few hours each morning getting acquainted with the ship and the crew members. He had an idea he wanted to try. As he met the crew, he would snap a photo of each man. It would help him to learn faces quickly; it would make most of them feel good. After all, who doesn't like to have his picture taken? A spy, that's who. A crewman with a hidden agenda would tend to be camera shy, and *that*, Buck thought, could be a real help to me. The rest of the time will go into my outside intelligence work. He smiled at the title he had chosen for it.

Arriving at the office, he grabbed his Canon and micro-recorder and headed out to the ship. He was glad he had opted for the blue jeans and sport shirt. Suits were completely out of place aboard the ship. When he had climbed the springy steps and found himself on the forecastle deck, he paused. How was that pronounced? Seems like Ed called it the focusle, or foc'sle. "Foc'sle, foc'sle," he repeated, surveying the ship from fore to aft. Two seamen were chipping and scraping paint from separate cargo hatches, and beyond them was a group of silver hardhats clustered around a white one.

Unsure of shipboard protocol, Buck decided that the captain should be his first contact. He started toward the watertight door of the forward house. On impulse, he stopped. No, damn it! he thought. This dude is going up the *outside* steps. Pausing at the landing of each succeeding deck level to deliberately subject himself to the height, he made his way to the top. He hoped, after all that, the door wasn't locked! Going up is a whole lot easier than going down.

The lever moved and he made his way through the tiny vestibule to the bridge. There was nobody there, but Buck decided to look around a while before heading back down. It was while Buck was taking pictures of the collision-avoidance radar monitors that he noticed the two video cameras. One was mounted above the radar apparatus, obviously focused on the equipment. The other hung from the ceiling in such a way as to take in all activity at the ship's controls along the front windows of the bridge. He remembered reading that in an emergency mode the cameras are activated to record the radar scopes, as well as human reactions by those controlling the ship. I guess that's their version of the airlines' little, black boxes, he mused. Another good idea. Following a flurry of shutter clicks, he left, choosing the inside stairs down to the captain's cabin on the deck below.

"Come!" was the reply to his knock beside the open door, and he stepped into the captain's dayroom.

"Captain Portner?" Buck asked of the slender, khaki-clad man who was seated at the desk to his right. The middle-aged officer with wavy, gray hair swiveled his chair. He stared briefly from behind wire-rimmed glasses and then stood mechanically to shake hands.

"Gene Portner," the captain said with a resounding lack of expression, like he was bored with the sound of his own name.

Buck was surprised at the man's size, perhaps five-eight? Five-nine? He couldn't help glancing at the shoulder boards to be sure this was indeed the captain.

"You the man Ed Roland was telling me about? Publicity man?" the captain asked.

"Right." Buck wondered if Captain Portner knew of his real assignment. Portner struck him as one of the most expressionless men he had ever met. His demeanor suggested no hostility, but no friendliness either.

"This," the captain said, pointing to a large man in white coveralls who was seated across from the doorway on a sofa, "is Chief Johnson."

Buck recognized the size and shape as the chief came up off the sofa. While Johnson wiped his greasy right hand on his coveralls, Buck studied him intently. His rugged, dirt-smudged face was not handsome, but his dancing eyes and fixed grin gave it a friendly appeal. He had straight, brown hair combed to one side in a style from the thirties and enormous, bushy eyebrows. When Buck's sturdy hand disappeared within Cliff Johnson's grasp, he feared that he might get it back in pieces.

"We almost met yesterday," Buck said with a smile, relieved that he still had feeling in his hand. "In fact, if I hadn't heard you coming, I'd probably be dead."

"Oh? Oh, that was you with Ed Roland? Sorry 'bout that. I'm always in a hurry. Speaking of . . . Cap'n, I'll have those starboard valves checked. Nice to meet you, Buck." The large man plunked his helmet on his head and hustled from the dayroom. There was an awkward silence.

"Uh, Captain, I'm new to ships, but I'm certainly here to learn."

"You mean, do I have an orientation program for you?"

"Well, something like that."

"No, Barnum, you have the run of the ship. Observe, ask questions. But don't get in the way. My concerns are the efficiency and safety of this ship, not what the newspapers say." Then, turning his back on Buck and reaching for some papers on a nearby shelf, he added, "Stop in anytime."

"Captain, do you mind pictures?"

"Yes . . . but go ahead," Captain Portner replied without looking up. Buck hurried around the desk for a shot, thanked him, and left.

As he slowly made his way down to A-deck, he muttered to himself, "I think I just met a robot."

He poked his head into the officers' lounge on A-deck, and finding it empty he descended past the forecastle deck to the main deck. The passageway here was L-shaped, extending from the right side of the house structure to the center where he stood, and then straight ahead toward the bow. The latter portion of the passageway was flanked on the right by the galley and on the left by first the crew's mess and then the officers' mess.

The clank of metal broke the silence, and the aroma of fresh pastries reminded Buck that he was hungry. Seeing no one in the crew's mess, he went for the officers' mess. It was surprisingly small, with painted off-white walls and the standard green carpet. Three small, circular tables were surrounded by orange Naugahyde chairs. The metal lips around the table tops reminded Buck that he was on a ship, and the future could bring some rough seas.

"Hi there, Mr. Barnum!" came a cheery voice from across the passageway.

Buck turned to see the back of a white-clad figure over in the galley. The man wiped a kettle and tossed it carelessly onto a countertop. His white paper hat was jammed down over long, shaggy black hair, and his white T-shirt revealed massive shoulders that tapered only slightly to a roll of fat above his waist.

"Coffee and rolls over there," he said, turning toward Buck. While the reddish-brown skin of his smiling fat face suggested American Indian, Buck was surprised by the large, round eyes. "You officer or crew?"

"Don't know, I guess," Buck replied. "Could be both, or neither."

"Then start at the top and work down," the friendly cook said, pushing Buck ahead of him into the officers' mess, pointing to the coffee urn and Danish pastries on a small counter to the left.

"You must be," Buck began, pausing to pour his coffee, grab a roll, and try to recall the name from the ship's roster. "Ah, you must be Joe Morse."

"They call me Indian Joe," the young man said with a nervous laugh that reminded Buck of a bleating goat. Placing his own coffee on the table, Joe reached across for a belated handshake. "'course after chow, they call me other things, too."

"How'd you know me?" Buck asked, taking a huge bite of the tasty, apple-cinnamon pastry.

"Not much that goes on 'round here that Joe don't know," he said, punctuating his answer with another chuckle. "Yer s'posed to be a writer, but the word is, yer a spy fer the company." Joe's friendly grin became a devious smile that changed the statement to a question.

"A spy? Is that what *they* say? Or is that what *you* think?"

"Both." Another chuckle.

"Well, in a way, I guess you're right. No writer can be worth a damn if he isn't alert to what's going on around him." Buck laughed and watched for a reaction. None. "Tell me, Indian Joe, how did *you* get into this?" he asked.

"Which question you askin'?"

"Pardon me?"

"You askin' how *Joe* got this job? Or you askin' how an *Ojibway Indian* got the job."

"Ojibway—are you Chippewa? Wisconsin or Minnesota?"

Joe's eyes brightened. "Minnesota. Little village called Inger, up there east of Bemidji, south of International Falls. You ever heard of it?"

"Heard of it! I used to do some fishing right in your neighborhood—Big Sand Lake. I came originally from Woodridge in southern Minnesota."

"No shit! Big Sand's just two miles up the river from Joe's house. Joe grew up on that lake, ricin' and fishin'. 'Course Joe's walleye limits were a little bigger than yers, and sometimes Joe used gill nets 'stead of fishin' line." He laughed heartily and then stuffed the last of his roll into his mouth.

"Ohhh, so you're one the guys that nearly wiped out the walleyes," Buck accused with a laugh.

"Our fish." The smile was gone.

"Maybe so. Tell me, how did Joe—how did *you* end up out here?"

"How much time you got?" He chuckled and then continued,

"If you know anythin' 'bout the reservation, you know they got some problems." Indian Joe's face turned serious.

"You mean the alcohol?"

"Allus had alcohol problems." Joe went on, "The whites say, 'That's yer own fault for bein' a bunch o' drunks.' The Indians say, 'It's their fault for takin' our land and sellin' us the booze.' None o' that don't change nothin'. But like the poison weren't enough, then come the drugs, then come the lawyers who know how to work the gover'ment for more money, an' then come the *educated* Indians." He bracketed the last two words with quotes, using two fingers of each hand.

"Educated Indians?"

"Yeh, the *good* ones that got through college. They come back to the reservation as gover'ment agents, college perfessors, and teachers."

"So what's wrong with that?"

"Nothin' 'cept their doubletalk and their chest pounding. They tell us we should fight our way through the white man's university so we kin fight for the right to *what?* Live like washed out Indians? An' they're allus sayin', 'Look at *me*. Look what *I've* done.' Makes it shittin' confusin' to a high school guy, that's all. My dad pulls his head outa the bottle an' says, 'Joe should stay right here an' be a Indian.' The educated ones say, 'Joe should go to college an' then come back an' be a Native American.' My buddies say, 'What the hell ya wanna do that for, too good for us?' Shittin' confusin' that's what."

"I guess that would be. So, what did Joe, uh, you do?"

"Well, Joe should do this. Joe should do that. They all talked at Joe. They all talked 'bout Joe. Nobody never talked *with* him. So Joe quit school in his junior year, hitched his way out here, an' got a job in a rest'rant. Sorta like that Frank Snotra guy—did it *my* way."

Buck laughed, then caught himself. It wasn't meant to be funny. But Indian Joe was laughing, too.

"You're all right, Joe! Did you have any trouble finding work?"

"Nah, the 'stablishment has to take some minor'ties, so I had a big 'vantage. They don' wanna get stuck with big gangs o' minor'ties, an' if they hire even one of them damned Blacks, Mexes, Chinks, or Gooks, that's what they'll end up with. But how many Ojibways out here?

Got a job cookin' in a fast food. Then pulled some strings an' I got on here."

"You know, in some ways my background and reasons for escaping to California were a little like yours, Joe."

"Oh? Which reservation you come from, *White* Earth?"

"Worse. My mother was a librarian."

"No shit? That *is* worse. Allus got my ass chewed fer makin' noise in the lib'ary." They laughed together and then chatted on, mostly about fishing on Big Sand Lake.

"Joe, were you serious about the spy stuff?"

"Uh huh." The sly grin reappeared.

"Why would the company want a spy out here?" Buck tried to appear as casual as possible. If everyone knew his real purpose, it could be difficult. He'd get little cooperation from anyone.

"Well, after the shakedown cruise, they fired four guys an' brought new ones in. So ever'body figgers yer here to see if there's any more that should be whacked outa here. Right?"

Buck laughed, a big, deep, genuine laugh.

Indian Joe Morse looked confused. For the first time, he seemed to have lost his control of the situation.

"Joe, let me tell you something—straight up. I've *never* been on a ship before in my life. How the hell would I know who is and who is not doing his job! So far, I know only two things—the captain gives the orders, and Indian Joe makes damned good rolls."

"*Never* been on a ship?"

"Never."

"So what the shit you doin' here then?"

"Here to learn about the ship, and guess what? To write about what I learn." Joe sat back. He looked embarrassed. "And now, Buck's got to go. Got a lot to learn." He chose to leave it at that and started for the door.

"Hey, Buck White Earth!"

Buck stopped and turned.

"Put yer dishes on that yella' tray over there!" There was the infectious smile Buck had first encountered. While Buck followed instructions, he coaxed the young man back to his galley for a picture. Just as

Buck was ready to shoot, Indian Joe grabbed a pan, slapped it on his head, scrunching the paper hat, and mugged for the camera.

On his way topside, Buck thought about the young Indian. Certainly not camera shy, and he was really quite likable. Even his blunt approach to things was refreshing. But Indian Joe Morse was definitely one shrewd character, dumb like the proverbial fox.

Chapter 8

Buck meandered aft along the central catwalk snapping shots of pipes, valve assemblies, access hatches to the twelve storage tanks, anything that caught his eye. Two officers headed his way. He recognized one, the large figure of Cliff Johnson. The other man was about Buck's size and a few years older. As they met, Buck made out the label on the man's white hardhat, RUNKLE—1st ASST. ENG.

Chief Johnson introduced Buck to Mal Runkle. "Buck's the PR man—be with us on the burn." The man ignored Buck's hand. He stared briefly into Buck's eyes, sneered, and continued on.

A grin flicked across the chief's face and he said, "Coffee time. Join us?"

"Thanks, Chief. Just came from there. See you later." Buck watched the two men as they headed forward. That's not a nice man, he thought as he watched Runkle swagger along the catwalk. I've seen faces like that across the line of scrimmage in games, but a first meeting with a fellow employee? Buck activated his micro-recorder and dictated his impressions of the people he had met so far.

"Runkle," he said, "very, very unfriendly. And it seems to be personal. Calls for some special attention."

On his way aft, he stopped for a couple of shots of the white, five-hundred-gallon liquid nitrogen tank, the reservoir for the IGS system. As each tank is loaded with chemicals, the nitrogen is used to top off the tank, thereby eliminating all oxygen and the potential for fire. He remembered reading something about old tankers that blew up when the sloshing of crude oil generated static electricity. What if this IGS system doesn't work right? He shuddered as a quick vision came to him, a vision of Buck Barnum standing on deck when the tanks suddenly explode.

Climbing the white steps to the after structure, Buck shot pictures of everything from the tall signal light mast to the forward house. He started down the steps that led below to the first of the three separate divisions within the stern. The first two flights of steps took him down past large flume tanks used for ballast, little of interest.

Descending still farther, he found himself in the pump room. There, lined up side-by-side, about two feet above the deck and spaced out nearly the width of the ship, were twenty-four gigantic electric pumps. The orderly mass of large pipes showed clearly that the pumps drew the cargo from the tanks amidship and fed it to the incinerators somewhere aft of the pump room.

Buck's attention was drawn to an assembly of strobe lights attached near an audio alarm on the forward bulkhead. He recalled reading that there were some two dozen of these alarm stations. Let's see, he thought, the red means general alarm, blue is for fire, yellow means phone, and white is . . . all clear? Good thinking. With all the noise during a burn, a guy might not hear his walkie-talkie or the audio alarms, but with those strobe lights reflecting around corners and everywhere, anyone should get the message. Some good, though, if she blows up.

When he had climbed back topside, he entered the incinerator control room. The simplicity of the room surprised him. He saw a couple of work tables with chairs, shelves of books and three-ring binders along two walls, and a control console that occupied most of the aft wall. Two men standing at the console turned as Buck entered. Both wore white coveralls, but while one wore a white hardhat, the other wore orange.

Buck introduced himself and asked where he might find Dr. Keene. The tall, skinny, young man beneath the orange hat smiled and waved Buck toward them. He had a slender face, high cheekbones, a pointed nose, and a tiny mouth. Small, green eyes peered through large, plastic-rimmed glasses. He appeared to be in his early twenties.

"I'm Dr. Keene," he said, extending his hand.

Buck was startled by the resonant bass voice that came from such frail stature.

"And you're Mr. Barnum? Welcome to the garbage department."

"*You're* Dr. Keene? Oh, I'm sorry—"

"Quite all right." Dr. Keene laughed. "It happens all the time," he said, flashing a knowing look at his compatriot. "Actually, I'm older than I look—three years older." He laughed again. "This is Craig Gantsky, second assistant engineer."

"Glad to have you with us!" Gantsky said.

He was in his early thirties, about five-foot-ten, and he had a slender but athletic build that showed even through his loose fitting coveralls. His handsome, smiling face provided the perfect setting for bright blue eyes like Buck had never seen before. They radiated a glowing quality that seemed say, "I'm special, and so are you."

"Please don't take offense," Buck said, his gaze still locked on the mesmerizing blue gems, "but you don't belong here. With eyes like those, you belong in Hollywood." A brief memory flashed through Buck's mind as he spoke the word.

Gantsky grinned and lowered his head modestly.

"You're a jock," Buck added. "Baseball?"

"Football, played guard in high school. Too small for a college lineman, so I wasted a couple of years of my life and then went to the Merchant Marine Academy."

"My guess is, you were pretty good, though," Buck said, resisting the urge to mention that he himself had succeeded in college football despite his size. I think he could have made it, Buck mused. He just didn't find the right opportunity.

"Craig is a tech-nut, crazy about computers," Dr. Keene injected. "His responsibilities are in unrelated areas, but he comes back here whenever he has time. He soaks it up faster than I can teach him. In another week, he'll be teaching me."

Buck looked back to Gantsky, who seemed embarrassed. Then, with a quick step toward the computer cabinet, Gantsky flipped open a compartment and reached inside. His hand came out moments later with a rectangular metal device that was about one inch by two inches and perhaps a half-inch thick.

"Look at this!" he said with the enthusiasm of a child who has found the prize-winning Easter egg, "just look at this!" He waved the object before Buck. "This is the chip that runs the whole thing—tank controls, line monitors, pump controls, temperature controls, incinerator jets, sensors, IGS, everything! Isn't that incredible? This little hunk?"

"I'll never understand my little PC, let alone how that tiny piece of junk can do all those things," Buck acknowledged, as Craig Gantsky replaced the chip and Dr. Keene's youthful face beamed fatherly approval. Having restored the vital chip to its place, Gantsky looked at his watch.

"Damn! You're right, Mr. Barnum. I *don't* belong here. I'm supposed to be in the chief's dayroom in two minutes."

With that, the enthusiastic second engineer jerked the door open and took off on the run. Dr. Keene simply crossed his arms, smiled, and shook his head.

"Kind of sad, really, a waste of talent," Dr. Keene said. "Do you know what the second's duties are? Maintaining lube oil levels, water purifiers, the laundry, and mundane things like that." He stared past Buck for a moment. "But you're here to learn about the process, I imagine. What have you covered so far?"

"I've worked my way back as far as the pump room, then here," Buck replied, slipping the strap of the micro-recorder over his head so that it dangled against his chest. He turned it on. "Do you mind?"

"Of course not. Now, depending on which tanks we're drawing from, their related pumps pull the cargo, send it through the heating system," Keene casually flipped a hand to point up and behind him, "where its temperature is altered to provide the best flowage and combustion. Oh, and along the way, the cargo is run through the correators to grind up any particles that might foul things up. Then, it's on to one of the two incinerators. All through the system, we have electronic sensors to give us a readout on temp and flowage. Anything beyond our preset limits—she shuts down. Here, take a peek at the control console." Dr. Keene's enthusiasm seemed to drive him faster as he went on.

Buck knew at a glance that complete comprehension of the switches and digital monitors was out of the question. But still, the array before him did make sense. "Obviously, some pretty bright heads put all this together," Buck said. "Have they considered all of the what-ifs?"

Dr. Keene laughed. "As a scientist, I should be able to analyze all of this theory and application and pick it apart." He paused and gestured helplessly. "I can't. The remarkable thing about *Ark II* is the combination of fail-safe principles in terms of both ship design and incineration control. In short, it pushes Murphy's law almost to obsolescence."

"Human error?" Buck quizzed, taking a photo of the young scientist at the console.

The incineration chief smiled and continued. "It would take a perfect and highly improbable combination of numerous events to beat the system. No single error would do it."

Buck snapped a sequence of photos as he followed his guide through the fan room, the maintenance shop, and the laboratory, with its unique paraphernalia and refrigerator for storing samples.

"I assume these heavy steel fire doors are closed during the burn?" Buck asked.

"Right. Open this one that leads to the incinerator room during a burn and everything shuts down automatically."

They stepped through the door, and Buck found himself on a landing three steps above the incinerator room floor. Before him, side-by-side, were two immense round structures, each perhaps twenty-five feet in diameter and tapering near the top.

"There they are," Dr. Keene said. "Aren't they beautiful?"

Buck followed the younger man down the steps and over to a door-like panel in one of the structures. He peered into the room-sized chamber. Its walls were lined with clean, new firebricks.

"Suddenly the Biblical fiery furnace takes on new meaning!" he said. The Canon clicked and clicked. "It's so big—you could cook a whole football team in there!"

Dr. Keene laughed. "Are you familiar with the common fuel oil furnace?"

"Somewhat."

"That's basically what you're looking at," Dr. Keene said, jerking open a panel, "two oversized and technically advanced fuel oil furnaces. Basic function is the same."

One level below the two behemoths was the draft room. Dr. Keene explained that air was to be drawn through and forced upward to the burners in controlled amounts to aid in maintaining the proper burn temperatures. Fuel oil would be used to ignite and preheat the incinerators, and it would be fed, in varying amounts depending upon the particular chemical to be burned, to aid in the burning process.

"Thanks, Doc—can I call you that?" Buck asked as they wound their way back to the control room.

"Why not? One syllable beats three," he laughed.

Buck thanked Dr. Keene again and started for the forward house. Emerging from the secluded, narrow passageways among the aft structures, he paused for a moment to adjust to the bright sunlight and then moved on.

As he walked along the main catwalk, he spotted two seamen working on the starboard loading manifold. He turned off on a narrow catwalk that led to their platform. They were attacking the faded, red assembly with wire brushes. Buck introduced himself. The slender young man with blond hair showing beneath the rim of his silver hardhat seemed friendly. His name was Spencer Callin, and he was one of the recent replacements on the crew. Buck caught nothing but the friendly smile as he took Callin's picture.

"Just give me a week or two," Callin boasted, "and I'll have the chief's job."

Buck decided the energetic young man in his twenties must be Irish. He seemed to alternate between a self-confidence that bordered on arrogance and a self-deprecating humor that had a certain appeal.

"How much do you have to repaint?" Buck asked.

"Just the manifold—I think." Callin scanned the maze of red fittings on the main deck, "Jesus, if they ever decide to brush down the whole damned thing, I'm over the side!"

Buck laughed and directed his attention to Callin's partner. It said MAINE on his helmet. The one-syllable answers the man gave to questions suggested that the label on his hardhat might tell as much as would be learned from him. As Buck lined up his picture, Maine turned his head back to the work at hand, and a profile shot was the best Buck could get. He returned to the friendly banter with Callin, but he was conscious of the occasional glances the silent one sneaked in his direction. Might pay to keep an eye on this one, he thought.

He roamed for another hour, breaking ice, as he preferred to think of it. He ate lunch in the officers' mess, sharing a table with Craig Gantsky and Chief Johnson. Both men were friendly, and the conversation was easy and relaxed. They added interesting data to Buck's rapidly growing bank.

Occasionally one of them would suddenly toss a friendly jab at the other.

"What do you mean, the old man will never let me go aft during a burn?" the chief challenged his second.

"Got to tell you about my boss," Gantsky said to Buck. "He's the best damned trouble-shooter in the West. He goes right at the glitch. Hell, if one of those burners were to act up, the chief would go right down there, open the service door, and stick his head inside the furnace to find the trouble. Then he'd pull his head out," Gantsky went on, "turn around, his face burned to a crisp, and say, 'Gawd damn, it's *warm* in there!'"

As they laughed, Buck glanced through the open door to the galley. There stood Indian Joe, watching and listening.

Chapter 9

After lunch and an hour with Ed on strategies, he sat down to his computer. He inserted his digital card and transferred his collection of photos, splitting them into two files: SHIP and CREW. It took another hour, however, to run through the photos and label them. Then he took off for the library. There, he spent the afternoon pouring through newspapers, the yellow pages, *Standard and Poors*, and every source he could think of, searching for additional information on the companies he had listed as potential adversaries. He had no idea what he was looking for, and nothing he found struck him as valuable. But he scribbled notes rapidly, getting what he could for names, positions, addresses, phone numbers, and specifics on the services offered. Better to copy a lot of useless crap, he thought, than skip over something that might help later.

He had decided to visit the meeting of ASH that evening in Long Beach. When he had mentioned the idea to Ed, it hadn't gone over well.

"No need," Ed had said. "I can handle it."

But Buck had decided to follow through anyway. He wanted to get a feel for organizations such as ASH. He would simply drop in as a concerned citizen. And since he had to stay in the area, he stopped at Dante's for dinner. This time, Dante greeted him warmly.

"So, Buck Barnumini, how you lika my frienda?"

"Wow!" Buck rolled his eyes and warmed at the thought of Lenny Bercovich.

"I thoughta you would. Really hurtsa to be so old, right?" Dante hustled away, busying himself with incoming customers, and Buck was left to eat alone.

He had wanted to ask about Dante's strange behavior on Monday, but there really hadn't been an opening. Buck found himself leaning over to check the other booth, hoping Lenny might be there. Certainly no reason to expect her, he thought, but wouldn't it be nice? A gentle surge of energy, coupled with heightened senses, flashed through him at the thought. Yeah, he mused, that old song's right, ". . . .you make me feel so young."

Finishing his meal, he paid the check and started down the narrow, dank hallway toward the rear exit. He was still checking each face that he saw, and as he unlocked his pickup, he felt a hollow letdown. Buck, he thought, you're acting like a crazy teenager.

When he had located the private school where the meeting was to be held, he took a seat in the tiny auditorium. He guessed that there were about a hundred people there, all seated in the center section. He chose an empty aisle seat six rows from the back. Just like church, he thought. The first few rows and the last rows are the most conspicuous, and he wanted to blend in.

The group seemed to represent a cross-section of people, men and women of all ages attired in a range from fine suits to jeans and work clothes. While the assemblage was predominantly white, there were Asians, Hispanics, and blacks as well. Some were talking quietly with their neighbors, while others studied the one-page handout.

Clustered near a music stand and a microphone in the space between the first row and the stage stood four people, apparently the leaders. They were too far away to be heard, but it seemed to Buck that they were doing some last minute organizing. From Ed's description, Buck quickly picked out the president, Juanita Railsback. She was wearing an extremely rich-looking business suit, but despite her dress, the large, buxom woman reminded Buck of a female Russian shotputter. And the hard lines in her face did nothing to belie the image. Buck had just begun to read the sheet which presented the officers, history, and objectives of the Alliance to Save the Harbor when he heard the popping noise of someone testing the microphone. He scanned the front, but no sign of Ed Roland. A no show? Buck wondered. No, not Ed.

"Ladies and Gentlemen," Juanita Railsback said, "welcome to the Alliance." Buck was startled by the sound of her voice. He had expected the gruntings of an NFL nose tackle. Instead, a satiny, irenic quality drifted across the audience with a seductive appeal that quickly silenced the last of the conversations. The first segment of the meeting consisted of a series of statements, complaints, and testimonials by volunteers from the audience.

"My name is James Dolen," the first man said, rising as he spoke. Buck could see only the man's gray pinstriped suit and the round bald spot on the back of his head. "I'm a new member, joined tonight. I'm firmly dedicated to the elimination of all pollution, but particularly the terribly threatening plan of these sea-going incineration people."

As the short presentations went on, Buck concluded that the speakers were carefully chosen and planted in the audience. Then, an awkward, boney woman stood in the center of a middle row.

Buck couldn't help but notice her greasy black hair and the dirty sweater she wore.

"Natalie Groneveldt! Ain't a member yet, might join, don't know yet," she nearly shouted in a raspy voice. "We got kids tippin' the garbage in our alley alla' time, and I wanna know what yer gonna do about *that!*"

Railsback cut through the laughter quickly and moved the business on. She left no doubt that, despite her warm, soft voice, she was in control of the meeting. She spent a few minutes paraphrasing the background material in the handout and then called for reports from the Fundraising and Political Action Committees.

Buck took note of the fact that the group's treasury was anemic at best. With a little over two hundred dollars, they can't do too much damage, he thought. You can't even make very good signs with the money they have. He was feeling better about this as the meeting went on.

His feelings began to change, however, when one Joseph Simons, an attorney, was given the floor. Buck recognized him as one of the leaders who had gathered up front prior to the meeting. Simons, a slender man about Buck's age, stood and faced the audience. He outlined a two-pronged "attack," as he called it.

"We must coordinate our efforts with the other environmentalist groups to gain the benefit of collective strength, and we must pursue every avenue through the justice system, state regulatory agencies, and the EPA."

Buck shuddered.

Simons went on to announce, with an air of pride that smacked of arrogance, that he was busy researching the zoning laws and establishing contacts with the right agency officials. This guy could give us trouble, Buck thought. He may only be on an ego trip, but he sounds like he knows his way around. But then, he's also hamstrung by the lack of funds. Simons finished his proposals and took his seat.

Railsback smiled at him as warmly as a face like hers could. Then she announced that there would be presentations by two guests to be followed by the last portion of the meeting, the registration of new members. She proceeded to introduce the first guest, a tall, blond-haired man named Don Murrell.

"I'm not a public speaker," the handsome, young man began, "and I won't pretend that I am. But the bottom line is, I—*we* want you to know that you aren't alone in this battle against polluters. And we also want you to know that this isn't a battle between ordinary people and the business world. A while back, several companies that are very concerned with solving the hazardous waste problem got together and formed the Kersting Foundation. The members of the Kersting Foundation prefer to remain anonymous, but their goals are the same as yours."

Murrell paused and groped about the inside pocket of his sport coat, finally retrieving a piece of paper.

"I'm here to offer help from the Kersting Foundation," he continued. "It's going to take money—that's the bottom line. And for starters, I'd like to present this check for ten thousand dollars."

Railsback motioned for applause, leaned into the microphone, a wide Hollywood smile on her face, and crooned, "Isn't—isn't that just *wonderful?*"

Damn, Buck thought, that's *all* we needed. He feigned applause and glanced about the audience, deflated by their enthusiastic response to the donation. As he turned to look over his right shoulder, he noticed something peculiar. He had turned back to the front before the imprint took shape in his mind. That strange, little man in the row behind him, the one with the pony tail, was not applauding. Instead, he was slouched in his seat, one leg cocked across the other, a strange grin on his face, looking directly at Buck.

Do I know him from somewhere? Buck wondered. He resisted the urge to turn for a second look.

Murrell finally made a move to his seat, and the boisterous approval began to fade. Juanita Railsback repeated her "just wonderful" remark several more times through the fading din.

Concentrating on the drama, Buck felt sympathy for Ed Roland. Ed has to follow that with the Essee Beecee point of view, he thought. Talk about a lions' den. He was glad he was not up there facing this crowd.

"And now, in the interest of fairness," Railsback crooned, "our last speaker for the evening. He is the *propaganda chief*," she said, pausing to see that the audience had caught her point, "for Southern California Boatbuilding Company, our opponents in this matter of incineration at sea. He *tells* us that we're all on the same side. We'll see." Rustling noises, as people turned to one another, were accompanied by a drone of murmurs. "Mr. Edward Roland."

Suddenly, from nowhere, there was Ed striding, almost trotting confidently down the aisle, a smile fixed upon his scarlet face. Buck wanted to stand and applaud, but instead he hunkered down a little lower in his seat. Ed reached the speaker's area and deftly set up a tri-pod that held a set of large flip charts. Buck admired his new friend's poise and agility under such pressure.

"Ladies and Gentlemen of the Alliance," Ed began, still smiling, "thank you very much for being here and allowing me to speak to you this evening. You are truly members of a rational, democratic group, and only through such rational, objective democracy in action can we hope to gain the knowledge we need to make the important decisions that will so profoundly affect our great country. I wish to commend the Kersting Foundation and the companies that are part of it. It's going to take help like this to rid ourselves of the toxic scourge that threatens our nation."

Ahh, good shot, Ed, Buck thought. He wondered what this great Kersting Foundation really was? Maybe Ed already knows something about them. Buck observed that Ed's remarks had quieted the remaining talkers. Ed paused. Reflecting dignified confidence, he looked over the audience. He smiled again, and with perfect timing, resumed.

"Now, some of you are wondering, what's this guy up to? What's he trying to do?" Another pause, and the telltale bulge in Ed's cheek told Buck that his friend knew exactly what he was doing. "Let me ask you—how many of you drew water from your tap for cooking or drinking in the last twenty-four hours?" Less than half of those present responded with reluctant hand gestures. "Okay-y-y, so did I," Ed went on. "Now, how many of you are willing to bet everything you have—including your family's health—that you'll be able to do that—safely—in another ten years?"

Ed paused, giving the people time to gauge for themselves the obvious lack of response to the question. Buck caught himself almost saying aloud, Man, he's good, so controlled, so in command. The people remained quiet, apparently trying to figure out where this was going.

Buck glanced back. Just as before, the hawk-faced little man with the beady eyes was staring directly at him. What's with this guy? Buck thought. Is he gay? He chanced another look. No, no love in those cold eyes. He shuddered and forced his attention back to Ed.

"Good! Good!" Ed was saying. "I wouldn't answer 'Yes' to that question either. For unless we find ways to deal with the disposal of hazardous wastes, many of us, nationwide, are going to be without drinking water in the near future. Did you know that the U.S. produced an estimated four hundred million tons of hazardous waste last year. Think of that—*four hundred million tons!* And where did most of it go?" Ed paused and scanned his audience. There were murmurs again, but no one volunteered an answer.

"I'll tell you where it went." He paused again for effect and then pointed an index finger toward the floor, "It went in—to—the—ground! That's right, into the ground. And where does most of the nation's drinking water come from?" Tongue in cheek again, he smiled, "Uh huh, you got it. Even our reservoirs here in California, those all-important reservoirs that collect the rain and melting snow, are contained by what? Uh huh, Old Mother Earth."

Buck knew that Ed Roland had the attention of his audience. Undoubtedly, many were still wondering where this was leading, but he was speaking their language. Ed detailed the danger with a series of short, threatening, historical anecdotes. Then he presented the Essee Beecee plan, dividing it into three segments: Collecting and Hauling; Storing, Mixing, and Loading; and *Ark II*—Incineration At Sea.

He moved along quickly, flipping the pages of his charts as he spoke. Some pages contained professional quality illustrations, and others were simply lists of key words he chose to emphasize, key words that supported his basic theme, effectiveness with safety.

As Ed continued, varying his gestures, inflections, and rhythms to accent his points, Buck's mind drifted to an earlier conversation with him.

"I love these gigs," he had said. "It's attack and counterattack. I hit them with the presentation—that's the attack. But," he had emphasized, "I always get them to promise me a question and answer period—that's the counterattack. Their arguments are no match for mine, and they are no match for me. That's when I *really* score."

Boy, I can't wait for the counterattack, Buck thought. This will be good. When Ed was nearing the end, Buck checked his watch. In fifteen minutes, Ed had deftly and thoroughly covered the important facts that had cost Buck hours and hours of study. And in the process, Ed had stressed and restressed the ninety-nine and ninety-nine hundredths percent effectiveness and the amazing network of high-tech, safety features. Buck heard movement behind him. No, he thought, don't give the little weirdo the satisfaction. Don't look.

"Ladies and Gentlemen, right here in Los Angeles and Orange Counties we have millions of tons of hazardous wastes being produced each year, wastes that will come back to bite us if we simply continue to bury them. We *must* eliminate them, and the incineration-at-sea program will do just that—and do it *safely*." The smile had gradually faded, replaced by dramatic intensity. "As you determine your course of action, the questions are not, 'Shall we incinerate these wastes? Or shall we continue to bury them?' The questions are, 'How soon can the program begin? And how can *we* help?'"

He paused and then allowed a warm, friendly smile to cement the presentation. A smattering of polite applause faded into the buzz of voices that followed. Now, the good part, Buck thought, as a sober-faced Juanita Railsback stepped to the microphone.

"That was . . . interesting," she said. "Now, for the main event of the evening."

Reading the anticipation on Ed's face, Buck smiled broadly and turned to face the strange, little man behind him. The seat was empty.

"Ladies and Gentlemen," Railsback continued, "seated at the table to my left is one of our board members, Mr. Ralph Pankonen. At this time, we invite those of you who are not already members to see Ralph and join the ever-growing ranks of the Alliance to Save the Harbor. Thank you for coming, and I thank you in advance for joining us."

Buck was stunned. "Of all the dirty, damned tricks," he muttered.

People shuffled about, some headed to the front and others to the exit. Buck started down the aisle. His temper had already boiled past anger and was headed for the point of rage. He had no idea what he would do when he reached Railsback and her cronies, but he'd damned well do something! He got as far as the second row from the front when he was blocked by the group of people waiting to register.

Stepping off into the row of empty seats to his left, he was about to step over the necessary seats to make his assault. But he stopped. There, not ten feet away stood Ed Roland and Juanita Railsback, smiling at one another and chatting as if they were discussing a recent movie, or a book they had read. Confusion iced Buck's anger. Moving farther to his left brought him closer to the bizarre conversation. Despite his flaming red face and angry eyes, Ed Roland maintained his trademark smile. But he pointed a finger at Juanita Railsback as he spoke. Buck leaned forward to catch the words.

"You're right about *that*, Ms. Railsback. You didn't *have* to let me speak."

Railsback said something, but Buck couldn't pick it up.

"And you're right about that, too," Ed replied. "No laws were broken."

Ed turned and saw Buck. With a jerk of his head he gave Buck the order to leave. Buck hesitated, and Ed turned back to Juanita Railsback, his smile broader than ever.

"But we had agreed on the terms," he continued. "You broke your word, and such things aren't forgotten." As Buck turned to leave he heard Ed say, "And for that, Juanita Railsback, I promise you this. You are going to get your ASH kicked."

Chapter 10

No, it didn't really alter the outcome, Buck thought as he drove along the Pacific Coast Highway toward home. But Ed's closing remark to old Razorback, as Buck had come to think of the ASH president, certainly helped close the wound of defeat. I'll never forget the look on her face when Ed delivered that "kick ASH" remark. Stopped her cold. Boy, speaking of cold, that old Razorback is a forceful, ugly woman who knows she is forceful but doesn't know she's ugly. Got to hand it to her, though. She did her homework. She must have known how effective Ed is in a question-answer session. So she cut him off at the knees. Kind of sad, really. We should all be on the same side.

Funny thing, I used to fight off all kinds of tricky, dirty, and illegal moves by big linemen. Sort of got used to it, expected it. But lately, I've had a real initiation into the wars of words. Got to sharpen up there.

As he cleared Sunset Beach and continued south with the open beaches and dunes between the highway and the ocean, Buck began to relax. Easy driving, few cars, and a beautiful summer evening. He glanced out at the lighted oil platforms. A pair of bright headlights were pulling up on him from behind, so he eased over into the right-hand lane.

Suddenly brilliant lights reflected from his center mirror. He realized that the car he'd given the fast lane to had pulled in close behind him, and the driver had his high beams on.

"Come on, dummy!" he said aloud. "I moved over for you. Go around."

The lights nearly blinded him. Buck glanced at his side mirror. He was about to swing left into the left lane again when he saw a truck coming up fast. Well, that explains it, he thought. The guy behind me moved out of the truck's way. If he'd just back off and dim his lights. Easing up on the accelerator, Buck risked a glance out the left window. There beside him was a large, black shape, its front wheel topping off at Buck's eye level. His eyes darted from the truck to the mirror and back again. As soon as he's past, Buck would swing over into that lane and drop back behind that idiot in the car.

His instincts told him to concentrate on the road, control what he could control. He had reached the point along the beach where the sand had built up to high dunes. A ditch fifteen feet deep separated the dunes from the highway. The car behind him drew still closer. Focusing on the highway, Buck reached up and turned the mirror off to one side. Good! That feels better, he thought. But the truck is still there. Why doesn't he pass? What the hell's going on here?

A quick glance to the left. The black monster was right there, its husky diesel engine roaring a dissonant harmony to the growling of the huge tires. Buck could almost reach out and touch it! *Thud!* The truck's huge bumper rammed into Buck's front left fender. His head thumped against the side window frame as the collision jarred the small vehicle and moved it over a couple feet. He eased the wheel slightly to the right to escape, but the beast stayed right with him.

"Cut it out! Don't—!" Buck yelled, pulling hard left on the wheel to resist the pressure. It was as though his steering was gone. With his wheels turned left he was moving steadily to the right. Nothing he did made a difference! He braked hard. His right wheels hit the shoulder. The nose of the little red pickup was angling toward the ditch.

"No! Damn it—no!"

The gravel shoulder dropped off at a sharp angle into the deep ditch. As Buck went over the edge, he felt the bottom drop out— airborne! He squeezed the wheel, trying frantically to resist turning it. Too much left and he'd roll for sure when he landed. *Kump-Whump!* He was down, tilted dangerously to the right, but still on the wheels. He turned hard left as he reached the wide, flat ditch bottom.

Scrantch! The pickup lurched as it scraped against the opposite bank. He found himself bumping along the flat bed of the ditch parallel to the highway. Then he saw it. Ahead and coming at him fast—a huge, rock wall, the base of a driveway from the Coast Highway into the seaside park on his right! He locked the brakes. The little pickup rumbled and shook as it slid through the rocks and gravel toward the stone wall. A round culvert in the wall grew larger by the second.

"Not going to stop in time! Not going to—" Buck let up on the brakes, giving traction to his front wheels. He pulled the wheel hard left, held it there, and locked the brakes again. The maneuver spun the pickup violently to the left. *Crunch*! Every nerve, every muscle, every organ in Buck's body screamed at the impact. Only the cutting seat and shoulder belts kept him from flying into the right side glass. The little pickup gave two feeble lurches, and died.

Buck slumped in his seat. He took several deep breaths and just sat there, tilted back against the headrest and facing up the steep bank toward the roadway above. Something told him to jump out quickly to see what he could of the other two vehicles, but the thought left as quickly as it had come. He simply sat there and stared, his eyes following the beam of his single remaining headlight as it streamed upward like a spotlight into the night sky. He heard a car pass beneath the beam but it didn't stop. His brain began to kick in, but along with it came the raging temper.

"Damn you!" he roared, thumping a hand against the wheel so hard a sharp pain ran up his arm. "No accident, you bastard! And when I find you, you'll need more than that damned truck to hide behind!"

Then, as though his threat had injected some purpose into the bizarre experience, he went into action. He pressed the belt release, grabbed the flashlight from the glove compartment, forced open the door, and stepped out. As he straightened, trembling began in his knees. It surged upward through his body, blending with the pounding surf he could hear from over the embankment, to produce an ethereal disconnection from reality. Somehow, he commanded his slow, mechanical arms to reach into the pickup and turn off the ignition and lights. But the lights might bring help, he thought.

"What kind of help?" he mumbled. "Whole world's screwed up." The tremors rattled steadily, and the rage burned furiously.

"Mister? Mister?"

Buck looked about for the tiny voice that filtered through the sounds of the crashing surf. There, high above him on the oceanside embankment, were two people, a young man and a woman.

"Mister? Are you all right? Can we help you?" the man called.

"Just buzz off!" he shouted. "I've had enough of stupid people for one night!"

"Well, up yours!" a fading voice said as the two disappeared behind the dune.

Buck drew a deep breath and slowly exhaled. Did it again, didn't you? he thought. But the shakes were easing. The rage diminished, changing to a familiar, adrenalin-fed determination to take action, to overcome the situation. Using the flashlight, he picked his way around to the right side of the truck, afraid of what he would find. He knew it was silly, but he loved his little Chevy truck and the independence it provided.

"Oh, man," he moaned as the light showed the mangled right side of the truck. He bent over, picked up a hubcap, and examined the right rear wheel. The tire was still inflated, but even in the limited light he could see a twist in the wheel. His last sideways skid had turned him parallel to the entry road, slamming the right side of the vehicle into the rocky structure. The body was a mess, but he still had four, no, three-and-a-half wheels. He slid on his back under the truck. The flashlight showed no sign of leaking oil or coolant.

"Okay, Little Red Wagon," he said as he struggled to his feet. "Think you can get me home?"

He climbed into the cab, started the engine, shifted into four-wheel drive, and planned his move. He was perpendicular to the highway. There was only one option—straight up the fifteen-foot slope. When he saw no headlights approaching, he put the red truck in gear, revved the engine, and snapped the clutch out. The vehicle roared and bounced up the incline, the four wheels spewing rocks and gravel as they clawed their way upward. Once again, Buck felt the front wheels leave the ground as he cleared the ridge.

Kump-Whump! The thundering reunion of wheels and pavement jarred all of the painful places in his body. He turned hard right. Shifting back to two-wheel drive, Buck started down the Pacific Coast Highway, listening to the squeaks, screeches, thumps, and moans of the truck. At least two wheels were badly bent, for any speed above twenty-five miles an hour prompted a shuddering that neither the pickup nor Buck could withstand for long.

With only one headlight and two round wheels, it was to be a long, slow trip. Despite many lectures by his mother, and then by Roberta, patience was a quality Buck had come to believe he would never acquire. *Thump, thump, thump* reverberated through the truck with every revolution of the twisted right rear wheel, answered by *whap, whap, whap* from the front. He tried unsuccessfully to relax as he eased the wounded hulk down the highway.

"Come on, Baby," he said occasionally, "you're doing fine. Keep it up."

He imagined himself as Don Quixote, riding a crippled horse across the desert, tired, thirsty, struggling desperately to make it home. By the time he started up Marguerite Street hill, his anger had been blanketed by fatigue. His single headlight swept across the Lees' front window as he turned into his driveway. He punched the door opener, waited a few seconds, and drove into the garage.

Once again, the telephone rang precisely as he entered the kitchen.

"Barnum here," he said.

"Pretty cute trick, coming to that meeting tonight," a man's voice said. "Hope you learned something."

"What? Who is this?" Buck demanded.

"Don't worry about that," the voice said with a sarcastic laugh. "The bottom line is, we're done playing around. The next time—you're dead."

The caller punctuated the message with a *click* as he hung up.

Chapter 11

"Damn it," Buck muttered to himself. He was awake again, the third time. He lay still for a while, listening to the silence, trying not to think. But there was so much not to think about. His mind was a kaleidoscope, images popping in and out with no sense, no order to the parade. He tried again to shut it down, but there was Peter—Juanita Railsback—Hudson and Grigsby—the big, black truck—

"That's it!" Buck exclaimed, jerking to a sitting position, electricity sizzling through his veins. That's it, he thought—*the bottom line!* It's Murrell, the guy from Kersting Foundation who gave the money to ASH. He's the one who called last night. That cliché Roberta hates so much—*bottom line.* He used it at the meeting, and again when he called. And no doubt about it, it was *his* voice on the phone. And he was probably one of the drivers.

A glance at the digital clock on the nightstand told Buck it was five-thirty. He had slept longer than he thought. As he bounded up and flipped on the light, the tender spots made themselves known. Bruises he could tolerate, like those the day after a tough game, but the stiff, sore neck pronged him with every movement. The excitement of his discovery, however, helped him past the pain. He made his bed, laid out his clothes, and headed for the kitchen. He poured a cup of coffee and sat down at the table.

"Okay, Mr. Don Murrell, you're on my radar. Now it's *my* turn," Buck said aloud.

He heard a noise and looked up. The door to the patio opened slowly. A doll face with blue eyes, a pug nose, and an impish smile appeared through the opening. Her long, blond pony tail swished as she rotated her head back and forth, surveying the situation.

"Safe to come in?" she whispered.

"Sunny! I didn't know you were here. I thought you were at your apartment in Long Beach." Then, lowering his voice, Buck said, "Sure, get in here!" He smiled as his tall, lovely daughter edged into the kitchen.

Jennifer was her name, but her golden hair, radiant smile, and irrepressible personality had brought him to tag her with the nickname nearly twenty years before. Sometimes he had examined the love he felt for others, and many times he had questioned his faith in God. But he loved the love he felt for his daughter, and to put a creature like this on earth? There *had* to be a God.

"I stayed over last night. Heard you come in, but I was too drousy to get up. Went out running at five o'clock. I've been sitting out on the patio with Bobby. He came over for breakfast, too."

"Well, get in here, you guys!" Buck got up, kissed Sunny on the forehead and moved toward the door. "Just in time for breakfast, Bob!" Buck said, wrapping one arm around his son's shoulders. He felt Bob stiffen.

"Who's cooking?" Buck asked.

"Jennifer," Bob said cooly, leaning against the counter top, his hands in the pockets of his tattered jeans. The slender six-footer's sinewy arms were bared to the shoulders where the sleeves of the faded BARTHOLOMEW COLLEGE ATHLETIC DEPT. sweatshirt had been torn off.

Buck sat down, sipped his coffee, and studied his twenty-two-year-old son. Bob had short but thick brown hair that topped his mother's face. The kids' blue eyes were a given, but while Sunny's were warm and smiling, Bob's had a peculiar, penetrating glint, as though he wore ultrathick contacts. Only the brown hair and strong jaw were Buck's. Bob had always resisted suits, and now that his career with a high-tech firm in Irvine required coats and ties, he had become even more of a slob on weekends. Buck smiled. Bob had always been immature, as if determined not to grow up. When he was a freshman on the college baseball team, he played like a senior, but acted like a freshman. Four years later, nothing had changed.

Sunny began work on the pancake mix, but Bob just stood there staring downward at the white tiles.

Oh, oh, Buck thought, was his sensitive son really upset? Or is he just in one of his 'not sure I want to be here' modes? Buck would see if he could give this scene a little lift.

"I—ahh—got that job, kids, that job in PR with the ship company."

"Ohhhh! Good, Dad!" cheered Sunny. "Bobby, get me the eggs, will you?"

"It's early to tell, but I think it's going to be an interesting position—with a future, I might add," Buck said. "And it's the best money I've ever made, *ever!*" He thumped the table top with a fist. His cup hopped, spilling coffee on the formica. Bob flinched and dropped an egg.

"Jeez, Bobby!" Sunny shouted. "Don't step in it! You'll fall and break your arm again!" When she turned around, she was laughing. Buck couldn't help joining her. Bob looked from one to the other sheepishly, then at the egg, and broke into a cautious grin.

"My fault," Buck said quickly. "Bob, grab a cup of coffee and come sit down. It's safer. Haven't seen you for a couple of weeks. Ought to have a talk."

Bob cleaned up the last of the splattered egg, poured himself a cup of coffee, and said over his shoulder, "How long?"

"Well . . . long as it takes, whatever," Buck said.

"Okay," Bob said as he took his seat. Then he added, "But I can't stay long. I told Tim I'd be right back. Look, can we use the pickup today? We're moving."

"You're *what?*"

"Moving. We got a new apartment that's closer to work for both of us," Bob replied. He went on to explain that Tim had gotten a job with a real estate firm in Dana Point. In time, he would get his license and work into sales. "Tim's really excited about the job. It's like his boss has never even noticed that he's black."

The tempting aroma of Sunny's pancakes drifted across the kitchen.

As Sunny set the table, Buck's thoughts were on Tim Lee who grew up next door and had been Bob's best friend forever. He remembered the first double play they had pulled off as little leaguers on Buck's team and the records the duo had set for similar plays through high school and college. Tim is a fine boy, Buck thought, actually much more receptive to coaching through the years than Bob. Tim's like one of the family. But his father? Buck had tried and tried, but he never could get close to Herbert Lee. Most of the neighbors saw him as arrogant. But really, Buck thought he was smuglent—*smug* with the satisfaction that his business success has enabled him to live in an affluent white neighborhood, and *silent* out of fear that he might say something to spoil it. Buck suspected that the wildest thing Herbert Lee had ever done might be a wheelie on his stationary bike.

"Bob?" Buck began, as Sunny placed the steaming hotcakes on the table and sat down. "Did we ever talk about—about this being a good time to spread out? To make some new friends?"

"Dad!" Sunny said.

"It's all right, Jennifer," Bob said. "Yes, Dad, *you* talked about it. But Tim's my best friend, and it's *our* choice."

"I'd never suggest that you dump Timmy as your friend. I'm talking about broadening your professional contacts, networking."

"You also said something about forming convictions and standing by them." Bob's face hardened, his squinting eyes radiating the challenge. He stuffed more pancake into his mouth.

"Dad," Sunny said, "I'd like to hear about your new job."

Buck looked at his son. Those eyes and that red face. He was angry again. "Bob, I'm sorry. I think you misunderstood me," he said.

"Why is it, Dad, that *I'm* always wrong and *you're* always misunderstood?" Bob pushed the last enormous glob into his mouth and started up from his chair. "Can we use the truck?"

"Afraid not," Buck answered. "The pickup's down."

Bob stopped and looked down at his father. The glaring eyes and the angry set of his jaw tore at Buck's insides. Bob swallowed hard to clear his mouth.

"You trying to teach me something?" he asked. "You'd even resort to obvious lies? Mom was right. Your head *is* on sideways." He wheeled and disappeared into the garage.

Buck started up from his chair, but something stopped him. Moments later, the service door to the garage slammed, slammed hard on Buck's heart. Poor Bob, he thought, now he's embarrassed and running away.

"Ohhh," Buck groaned. "I don't know. I just don't know."

"Chill down, Dad." Sunny's soft words worked their magic on Buck as she crossed the kitchen.

"Sunny, what the hell's going on? Bob's never talked to me like that. I expected some rebellion when he went to college. It never came. Now, when we should be friends, he declares war. Have I screwed up that badly?"

"No, Dad," Sunny replied as she returned to the table. "In fact, you're the best father *I* ever had!" She laughed and hugged Buck from behind. As she moved to her chair and sat down, with one leg curled beneath her as always, Buck grinned.

"You con artist!" he laughed. "You know just when to turn my pages, don't you? Why is it that you and I never have these misunderstandings?"

"Oh, that's simple. I'm *your* daughter, and Bob is *Mom's* son."

"No you don't!" Buck snapped. "I worked—"

"Yes," Sunny cut in, "you worked just as hard with Bob as you did with me. You're talking about parenting, Dad, and that's why you get defensive every time this matter gets close to the surface. I'm talking genetics. Their personalities are similar. Our personalities are even closer. I think you should quit denying it. See it, accept it, and work with it."

Buck thought for a moment. Maybe, maybe she's right. He visualized the angry face he'd just confronted. She *is* right. He smiled.

"How'd you get so damned smart?" he asked.

"We just covered that," Sunny said with a warm smile.

"Your mother deserves some credit, too." Buck shook his head slowly, "But, lately—anyway, I'll give some thought to your genetics theory. Now tell me, what's the status with ol' Bongo Bongo?"

"Dad!"

"I'm sorry, Sunny. Really, I think he's a nice guy, extremely intelligent, and very well-mannered. And you know I'm not a racist, so his Samoan heritage is no problem to me. But when I look at him, can't help it, I just think, *Bongo Bongo.*"

"And what if he looks at you and thinks, *Beverly?*"

Buck flinched.

"Damn, but you're sharp," he said. "With one word you just deleted

Bongo Bongo, permanently! Now, what's the latest with Daniel? Haven't seen him around."

"At the last minute he landed that internship for the summer with the government. He'll be in D.C. through August."

"And the relationship?"

"About the same, pretty cool," Sunny responded, her expression matching her choice of words.

"This does sound cool," Buck said. "Problems there?"

"No, not really. We like each other very much, but it's not a passionate connection. To be honest, I think we'll probably just date until the right person comes along—for either of us. And I'm comfy with that. At least he doesn't try to drag me around like a trophy on its way to the bedroom. I have tremendous respect for him. He's so interested in everything, wants to learn faster than he can find things to learn. Now, tell me about your new job, Dad."

"Well, it's turning into a strange situation. Right this minute I don't know what I'm facing or what I'm doing. In one week, the job has gone from a writing job to a detective assignment and then to the front lines of a war zone." He went on to explain the *Ark II* project, the anticipated opposition to it, and the events of the previous evening.

Sunny jumped up and scooted for the garage. In a few minutes she returned.

"Oh, Dad, that's scary! You could have been killed!"

"That's exactly the message they sent, Sunny."

They sat quietly for a couple of minutes. Then Sunny perked up and clutched Buck's arm.

"You know what? I think Peter made a great choice! You're sharp, you're gutsy, and you've been around the mountain a few times—just what they need!"

"I wish I felt that confident," Buck said. "The bad guys want me out, but they went about it wrong. After last night, I'm motivated." Sunny was watching him intently. "But my problem is—I'm still ignorant. I've got to get smart fast, and there's nobody to teach me."

"I guess it's *your* turn," Sunny said.

"My turn?"

"Remember that tennis tournament I entered when I was eight or nine? I had never played before, and just before my first match I found out that the other girls had been taking lessons for a year. I was scared to death. I came to you, Dad. Remember what you told me?"

"No." Buck hesitated. "But that was back when I was still smart. It must have been something quite profound."

"I think it was, Dad. I couldn't have won without it. You said," Sunny's face took on a scowl, and her voice dropped to a pseudo bass, "You said, 'So go get 'em! Go out there and beat their pants off before they figure out that you don't know what you're doing!'"

"Pretty good, Sunny," Buck laughed. "Do you have total recall? *All* the advice I ever gave you?"

"Yes."

"Did any of it turn out to be bad?"

"Yes, but not *that* piece."

"Thanks. Comment well taken." He got up, picked up the dishes, and began rinsing them in the sink. As a plate began to shine, he saw Lenny Bercovich's face in it. He could hear her voice, "No zebras out there. They make their own rules."

"Something heavy, huh, Dad?"

He refilled his coffee cup. "Want more?" he asked, his face becoming even more serious.

"No, thanks. I'm drowning now. What is it, Dad?"

"It's—I guess it really *is* heavy," Buck said, "no idea how heavy until now." He reached across the table and took Sunny's hands in his. Her eyes showed love and trust. Would that love and trust be there if he screwed up on this thing? he wondered. "Sunny, until last night I had no idea what I was getting into. Now, I do, and I don't like it one bit. We don't know what these hoods might do. Obviously, they're not bound by any rules, at least no rules that *we* know."

"What's this, Dad? You thinking about quitting?"

"I'd have to be downright stupid not to consider it," Buck replied. "I'm in this business to provide a needed service and make a decent wage while I do it. These guys I'm up against? They're in business to make sure I don't stay in business."

"Dad, do we really face serious threats from toxic wastes?"

Buck looked at Sunny. There was no smile. Isn't that something? he thought. Even when she's dead serious, those eyes radiate a sincerity that warms your heart and makes *you* want to smile.

"Yes, Sunny, big ones."

"And you believe the *Ark II* project can work?" she asked, tilting her head slightly to one side as she often did when wrestling with heavy thoughts.

Buck slowly nodded. He could sense the direction his daughter was taking, and he considered shutting her down.

"And you promised Peter?"

"*That* promise doesn't count. I didn't promise to fight the damned Mafia."

"Still, they're three pretty good reasons to finish the job, Dad. Nobody ever won a game by heading for the showers in the first quarter," Sunny said. "And if you're concerned about us, we didn't just get off the bus. We can take care of ourselves."

"Sunny, it's easy to be cavalier, to play John Wayne, sitting here in our own kitchen," Buck said, watching his daughter's face for a sign of anything but sincere conviction.

"Look, Dad, I'm not some starry-eyed kid who just came out of a movie theater. But you told me before you left for the job interview, 'Boy, I need to win one.' Remember? Well, you *do* need to win one!" Sunny slapped the table. "What can I do to help?"

Isn't that just like her? Buck thought. "What can *I* do to help?" There isn't another father in the world with a daughter like that. But the mushrooming pride was cut off at the stem, for Sunny's question provoked a sobering thought.

"Yes, there is something you can do for me. It'll help take some pressure off," he said.

"Good! What is it?"

"You—both of you—keep your eyes open, where ever you go. Watch for anyone, on foot or in a car, who might be tailing you. Especially watch out for a big, good-looking blond guy, about six-two, early thirties. That's Don Murrell. He's the only one I'm sure of right now. You see him, or anything suspicious, call me immediately—or sooner!" Buck felt like shouting to get her attention, but he couldn't. Instead, he glared, glared at her with his fifty-volt charge, the one she'd rarely seen but always obeyed.

"Aw, Dad," Sunny complained, "that's easy. That's no challenge."

Chapter 12

By eight o'clock that morning, Buck had extracted a promise from Sunny that she'd be careful, and he was off and running, but roughly and slowly. *Thump, thump, whap, whap,* argued the damaged wheels, and *screetch, rrrawwk, screetch, rrrawwk,* complained the twisted frame. The truck seemed to shudder even more violently than it had on the long trip home. Buck had carefully mapped his morning travels, but the gauges showed rising engine temperature and falling oil pressure, prompting a change in plans. Bypassing the sheriff's office and the insurance company, he nursed his mortally wounded friend straight to Zeke's Auto Repair Shop.

After a quick check, Zeke predicted a "total" by the insurance company. Buck covered his feelings. Kind of like losing a pet, he thought. But, as the shop owner gave him a lift to the car rental agency, Buck felt his sadness turning to anger.

"I want the fastest, inconspicuous road-hugger you have," he told the rental clerk, tossing his overloaded credit card on the counter. Minutes later, he drove off in a gray Camaro with a V-8 engine. He hoped the choice would give him two advantages, a marked contrast in style from what he had been driving and the low slung chassis and speed to get him out of trouble should it arise.

He reported the ditching incident to the sheriff's office and then to his insurance company. Both representatives perked up when he told them the force-off had been deliberate. He described the vehicles the best he could, but then they pressed him to explain why he might have been targeted.

"I've no idea," he said simply. "Never saw either of them before. You'll probably never find them, but I want it on record." As he headed for the office, the wheels in his mind were turning as fast as those of the new Camaro.

He found Ed Roland at his desk in the grungy, little office, pouring over some marketing materials. Ed looked up, saw Buck, and seemed to switch on his affable personality. But when Buck told him the story of the previous night, Ed's jaw dropped and his face turned crimson.

"You really sure it was intentional?" Ed asked incredulously.

"No question about it. The phone call confirmed it."

"My God! I knew we had some adversaries, but I—I just can't believe they'd—"

"Believe it," Buck said. It was the first time he'd seen Ed Roland flustered, almost speechless.

He's really shook, thought Buck. I might as well finish the job. "I think you and Peter had better be alert. It seems like I'm their target, but actually, you're both more important to the project than I."

"Well, yes—but there must be something we can do, isn't there?"

I can hardly believe this, Buck thought. This picture of poise, this confident, almost arrogant man has waltzed through stress sessions I'd run miles to avoid. And after *I* get bounced around, *he* comes unraveled. I guess we each have our own strengths and weaknesses. An old, familiar feeling, a surge of confidence sifted through him as Buck realized that, for the first time since he had hooked up with Essee Beecee, he was in a position to be the strong one, to provide the leadership.

"Yes, Ed," he replied, "there are things we can do. And we start by trying to plug the leak." He extended a thumb and jabbed it horizontally toward an imaginary wall. "It's bothered me all along. The same evening I get hired on, I get a threatening phone call. They sure didn't read about it in the papers."

"You're saying—somebody in the company?"

"Either that, Ed, or termites have telephones."

"Sorry, Buck. I'm so startled by all this, I'm having trouble dealing with it. What do you think? Office people? Shop workers? Crew?"

He seems to be coming around, Buck thought. "I've noticed we have almost no office help," Buck said, "only Viola and two other secretaries. And very few shop workers around. Why is that?"

"We bought the ship intact. The chief has supervised most of the renovations, so with no design and construction involved, we've cut way back. Three office girls and four guys in the shop, unless of course, we count ourselves." Ed laughed weakly, but it showed he was on his way back.

"Okay," Buck commanded, "let's get on it. I can't accomplish much—in fact, I might end up dead—if they always know what I'm doing before I do. So Ed, I want you to make copies of all the personnel files, that is all but the big wheels here in the office."

"Sure." Ed agreed, his confidence seeming to feed on Buck's words. "I'll get Erica right on it."

"No. I want *you* to do it, and do it inconspicuously. No one else in on it," Buck demanded. Ed might not like taking orders from me, he thought. "Then you get the crew's folders to me, and you check out every detail on the office people. Everything! Okay?"

Now, Buck thought, we'll know how you're going to handle this. Certainly, this little job shouldn't be too confrontational for you, Ed.

"Any hunches?" Ed asked. He seemed more comfortable with his role.

"Obviously, on the basis of numbers alone, it would seem to be a crewman," Buck said. "By the way, Ed, I thought you were absolutely incredible, the way you handled things at the ASH meeting."

The red face looked up, blinked, and broadened into a wide smile, the smile that was Ed Roland. "Why, thanks! Thanks a lot! In spite of the rotten finale, it was kind of fun." Then he sobered quickly. "But this violent stuff—I don't handle it very well. Bear with me, will you?"

"Sure, Ed. But we've all got to change the way we think or we're in real trouble. I saw a World War II poster in an antique shop once, and I've never quite forgotten it, 'A slip of the lip can sink a ship.' Kind of fits, doesn't it? Last night, they sank my little red boat. And very soon they mean to sink this ship."

Buck grabbed his hardhat, recorder, and camera, and headed for the pier. The morning was nearly gone, but if he moved fast, he might get pictures of the rest of the crew, along with shots of a few more of the *Ark*'s unusual features.

He was beginning to feel comfortable on the ship. There were few places he had yet to see. Several crew members greeted him as he moved about the main deck. The number of crewmen had increased, and he quickly added a dozen faces and photos to his collection. Buck hadn't been below the galley, deep in the bow section, so he headed down the tight staircase. The bow narrowed at second deck level, and since the hull was narrower at that level the lateral passageway was considerably shorter than those on the upper decks. On the aft side of the passageway was the auxiliary machinery room, which also contained two large, potable water tanks. The fore side was divided into several smaller compartments, including the laundry room, a storage room, linen storage lockers, and the bowthruster machinery room.

A seaman with a silver hardhat stood before an open, electrical circuit box that was labeled: BOWTHRUSTER. Buck maneuvered to catch a shot of the open box and the man's profile. He squeezed the button. *Click*—

"What the—" The sailor jerked and turned to face Buck. It was Spencer Callin. "Oh, it's you, Buck." Callin heaved a sigh and smiled. "Didn't hear you coming. Scared the bejeesus outa me."

"Sorry about that," Buck said amiably. "With my big feet, I was sure you'd heard me."

Callin laughed and slammed the cover of the box shut. Then his face sobered, and he said, "I, uhh, I think this career has cost me some of my hearing—just between us, of course."

"Sorry to hear that," Buck said, pointing to the box. "So *that's* the bowthruster control?"

"Right, well, sort of. This is the circuit breaker box for the bowthruster. It's actually controlled from the bridge."

"Looks simple. Having trouble with it?"

"Naw, no trouble. Just checking a couple of things. It really is simple. Wish I'd invented it. Got a prop set sideways in a round tunnel right through the hull down there," he said with a gesture. "Got a big Cat, just like the main engines, to power it. Just start her up, determine the pitch you want, and she pulls the bow right or left, whatever you want. God, I could retire if I had the royalties from that," he laughed.

"Well," Buck kidded, "maybe you can invent a *better* mousetrap!"

"Be hard to do much better'n that," Callin said. "See you later."

Buck headed up to the galley. He stuck his head through the open door and greeted Indian Joe Morse. The hefty cook with the wide, toothy grin sidled over to him.

"Joe took care of it," he said softly.

"Took care of it?"

"Put the word out you weren't no spy. Tell any differnce?"

"Hmmm, now that you mention it, seems friendlier around here today. Thanks, Joe. You're a good man. See you later."

"Got a good lunch today. Got time, c'mon back!" the congenial cook called out. Buck acknowledged with a wave and went topside. He spotted the first engineer, Mal Runkle, climbing out of a main deck hatch from a storage tank. Remembering that Runkle was among the few not yet photographed, Buck started aft. Along the way, he met Craig Gantsky, the friendly second engineer who was such a computer nut.

"Hi there, Mr. Barnum," Gantsky greeted him.

"It's Buck to my friends," he replied. "So next time I'll know where I stand with you," he admonished, aiming a finger at the second.

Gantsky laughed. "Got it—Buck. How are you doing? Finding your way around?"

"Almost like I was born and raised here."

Gantsky's walkie-talkie crackled. He unhooked it from his belt and responded, his bright, blue eyes fixed upon Buck as he talked into the green plastic device. Another good idea, Buck thought, as he eyed the time-saving, step-saving piece of electronic wizardry. He noticed that the white marks etched into the plastic dial and switches were all but obliterated by grease. Of course. These guys always have their hands in greasy projects. Bound to happen.

"Be right down there, Chief," the second concluded. "Gotta run, Buck. Anything I can help you with, just let me know."

"Sure will, thanks."

Buck continued on his way aft, turning left on the narrower catwalk that would take him close to the first engineer, Mal Runkle. The engineer had just directed a seaman down through the hatch and was bent over the opening, talking to his helper. Buck moved to get a better camera angle. The stout man straightened, looked up at Buck, and smiled. As Buck hurriedly placed the viewfinder to his eye, he realized that the smile was actually a sneer. He was about to squeeze the button when Runkle turned his back. Buck waited a few seconds, his Canon aimed at the broad back topped by the white hardhat. No change. He'd have to ask the first engineer to turn around.

"Don't point that God-damned thing at me!" the burly first said without turning.

"I beg your pardon?"

"Don't point that son of a bitch at me!"

No mistake. Buck's face flushed with anger and embarrassment. "Ah, Mr. Runkle, I'm just doing my job. Part of it is to get pictures of everything, and that includes the people."

No answer. The first remained where he was, bent over the open hatch. Buck lost the standoff. He decided to retreat. I guess that marks *him*, he thought. Oh well, I got most of what I came for. I'll quit this and head back to the office. As he bounced down the springy steps to the pier below, he vowed that he would win this battle. I'll get his damned picture. He strode off across the pier, laughing to himself. I'll bet, he thought, when Runkle's picture does come up on the computer, it'll be round and puckered.

Back in his office, Buck sat at his table and reviewed the strange event. Wonder if it *could* be Runkle? he thought. Good chance, but right now there's a better lead to work on. Let's get on to the ASH-Murrell-Kersting connection.

Consulting his notes on the ASH meeting, he refocused his mind, recalling the facts and events that related to ASH. He listed them on a sheet of paper:

1. ASH Officers—Railsback, Simons, & Pankonen.

2. Kersting Foundation—Don Murrell—black truck—car—crash—phone call.

Okay? Now, what would he do with it? Then, he remembered the one-page handout from the ASH meeting. Conveniently, or perhaps egotistically, the ASH leaders had included a short paragraph of biographical information, including phone numbers, on each of the officers. Buck was deliberating between Railsback and Simons for the first contact, when it struck him. Don't try to weasle information out of the tough ones. Find the weakest link in the chain. That's Pankonen, Ralph Pankonen. He reached for the phone. "Here goes," he said under his breath. "I hope this guy's the accommodating wimp I think he is."

"Pankonen's Ladieswear," the voice said. "This is Ralph. How may I help you?"

"Oh, Ralph Pankonen!" Buck said in a thin, excited voice. "I'm so glad I found you, Ralph. My name is Herbert Wotzheim, Wotzheim Steel Fabrications. Ralph, one of my employees attended your meeting of the Alliance last evening, and she was telling me about some Kersting Foundation," Buck rattled on as rapidly as he could think. "She was telling me that the foundation is made up of business people who want to help fight pollution. She thought the young man's name was Morgan, or something like that. Is that correct? She said, if anyone would know, it would be *you!*"

"Uh, Mr. Wotzheim, can I ask the nature of your inquiry?"

"Ohhh, of *course!*" Buck sang into the phone. "Of course! I'll be very frank with you, Ralph. We've had a good year, and I'm vitally interested in helping the cause. Contributions are deductible, of course?"

"Why, Mr. Wotzheim, I'm sure they are."

"Ah, good, good! Then, Ralph, can you tell me how to get in touch with this Mr. Mornwell?"

"It's *Murrell*, Mr. Wotzheim, Don Murrell. Please hold for a second. I have it right here." Buck could hear papers rustling. He smiled to himself. "Here it is, Mr. Wotzheim . . . Don Murrell, Kersting Foundation, P.O. Box 4536, Long Beach, Zip 90804. Will that help?"

"Ah, Ralph, we'd like to get involved in this as quickly as we can. Would you have their street address, or their phone number?"

"No, I'm sorry, sir. I don't have either of those. The box number is the best I can do. By the way, Mr. Wotzheim, since you are so interested in these matters, we'd love to have you join us in the Alliance as well. Would you be interest—"

"But of course! Of course! I'm planning on it—plan to be at your next meeting! Thank you, Ralph. I can see why you are such an effective leader, and such favors are not forgotten by Herbert Wotzheim. Good bye, Ralph."

Buck sat back, chuckling to himself. It worked, he thought, and what's more, it was kind of fun. Then, recalling a research trick he had learned at a job hunt seminar, he called the East Long Beach Postal Station and requested the business address of the box holder. In a minute, he had his answer—3220 East Seventh Street, Long Beach.

"All *right!*" he said aloud, his enthusiasm bubbling to the top.

Throwing his notes into his briefcase, he grabbed the Canon and the recorder and headed out. As he passed the demarcation line, he slowed his pace and glanced in through the open door. Viola Erichs looked up as he knew she would. He turned on a beaming smile and waved. She blinked and then tilted the stone face downward toward the papers on her desk. After a quick lunch, Buck aimed the gray Camaro east on Seventh Street in Long Beach, watching the address numbers creep upward.

Amazing, he thought, the contrast between this rather dumpy neighborhood of one- and two-story buildings and the elegant structures of nearby Ocean Boulevard. He felt the strange blend of curiosity and tension as he passed the 3100 block. He moved into the right lane and slowed. He watched the numbers carefully, 3200—3208—3216. There it is—3220!

It was a sprawling one-story building that devoured half of the block. The entire facade of old tan bricks yielded only two single-door entrances, each flanked by a small plate glass window. Above the first was a small blue and white sign: M & S SAND & GRAVEL. Over the second door, hung a large, faded yellow sign with black letters: OSMUNDSON'S TRANSPORT CO. The door to OSMUNDSON'S bore the 3220 number.

But where's the Kersting Foundation? Buck asked himself. Maybe there's a small sign I missed. Before he could take in more, he was past the building. He circled the next block on his left. Arriving back at the Seventh Street intersection, he pulled to the curb and snapped shots of both entrances to the building across the street. He double-checked his notes, then studied the building. The number was right, but there was no sign for the Kersting Foundation.

Buck decided to check the rear of the building. While he waited for his green light, he found himself looking at the OSMUNDSON sign and repeating the name to himself. When the light switched to green, it was as though it completed a circuit in his mind.

"Yo, that's it!" he said aloud. "Osmundson—on the list of competitors—the hazardous waste business!"

A loud blaring horn behind Buck jolted him. He snapped a left turn back onto Seventh Street and headed east. His first impulse was to put distance between that building and himself. He needed time to think. After two blocks, he pulled off on a side street and parked. He could concentrate without the distraction of driving.

Okay, he thought, Kersting Foundation gives the money to ASH. At this point, it appears that Kersting shares the offices of Osmundson, or might even be an offshoot of Osmundson. Perfect! What a simple, indirect way for Osmundson to funnel money to our opponents. Okay, what about M & S Sand and Gravel? It *was* a gravel truck that ran me off the PCH. Buck started the Camaro, and soon he was discreetly parking in a small parking lot across the back alley from the warehouse. A van partially hid his car, but he could see across the open lot to the rear of the building.

There were two immense, retractable doors, large enough to accommodate any truck, and the approaches to both doors led down inclines to perhaps four feet below ground level. The door on his left would be M & S, on his right, Osmundson. He snapped a shot of the layout and then settled down to wait. He wasn't sure what he was waiting for, or even *if* he should be waiting.

Something caught Buck's attention. The Osmundson door was slowly rising, rolling back, and disappearing overhead. As the opening in the wall grew larger, Buck could see the silver grill, blue cab, and aluminum trailer of a semi-truck facing outward. It was in a sunken, loading dock structure, and along one side, Buck could make out a concrete platform on which sat scores of fifty-five-gallon drums, all standing on end.

He grabbed the camera and snapped two quick shots. Then he switched the key on and touched the button to lower his window. The voices he heard were too distant to be understood. But the sound of the diesel engine starting up, sending puffs of black smoke into the upper reaches of the warehouse, was unmistakable. Finally, things are happening, he thought.

Buck had just made the decision to follow the semi, when a flourish of activity almost overwhelmed him. The crackling exhaust of another big engine at the entrance to the alley on his right was followed by a single blast on an air horn. Entering the alley was a black gravel truck, its box covered by a heavy, black tarpaulin. Buck slid down in his seat, and as the truck eased past him, he raised up and snapped a shot.

"That's it!" he said softly. "It's a Peterbilt! That's it, or it's one just like it!"

As he lowered the camera, he glanced at the driver's door. Small, white letters spelled out:

M & S SAND & GRAVEL. He felt the increased adrenalin as he watched the black truck backing down toward the opening on the left. The semi-rig was now laboring up the other ramp directly toward Buck, its long snout blocking Buck's view of the driver. Good, he thought. It means he can't see me either, at least not yet. Let's hope he's looking at where he's turning when the tractor levels off. The semi stopped. Buck slid a little farther down in the seat.

Just then he spotted yet another movement to his right. A blue, tandem-axle truck roared into the alley. Just past Buck, its airbrakes hissed as it lurched to a stop. He chanced a shot of it. On the driver's door was the yellow and black Osmundson sign. The truck had a large black box with low sides and a tarp stretched over the top. At the rear, Buck saw a hydraulic lift platform retracted against the box. Through the open space between the lift and the tarp, the bottoms of more steel drums could be seen.

The semi started moving again and was almost on top of Buck now. He froze. No time to hide *or* take pictures! At the last second, the driver spun the wheel, and the big rig turned left and headed toward the street. On the right side door was the Osmundson sign. As soon as the tractor-trailer rig had cleared the inclined ramp, the latest arrival began backing down into the Osmundson opening. The overhead doors of both buildings began to close, almost simultaneously.

Buck looked out toward the side street. The semi had turned left toward Seventh Street. Now what? he wondered. They might have seen me. Better not stay here. He checked to the sides and behind him. Nobody else in sight. In the process, he noticed an old single-car garage nearby. Its wooden doors hadn't seen paint in decades, and jagged edges outlined the pieces of glass missing from its windows. He decided that if—when—he came back, the old building would provide a better vantage point. For now, he thought, I'd better get out of here and see if I can find that semi.

On a hunch, he headed east on Seventh Street. Sure enough, he caught the rig just as it chose the entrance ramp to the eastbound Garden Grove Freeway. Buck dropped back to a slot a good block behind the truck. The hard part was over. The highly visible semi would be easy and safe to follow. He trailed it all the way across the Garden Grove Freeway to the Costa Mesa Freeway and then on to the eastbound Riverside Freeway.

As they climbed into the first of the mountains, Buck began to question his plan. Where does this end? The trucker might pull off at Corona, or he could be headed for Riverside, San Bernadino, Las Vegas—or even *New York*! Might as well be Paris, you dummy, he scolded himself. You could follow this guy for two days and then find he's hauling to a legitimate dumpsite in Nevada or Utah. When the truck continued its easterly course past Corona, Buck abandoned the project and pulled off. Before heading back to Long Beach, he stopped and dug out his cell phone to make a call. He caught Lenny at home. His spirits flew when he heard the soft, warm voice. But he hit a down-draft when she sounded as if she hardly remembered him. Reluctantly, she did agree to meet him at Dante's.

"And would you have time to check something out yet this after-noon?" he asked.

"Maybe. What is it?"

"Could you see what you can find on Osmundson Transport? And on M and S Sand and gravel? No, that's M, as in Mary. I'll tell you all about it tonight. Good. See you at five? Thanks, Lenny." He was grop-ing for words to keep the conversation going when he heard the click.

He felt guilty when he admitted to the giddiness that the contact with Lenny had renewed in him. You're not going to bed with her, he reasoned. You're only meeting her on business. But maybe it's time you started building *other* bridges. Could you possibly do any better than Lenny? Don't know. Don't even know her, he told himself. It took nineteen years to find out you didn't know Roberta. You ready to do *that* again?

Buck's thoughts rambled on as he cruised down the Riverside

Freeway into the increasing smog of the Los Angeles basin. His gut told him that he had tumbled onto something big, something that was close to making sense. It was like that point late in the first quarter, when you've begun to get a feel for the other team's offense. You're still not sure what they'll do next, but some of the blanks have been filled in. A few more answers, and you can shut them down cold. He checked his mirror, then shuddered slightly. It was the *first* time he'd thought to check the mirror since leaving Long Beach!

Chapter 13

It was after five when Lenny Bercovich appeared beside the secluded booth. She wore a black pants suit with a light blue blouse. The gold loop earrings had been replaced by small blue stones that matched the blouse. This time, every hair was carefully combed in place. The face was not smiling. It was a serious, perhaps sad face. Buck couldn't tell which. But she looked *good*.

"Hello," she said as she slid into the booth. "What's happening?"

Buck wanted to direct the conversation to more personal things, but he responded to the question. He gave her a running account of the events, from the ASH meeting through the PCH ditching, the phone call, the confrontation with Runkle, and the afternoon stakeout. He felt a little embarrassed at his use of the police term "stake out," as though he were trying to be something he wasn't. Lenny listened seriously and jotted notes in a small spiral-bound notebook. Buck watched her as he talked, eager for a positive reaction. But she showed nothing.

"Whoof!" she said when he finished. "You are a mover, aren't you? Do you know what you've gotten yourself into?"

"I think so," Buck replied. "I've been in situations before."

"Not like this you haven't. You still don't understand, do you? You're an amateur, and these guys are pros."

Buck felt the heat turn up inside. "This is my job," he said indignantly. "I'm getting paid for it, and that makes me a pro—a bad one, maybe—but a pro." It wasn't what he had intended to say to her, but—too late. "Anyway, what's the difference? I'm ahead of them now."

"Maybe."

"What do you mean, *maybe?*"

"You thought you were ahead of them at the ASH meeting, too, didn't you?" she asked.

Buck nodded. "And now, this afternoon's adventure. You got away from that all right, too?"

"Uh huh."

"Are you sure?"

"Well . . . no, can't be sure," he answered reluctantly.

"Right, you can't be sure. And, if you haven't figured it out, these guys send one, maybe two warnings. Then they just eliminate the problem. According to my count, you've already used up *three* warnings—two phone calls and the ditching. Are you reading me, Mr. Barnum?"

Buck was surprised by her stern, cold demeanor, but more so by the "Mr. Barnum." At least, he thought, she didn't use *Beverly* like Roberta had when the steam reached a certain level. He was struggling to formulate an answer when the waiter appeared with their drinks, bourbon and water for Buck and iced tea for Lenny. Buck ordered his meal, but Lenny declined.

"You're not eating?" Buck asked when the waiter had gone.

"No."

"Why not?"

"I don't have to give you reasons," she said.

Buck felt like he had been doused with ice water. What's gotten into her? he wondered. Maybe I read her all wrong. I got enough of this stuff at home before Roberta finally took off with her Howard.

"Now," Lenny said, "anything else? What about crew members? Any likely prospects there?"

Buck rattled off the names, Runkle, Maine, and Morse. "What have you found out?"

"A little. Some of it I'll share with you. Some, I won't."

"Why not?" Buck asked. It seemed the hole he was sliding into was growing deeper by the minute.

"Tell you why." She leaned forward, her face softening slightly. While she was still serious, she no longer seemed angry. "I let you go ahead with your amateur investigations because, at that point, we had nothing. Now, we have at least the beginnings of a case."

"Lenny, don't abandon me now. There's a lot more than my job riding on this."

"I understand, Buck. I really do," she said with a sudden warmth. "I *can* tell you this. I checked with the HAZ-MAT people. There is a set of laws on the books, what they call the cradle-to-grave laws. These laws require strict record keeping and filing of all shipping manifests that involve hazardous wastes. The idea is, the stuff that's dumped in the safe-sites must match up to the amounts collected by the commercial disposal companies. Now, the state knows there is cheating going on, but they don't have the manpower or the money for a lot of long, dragged out investigations.

"They don't have the money or manpower? That's really encouraging," said Buck. "How do the cheaters work?"

"It's often the same, really quite simple. A company's licensed trucks pick up the waste, usually in drums, and return it to a central location. From there, a small portion, with doctored shipping manifests, is hauled to the legal dumpsites, usually in Nevada or Utah. The rest is hauled out into the countryside and buried."

"But how do they get around the fact that their total collections and disposals don't match up?" Buck sipped his drink, relieved that their conversation had reached some level of normalcy.

"Some of the out-of-state people receiving the stuff really don't care what the paper says. They'll sign a phony manifest. They'll sign anything. They're only concerned with getting appropriate payment for the amount actually dumped there."

"That figures," Buck interjected.

"And some of the haulers go on and on, letting the discrepancy between collections and disposals grow and grow, knowing that the government will probably never catch up with it. If they see suspicious clouds on the horizon, they just move, or change names, or disappear completely. They can afford it with the profit they've made," Lenny said with a shrug.

"What did you find out about Osmundson and the M and S outfits?"

"Osmundson is approved for hauling hazardous. They have a fleet of seven regular trucks and two big rigs, all blue. The M and S Sand and Gravel Company is not approved. They drive five dump trucks, all black."

Buck nodded and smiled knowingly. "And did you find out who heads up these two companies?"

For the first time, Lenny smiled, a big smile. "The applications for the Osmundson registrations were signed by one Michael L. Schutte."

Buck pondered the name. Unfamiliar to him. Suddenly, his face lit up. He reached across the table, taking Lenny's hands in his, and said,

"And the M and S applications were signed by Michael L. Schutte. Right?"

He felt excited. He looked over at Lenny. She was looking at their joined hands. The angry face was gone. Man, she's gorgeous, he thought. He squeezed her hand once more, then released it. To his surprise, she took his hand. Her eyes told him what he needed to know. Then, she withdrew and smiled at him.

"Uh, let's stay on the business," she said. "You may be a pro, but you're still a little slow. Has the bell rung yet?"

"Oh, I had it figured out this afternoon," Buck lied. "The Osmundson trucks pick up the wastes and drop the barrels off at the warehouse. Some are loaded on the semi that I followed to be hauled legally to approved dumpsites. Glad I quit when I did and came home. But most are rolled right next door. They're loaded on M and S trucks and hauled out into the country some place to be dumped. And I'll bet that when I follow an M and S truck to their gravel pit, I'll find the dumpsite."

"You've done well," Lenny said, "but as of now, Sherlock, you're out of the loop. We have enough to light up the D.A.'s eyes. And we have a very aggressive local strike team to finish the job."

"But when, Lenny, when?" Buck demanded in a half-whisper. "I need this right now! We're getting ready to go, and we've got to discredit Osmundson, Kersting, and ASH. Got to sink *them* before they sink *us*!"

"Tell you what, Buck," she said, taking his hand again and looking directly into his eyes. "I'll bring my boss in on this. He's a mover, too."

"Stop that. You're trying for a melt-down. Can't you see my problem?"

"Of course I can! And I'll go way out on the limb to help you. Now you try to see it from my perspective. If you go out there, wherever *out there* is, and blow it, we might lose them. When we get them, we'll need you as a witness. Will you still be *alive?*" Lenny hesitated, lowered her voice and added, "And besides, I—I don't want anything to happen to you."

Something in Buck quivered, and his emotions rode a rollercoaster to the top.

"I'd feel responsible," she added.

Buck's rollercoaster crashed at the bottom.

"But the sooner we expose them," he argued, "the sooner we disarm them. I've got to have them hogtied before *Ark II* leaves for the test."

"Okay," Lenny conceded, "promise me one thing? Promise me you won't go near these guys until I've talked with my boss?"

"How soon?"

"I'll corner him tonight, have an answer for you in the morning. Okay?" she asked.

Buck nodded agreement. He was caught up in an emotional whirlwind, tossed about by her overwhelming appeal and her concern for him. At the same time, he could not simply abdicate his responsibility to the project, especially after such a giant stride forward. Lenny stirred, snapping Buck's attention back to the present.

"I really have to go now," she said, "but if you'll promise to be careful, I'll give you something else to work on. Promise?"

"I—I promise," Buck sighed. I'd promise anything you asked, he thought, if it would keep you here.

"You might want to see where this leads," she said, tearing a page from her notebook and handing it to Buck. On it was written: Groundswell—Jim Reicher—Jim's Marine Shop—Seal Beach.

"Jim Reicher," she continued. "I'm told he's a mean dude, kicked out of Greenpeace for being too radical. A real monkeywrencher." She slid out of the booth and turned to leave. Suddenly, she spun back, took his face in her hands, and kissed him quickly on the forehead. "Please be careful around this guy, Buck, and watch your mirror?" She wheeled and was gone.

Buck sat there, a paper bombshell in his hands and the touch of her lips on his forehead. "Barnum," he said aloud, "you're really screwed up now."

Chapter 14

"Where you from?" Jim Reicher asked. He jerked the heavy outboard engine from the testing tank as though it were a toy and carelessly plunked it on the dirty, concrete floor. His pudgy grease-stained face turned while he was bent over. Angry eyes, magnified by thick bottle cap lenses, seemed to measure the newcomer from bottom to top as he slowly straightened to face him. Beads of dirty sweat clung to Reicher's forehead, threatening to launch themselves with the slightest provocation. The grungy marine shop owner brushed the back of one greasy hand across his black goatee and waited for an answer.

"Local—this area," Buck said

"What you want? Boat? Motor? Trailer?"

"No, I came to see what I can do for you."

"Ha!" Reicher retorted. "What the hell *you* gonna do for *me*?"

"Well," Buck began, "I've got some pretty heavy feelings about the way big business runs everything these days, especially the way they go around polluting things and getting away with it."

"So?"

"Well, I got to talking with a guy after the Alliance meeting the other night, you know—the ASH group?"

"So?"

"Well, I'm really concerned about this new incinerator ship, and we got to talking, and this guy tells me that ASH is just a bunch of sign wavers. 'If you really want to get something done,' he says, 'get in with Jim Reicher's Groundswell group.' Now, I don't have lots of money to throw around, but I got some, and I'm not afraid of a little action, if you know what I mean."

"C'mon," Reicher said curtly. He led the way past two day cruisers and out through the large opening at the rear of the shop. They cut between two trash barrels and followed a worn path to the rear of an adjacent, store building. The steel bars and loose window panes rattled as Reicher jerked the dilapidated door open. "What's your name?" he demanded, leading Buck into a small, empty store. Long sheets of brown wrapping paper had been carelessly taped in place to cover the front street-side windows.

"Huh? Oh . . . Bob . . . Bob Bernhardt."

"Bob Bernhardt, shit!" Reicher hissed.

Two men were painting on a large banner that was stretched out on the floor. They stopped and looked up. Their eyes flitted from Reicher to Buck and back again. Their faces told Buck they were uncomfortable with the tension Reicher was creating, and their reaction suggested to him that a change of tactics was in order. They're scared of him, he thought.

He turned on his fierce face and glared at Reicher. "That's the name I gave you, Reicher. You got trouble with that?"

Reicher laughed. "Hell no, I got no trouble. You got the problem."

"You sure as hell didn't think I'd come in here, offering my money and my help to a bunch with your reputation, and give you my real name, did you?"

"They did," Reicher replied, nodding at the two men on the floor. "Let's try it once more. What's your address?"

The first test had served as a wake-up call, and Buck reacted quickly, "Thirteen, seventeen," he began, recalling the number for Reicher's shop, "Thirteen, seventeen, Reicher Drive, Reichersville, California, and it's *your* problem, punk, because I'm outa' here." He started for the door.

"Hey, Bernhardt!" Reicher called when Buck had almost reached the back door. "You want a beer?"

Buck stopped and turned slowly. Reicher's magnified eyes looked as cold as before, but he was smiling. "Well—yeah," Buck said, "but don't try to card me."

Reicher laughed and headed for a nearby refrigerator. He opened the grease-smudged door, pulled out a can, and tossed it. Buck reached up deftly with his left hand and plucked the missile out of the air.

"You might be all right, Bernhardt. We'll see."

The mechanic gestured to one of four folding chairs surrounding a flimsy, old card table.

Buck sat down, casually popped the ring on the can, and took a long drink. He surveyed the surroundings. Hanging from one wall was a collection of signs and banners, each headed with the word, GROUNDSWELL. The banner headings were followed by slogans:

Care for the planet—We don't have any spares!

Lies! Lies! All lies!

Just move the crap from earth to ocean?

Profits in their pockets—Poison on our plates!

Save the baloney! Sink the BURNER!

"Bernhardt, this is Ken, and Al." Reicher motioned toward the duo working over the sign. "They're members of our board." The two men looked up from their positions on their hands and knees and nodded.

"Nice signs," Buck observed as Reicher plopped onto the flimsy chair across from him.

"So, who'd you say this friend was?"

"Didn't say. Doesn't really matter," Buck said, forcing himself to focus on the enlarged eyes. Don't know if it's the eyes or not, he thought, but Lenny was right. He looks like one mean dude. "Really, Reicher, only two things that matter right at the moment. What are you guys doing to stop the burner? And are you and your plans convincing enough to make me want to invest in them?"

"Shit!" Reicher scoffed. "You think I'm gonna turn my guts inside out for every little do-gooder that comes along, especially one that doesn't even know his own name?"

Don't know yet if the guy's smart, Buck thought, but he isn't stupid. He was hoping it wouldn't come to this, but he'd have to go to Plan B. Sliding a hand into his trouser pocket, he came out with the wad of bills he'd just picked up at the bank. He methodically counted out two hundred dollars and pushed the pile to the middle of the table. He sure hoped Peter would back him on this. He couldn't afford it.

"Okay," he said, "you've got a point, Reicher, so listen up. This little pile of beer money is to get and hopefully hold your attention. You with me?"

Reicher shrugged and looked at his watch. "The timer's running."

"As far as you're concerned, I'm still Bob Bernhardt. But I can tell you this. I represent a company in the waste management business. I have to spell out what that damned burner means to us?"

Reicher tilted back on his chair, folded his hands across his belly, lowered his head so that his short beard rested on his huge chest, and smiled.

"Your nickel," he said, a touch of triumph in his voice.

"Here's how we handle our doubts," Buck began. "Really very simple. For the little bit of earnest money on the table, you give me reasons to stay interested. If your reasons are good enough, I'll be back Monday with a thousand—cash, of course. If what I hear Monday is truly inspiring, I'll see you on Wednesday with ten grand."

Reicher said nothing, simply locked onto Buck's eyes. Buck held his ground, determined not to be the first to break. Sooner or later—there! Reicher's big eyes glanced ever so briefly at the money.

"At that point, Reicher, we change the game," Buck went on, "and you play first. *If* I'm completely captivated by the story, motivated by your integrity, and awestruck by your ability to carry the story to its proper conclusion, then Groundswell gets the ten."

Buck swigged the beer, thumped the half-filled can on the table, and stood up. He glanced at the two seemingly paralyzed helpers. They were silent, but their faces said, "Do it, Reicher! Do it!"

Buck turned toward the door and paused. "Timer's running, Reicher," he said, "and I need reasons to come back."

Reicher plunked his chair back to all fours, looked up with a smirk and said, "For reasonable expenses, we can make the burner look very bad in the press before she ever leaves the dock."

Buck said nothing. He simply extended a hand and, with a couple waves toward himself, he motioned for more.

"For *real* money, there's a chance of enough accidents aboard her that she'll have to abort the test."

Buck motioned again.

Reicher leaned back on his chair. "That's all for now, Bernhardt. Two pills for two bills. Your play."

Buck's instincts told him he had pushed Reicher as far as he'd go. Better to make a businesslike exit than to try again and fail.

"I'll think about it, Reicher." He moved toward the door, forcing himself into a cool, deliberate pace. He pulled the noisy door shut behind him and fought the urge to break and run.

He had parked the Camaro in the fourth row of the lot next door and deliberately left it facing *away* from Reicher's place. As he casually strolled along the main driving lane, he surveyed the area thoroughly. A couple of glances over his shoulder showed no sign of Reicher or his associates. Satisfied that nobody was watching or following, he darted in among the cars and then bent into a hunched-over walk. Seconds later, he quietly eased the Camaro door shut and exhaled a giant sigh of relief.

"Won't win an Oscar," he said softly to himself, "but might have a chance at the Ed Roland Trophy for Biggest Bullshitter." He thought for a moment about what had been accomplished. Certainly, he had no incriminating evidence, but he had reason to believe Reicher was serious and willing to wage war against the *Ark*. I think, if Peter will ante up the thousand, we might get enough to nail the— Stupid! he thought. How dumb! You sit here in the enemy's backyard—*thinking*?

He was glad he had picked a spot some distance from Reicher's back door. He would be driving away from the shop, not toward it. He had just inserted the ignition key when a large, black shape flashed past his rearview mirror. Buck had the engine running and the automatic transmission in reverse when the thought crystallized. A big, black car? He eased halfway out of his stall for a better look. It was a new Cadillac with an out-of-state license that read: D'COBRA. It seemed familiar— but ominous. Why? His first thought was to get out of there.

"No, calm down!" he told himself. You can't peel rubber every time you see a black car or truck. He backed out of the stall and straightened out in the lane, facing the street. Leaving the Camaro with the door open and the engine running, he got out, stooped over, and moved among the parked cars, working himself closer to Reicher's shop. The black Caddy stopped before Reicher's drive-in door. Two men got out, and Buck felt prickles run up his back. The one closest to Buck, the driver, was a small, wiry man with a ponytail, and the other? No doubt about it, that Kersting guy, Don Murrell, the tall, blond man, the one who gave ASH the check and made the "bottom line" phone call. As they approached the service door, Reicher stepped out to meet them.

Buck couldn't hear anything from that distance, but Reicher's gestures told him they were getting a much warmer welcome than he had received.

That little guy, he wondered, is that the one who was staring at me during the ASH meeting? Peering through two panes of auto windows distorted the figures, but Buck was reluctant to raise up for a clear line of vision. Staying low, he moved around the vehicle and worked his way to the second car in the row. He was still too far away to hear, but he could see much better, even through the windows of a parked Ford. The little guy? It's him! Buck thought, recalling the chilling, steely eyes and the 'I know something you don't' grin.

No wonder, Buck thought. He knew me the minute I walked in. He knew what he was going to do. And what did I know? I knew I was playing Mr. Anonymous to the hilt. Several of Lenny's warnings zipped through his mind on fast forward, ending with, "Remember, they make their own rules." He was about to leave when a change in the scene before him caused his body to freeze. The big man, Murrell, was staring directly at him. If Buck could see them through two tinted pains of glass, it was reasonable that they could see him.

"Down!" a voice within him said. "No, don't move—the movement will give you away!" another answered. He watched Murrell closely for any body language, any sign that he'd been spotted. Murrell continued talking, and the focus of his gaze seemed unchanged. Discomfort set in. The Saturday morning sun suddenly turned hot. Perspiration gathered on Buck's forehead. And holding his awkward position was bringing a severe cramp in his right calf. He held to the challenge, waiting for Murrell to look away, or even blink his eyes.

An auto horn sounded twice from somewhere behind Buck in the parking lot. Murrell was like a statue. The horn honked again. No reaction. Damn, thought Buck, he *must* see me. Most people would turn toward the noise. The horn seemed even louder the third time.

Oh, no! Buck thought. That's coming from where I left the Camaro. Someone's honking at *me*! He ducked, turned, and scooted back among the cars, zigzagging his way toward the Camaro. He expected to hear shots at any second. Stay low, he told himself, make like a midget. As he approached his car, he slowed to a walk, gradually raised up, and chanced a look back over the tops of the automobiles in the crowded lot. He couldn't see the little guy, but Murrell and Reicher were still standing there, facing one another.

The vehicle behind Buck's was an aged though immaculate white Olds 98, early seventies vintage, and it looked like it had just left the showroom. Its enormous front and rear decks reminded him of an aircraft carrier. The driver was a spindly, little old lady—somebody's Aunt Esther, Buck thought. She seemed to be smiling, a really sweet, little lady.

"Very sorry, Ma'am," he called to her as he reached the Camaro. "Sorry," he repeated with a smile as he slid in behind the wheel.

"Sorry doesn't cut it!" came a squeaky reply. "Get that mother fucker out of my way!"

A lot of nice people in this neighborhood, Buck thought as he eased out of the parking lot and blended in with the traffic. He headed for the office, his frequent mirror checks alternating with his attempts to relax through deep breathing. Funny, every time I begin to unwind a little, I look at the rear-view mirror and tighten up all over again. I wonder how many times I'll check that mirror in the next two weeks? The question sent a chill through his hot, sweaty, and tense body.

Chapter 15

Buck let himself in, turned off the alarm system, and headed for the dingy office. He called home. As his recorded message came on, he entered his retrieval code. He felt a gentle, warm thrill when Lenny's voice came on.

"Mr. Barnum," the businesslike voice said, "Detective Bercovich has some information regarding the matter you discussed. You may reach the detective at. . . ."

Buck's excitement churned as he scribbled the number down. He loved the sound of her voice, and he recognized her home phone number. Her message set him to reading between the lines. After hanging up, he sat there for some time, thinking about Lenny and the possibilities. Finally, he shook it off and reached for the phone.

"Hello," the warm, musical voice said.

"Hi, there! This is Buck. Thanks for calling, Lenny," he opened enthusiastically.

"You're very welcome. You weren't out getting into trouble, were you?"

While her words hinted at humor, her soft tone suggested real concern. He had intended to keep the conversation a personal one as long as possible, but he suddenly found himself relating the morning's adventure. As he went on, he realized that he was quite proud of the way he had handled things, at least up to the episode with the little, old lady in the white aircraft carrier. It brought a laugh from Lenny.

"You know," Buck went on, "I couldn't hear anything the three of them were saying outside the shop, but I had the feeling this wasn't the first time they'd met."

"Very good, Buck. You're probably right. The car?"

"Black Caddy, four-door, looked new."

"License?"

Buck read off the New Jersey numbers. "Plate says, 'D Cobra.' Good match," Buck added. "He looks like a cobra, definitely the one coiled up behind me at the ASH meeting."

"You should know him pretty well. He's got his fangs right in your butt."

"What do you mean by that?" Buck asked.

"Buck!" Lenny said sternly. "You'd better become a hundred percent more alert and two hundred percent better with your memory if you hope to keep up with these guys. You really *don't* remember the little drunk at Dante's the other night?"

When the light finally went on in Buck's mind, it illuminated an image of the little drunk, but more than that, it exposed a sizeable chunk of embarrassment. "You're—right. That *was* him," Buck agreed humbly.

"Can you describe him?" Lenny asked.

"Oh, he's—he's not very big, and he has a pony tail—"

"He's five-seven, a hundred and thirty-five, and he carries a blade," she said sharply.

"Oh, come on, Lenny," Buck said, "I admit I'm still an amateur, but don't tell me you spotted a knife *that* fast."

"Dante spotted that. He saw him come in right after you did. The punk had followed you again. Dante flashed me a warning right away—motioned to me that the guy wears it under his shirt."

Buck went cold. He'd fought it out many times on the field and a number of times off the field, but a knife?

"Are you thinking? I told you, these guys make their own rules," Lenny said. "Now, put it all together, from their perspective. What do they have?"

"They know me. Know I eat sometimes at Dante's. They've seen you, but—"

"By this time, we have to assume they know who I am. Now, I can take pretty good care of myself, and I'm usually with my partner. But that makes you a much hotter burr under their saddle. You understand?"

"Yeah, I'm learning. Bear with me. Does this put Dante at risk?" Buck asked.

"Dante's been at risk most of his life. But we could relieve him of some of the heat," she replied, "by not meeting there all the time."

Buck agreed, but his mind took a detour. This had become a

threatening conversation, and Lenny was setting the dangers front and center. Yet, he found himself calmed and encouraged by the soothing voice and the deep concern it carried. He wondered, can a well-balanced, perfectly sane man fall in love with a voice?

"Buck? Buck, are you still there?"

"Huh? Oh, you can bet on it," he said. "The day I hang up on you, you'll know there's something very bad happening to me. Any chance I could come over to see you? I mean, we could talk, or go for a ride, or get a cup of coffee, or—"

"I'd like that, Buck," she cut in, "but the answer is, 'No.'"

Buck processed her reply in reverse. The "no" was firm; she meant it. But the expressive, "I'd like that," washed the negative aside. He knew, he was certain that there would be a relationship with this fascinating woman. Just what it would be, how it would go, or how long it would last, he couldn't know. In fact, until that glob of nervous teenage drivel that was meant to be an invitation had spewed from his mouth, he hadn't even meant to push the issue. While Lenny continued talking, explaining that she was due for her volunteer stint at a nursing home, Buck sat back, relaxed, and smiled.

"*You*—helping at a nursing home?" he asked.

"Certainly! Is there something wrong with that?"

"Oh, no. Do you ever have trouble with dirty old men?"

"No, most of them are really sweet. Well, there was one. On my first visit he started to hit on me—pretty bad, really."

"And what did you do?" Buck asked.

"Oh, I just looked him in the eye and said very quietly, 'Please clean up your language—or I'll kick you in the balls.'"

"And?"

"He started laughing. He flailed his arms and laughed so hard, he forgot *two* things—what he'd wanted to do to me—and that he couldn't stand without both hands on his walker. Really though, I enjoy helping out there. They're such nice people. But sometimes it seems so unfair. As they've grown older, they've had to adjust to getting their kicks out of simple, little things. And then, they get to a point where they're even denied *those* little pleasures. If I can provide just a few, it's worth the effort. Don't you agree, Buck?"

"Pardon the cliché, Lenny, but you never cease to amaze me. If you keep it up, you're gonna larn me ta be a right, smart ole man!"

"Oh, Buck, I've got to get going. I'll be late. Got to tell you, though, I talked to my lieutenant. He thinks we're onto something big, *really* big, much too big to jump the gun. He said we should back off, do nothing for now. He'll talk to the captain Monday morning."

"Lenny! I'm running out of time. Did you tell him that?"

"Of course I did. The lieutenant's a tough, by-the-booker, but he understands, and he'll make sure the captain understands, too. But if I read this right, Buck, they'll probably need a week to make sure they're on solid legal ground, get organized, get warrants and everything. If we rush in and blow it, our chances for a complete sweep go down the toilet. Can you handle that?"

Only Buck's feelings for Lenny held the burst of locker room profanity that threatened to erupt. "Can't you do any better than that?" he asked in stilted, strained tones.

"I'll try. I'll call you Monday afternoon with the latest. I'll even go in early," she said.

"And what am I supposed to do, Lenny, just wait?"

"You work on your other angles, and most important, you concentrate on staying alive and well. That's more important than snagging the whole damned Mafia! Got to go, Bye."

Chapter 16

Buck felt a boiling volcano within him Monday morning as he flashed his badge at the pudgy guard and headed for his parking place. Even the deep breathing exercises he had done on the way in had failed to relieve the stress. He had tried to shake off the negatives and concentrate on the positives. What positives? The fog is unusually heavy this morning? This rental car is costing way too much? Friday is his first payday in a long time—and maybe his last?

Then, there's Bob. He should have followed up on the one encouraging talk they had, but there just hadn't been time. The Osmundson-Kersting-ASH hookup? He should feel good about the progress there, but now he's supposed to just sit on it and wait? Unless—he found their dumpsite. Yeah, maybe that would get things moving.

And Lenny Bercovich, the irresistible enigma, the little doll. Little? He don't even know how tall she was. They'd never even stood beside one another, or walked together, or—shut that down, Barnum. But even Lenny. She helps him get things rolling, then tells him to back off.

"Good morning, Mr. Barnum," the outer receptionist said cheerily as Buck entered the office.

The words didn't penetrate. Buck flipped an automatic wave and looked straight ahead as he started down the long hallway, his mind skipping from one thing to another. Ahh, quit wimping, he thought. You've always thrived on competition, so get with it. Remember what Coach used to yell. "If you can't hit *your* man, hit *somebody!*"

They were all around him, taking whacks at him—Hudson, Grigsby, Murrell, the Snake—but he didn't seem to get any whacks of his own. He was letting them catch him off guard. Going to change that. You hear that, Lenny?

Once in the office, Buck grabbed a cup of coffee and organized his plan for the day. After the first mate Dick Hobbs, he had one remaining seaman, and good old Mal Runkle, the uncooperative first engineer left to photograph. As he thought of the sneering engineer, he felt a chill, followed by a tinge of anger, and finally a swelling of determination.

He'd get him yet, and while he's at it, he'd better do some serious checking on Runkle. No doubt, *we've got a spy here somewhere, and he's still the most likely prospect. Nobody could be such a dunk without a reason.*

He decided he'd work the ship for a couple of hours, watching and listening. Then, after a couple of hours going over the personnel files, perhaps he'd hear from Lenny. After that, depending on what she said. . . . It amazed him, just how fast the decision was made, especially after slogging his way through a muddy mind all morning. Sure, why not? he asked himself. *If Lenny tells me to stay on hold, I'll get something accomplished* my *way.* He grabbed the Canon and headed for the ship.

Buck chose the outside steps up to B-deck. Each time aboard, he had deliberately subjected himself to the exposed heights, and with each trip he gained a victory. He still didn't feel comfortable up there, with nothing but the small railing for security, but at least the queasy feelings were subsiding. He had never actually felt dizziness, more the fear that he would become dizzy.

"Ho!" came a shout from the first mate's quarters when Buck knocked.

"Ho?" *What does* that *mean? Come in?* He knocked again and slowly opened the door. Dick Hobbs stood just inside, hanging his clothes in the wardrobe cabinet to the left of the door. He appeared to be about Buck's height and age, but the immense, curly bush of red hair and the splotches of freckles on the pudgy face ended any similarities. Buck had never seen such vivid freckles on a middle-aged man. He had assumed such markings disappeared with adolescence.

"Jump the chair over there," Hobbs said, his smile revealing a conspicuous, gold-capped tooth. "You must be Buck Barnum. Be right with you."

"Thanks." Buck dropped carelessly into the orange chair. "I've wanted to meet you and add your picture to my collection, but you're a hard man to find."

"Haven't been hiding," the first mate said. "Been in for a few meetings, but not officially on duty until today." Buck watched the man, clad in khaki trousers and a white T-shirt, as he finished his chore and wiggled into a khaki shirt. Hobbs had the rotund body of a man who ate well and was not given to resisting the bloat of time. He turned toward Buck as he buttoned the shirt. Then, he nonchalantly unzipped his trousers, tucked the shirt in, sucked in his belly, and rezipped.

"Man-o-man! This tumor just keeps growing and growing. Guess I need more time at sea," he laughed, reaching to shake hands with Buck.

"I've got a cure for that, if you're interested," Buck said.

"No-o-o thanks! You're talking about diet and exercise. I will not diet, and I'm allergic to exercise. Makes my face break out in spots," he laughed. "So you're Buck Barnum, the sportswriter. I used to read your stuff in the *Chronicle*. Have a couple of younger brothers who played ball. You were pretty good. Why'd you quit?"

"Evolution, I guess. Just got bored with it, sort of outgrew it. Same story over and over. The names change, but the stories don't. Then, when the paper went weekly, I found myself getting assignments that ranged from covering the women's clubs to cleaning the coffee pot."

"Boy, I follow you," Hobbs replied. "A lot of people changing careers these days because of changing priorities in this society. I'm lucky. Made a good choice, happy with it, and it's been good to me. Twenty years in the coast guard, nice retirement, and now I get to do it again, with better pay than I got the first time around."

"I envy you," said Buck. "It's too bad we have to make such important decisions at an age when we're blessed with energy and blinded by ignorance. Good to know your choices worked out so well."

Buck liked Hobbs, easy to talk to, outgoing, and friendly. In a short time, he learned that the first mate had served in the coast guard with Captain Portner for several years and had then elected to retire and come aboard *Ark II* at the captain's urging. If the endeavor proved successful, the affable first mate had first shot at the next command available.

Buck asked Hobbs to don his black, baseball-style cap with the S.C.B.C. logo and pose for a picture. His subject consented willingly, but when Buck was ready to shoot, Hobbs waved him off.

"Hold it!"

The cap climbed upward, as if by magic, on the balloon of red curls. "Worst thing about this job," Hobbs muttered, mangling the cap into a ball in his hands, wringing it this way and that, "got to break in a new cap."

He pulled it on firmly, tugging on the brim in front and the adjustable band in back. The bulge of brilliant red that popped out beneath the cap reminded Buck of a clown.

"There. Now you can shoot. But be sure you get the shoulder boards, gotta get the boards to show. Nobody ever gets the boards," he laughed.

After the picture, they left and went separate ways, the first mate toward the galley, while Buck headed aft. The congenial encounter had lifted Buck's spirits. But no sooner had he recognized the welcome change than he was reminded of his next mission. He found the seaman, Martinez, moving some gear about the top deck of the afterhouse. The young Mexican smiled proudly as Buck snapped the picture, but his face showed disappointment when Buck thanked him and walked away after only one shot.

An inquiry along the way told Buck that the engines were among Runkle's responsibilities, so he set out for the engine room. He quieted his steps as he started down from the second deck. A smile crossed his face, and the analogy almost made him laugh aloud. Down here, in the lowest level of the rear end of the ship, exactly where you'd expect to find the anus. He slowed and stealthily made his way down to the floor plates of the engine room.

Three men bent over a housing at the rear of one of the twin, two-thousand-horsepower Caterpillar engines. Gantsky and Runkle had their backs to Buck. The other, a seaman, glanced up briefly, then rejoined the project. The light was barely adequate for a no-flash shot, and Buck quietly made his way closer to the group. Gantsky was hammering vigorously on something metallic that Runkle appeared to be holding. The clangs of the hammer reverberated about the large, steel chamber.

It suddenly occurred to Buck just how silly this thing had become. He didn't really need Runkle's picture, and he certainly didn't have to read body language to pick up Runkle's attitude toward the picture-taking. He knew what the first engineer looked like. What's the point?

he asked himself. Simple, came the answer. Runkle's challenged me. Okay then, he thought, let's do it. He could get close and time his shot to Gantsky's hammering. One last camera check. Okay.

Clang! Clang! Clang! Just as Buck snapped the shot, Gantsky checked his swing with the hammer. *Click* – The shutter had never sounded so loud.

"What the—" Runkle turned his head. Buck felt his own face flush. Oh, hell, he thought. Just my luck. Now what? He saw Runkle twisting toward him as he straightened.

"Don't let me bother you," Buck said, faking a smile. "I'll learn by just watching."

"You sneaky son of a bitch!" Runkle roared as he approached Buck. His face was contorted beyond the sneer—pure, unmistakable anger, a rage that was incongruous with the situation. A chill quivered through Buck, followed by the hot flash that primed his own anger.

"Who the hell you think you are?" Runkle shouted. "I said, 'no pictures,' and that's what I meant! I'm on this ship to do my job and collect my money, and that don't include no pictures!"

"Christ, you'd think I caught you on the toilet or something," Buck said. "I'm just doing my job."

"I don't know what your job is, but I'm sure as hell gonna teach you what your job *isn't*! Now, gimme that camera!" Runkle grabbed the camera and jerked. The strap cut into Buck's neck, but he deftly managed to jab his left arm through the opening of the strap, securing his hold on the black device. Runkle pulled again. *Click*— went the shutter. The protest of the camera triggered Buck's compulsion to protect his treasured partner.

"Now, back off!" he demanded. "You're acting crazy!" The tugging became more violent, and Buck wondered if the strap would hold.

"I'll take that damned thing and shove it up your ass!"

"What you so scared of? Got something to hide?"

Runkle blinked. "Why you—" He kept his grip on the camera with his left hand and cocked his right arm. Buck caught just a glimpse of the massive, greasy fist and reacted instinctively. His left arm came up, deflecting the blow. He felt the searing heat as Runkle's fist grazed his left ear, knocking his hardhat to the deck. Following by a split second,

Buck threw his right with as much force as he could muster. The leverage began at his feet and worked upward through his strong legs, shoulders, and right arm. He had learned many years before that breaking a
fist against bone was Hollywood stuntman stuff. His blow caught the
extended body of the husky engineer in the midsection.

"Oooff!" A venomous burst of foul breath sprinkled with spit
exploded in Buck's face. Runkle's eyes rolled upward. His grip on the
camera released as he dropped to his knees. With the first sight of
Runkle's fist, Buck's self-control, his ability to reason had left him. He
was half animal and half little boy, and the bully before him must be
beaten! He kicked upward with a knee. It caught the distorted face
flush on the jaw, sending Runkle to his back on the steel plates. Buck
was on him instantly.

"Cut it out! Break off!" a voice shouted from behind Buck. He felt
his arms pinned back, and he was being pulled over backward. When
he looked up from his helpless position, he realized it was Gantsky and
the seaman, Simpson, who were holding him down. "Ease off, Buck!
You wanna kill 'im?"

"Huh?" Buck's body began to tremble. He recognized the feeling
from the all too recent past, and he hated it. It was like fear, and there
was no room for it in his life. After a few moments, the two men
relaxed their grips, and Buck remembered that the dreaded trembling
also signaled something else. The battle was over.

Slowly, he got to his feet. Gantsky and Simpson were kneeling over
Runkle. His eyes were open, but they were blank. There was blood
coming from his mouth.

"Looks like he bit his tongue," the second was saying. "We'd better
get him up front."

Buck leaned against the aft bulkhead while the two tended his
adversary. The trembling was almost gone, but the burning sensation
told him his left ear had been battered, maybe torn off. He touched it
gingerly and found it hot and swelling rapidly, but at least it was still
there.

"Come on, Mal," Gantsky said. "You're going to have to help.
There's no way we can carry you up those narrow steps. Come on, get

up! You have to help!" Ever so slowly, the two got Runkle to his feet. Shuffling along, half dragging him, they made it to the steps and began the tedious climb.

Buck waited in the engine room, cooling down, trying to think. He checked the camera. When the others had disappeared up the steps, he picked up his hardhat and put it on. He had started across the engine room when he spotted the other white helmet on the deck. A tiny wave of compassion eased through him. It felt good as he bent to pick up Runkle's hardhat. When Buck had completed the strenuous climb from the bowels of the ship and descended on the outside to the catwalk, he could see the threesome far ahead, just disappearing into the forward house. The small groups of crewmen, scattered about the main deck, had stopped their work. As Buck stepped onto the catwalk, their eyes turned to him. They talked quietly among themselves and watched as Buck made the long trek, the extra hardhat dangling from his fingertips.

He wondered what they were saying, what they were thinking. They might become very resentful toward him, toward the newcomer. Or, there might be some who felt Runkle's beating was long overdue. At this point, I don't much care, Buck thought. But something made him walk a little taller, add a zip to his steps, and effect a nonchalance that said, "No big deal. Any other takers?" His rational mind told him this victory march of the fast gun in a western movie was corny, but something else said, "It feels good."

As he completed the long, exposed walk, he considered his options. Leave the ship? Report to the captain? Or just wait? Unable to sort it out, he chose to wait. He headed for the officers' mess, hoping he could be alone there. But as he stepped from the passageway, he saw Chief Johnson and the second mate seated at a table. Indian Joe Morse stood across from them, leaning over the table and gesturing as he talked. When Buck reached the coffee urn, the voice stopped. Buck ran his coffee. He started for the empty table. As if on a signal, the second mate and the cook abruptly left the mess.

"Care to join me?" the chief said.

"Is it safe?"

Chief Johnson laughed and shoved a chair back from the table with his foot. Buck sat down and raised his coffee mug. To his surprise, the coffee rippled as the mug came up. He wasn't completely past the trembling. The chief said nothing, just watched. His face seemed serious, but Buck thought there was a twinkle in his eyes.

"You heard?" Buck asked.

"News like that travels faster than sonar."

"I just don't understand. All I wanted was a picture."

"Yeah, you *don't* understand," the chief said in his slow, comforting drawl. "You don't understand the first. What you wanted and what he wanted were two different things."

"Does he always react like that when he doesn't get his way?"

"On shore, yes. Aboard ship, no."

"So why did *I* get such special treatment?"

"Don't know. For some reason, he doesn't like you."

"What's with him? Is he hiding something?"

"The first? Naw. But he might think *you're* hiding something."

"What? Ohhh, is he the one who started the bit about my being a company spy?"

"Don't know if he started it, but he might believe it."

"That's ridiculous. I think *he's* hiding something."

"I've known the first for a long time. He's not a very nice guy, but he's a good engineer. And if you're thinking what I think you are, forget it. I'd trust him with my life—aboard ship. Anyway, you must handle yourself pretty good. Nobody's ever put him down when he's sober. I *think* I could," Chief Johnson said with a grin, "but I've always been glad I never had to find out."

Buck tried his coffee again. His hand was steadier this time. He found the huge, easy-going chief relaxing and accepting. He needed both.

"Is Buck Barnum still—oh, there you are," came a voice from the doorway. Buck turned to see Craig Gantsky. The second engineer poured a mug of coffee and joined them. "The old man wants you in his dayroom."

Buck searched Gantsky's face but learned nothing. "Is he pissed?" he asked.

"Uh huh."

"How bad?"

"Don't know yet." Gantsky's face was still expressionless, a face that was new to Buck. It was disconcerting. The second's blue eyes radiated the same warmth, but without the smile, they disturbed Buck. "The old man got my story. Then he got Simpson's. Tried to get the first's. Couldn't understand much of what he said."

"Is Runkle okay?"

"Think so. The first mate took him to E.R. Probably need a couple of stitches in that tongue."

"Damn," Buck said, shaking his head. "I still don't understand."

"Well, you'd better understand two things," Gantsky said. "One, you'd better get up to the old man's dayroom. Don't like to be kept waiting."

"And the other?" Buck asked.

"You're never going to see *me* lay a hand on that camera of yours!" Gantsky grinned. "Now, you'd better haul ass."

Hustling up to B-deck, Buck found Captain Portner alone in his day room. To his surprise, the captain's manner was exactly as it was in their first meeting.

"Barnum, I don't allow fighting on my ship. Never have, never will. What's *your* version?"

Buck described the episode as concisely as he could. The captain's expression never changed.

"I don't understand it, but that's what happened," Buck concluded. "He swung first, about took my ear off, and I decked him."

"I don't understand it either, and I don't like things I don't understand. Your story matches the others, but I'll not take action until I hear what the first says about it. I am reporting the incident to Captain Hudson, of course."

Oh, oh, Buck thought. It hadn't occurred to him that the matter would go all the way to Hudson. And the way Portner referred to the CEO—*Captain* Hudson—said something about their relationship. Maybe, he thought, maybe he *should* just cut and run.

"That's all for now, Barnum." The captain simply turned his back. The conference was over.

As Buck left the dayroom, he felt his temper surging again. He had won the fight, but had he really won anything? He needed a victory, an absolute, unqualified victory. By the time he reached the springy steps down to the pier, a course of action had cemented itself into his mind. Get off this damned ship before something else goes wrong! Go find that Osmundson dump site.

Chapter 17

Once in the office, Buck tended to his faithful camera. Not exactly a high-tech examination, he mused, but everything seemed okay. Test photos he shot turned up fine in the viewer. Satisfied with the results, he decided to escape the S.C.B.C. world for a quick lunch. In no time the Camaro was headed into downtown Long Beach where he found his favorite deli.

His Reuben sandwich was excellent, tangy but not bitter, moist but not soggy. His mind raced while he ate. Why would Runkle go wild over such a silly provocation? He *had* to be hiding something, perhaps *himself*? Or is it only, as the chief suggested, that Runkle believes I'm a spy for the company? The way things have happened, there has to be a spy in the company or on board the ship, and Runkle is still the prime suspect.

Could there be others? Until now, he'd not given the possibility much serious thought. But the Groundswell leader Reicher's indication that accidents could be made to happen—for all Buck knew, there could be a *dozen* spies aboard that ship. When he got back to the office, he would spend some heavy time on the personnel files.

His attention drifted to a neighboring booth where a middle-aged couple sat facing one another. As he watched he realized that the woman talked incessantly, nonstop, a real motor-mouth, while the man, presumably her husband, simply sat there quietly, rhythmically spooning his soup to his mouth. Buck watched for several minutes to see if the pattern would be broken. Nothing changed. And it looked like nothing would change, until the man ran out of soup.

But the monologue somehow led Buck back to himself. He became conscious of the vast amount of his time that he was spending recently in thought, in introspection. Like the woman in the other booth, was this becoming a non-stop habit also? He had always been one who simply identified a task and got busy performing it. Now he found himself thinking, thinking, thinking . . . about the new job . . . about Bob and dangling residue from his marriage . . . and about Lenny Bercovich.

He wondered if all this thinking was productive. Was he simply becoming a worrier? No, he decided. Right now he was faced with an extremely challenging project. The job was like nothing he had ever done before. To this point the job had been nothing *but* problem-solving, and that meant thinking. Bob? He would never stop thinking as long as there was a chance to bring his son closer. And Lenny Bercovich, the recent addition to his list? She was the only one who brought strong, positive vibes. While the brief analysis helped his perspective, the puzzle was still missing a piece or two.

But generally satisfied with his answers, he drifted back to the morning on *Ark II* as he finished his soft drink. He was grateful for the friendly support of Chief Johnson. Although the chief defended Runkle's integrity, Buck thought, he didn't turn on me. He could have. That was *his* first assistant that got whipped. But he seemed to treat the incident with humor, almost as though he was glad it had happened. And Gantsky? I forgot to thank him. He only told the truth, but he could have really fixed me up bad with the captain. I owe him one.

Buck returned to the office where he began pouring through the files of the crew members. He printed out the photos he had taken, and as he opened each file he added the appropriate photo. Buck studied the background information. While some had done a hitch or two in the navy or coast guard, the majority had come over to Essee Beecee from tankers. In most cases, their positions aboard *Ark II* represented promotions, and in all cases, their salary levels rose. Buck remembered something Peter had told him. The crewmen on *Ark II* were drawing premium wages, "not *because* it's hazardous duty," Peter had said, "but to *keep* it from becoming hazardous duty."

First Engineer Runkle had also received a promotion with his assignment. He had last served as second engineer on a small tanker. Buck tried to be objective as he reviewed the first's file. He noticed some curious things about Runkle's career. Twelve years in the navy? Twelve? It seemed to Buck like an unusual number. Most people who stayed in the armed services beyond a couple of hitches followed through to the minimum twenty years required for the retirement pension. But, twelve years? After leaving the navy, Runkle had not exactly jumped from ship to ship, as Buck might have expected, but he had never stayed with one company for more than five years either. What does *that* say? he wondered.

At four o'clock, as Buck started putting things away, the phone rang. It was Lenny.

"I've checked out a couple of things," she said, "but understand, you didn't hear any of this from me. The Kersting Foundation is so new it's not even listed in the standard sources. It was chartered only a month ago, and the executive director is Donald Murrell. Does that surprise you?"

"Certainly doesn't," Buck said. "Anything else on it?"

"No. You already have the mailing address and, for that matter, the operating address." The soft, soothing voice was reassuring, and he needed that. He wanted to prolong the call to keep the pleasant sounds in his ear, but there was the big question to be dealt with, and that was undoubtedly her reason for calling.

"What does your boss think?" he asked.

"And I've traced the Caddy, DCOBRA. The snake's name is Lester Amato. New Jersey knows him. He's been a suspect in a couple of homicides, but their evidence was too weak to nail him. They have an APB out on him now for assault.

Buck tried to ignore the tingle that went up the back of his neck. "Can you pick him up?"

"No," she said. "Think, Buck. What would that tell the Osmundson-Kersting guys?"

"Yeah, I suppose so. What does your boss say?"

"He's grateful for what you've done. He appreciates your situation, and he promised me that he'd get the agencies moving on this right away. Unfortunately, he couldn't promise a quick conclusion to the investigation. Before they'll come swooping down, they want to be sure that they're not missing some bigger elements," she explained.

"Somehow, I knew I'd hear that," Buck said, "and I can guess what you're going to say next."

"Afraid so. He doesn't want you to go near them. Says you'll blow the whole thing and get hurt in the process. He can't take the responsibility."

"Aw, come on, Lenny. Don't give me that old saw about

responsibility. What does *that* mean? If something happened to me and he *was* responsible—does that mean he'd present my family with a big bucket of money? I doubt it. Or does it mean he'd have to say, 'Sorry, it was *my* responsibility?' Uh, uh, none of the above. That line is just a copout, and you know it."

"Please, Buck. Try to see the larger picture? This operation might be miles wider than you can see. If we jump in too soon, we might miss ninety percent of the catch that a thorough investigation would get."

It was more a plea than an argument.

"Lenny, I've got to lay that larger picture thing right back on you. This incineration project is vital. It's already had its butt kicked once. Another failure, and I doubt anyone will pick it up for a third try. We want to see criminals caught, too, but our first priority has to be putting them in the public spotlight so they have to think twice before they move on us."

"Buck—"

"And, Lenny, I've got several bosses—I've got people breathing down *my* neck. If I don't nail these guys right now, I'm back on the streets, packing my resume around town."

"I—I'm not going to change your mind, am I?"

Her tone conveyed deep, personal concern that overrode the concession of her words. For a moment, Buck was tempted to change his stance, to do anything to please her. He remembered their last meeting when she held his hand and allowed him access to her feelings through her eyes. His resistance was about to crumble when she spoke again.

"Buck, you're going after that dumpsite?"

"I have to."

"When?"

"Don't think I'd better tell you that."

"Buck, nobody else, just me. Someone should know in case. . . ."

"Hey-y-y, I'm not a commando going behind enemy lines. I just want to find it, watch, get some pictures if I can. For me, there's a vivid line between bravery and stupidity."

"And *that's* not going behind enemy lines?" There was silence. "When?"

"Tonight, if it works out, if they cooperate."

"Buck, be careful. And call me, at least leave a message as soon as you're back."

The phone clicked, and she was gone.

Buck's bravado was replaced by a hollow feeling, the loss, at least for now, of this wonderful woman who openly displayed such concern for him. Who else cares that much for me? Buck wondered. I don't have a dog. Bob? Doubtful. Sunny? Yes, Sunny. In fact, Sunny and Lenny are a lot alike, positive, assertive, but concerned and compassionate. That's interesting.

The phone rang again. Ah, he thought, she's calling back. A charge of electricity surged through him, and he snatched up the phone. It was a wrong number.

The disappointment seemed to trigger a light descent into Buck's land of little confidence. But he was learning to slog his way out of the pit. He started immediately.

You were never a loser. Don't start now. He built a mental checklist: public school—good student; lumber yard—good worker; college classes—three-point average; football—all-conference for four years; newspaper work—good job, well respected by superiors and peers alike. Did you put yourself through these painful self-analyses in these areas? Hell no. The job was there to be done. You just went ahead, did it, and things seemed to work out fine.

He drew a deep breath, exhaled, and sat back to relax. Now that he was *thinking* positive, it was time to *do* something positive. A smile crossed his face as he recalled the handsome young Gantsky who had said, "Better haul ass." He opened a duffel he had brought with him to work. After changing into dark brown twill trousers and black sneakers, he grabbed his dark brown nylon jacket, his camera, and a large flashlight and headed for the parking lot.

Chapter 18

Buck peeled out of the day's end rush hour traffic and parked the Camaro on a side street near the alley to the Osmundson Transport Company. He watched the facility for twenty minutes. The two overhead doors remained closed. There were but three windows in the rear of the building, and he focused his attention on them. No sign of activity at any of them.

Finally, he strapped his camera on under his jacket, grabbed the flashlight, and left the car. He strode purposefully down the alley toward the old, dilapidated garage, but his eyes roamed, searching for anyone who might be watching him. It was risky, walking down this alley in broad daylight right past the Osmundson warehouse. And what if the old garage was locked?

"This is *your* alley," he repeated to himself. "You *belong* here, so *look* like you belong here. And if you can't get the door open, just walk away like nothing's wrong."

Second story apartments on his left, across the alley from Osmundson's, overlooked his route. His eyes swept over the outside stairs and balconies, as well as the windows, for any movement. So far, it looks good, he thought. Now, let's hope that service door isn't locked.

The frame building was decades overdue for a paint job. Facing the alley, it had an old-style one-piece overhead door for automobile access in addition to a standard wooden service door. The large door had a horizontal row of windows about head high, their jagged panes testifying to vandalism. With one last check around, he veered left, directly to the service door. He grabbed the rusty knob, twisted it, and pushed. The door held firm. Quickly, he put a shoulder to the door, driving with his powerful legs as though attacking an opposing lineman. It popped open, its hinges screeching and its bottom scraping noisily across the concrete floor. Buck pulled upward on the flimsy door, hoping to avoid the scraping as he closed it. It worked.

He stood motionless, hardly breathing, listening for any indications from outside that he had been seen. He held the pose for several minutes and then began to relax. Carefully shrouding the flashlight beam with his hands, he surveyed the garage. It was piled full of odd shapes, boxes and cans of all sizes, several old rolls of carpet, and a collection of old furniture. The mass reached nearly to the rafters and extended almost to the front, leaving Buck only a narrow space just inside the door.

The place reeked of dust, mildew, and rancid engine oil. Buck felt a powerful sneeze coming on. He moved his face close to the fresh air coming in through the first window opening. Broken glass crunched beneath his feet. The tantalizing sneeze continued to swell. It's the dust, he thought.

Suddenly, he realized something else. Because of the low angle of the setting sun's rays, there was darkness behind him. Outside—brilliant sunlight. And here, framed in the window, was the face of Buck Barnum—who was about to sneeze! He turned from the window and ducked down, smothering the outburst the best he could. He listened again. Still quiet. He crouched and waited while he stifled several more sneezes.

Buck reexamined his observation post. A slot of light showed through the door at waist level. He had almost missed it. He bent over for a closer look and found a split in the wood. He grabbed the splinter and wrenched it inward, enlarging the flaw to make a jagged peephole about two inches high by four inches wide. In a quiet flurry of activity, he moved some of the junk around to make a space for himself just inside the hole. From the top of the pile he dragged down an old, wooden, straight-back chair.

Ah, pretty cozy, he thought as he took his place on the chair, bent over, and peeked out. He could see both warehouse doors while remaining hidden.

He watched intently for some time. An occasional auto tore through the alley. Otherwise nothing of concern, except that he was getting a stiff neck from the bent-over position. Really stupid, he thought. Get smart, Barnum. He straightened up. He didn't need to remain bent over to the hole. By simply listening closely, he could pick up on any sounds that needed to be checked visually.

As he relaxed his thoughts wandered. For some reason lately he was beginning to fall back into the old Roberta rut. He had worked his way through the terrible hurt she had inflicted. No need to cut through that again, he thought. That was behind him. Then why was he regressing, thinking about her?

Suddenly, the sounds of a loud engine invaded the alley, followed by the explosive hiss of airbrakes. Buck peeked out through the hole. There, not three feet from him, was an immense, silver-hubbed wheel. As it backed toward the opposite side of the alley, the wheel nearly scraped against Buck's door. The huge overhead door rolled upward as the blue Osmundson truck backed down the ramp. He readied the camera. *Click— Click— Click—* Even before the truck was completely inside, the door reversed and began to close. In seconds, the innocu-ous-looking building had swallowed up the large truck. Soon, he could hear what he decided was the sound of a forklift amid the rumbling of heavy drums being rolled about. Other than the sounds, there seemed to be nothing else to demand his attention.

Why was he thinking about Roberta? He didn't love her. He didn't miss her. He certainly wouldn't want her back. Then why? Perhaps it had something to do with Bob, who had never been the same since the divorce. He seemed to be overly quick to defend his mother. Indeed, at times Buck got the feeling that in Bob's mind the whole shabby affair might be Buck's fault. But there might be an even more plausible explanation for retracing the Roberta episode—Lenny! The powerful feelings he was developing for Lenny brought on the fears that still lingered, that inevitably sounded off when he thought of the beautiful detective.

The sound of voices drew Buck down to the opening. Two men had emerged from the Osmundson building and were headed toward the cars parked to the left of the Osmundson truck ramp. He recognized them, one tall and one short, Murrell and Amato! His pulse quickened. He stood up slowly and snapped a shot through the open window. This wasn't exactly what he'd been watching for. But seeing them there cemented their connection to Osmundson.

The two got into a black Cadillac, with Amato driving. As the Caddy emerged toward the alley it headed straight toward Buck. He dropped back down to the peephole. The black auto came closer, and

Buck had to tell himself that the occupants hadn't seen him. Through the hole, he got a good close-up of Murrell as the Cadillac screeched to Buck's right and accelerated rapidly down the alley.

Moments later, he heard the sound he had waited for, the rumbling of the overhead door in the neighboring warehouse. The door had no sooner opened than a black tandem-axle gravel truck came up the ramp and made its sharp left turn. As the truck went past, he got a shot of the cab, centering on the M & S sign and the white No. 4. The big door closed and the truck went on down the alley. He popped out of the old shed, pulled the rickety door shut, and walked briskly to the Camaro.

Buck caught up with the black truck as it headed east on Seventh Street. Its tarpaulin covering rippled slightly in the slipstream despite the taut tie-down job done on it. Through a small open space at the rear, he could see drums backed up against the tailgate.

"Bingo!" he sang out. "Game time—and this time I kick *your* butt!"

He eased off, allowing several cars to fill the gap between the two vehicles. The driver took the southbound I-405, the San Diego Freeway. When he continued on past the 55 Freeway, Buck knew their destination was not Nevada. It was somewhere to the south. There would be no more intersections with major east-west freeways until San Diego. But how far? Where? In certain stretches of south Orange County there was still open land to the west among the coast range of hills between the freeway and the ocean. And to the left of the freeway the Santa Ana mountain range paralleled the highway. But, how much farther? This jaunt could end up in Mexico! It was a possibility he hadn't thought of. Each time he passed a highway sign indicating an off-ramp to another city, he framed a shot showing the truck and the sign. His camera was set to imprint the time on each photo.

The black truck passed Irvine and rode the line between Laguna Hills and Lake Forest. The Lake Forest sign brought a smile to Buck. The people of El Toro had passed referenda to incorporate and rename the city. Many had grown tired of, perhaps embarrassed with the name, El Toro, so "The Bull" became Lake Forest. More Southern California imagery. A couple of little ponds and some trees, and they call it Lake Forest.

When Buck had passed Mission Viejo and was approaching San Juan Capistrano, he felt the mounting tension. How *far* is he going? he asked himself. Could he have spotted me? He dropped still farther back and moved over two lanes to the left. It's getting dark, he observed. Almost nine o'clock. Reluctantly, he reached for the headlight switch.

Suddenly, with no signal, the black truck veered off to the right onto the Ortega Highway exit ramp. Horns blared as Buck cut across three lanes of traffic. He hoped the truck driver was too busy to notice. The truck turned east and began the gradual climb into the Santa Ana foothills. Buck followed cautiously. Now that they were off the busy freeway and headed up the winding, two-lane highway, there were no cars between the red tail lights and himself. He dropped as far back as he dared. Each time the truck rounded a curve, the lights disappeared from sight, and the farther they climbed, the sharper and more frequent the curves became. The roadbed had been carved out of the hills on the right. To the left, the shoulder dropped off into darkness.

He eased out of a sharp, right turn. His headlights revealed a straight stretch ahead, but the truck lights were gone! He slowed a little and watched to his right. As he passed a huge, rocky outcropping, he spotted a gravel road that led off into a canyon. There sat the truck with its lights on, perhaps thirty yards from the highway. He dared not reduce speed. In the glare of the truck's headlights, he saw a figure pushing open a large gate. When he had gone some distance, Buck slowed, waited for an oncoming car, and then carefully turned the Camaro around. He backtracked slowly, hoping he'd be able to find the road again.

"Man, it's dark up here!" he muttered. When the sun had settled behind the coast range of hills to the west, it was as though a curtain had been pulled. He punched the left window down and was greeted by several large raindrops. Dog dew! he thought. That's *all* I need. Driest summer in years, but tonight it decides to rain! Spotting the rocky structure, he stopped and aimed the large flashlight to his left. There it was—the road where he'd seen the truck! He couldn't park anywhere close. Their truckers would spot the car for sure. In a minute, he had done two more reversals and left the car parked several hundred yards above the canyon entrance and facing downhill on the right-side shoulder.

He strapped the camera on, grabbed the light, and headed for the gate. The raindrops had increased to a steady, cold drizzle. Miserable, he thought, but maybe that's better. Reaching the gate, he used the light. An eight-foot chain-link fence, topped with razor wire, extended around the outer slope of the hills on both sides of the winding driveway, disappearing into the rainy night. And the gate, of similar construction, was a sturdy one—no openings to slide through. The sign on the gate read: NO TRESPASSING—VIOLATORS WILL BE PROSECUTED.

Even if he could get over that gate, he'd have to climb it again to get out. Got to be a better way. He started off to his left, following the fence around the base of the hill. The terrain was treacherous at first. It was not walking country. He stumbled and fumbled his way over the slippery, wet rocks, their unpredictable shapes offering one challenge after another. He was grateful when, after about two hundred yards of the violent struggle, the rocks gave way to spongy, wet sand. While he was forced to navigate the slope of the side hill with a crabwalk, he could make better progress. It would help to have one leg longer than the other.

He had gone on for some distance when he was blocked by a gulley that led down the steep hill from his right to his left. He slid the five feet down into the gooey mud and water. About to climb up the other side, he stopped and pointed the light at the bottom of the fence. There was an open space of two feet where water runoff coming down the steep slope had washed out the dirt beneath the fence. Protecting the camera with one hand, he dropped onto his back and slithered upstream through the hole. Getting to his feet, he slipped, nearly dunking the camera as he went back down.

"Moose mud!" he exclaimed. If he wrecked the Canon the whole trip would be for nothing. He adjusted the camera strap so the device hung inside his jacket and against his back. There, if he went down again the camera was protected. He slipped and grunted, pawed and clawed his way up the winding trough. Finally, it narrowed, became shallower, and disappeared completely, blending into the smoother ground around it. He found himself climbing the remainder of the grade on solid ground. He switched off the light.

By the time he reached the crest, he was breathing hard, soaked through, and covered with slimy mud. His condition combined with the throbbing in his chest and neck to remind him of those rainy football games of so many years past. He had been a pretty good mudder back then. And now? Definitely older, but still he drew a charge from the familiar feelings. He stopped to get his bearings when he found himself on the relatively flat hill-top ridge about ten yards wide. Below, on the opposite side from which he had climbed the hill, was the canyon the truck had entered.

Then he picked up the distant sounds, the unmistakable exhaust noise, the squeaking and screeching of drive wheels against treads—a bulldozer! The noises directed his eyes to the left, to a dimly-lighted area, perhaps a half-mile farther into the canyon and about two hundred feet below the crest of his hill.

"That's it!" he said. "Got 'em!"

The throbbing in his chest and neck became stronger. He looked back at his escape route. From where he stood, the gulley and the fence were obscured by the rainy darkness.

"*Never* find it coming back," he mumbled. He contemplated laying the flashlight on the ground, beaming toward the direction he would go. No good, he thought. He might need it, and besides, the batteries would probably go dead. In seconds, he came up with his best alternative. He whipped out his white handkerchief. After using it to wipe his face, he placed it on the ground, weighting it down with a small stone. Retreating to a slightly lower level behind the ridge, he started toward the sounds.

When he had reached the point just above the lighted area, he pocketed the flashlight, worked the camera out from under the jacket, and made some preliminary settings. Under such conditions, fast shutter speeds or maximum zoom would not yield good pictures. But, he might get some clear enough to show what was going on—about the best he could hope for. He set it for manual, with wide open aperture, and checked the telephoto lens. He'd have to find something on which to rest the Canon for steadiness. Then, he'd try various slow shutter speeds.

Dropping to his knees, he edged upward toward the crest, cupping one hand over the lens to shield it from the rain. As he reached the top, he flattened to a prone position. He was in luck. There to his left were several large, weathered rocks. He wiggled over to them. He'd use them for cover as well as a solid base for the camera.

From his place among the rocks, he could see that he was on a small bluff with almost a shear drop to the pit below. The pit was lighted by four weak floodlights mounted on makeshift posts around a perimeter half the size of a football field. They probably don't want any more light than that, he thought. On a clear night, people flying over would see too much. Parked to his right, facing back toward the highway, were two black trucks. The tarps had been removed from both. One was empty, and the driver was up in the box, folding up his tarp. The other was loaded with drums that Buck presumed were to be dumped. He couldn't see its driver. Probably waiting in the cab.

Extending from the trucks to his left, Buck saw two large trenches, each perhaps thirty feet wide and eight feet deep. They reached almost to the left edge of the clearing. The bulldozer was working in that area, pushing dirt from a large pile into one of the trenches. He could make out the shapes of several drums where the bulldozer had yet to complete the cover-up. Directly across from him, parked beyond the lights, was a white pickup truck. Seeing no other vehicles, he decided the pickup belonged to the dozer operator.

Buck rested the camera on a rock, checked to be sure the flash was turned off, and began shooting. *Click— click— click—* Fortunately, unlike in his morning encounter, there was no danger of being heard over the noise of the bulldozer. He was adjusting to a new shutter speed, when the bulldozer stopped moving, its engine reduced to an idle. The operator stood and waved toward the trucks. Buck got him three times. He had just snapped photos of the trucks, trying for their license plates, when both began to move.

The empty unit headed off toward the canyon gate, and the other began backing down into the trench. It stopped just short of the area that had already been filled in. Slowly, the hydraulic lift tilted the box upward, and at the precise moment the drums began to slide to the rear, the driver eased the truck forward. Buck snapped repeatedly, catching the action. He hoped that the No. 4 on the cab would show clearly in the photo.

When the truck had emptied its load, Buck stopped to reset the shutter. Wiping the water from his face with a wet sleeve, he marveled at what had transpired before him. It was really an artistic piece of work. The truck driver had moved his vehicle forward at precisely the correct speed, allowing the drums to slide off, bump against those already in the trench, and end up standing vertically, like soldiers in close formation. Amazing, Buck thought, so simple!

He did a sequence of time exposures, hoping that he hadn't moved the camera. The empty truck had moved to its original position, and Buck tried one last series at still another setting. Then he raised up to his knees, slid the camera beneath his jacket, shook his head to rid himself of the droplets that seemed determined to find his eyes, and prepared to move out. He was resnapping the jacket and reaching to his back pocket for his flashlight when a movement caught his eye. The bulldozer driver was standing again, waving an arm, then pointing. Waving again, then pointing. Now what? Buck wondered.

"Oh, no! He's pointing at *me*!" Buck glanced from side to side and suddenly froze. The two floodlights facing his position illuminated it more than he had realized. And when he had risen even slightly from behind the rocks—he had become an actor on stage! He looked to his left, along the ridge, to the spot that was the focal point of the driver's waves. A chill swept upward, up his back to the nape of his neck. Through the drizzle, he saw two white spots swinging frantically and moving toward him on the hill-top. Flashlights! And they couldn't be more than fifty yards away!

He jumped to his feet and took off, scurrying along the ridge top as fast as he could make his spongy shoes move. His flashlight beam moved violently, lighting only bits of his course on its downward swings. He fought the urge to look back. Another fifty yards and he was running well. The footing was surprisingly good along the crest, he told himself. But it's good for them, too! Hey, take it easy! You're in good shape. Unless they're young athletes, they're not going to catch you. You've got your sneakers on. They're probably wearing boots of some kind. Should I ease off and pace myself? Quite a ways to go. No. Might be the last time you'll ever pace yourself, Barnum. Move it!

He was trying to estimate the distance he'd run when panic hit him. Where's the handkerchief? Should've seen it by now! Maybe he'd gone too far! Better drop down along the side of the hill. Don't worry about the *marker*. Find the *ditch*. Passed it! He knew he had! And running on the side of the slope was slowing him down! He would go a little farther, then double back and hunker down with the light off. They might go right on past.

But suddenly, the ground disappeared, and for a moment Buck hung suspended in mid-air. He crashed into the far bank of the gulley, landing in a heap and dropping the light. Without stopping to recover it, he ran, slid, and tumbled down the enlarging wash. What if it's not the same one? he asked himself. Should still have a hole under the fence. Fatigue was setting in. Rhythm was gone. And for all he knew, they were right on top of him. The fence came out of nowhere, rising up and slamming him to his back before he even saw it. He wiggled his way downhill, scraping the bottom strand of the fence with his nose as he went under it.

Scrambling to his feet, he paused to look back up the hill. The lights had almost reached the gulley. Maybe they hadn't seen his move. He decided to wait quietly, hoping they'd go on past. His heart hammered, and his desperate gasps for air were uncontrollable. Buck was sure they would hear him.

The moving lights up on the ridge stopped abruptly, and just as suddenly Buck saw why. His own flashlight lay halfway up the wash, pointing the way like a beacon! Their lights turned toward him.

"There he is!" a voice shouted.

Buck turned and hurtled on down the wash. *Powmp! Powmp!* It felt like someone had sprayed his back with a garden hose while insects bit at the back of his neck. "A shotgun!" *Powmp!* He heard the pellets from the third explosion spatter among the scrubby bushes he was encountering at the lower level. If they're shooting, they're not running. He must be almost out of range. Go on down—bottom—go left. Faster'n those rocks! With a splash, he tumbled headlong into a rain-swollen creek. The cold water on his face seemed to chill the panic and sharpen his senses. His hands felt the smooth stones beneath the water. They were slippery and irregular, but Buck knew he'd made a good choice. He sloshed to his feet and started down the creek.

It seemed he had splashed his way for over a hundred yards when he rounded a slight bend, and there was a culvert beneath the roadbed! He clawed his way up the bank and then hesitated. Which way? Uphill? Downhill? Uphill, to the right! But despite the smooth highway surface, Buck's running had become little more than a swift stagger. His saturated clothing weighed him down. His heavy sneakers squished with every step. And his legs seemed to belong to someone else, unresponsive to his commands. It took all of his concentration to remain upright, to move forward.

If I—went—wrong way—I'm dead, he thought. No more— can't—go— He slogged unsteadily around a sharp bend in the road, and there it was. The Camaro—about fifty feet ahead—on the left! The sight of it fed one last shot of energy to his rubbery legs, and soon he was jerking open the door, grateful that he'd chanced leaving it unlocked. It took his shaking hand several tries to slot the key into the ignition. Finally, he had the V-8 humming. He paused for a few moments trying to think. His brain was scrambling on him. He drew a deep breath and exhaled slowly.

"Think, damn it, think!" he shouted. He locked the doors and started to reach for his seatbelt. "Seatbelt? At a time like this, you reach for the seatbelt?" He thumped a fist on the wheel. "Damn right, dummy," he said. "You're not out of this yet. This road's treacherous in broad daylight. And at night, in the rain, with those hoods out there?" He latched the seatbelt and jerked it extra tight. If nothing else, the process told him his mind was functional.

Now, he thought, if the first truck cleared the gate and left—Buck thought he should have—before they spotted him, there might be what, four of them left? The two who had chased him just might be trapped up there on the bluff. It would take them some time to get down. That would leave the other trucker and the dozer operator. Could they block the road, from shoulder to shoulder, with the dump truck and a pickup? Probably.

"And while you're sitting here thinking, Barnum, you're giving them time to do just that!" He shoved the console shift into drive and accelerated smoothly. He wanted momentum, but he had to control his speed in order to spin the Camaro around if his escape was blocked. It took several attempts to locate the wiper switch. He was tempted to turn the headlights on. No, not yet, he thought. He eased around the next bend. Was this the one?

The instant he saw the headlight beams crossing his path, he had his answer. He quickly sized up the situation. One truck, the big one, and it was moving out to block him. He floored the Camaro and hit the light switch. As the black truck grew larger and larger, Buck angled toward the right shoulder, the outer side with the shear drop-off. The truck jerked ahead to cut him off. Buck held his angle. The white No. 4 on the truck stood out vividly. It seemed that a broadside was inevitable.

Suddenly, he pulled hard left toward the mountain side, grateful for the firm suspension of the Camaro. He veered onto the driveway behind the truck before the driver had time to shift into reverse, and then he swung right again. His left wheels hit the soft shoulder, and he went into a treacherous skid. Jamming the accelerator down, he countered it. Correcting a couple more fish tailings as he returned to the pavement, he was quickly up to fifty-five. But with the first sharp curve to his left, he realized that he was about to accomplish what they had failed to do. The rear end of the Camaro threatened to let go, and Buck backed the off accelerator smoothly but quickly. He couldn't see the canyon floor far below on his right, but if he got close enough to see it he was dead.

The lights in his mirror told him the truck had gotten back on track and was following, but it was no contest. When Buck turned onto the northbound I-405, he blended into the traffic and it was over. A smile crossed his lips when he realized that the windshield wipers were chattering against dry glass. He switched them off, and as he snuggled down into the bucket seat, he thought, just give me a hot shower, a bite to eat, and my bed. It's been the second longest day.

Buck placed his sandwich and glass of milk on the table. He paused, gently sliding his fingertips over the two welts on the back of his neck. Damned lucky, he thought, just barely out of range. Twenty yards closer and he wouldn't be here. He had to get back to his daily running. He would do that.

He had nearly finished his peanut butter sandwich when his fanciful flight through the stratosphere of success crashed and burned.

"Oh, Buck, Buck," he moaned. "What if they figure out who it was out there? Or even guess that it *might* have been you? They've *got* to know where you live by now."

Despite his fatigue, he came alive instantly. He dressed and hurried into the garage where he nailed a piece of plywood over the window. Hours later, he was still on alert as he sat under the stars on his secluded patio, a thermos of coffee and his old .38 revolver on the table beside him.

Chapter 19

Prongs of pain jabbed their way into Buck's consciousness. Struggling to escape the stiffness, he turned over to his right side. His knees bumped against something firm. Still it was not right. Rolling over again, he became entangled in the blanket. His feet poked out from beneath the covers, protruding into the coolness of the night. In seconds, the chill triggered a switch, and his eyes opened. He blinked twice and lay there, staring through the strange darkness, wondering at the foreign shapes. Across the room, a rectangular face stared at him, then finally identified itself. The computer monitor—he was in the den. He remembered then that he had chosen the firm, narrow couch so he would be closer to the rear of the house where trouble would be most likely to come.

He stretched. The stiffness in his legs and back protested again. The bruise on his buttocks combined with the irritating bites on his neck to fully awaken him. Bites? No. He remembered then the welts left by the buckshot. The luminous face of the clock on the desk told Buck it was four o'clock. Four? He had slept less than three hours. While he didn't feel rested, he felt wired, charged by the tumultuous day he'd experienced combined with the anticipation of things to be done and the residual fears of a few hours before. But apparently, he'd had no visitors during the night. He struggled from the couch, reminded by his aching frame that he had neglected his running over the last two weeks.

Quietly, he made his way into the kitchen to start the coffee and then back to his bedroom. More by feel than by sight, he pulled his blue jeans and navy golf shirt from the closet and dressed. When the coffee had completed its cycle, he took a mugful into the lighted den and sat at the computer, carefully sipping the hot coffee while gathering his thoughts. Soon, he had created a document heading: ENVIRONMENTAL GROUP JOINS ORGANIZED CRIME TO OPPOSE ELIMINATION OF HAZARDOUS WASTES.

He proceeded into the text, his fingers dancing across the keys in perfect rhythm with his mind.

Although he was writing his way into strange territory, a world in which the writer had to be cognizant of legal responsibility, Buck found the words flowing. His carefully worded account of the Osmundson-Kersting-ASH linkup, along with the exposure of the illegal dumpsite, fell together faster than he could have hoped. It was one of those rare endeavors in the life of a writer when the rough draft *was* the finished copy. He proofed it carefully, wary of careless mistakes that could slip past beneath the camouflage of confidence and enthusiasm that he felt. But it was good. He *knew* it was good. He printed a copy, then copied the article onto four CDs, a back-up copy for himself, along with copies for the company, the Long Beach Police Department, and the newspaper.

The clock said six-thirty. Now, with the piece written, he had to prove the story. His hands trembled slightly as he pulled the memory card from his Canon, slotted it into the reader, and began uploading the photos into a new file he labeled: DIRTY PICTURES. His excitement went over the top as he worked over the photos, one by one, with his Photo Elements program. By adjusting the lighting and contrast slightly he came up with a surprisingly clear set of pictures, the best photo story of his career. He took a few minutes to copy them onto the four CDs, accompanying his article on each.

Some time later, as he walked into the decrepit office he glanced at the clock. It said: seven-fifty-five. Wow, he thought. After a night like that, he was still early for work at the office. *That's* dedication!

He got on the phone to Lenny.

"Buck! Where *are* you? I'd about given you up for dead. Are you okay?"

"I'm fine," he said. "Sorry if I woke you."

"Woke me? I've hardly been able to sleep. Couldn't you have called sooner?"

"I couldn't. No, that's not true. I could have, and I should have. I didn't think I should bother you in the middle of the night. I'm sorry."

"Did you do it?"

"Y-y-y-up!"

"Did it go all right? Any trouble?"

"A little hitch, nothing serious," he said.

"So you got what you were after?"

"Sure did, Lenny. We've *got* 'em, got 'em nailed to the wall! I have the report and incredible photos on a CD for your people, along with sets for my people and the newspaper. Now I'm going to print up a set of enlargements for our staff. Lenny, there's not a loophole in the series. I've got Murrell and Amato leaving the Osmundson warehouse. I've got the truck hauling the drums out to south Orange County, and I've got the whole dumping scene!"

"I'm going to be tied up all day, but your people should see this package as soon as possible, or sooner. Unfortunately, the dumpers know they were spotted, so they'll do everything they can to cover up. Can I leave your copy with the guard at our entrance guardhouse?"

"Why, yes, I'll pick it up there just as soon as I can get there. When can we get together? I'm off tomorrow."

"How about tomorrow at six at Dante's?"

"Maybe we should pick another place—oh, well, fine."

Buck tried to throw aside the implications that ran through his mind. The conversation that followed was principally a scolding by Lenny, a scolding for his cavalier attitude toward the risks of the venture and for not having contacted her sooner. The reprimand delighted Buck. He swelled within as she lectured. It was not the professional admonishment of the detective, but the warm concern of the woman, a desirable woman, who cared for him. About to put his feelings on the line, out in the open, he hesitated. Before he could recover the words, Lenny announced that she'd have to hang up.

"I'd better get over to pick up that CD right away!"

By nine o'clock, Buck had run Lenny's copy of the CD over to the guardhouse and had printed out five sets of the photos and his report. He assembled them in sequence, from the first shots at the warehouse through the finale at the dumpsite. The warehouse photos clearly showed the license plates and identification numbers of the Osmundson and M & S trucks, with the warehouse in the background. But the prize winner of the first group brought a smile to his face. The telephoto shot, combined with further enlargement, showed Amato and Murrell leaving the Osmundson side of the building. They were close enough to the viewer for a handshake.

"Gotcha!" Buck said under his breath. "Now it's *our* turn." He studied the pair for some time. Murrell looked much as he had remembered him, tall, blond, and fairly good-looking. Two things he hadn't noticed at the ASH meeting, probably too far away: Murrell was not just well-built. He was extremely well-built, the physique of an athlete—and his nose slanted a bit to one side. What does *that* say? Boxer? Brawler?

And the little snake Amato, he thought, studying the birdlike beak and squinting eyes. "I'd like to get my hands on that greasy little pony tail and break your neck," he said to the photograph. "I know you now. I know your car. We've almost evened the playing field, and it's my turn." Buck's eyes went over and over the tight blue jeans and matching jacket for any sign of the knife. None. But it's there, he thought, and from now on, my old .38 is with me or in the console box of the Camaro.

The last of the packets had been slipped into their envelopes when a note from Ed emerged from beneath the scatterings of his own project:

> C.H. CALLED A MEETING THIS MORNING. BETTER GET IN THERE AS SOON AS YOU CAN.
>
> ED
>
> P.S. BE READY!

"Man! Just what I needed. This time I'm ready!"

He grabbed the S.C.B.C. materials and took off. Halfway down the hall, he slowed to gather his composure. Don't make matters worse by going in there all shook, he thought. He improvised a smile and entered Hudson's office. The scene looked exactly as it had the first time. The same people, in exactly the same seats, with the same expressions on their faces.

"Sorry," he said as he slipped into his chair. Hudson glared at him. Nobody but Peter chanced a look in Buck's direction. Buck was surprised at his own reaction. He felt no fear, no intimidation this time. He had, whether *they* knew it or not, become a valuable asset to Essee Beecee, and *he* knew it. He squeezed the packets. He had something to offer. If Hudson tried putting him on the defensive again, he would be ready.

"It's nice you could join us, Barnum," Hudson said, looking at his watch.

"Thank you, sir," Buck replied with a polite smile.

Dale Craws fidgeted. Garland Grigsby smiled.

"I hope this meeting is no inconvenience to you," Hudson continued.

Buck felt the heater within him begin to activate, but he resisted it and found himself enjoying the increased intensity of the CEO's stare.

"No sir, no inconvenience." He looked toward Peter, expecting a signal to back off, that he was pushing his luck. But Peter's glance dropped to the packet. To Buck's surprise, Peter broke into a grin. Then, in a move that seemed totally out of character with his sophisticated savvy, Peter turned the grin directly toward Charles Hudson. The leader caught it. He flinched and then hesitated for a moment.

"Now, back to the business at hand. Peter, you've achieved a tremendous victory for Essee Beecee. With the EPA and London approval of the test burn, we're almost over the hump. The fact that they've moved the burn site out to two hundred and fifty miles will cost us, but I consider it a trivial tradeoff. And equally important," Hudson went on, "is the fact that you have it in writing. No more of the broken promises that sank our predecessors. What about the Europeans—their support in repealing the permanent ban by the London Convention?"

"I've been in contact with my counterparts. I'm optimistic about the position that will be taken by the English, Japanese, Swedes, Dutch, and Belgians. But my optimism is somewhat less with regard to the Germans and the French."

"The French, I understand," Hudson said. "They relish playing the devil's advocate in international issues. But the Germans? I thought they were our biggest supporters."

"Considering intent, they still are. But, despite the time that's passed since the unification of East and West, the country still faces enormous domestic challenges. And now, with the downturn in the economy, it's become a matter of priorities. At-sea-incineration is not at the top of their list. However," Peter paused for effect, "some of the

German industrial leaders, along with the committed politicians, are hoping they can still slip the matter through."

"Your next step?"

"We're setting up an international conference of industrial and political leaders, those who are known to be firmly in our camp, or at worst, marginal. It will be held in Brussels. Only the date remains to be set. I'm hoping that we can time the meeting to directly follow EPA's confirmation of *our* success."

"Excellent—excellent!" Hudson smiled, the first broad smile Buck had seen cross the cold face of the militaristic leader. "We'll begin loading on Thursday, and we'll ship out for the burn early Sunday. I think we've covered all the reports."

Buck leaned forward. He was being passed by?

"We all have a lot to do," Hudson said, "so the meeting is ad—"

"Sir!" Buck nearly shouted. Hudson turned and looked right through him. "You asked me for a progress report at the next meeting," Buck said. He recognized the old feeling that drove him. It was not the blind anger of the unsure newcomer, the heated frustration that had so frequently overwhelmed him in recent days. It was the confident spark of his competitive spirit.

"Yes, yes I did, but since you have so little regard for this group, I hardly think we should take their valuable time now. See me in my office *after* the meeting."

Buck waved the packet. "Sir, I have a report here," he said, "that is of vital concern to the project, to everyone here. With all due respect, sir, this matter should be addressed by the group, *now.*" Buck looked around the table, pausing briefly at each member. "I have hard evidence that we're up against opposition forces, a conspiracy, that's dedicated to sinking this project. They're smart, ruthless, and capable of violent tactics."

He looked directly at Hudson. "And up to now," he said, holding the packet up again, "they've been *way* out ahead of us. You've no idea how far ahead."

Hudson's eyes narrowed. His face became a hardened mask, its ominous, authoritative lines deeply etched. "Barnum! You're nothing but a lazy, insubordinate troublemaker. You don't come drifting in here late and tell *me* how to run *my* meeting. I doubt that *report* has one ounce of worth to the company, but if you like, you can leave a copy with me. I'll get to it—when I have time."

Buck was startled at the rush within him. As well as he had always managed physical conflicts, he had been equally poor in verbal confrontations. The meltdown, he had called it, that point where the brain simply refused to come up with the right words. But now, the words seemed to come instinctively, as natural as the evasive tactics of a linebacker fighting off a block by a big, strong tight end.

"Sorry, sir," he said. "Of the last forty-eight hours, I've devoted forty to this project. I've been attacked physically, run off the highway, and blasted by shotguns!" Buck raised the five packets ceremoniously, aware of his voice booming through the silence. He eased off.

"But if the results of my efforts are of no interest, so be it. I'll run my own experiments with incineration—and, believe me, these suckers will really burn! In fact, there are people who would undoubtedly pay me a *lot* of money to burn them." He stood and turned to leave, determined to do exactly as he had said. His leg bumped the chair as he moved, and even that tiny thump was audible.

"*I* think we should see what he has," said Grigsby. "*I'm* in no hurry."

Hudson ignored the remark. His burning gaze had dropped from Buck to something, perhaps nothing, off to one side of the room.

"If I may make a suggestion," said Peter, "it might be a good idea for us to take a break here, get ourselves calmed down, and then hear what Buck has to say." Grigsby and Ed Roland murmured agreement. Dale Craws simply looked down at the tabletop. Viola Erichs sat motionless, biting her lower lip, her pen poised over her legal pad.

"Good idea!"

Buck nodded his agreement. Then he turned to locate the speaker. The voice was Hudson's!

"Good idea," Hudson repeated. "Let's take a break, and then let's see if we can't channel some of this enthusiasm constructively."

Peter pointed a finger commandingly in the direction of his own office. Seconds after Buck had seated himself in Peter's office, his friend entered with two cups of coffee. He closed the door, took his seat, and sipped at his coffee, saying nothing for a full minute. Finally, he spoke.

"Welcome back."

"Huh? You're the one who was out of town. What do you mean?"

"I mean, welcome back—to the *old* Buck, the one I chose for this job. Frankly, I was beginning to wonder if he was gone forever." Peter smiled.

"You think I did okay in there?"

"Under the circumstances—couldn't have done better."

"I guess I even surprised myself a little. Never been good at verbal engagements under stress. Frankly, I just don't know how to play the corporate word games."

"For the time being, just continue as you are."

Buck nodded. "Speaking of games, you're the only one who can cross Hudson and get away with it. How come? I know you're good, but so is his ego."

"C.H. may be a lot of things, but he's not stupid. He needs me." Peter hesitated, staring at his coffee cup. "The funny part is, he knows that if the project succeeds, I'm going to replace him." Peter smiled, that all-knowing smile that was Peter. "And if the project fails? If the project fails, I'm going to replace him."

"Why you sneaky devil. You quite sure about that?"

Peter nodded confidently. "Between you and me, of course. He's between the proverbial rock and you know what. But his resume would look a lot better with this success on it. Of course, as soon as he's sure we're going to pull it off, he'll try one last shot to blow me out of the water."

"You don't sound worried."

"Home harbor advantage."

"What about Grigsby? Isn't he ahead of you in line?"

"Garland's about ready to hang it up," Peter said. "His biggest concern is the value of his stock. Now, after challenging the black knight, have you got anything to back it up?"

Buck opened two envelopes, tossed Peter a set, and kept one out for himself. His friend read quickly through the pages of text and then turned to the photos. Buck followed along, still scrutinizing the copy for errors. An occasional glance at Peter found his rock-solid face changing to a smirk, and then to a smile, and finally to an ear-to-ear grin.

"*Very, very good*," Peter said. "Better than I'd hoped for. I know about the ditching and the fight with Runkle. Was that bit about shotguns on the level?"

Buck bent low over Peter's desk and showed his mentor the welts on the back of his neck. "I was lucky. Just out of range. But I do think they were serious, don't you? You and I have run a lot of miles together through the years, but you'd have had a hell of a time staying with me last night." Buck laughed.

Peter didn't laugh. "Buck—I've never intended for you to take risks like *that*. Why didn't you turn it over to the authorities? Let them take those chances."

"I tried to. They're interested, but they have to go by the book—wanted a week or more to get set up. We don't have a week, and certainly not more. Really," Buck said, tapping a packet with a forefinger, "what I've got here will fire up their interest. They won't look too good when this comes out in the media and they're still reading the book."

"What else do you have going? Not that I could expect anything else."

"Nothing concrete. But I have this gut feeling that there's more," Buck answered.

"Such as?"

"Two or three on the crew that bother me, especially the first engineer, Runkle."

"Is he the one—the fight?" Peter asked.

"You heard?"

"Bits and pieces. Hudson was ready to fire you when I walked in this morning. A breach of *his* discipline," Peter said, reaching for his coffee.

"So where do we go from here?"

Peter checked his watch. "We go back in. Tell your story, *this* one," he said, flipping the packet back to Buck. "If C.H. doesn't buy this, he's got a hole in his hull. He'll be on the bottom by morning. By the way, I'm sorry your nice little truck got mangled. That picture looks awful. Are you getting it fixed?"

"Totaled out. Got a rented Camaro. I assume the company will cover me?"

"You got it. I'll see to it today. But, a *Camaro?* You're a *truck* guy."

"For appearances, a big contrast with what I was driving. And I found out last night, it moves pretty well," Buck said. "I don't think I'd have made it with my little, red truck."

The meeting resumed, and it was a friendly, cordial CEO who invited Buck to present his report. Buck circulated the sets, keeping none for himself. He had it memorized. When the group had finished reading and studying the photos, Buck added some details.

"Keep in mind," he said, "this is headed for the police agencies and the newspaper. They want facts, not theories."

"Sorry, Buck," Ed Roland said, "no paper will print this, not even under *your* byline."

"Of course not." Buck waved a separate page before them. "Not without investigating and verifying. I have an outline for them to fol-low, step-by-step, locations, best times to observe . . . all the ques-tions they'll have to answer to verify. And I know an aggressive man on the *Sun* who'll jump at the chance. In a day or two, he'll have all he needs—without getting smashed up and shot at."

"Good—excellent!" Hudson said. "Do you have anything else?"

"Yes," Buck replied. He paused for a moment. "Our adversaries knew about me within hours of my hiring. Obviously, we have a spy among us. It might be a crew member, someone in the shop, or even someone in this room who's been bought off."

An uneasy hush enveloped the group. All eyes returned to the report, as if they were afraid they'd see guilt in the next chair.

"Remember," Buck added, "the Osmundson-Kersting group tossed ten thousand bucks into the ASH kitty like it was pennies." Buck recalled a technique Ed Roland had used at the ASH meeting. He stood silently for a few seconds, simply watching, moving his gaze from one to another of his superiors. Then, almost as one, they raised their heads. Suddenly, Buck's mind rose above the stifling silence and popped into action.

Incredible, he thought. Look at their faces—and their eyes! He knew it was impossible, but he swore he could tell what they were thinking! He saw Peter's eyes dart from one to another, then back to him saying, *Good move, Buck, you really got their attention with that one.* He saw Ed Roland stare at Peter, silently pleading, *Do something, Peter. Do something!* Dale Craws focused rapidly blinking eyes on Ed Roland. *Roland. You're the one!* Hudson's attention was on Craws, his red-hot beams searing Craws with the message, *It's you, you spineless, brown-nosing son of a bitch! You sink me on this and there'll be hell to pay!* Garland Grigsby? How interesting! Grigsby was laid back in his chair, his arms folded across his chest, with a big grin on his face! He was just sitting there and grinning at Hudson! It was fun! Great show! But Buck decided it was curtain time. Always leave them up in the air, wanting more.

"Ahhh, sir," he addressed Hudson, "if there are no further questions. . . ."

"Oh—yes, yes," replied Hudson, jerking his attention back to Buck.

"I want the individual to know—he's dead meat," Hudson declared. "Meeting's adjourned."

Hudson cornered Buck on the way out, congratulating him on the job done. No apology, just a sugary gush of congratulations.

"Oh, a couple of things," Hudson added, "I'll talk with the captain to see that he understands the Runkle thing clearly. I know that from now on he'll be *most* cooperative with you. Count on it. If you need anything, anything at all, you just see me. Got that? Anything at all. This thing *has* to go next week, and we can't let anyone stop us. Okay? And, keep me informed on any new developments. Okay? I want the latest on everything. You know what I mean. Okay?" He smiled and dismissed Buck.

Back in Peter's office, Buck luxuriated in his glory. It was more than a job well done. It was his biggest success in years, and it marked the turn-around of his self-defeating insecurity. Aggressiveness had worked. He was once again a man of action rather than reaction. He promised himself that he wouldn't forget the lesson.

"Care to critique my presentation?" he asked Peter.

"Good! Stunning, in fact—except for one thing."

"What's that?" Buck wasn't sure he wanted to hear it.

"You told them too much. Only mistake—too much. Never give them the whole store. They might decide that they don't need the storekeeper."

"Good point. Always out front, aren't you?" Buck said with a laugh. "But I *didn't* give them the whole store."

"Oh?"

Buck recounted the episode at Reicher's Marine Shop. He could sense that Peter's quick mind was absorbing every detail as he rambled on. He had concluded the terms of the deal with Reicher when Peter cut in.

"That, James Bond, was a real piece of work. Good move! Tell you what. We may or may not go the whole ten thousand, but we'll cover your two hundred and get you the thousand for step two. It's a chance to learn more. I'll send someone to the bank, and you can get over to Reicher's yet this afternoon."

"Don't think I'll do that," Buck said.

Peter blinked, obviously surprised by the sudden reversal.

"Now for the *rest* of the story. . . . As I was leaving Reicher's shop, I just missed Murrell and Amato. No, *they* just missed *me*," Buck corrected himself. He went on to describe the meeting of the three, the pantomime that he'd watched. "Pretty clear that the two hoods were not strangers to Reicher. And if, by chance, he told them about me . . . you see what I mean? In fact, it's even possible he called them to stop by and check me out."

Peter tilted back in his chair and straightened the silk tie that lay on his expensive Fonini shirt. Then, he looked up, his face almost grave. "Buck," he said, "You stay the hell away from Reicher's shop—*no matter what.*"

Chapter 20

"Good idea, Peter," Buck said as Peter's silver Porsche zipped through the front gate. "Now that the big show is over and I've calmed down, I *am* hungry. The Rum Barrel?"

"Unless you have something else in mind," Peter said, snap-shifting up. As they turned left onto New Dock Street, Buck glanced back over his right shoulder.

"Stop!" he shouted.

"What's the matter?" Peter asked, skidding to a stop.

Buck was twisting around, trying to see behind them. "Spin her around, quick!"

"Wha—"

"Quick, spin her around! It's the black Caddy, it's Amato!"

Peter snapped the clutch out, spun the low-slung vehicle around, and burned rubber as he accelerated in the opposite direction. But when they rounded the curve, the black car had disappeared. Peter slowed, finally stopping for a moment. Then he reversed direction again.

"Never find him in there," Peter said, "a dozen alleys he could have taken."

"Damn!" Buck exploded. "I'd like to catch that little punk."

"Oh well, no big deal. Obviously, he's watching us. But at least we know it."

"No big deal?" Buck snapped. "*He's* the one that helped push me off the PCH."

"Ohhh, that gives him a special spot on your list, doesn't it? Any idea what the other one, Murrell, drives?" Peter asked.

"Probably a big, black dump truck."

As they took an outside table on the deck at The Rum Barrel, Peter pulled a folded news clipping from his inside coat pocket.

"You've probably been too busy. But have you seen this?" he asked, tossing the article across the table.

Buck unfolded it and read the headline:

TOXIC TRACKING TRAILS FAR BEHIND OFFENDERS.

"Wow! Where did *this* come from?"

"Diana clipped it out last night. Go ahead. Read it."

Buck quickly scanned the article, but certain portions jumped from the page. The lead paragraph read:

> Although California's system for monitoring the transportation and disposal of toxic wastes has been considered a model for the nation, its effectiveness has come under question. The system, which costs taxpayers nearly $2 million per year, provides clues which readily identify offenders, but there has apparently been little follow-up.

The article went on to substantiate with statistics the explanation that Lenny Bercovich had relayed to Buck. There were thousands of cases where the manifests filed in Sacramento by the generators and the receivers of the wastes didn't match up. And in many cases, the responsible parties didn't even file the manifests. Despite the obvious discrepancies, the state agencies were investigating few of the cases because of insufficient manpower.

"Man," said Buck, "this is really sad!" Then a smile crossed his face, and he looked up at Peter. "But, at the same time, it's *great*! And perfect timing, too."

"I thought you'd catch that," Peter said.

"I like it! It sets up our expose perfectly. Now I know my man with the *Sun* will jump on the story."

"Good," Peter said. Tapping an index finger on the article, he added, "That's another pitiful accounting for bureaucracy."

"Thirty thousand holes in the dike," said Buck, "and only one thumb. So, the attitude becomes, "What's the use? Won't do any good anyway. But I'm told the county strike teams are aggressive and effective." He paused for a moment. "You know? This," he said, waving the article, "gives our Osmundson case another plus. With the regulatory system swamped, I doubt our boys have been at all careful about covering their tracks."

The discussion stopped as their sandwiches were served and they began eating. It was Peter who finally spoke.

"Good, really, really good."

"Oh, it's good," Buck agreed, examining his sandwich, "but I'm not sure it's anything special."

"No, I mean *you*. It's really good to see you back in action, back on top of things."

"Oh, that." Buck smiled. "I feel better about things. It looks like you scored well on your trip, too. Getting that EPA test permit signed and sealed was no small achievement. But government people still make me nervous. Is it possible for them to back out, leave us holding the bag like they did before?"

"With the bureaucrats, anything's possible. But we have the necessary signatures, and to back out on the test burn now would leave the agency wide open. Heads could roll. At this point, I'm more concerned about delaying actions by local groups. Ed says that attorney with the ASH group is a blowhard, that he'll never follow through. Is that how you read him?"

"Could be, but to me it sounded to me like he knew where he was going. Can he stop us?"

"A good attorney could find ways to slow us down," Peter said, "but I don't think he can sew us up. Our attorneys tell us that it's easier to get a temporary restraining order than to make one hold up for long. Anyway, if we can get off quickly and quietly next week, we might be done before they're ready for any action, legal or otherwise."

"I don't think that's going to happen, Peter. Every time I move my nose, somebody takes a whack at it. Can't be coincidence. I think those hoods know everything that's going on. The *Ark's* got a big-time leak," Buck said, pausing for a drink of water, "and if we don't find it, and I mean *soon*, we're in for an exciting couple of weeks."

"Anything you're not telling me?"

"No."

"Okay, give me your list, in order," Peter directed.

"Obviously, this could change in the next hour, but right now I'd say: Runkle, Maine, Indian Joe, and Grigsby."

Peter's eyes opened wide with the last name mentioned. He reached for his shirt pocket, pulled out a yellow wooden lead pencil and flipped it at Buck.

"What's this for?" Buck asked, picking up the pencil.

"Turn it around—other end—the eraser—Grigsby."

"He's made it clear he doesn't agree with the direction we're going."

"The other three on your list," Peter said, gesturing palms up, "I don't know. But Grigsby, no way. He's ethical and straight forward. I'd bet the farm on him."

"That's exactly what you're doing," Buck said. "Okay, no Grigsby—at least for now. I guess I'm really concerned about Runkle."

"Maybe he's just crazy."

"Oh, he's *that* all right. The way he overreacted to me was absolutely crazy, but behind all that bluster. . . . I'm almost certain it was Runkle who put out the story that I'm a spy for the company. What better way to handcuff me than to get the crew united against me? And this business of the camera? He's got to be hiding something, or hiding *from* something. Most people are flattered to have their pictures taken. Remember, he knows an awful lot about the ship and what makes her go."

"Could be. What's your plan at this point?" Peter asked. His eyes followed the familiar, blond waitress as she brought their coffee and swiveled on about her business.

"When I get this report to Dick Ballenger and Lenny, there's not much more I can do on the Osmundson-Kersting-ASH thing for now. Just wait for the article to be published, and hope that they're smart enough to see that they'll be automatic suspects if anything goes wrong."

"Lenny?" Peter asked.

"Lenny Bercovich. Sh—that's the detective Dante connected me with."

"I see."

"I wish I knew more about Reicher's Groundswell radicals, what *they're* up to," Buck said. "It's a sure bet Reicher's hooked up with Osmundson somehow. Could be his group has become the action arm for the big boys. What if Reicher and the hoods *didn't* connect on me? Maybe it's still worth a try at Step Two of the deal I offered him. Might get something really valuable."

"Don't even *think* about it," Peter said. "We know they have plans. We'll just have to concentrate our efforts on our defenses. But I would be sure the police know about Reicher, your deal, and the possible ties between Reicher and the Osmundson hoods."

"Then my computer tells me," Buck said, tapping his forehead with an index finger, "that the closer we are to the burn, the more I should focus on the ship."

"Makes good sense to me. Tell you what. I was planning another trip to Brussels. But with things coming to a boil, I'd better stick around. I can follow up on the Osmundson thing or whatever else you need me for, especially while you're at sea."

"That doesn't make *me* unhappy," said Buck, "but what about Ed? Couldn't *he* help?"

"I—I don't think so." Peter's face became serious, his gaze fixed upon a tour boat as it churned inbound toward the bridge. "Ed is good at what he does, but when things get sticky? You know, he's been under some additional strain lately. I don't know just what the difficulty is. Something to do with his daughter who's going to school back east."

"Oh, family troubles I can understand," Buck said. "Could you spare some time this afternoon? I have an appointment with Dick Ballenger, the newspaperman, and I'd like you two to meet. Bring your copy of the report."

"Certainly. Then what? You still thinking about Groundswell?"

Buck nodded. "It's occurred to me that a blue-collar, action-oriented guy like Reicher, a guy who knows his way around the docks, might be just the kind to find a sympathizer among the crew."

"Reicher and Runkle?"

"Some kind of R and R, isn't it? Not exactly relaxing. Does that make sense to you?" Buck asked as they left the restaurant and walked toward Peter's car. "Strictly a theory. By the way," Buck said, "since you'll be following the Osmundson thing, here's the name and number of the L.A. detective. I'll stay in touch, too—but, just in case."

Peter's face took on a peculiar smirk. "Are you sure you want me to have this?"

Two hours later, they had met with Dick Ballenger at the newspaper office and were returning to Essee Beecee. After reading Buck's report and viewing the photographs, the newspaperman had nearly gone into orbit. Leaving Peter and Buck standing there, the veteran reporter had rushed to a phone, vowing that, if he could get the chopper from which to photograph the dumpsite, he'd have the story in Thursday morning's paper.

Chapter 21

Buck took Wednesday morning off work. With everything that had happened, and after so many long days, he decided he had the morning coming to him. And with the loading and test burn coming up, it might be around-the-clock duty for the next two weeks.

He had tried to make this one of those special mornings, the healthy, healing kind that he enjoyed so much. He'd really needed some time to wipe clean the slate of accumulated "to-do's" while absorbing the comforting security of his own little California kingdom, nestled so compactly behind the wooden walls that surrounded his postage stamp estate. He had done his early morning miles along the hilltop, enjoying the sparkling diamonds of the Pacific panorama, the ocean breezes cooling his sweaty body with new promise as they rustled the overhead palms. He had repaired the sticking garage door and mowed the tiny patch he called "the lawn."

Stopping for an early lunch on the way in, Buck arrived at the office about twelve-thirty. He browsed through the personnel folders again, searching for anything he might have missed, anything that might point to potential trouble. But there was nothing beyond Runkle's slightly unusual job history. Still, he had that feeling about Runkle, the feeling that there must be an explanation for such irrational behavior. Lenny's words came back to him, "If we had to analyze all the crazies we run across, we'd be crazy, too. We look for motives, of course. But sometimes, all we can do is gauge the act and decide whether or not to book them."

Lenny was back in his thoughts, and her presence invaded his consciousness with startling force. He was surprised by the vivid clarity of the images that came to mind, the smiling face with the turned-up nose, and the brown eyes that reached deep inside him, the thrill when she took his hand, the caress of her sensuous voice as the admonitions of the police detective turned to personal concern.

Whoa, he thought. A glance at his watch told him it was still over four hours before his meeting with Lenny. Better get your mind on something else. He left the office and headed for the ship. For two hours, he casually moved about *Ark II*, watching and exchanging banter with the men. Nothing in particular was accomplished, but with each visit, he felt more comfortable with the ship and her crew.

Back in the office, he changed into the camel-colored dress slacks and navy blazer he kept there. He checked out at five and headed for Dante's. For such a bad day, he felt good, really good, he mused as he reached Naples Plaza. Like a kid going on a date, only he was not nervous. He decided he needed the shock that morning to get his head back in line. He laughed to himself, switched down his window, and waved an arm at the car next to him.

"That's all right, Lady! You can cut in on me any time! Have a nice day!" he shouted. Even the Camaro's eight cylinders seemed to hum a smoother song than usual. In a short time, he had parked in the outside row against the far wall of Dante's parking lot. He reached into the console box for his revolver, then hesitated and put it back. What if it showed under his coat? Or if he dropped it? How embarrassing for Lenny if he somehow got nailed for carrying!

"Ah, Buck Barnumini! It'sa so good to see you!" The gregarious man's dark eyes flashed dual messages. There was the congenial warmth of any good host, but there was also depth that seemed to confirm Peter's analysis. Buck had the feeling that the friendly phony knew just about everything there was to know. "Your favorite booth?"

"Care to sit and relax a bit before the rush hour?" Buck asked as he slid onto the familiar bench seat. "I'd like to buy you a drink."

"Why, thank you, Buck. That's an excellent idea," Dante replied.

Without waiting for a request, he wheeled and was gone. Buck noticed that the adjoining booth in the secluded corner was again empty. Dante returned shortly with a Margarita for Buck and a red wine for himself. He swirled the wine several times, waved the glass gently beneath his nose, touched glasses with Buck, and took a sip. It was as though the delicate fluid tripped some mysterious switch. Buck sensed, before he could really know, that he was now sitting with the real Dante.

"That was a most interesting piece you left for Lenny," Dante said. "You *read* it?"

"Only when she asked me to. Sharing goes two ways. Bother you?"

"No, certainly not. I hope everyone in both counties will have seen it, or something close to it, by this time tomorrow. Your reaction?" Buck asked.

"Absolutely terrific—but absolutely terrifying." Dante's large eyes narrowed.

"Dangerous? I think it'll work the other way. Seems to me, exposing them to the public, as well as the authorities, should have a disarming effect. Not only will it put them out of business, but it'll also force them to be careful about what they do."

"Do you know who *they* are?" Dante shot back in a husky whisper. "How many *they* are? What *they* will do if *they* are cornered?"

"No, do you?"

"Not this group. But I've had some experience with the syndicate. Don't be fooled. They've cleaned up their act, gone legitimate, but they still have all the tricks they've always used for enforcement." Dante's intensity was something new to Buck. "Be advised, my friend, if they decide to take you out, you're history."

"Aren't you being a little dramatic?" Buck asked. "Sure, they wiped out my truck, but *I'm* here."

"You did a good job on them, got ahead of them. But staying ahead of them? You have cut off one tentacle, but do you know how many the octopus really has?"

"Do you?"

"No, but I know an octopus when I see one." Dante sipped his wine.

Buck waited, puzzled by his new friend's attitude. He sifted through Dante's unsettling remarks.

"Dante," he began finally, looking straight at the mysterious face across the table, "just what are you trying to tell me? Are you telling me to quit? Run? Hide?"

"You figure it out."

"Well, this is a shit-kicking game you're playing. I thought you were on my—"

"No—you *didn't* think. I'm trying to *teach* you to think." Dante sat back, sipped his wine, and measured Buck. "I remind you of something." His dark eyes glanced at the aisle that led to their booth. Buck realized that the eye movement was part of a regular pattern that had laced the entire conversation. Then, raising his left arm and patting the ribs beneath it, Dante added, "Remember, the little one carries a blade."

"Oh, man—" Lenny had mentioned Amato's knife, but suddenly a chill swept upward through him and then quickly evaporated. In its place there was a hollow numbness, followed by the sensation that his mind, which would not think, had been separated from his frozen body, which could not feel. Then slowly, the mind and body reconnected. He had been the target of distant shotguns, but to face a knife? He imagined movie scenes in which the heroes used various tactics to disarm knife-wielding attackers. He couldn't imagine himself succeeding with any of them. God, how awful, to have your belly ripped open, your guts spilling out, to stand there fully conscious and watch your very life fall to the ground! It was real fear, unlike any he had ever experienced. He sat there, before the watchful eyes of Dante, as naked as a man could be.

"Got your attention?" Dante smiled. Buck realized that the smile was not one of derision—it was compassion.

"You—?"

"Been there, done that." The swarthy man tilted his head forward, parting the thin layer of black hair that was combed across his baldness, and revealed a four-inch scar. He unbuttoned his shirt and pulled it open, baring his chest. There, protruding from the dark skin, was a wide, garish scar, a full six inches long and bordered on both sides by crude stitch marks. He quickly buttoned the shirt and leaned back against the cushion, staring coldly at Buck.

"How—where did *that* happen?"

"Afghanistan, just after the Russian soldiers came."

"A battle? A fight?" Buck asked.

"No—a warning. The Commies took me for a spy."

"Were you?"

"Yes," Dante replied simply with a casual palms-up gesture.

"Then what happened?"

"They—did some other things and then let me go, a warning to the others."

Buck's respect for Dante mushroomed. The pseudo-Italian buffoon was not only extremely wise; he was courageous and experienced. He *had* been there.

"What'd you do?"

"Just as soon as we got the bleeding stopped, I scraped together all the money I could find and got the hell out of Afghanistan. Came here and became Italiano," he said. "Armor made of courage doesn't repel a sharp knife, not when there are four men holding you before the butcher."

"If you came here to escape all that, why get involved with people like Lenny and myself, with projects like mine?" Buck asked.

Dante hesitated, looking upward as though weighing the question. "We have here," he began, "the first and the best democracy of modern times. But even here, when one compares our practice of democracy to our principles of democracy—we stink. Our leaders don't lead for the joy of leading.

They lead for the power and perks of leadership. And while they wrap themselves in power and perks, the criminals, organized or individual, go relatively untouched, sucking the system dry. You know, Afghanistan was run by a big mob," he continued. "They called themselves Communists and they professed to work from a platform of political purity. But they were just mobsters."

Dante drained his wine glass and slapped the fragile piece fiercely to the tabletop. It didn't break.

"When a mob gets that big and strong," he continued, "the only chance to defeat it is through war. But here in America, we are not quite yet in such a dismal state of affairs. By pecking away at the greed and corruption where ever we see it, there might still be a chance."

"You should run for office, Dante," Buck said, "but, to come here and take risks after what you've been through?"

"Oh, I try to avoid risks. I am about to leave you here, and the next time we face, I might not even see you." He grinned at Buck. "You might be too dangerous to see."

"You remind me of my ex-wife," Buck said laughing. "Sometimes she didn't see me either. But you also remind me of an old friend. He's become very active in a campaign to help throw the entrenched politicians out, to replace them with leaders who have what he calls 'capital conscience.'"

"He is right, you know," Dante said. "There is an American saying, something like, 'I've had enough, damn it, and I won't take any more.' Every two years, we sit in front of our TV's, inhaling the smoke of political rhetoric, trying to decide upon the lesser of two evils, Republican or Democrat. That's like choosing between Al Capone and John Gotti. Then we conjure up what little hope we have left, cross our fingers and vote, knowing deep down, even before the votes are counted, that we lost. We may have changed leeches, but still they suck the organism dry."

"You are so right," Buck said, "but it seems so hopeless." He raised his glass for a sip but saw it was empty.

"No, not hopeless. I see tiny seeds of grass roots government swelling in the topsoil, preparing to sprout and spread. If they multiply quickly before they are stomped dead by the donkeys and elephants, we could find this beautiful land covered by green grass like hasn't been seen for two hundred years."

"Incredible," Buck said. "Here I am, born, raised, and educated in this country. I've studied politics, sociology, and all the rest, and you, in a few years here—you've learned the language and identified the problems better than I. It's embarrassing."

"Too close to the trees and too busy being comfortable. Maybe if I were, how do you say it—in your shoes—I'd have done the same. And maybe, in my shoes, you'd have done just as—" Dante looked up suddenly, his serious face melting quickly into a warm smile. "Ah, Ms. Bercovichio! It'sa so good to see you!" He stood and leaned over to Buck, his soft voice penetrating like a satin-wrapped sword. "Be careful, my friend, very, very careful."

Chapter 22

"Hello, Dante. Hi, Buck."

Buck turned. His eyes swept upward, from the white shoes and nylon clad legs to the shapely, royal blue dress, and on to Lenny's lovely face with its smiling eyes, topped by the shiny, brown hair. Dante was on his feet instantly, motioning for Buck to switch to the side of the booth facing the aisle. As Buck and Lenny settled in, Dante looked seriously at Buck for a moment, tapped his own temple with a forefinger, snatched up his empty wine glass, and was gone.

"Well—" They laughed when their opening words collided over the table. Buck waited, taking in the large brown eyes, the pretty face with the ever-present dimples, the tiny nose that crinkled when she smiled, and the fresh, unpainted complexion. Adjectives whizzed through his mind. Beautiful, pretty, cute, each had its connotation, but she was all of them. He wanted to grab her and simply squeeze her, hold her.

"Buck," she said, "I'm *so* glad to see you're okay. I know you said you were fine, but now, seeing you I can really *believe* it."

"I should play the macho bit and tell you it was nothing, but quite frankly, I'm glad I'm okay, too."

It was then, hearing from Lenny that he really mattered, that he understood. The impact of Dante's message penetrated deep within him. It reordered his drives and his values, subordinating his own will to the instincts of fear and the need to survive. Boy, he thought, now I have to handle *that*.

"You did a great job on Osmundson's," Lenny said. "Have to confess, I really didn't expect you to come up with anything *that* good!"

"Your boss?"

"He's angry that you went ahead on your own, but he agrees with me on your results. The strike teams from L.A. and Orange Counties are going to hit the operation Friday morning with the support of the jurisdictional police agencies—and you don't tell *that* to *anybody*."

"Oh, oh," Buck hesitated. A creepy chill ran up his back.

"Way ahead of you, Buck. My captain's been in touch with the paper. They've agreed to hold the story until Saturday morning, an exclusive. It'll give them a bigger story and reduce the liability factor. Your writer friend, Ballenger, didn't want to risk the wait, but my boss went over his head."

"Good. I hope Ballenger isn't too upset with me for giving it to the police."

"You told him you were doing it, didn't you?" Lenny asked.

"Uh, huh. But it didn't look like your department would move this quickly."

"You were fair. There's no reason for him to be pissed," Lenny said in her calm, musical voice. Buck blinked. Lenny laughed.

A young waiter brought their drinks and took their orders. This time Lenny opted for a glass of white zinfandel.

"Really makes me feel good, Lenny, biggest success in a long, long time. I needed one. But you really helped me. Without that, I'd still be stumbling around, trying to figure out what I'm here for."

"I didn't do that much. You did most of the headwork, and *you* took *all* the risks. But you seem a little—different—today. A little more reserved, perhaps? You, uhh, had a chat with Dante?"

"Um hmmm. Made me realize how lucky this naive, bumbling amateur was. God, Lenny, he's the most fascinating man I ever met! When I think of what *he's* been through and what he knows, I feel *this* big," Buck said, gesturing with his thumb and index finger.

"Showed you some of his scars?" Lenny asked.

"Uh huh."

"Did he show—ah, *tell* you what else they did to him?"

"No. . . ." Buck raised an eyebrow.

"Let's just say he's missing some important parts. He told you he was a spy?"

"Yes." Buck's mind grappled with the implications—what *else* did they do to him?

"More than that. He was a well-known leader in the guerilla movement, but still he went regularly into the Communist-held towns to solicit information, recruits, and supplies."

"Wow! The stuff books are made of," Buck said. "I wonder if he would—we could—" He stifled the speculation. "One thing bothers me. I can understand an ignorant, little farmer abandoning a movement like that, but Dante? A superman who had done so much, risked so much? They don't quit, even when they should."

"That's in novels and movies," she said. "I think everybody has a breaking point, if he lives long enough to reach it, a point at which he says, 'That's it. I *can't* take any more.' Or his intellect takes over, and he says, 'That's it. I *won't* take any more.' Whichever it was in Dante's case, it was an excruciating decision to make, and he still suffers. He sounds flippant, but. . . ."

"I don't mind telling you, Lenny, he didn't sound flippant when he got me thinking about knives sticking into my old bod," Buck said. "I'd really like to get my hands on that little snake, Amato, but I don't much like the thought of that knife."

Lenny sat there quietly, looking into Buck's eyes, a trace of a smile on her face. Buck felt almost weightless, as though the warm, brown eyes were reaching far into him, examining every cell, every fiber, the very core of his soul. My God, he thought, it's scary what this woman does to me. Can I trust her? The thought helped him past the euphoria, back to the wooden bench seat of the café booth.

"Buck? Buck?"

"Huh?"

"Buck, I don't think you heard a word I said." Lenny's face and gaze were unchanged, but soft, soothing words came from her tempting lips. "I said, I'm so glad, so relieved to hear you talk of fear, to trust me with something like that. It makes me feel special—hopeful, I guess. Somehow, I don't think you're in the habit of sharing such thoughts."

"No," Buck said, acknowledging some embarrassment with a smile, "I'm not."

"Thank you." She reached across to place a hand on his. "Now, I want a promise from you. If you see Amato or any of those people, you'll turn and run. Promise?"

"Now, that's taking advantage of me," Buck replied. "I can't promise that."

"Promise?" Her eyes never left his, their demands anything but cold. Her other hand joined the clasp on his and squeezed firmly.

"Okay, I promise. I'll run."

"Good," she said, still holding his hand. "Do you own a weapon?"

"I have an old thirty-eight. Keep it at home for security. I've begun keeping it in the car."

"Any good with it?"

" Haven't used it for a long time. Used to be pretty good with it."

"License to carry it?"

"No," he said, wondering just where these questions were headed.

"Too bad," Lenny said. "You really ought to keep it with you. But then, as a police officer, I could never suggest a thing like illegally carrying a concealed weapon—never."

"You think I've opened up a hornets' nest?"

"I'd say you've got a cobra by the tail. If they haven't figured out it was you out there at the pits, when the publicity on the raid comes out, they'll know. It'd be great if we nailed them all in the raid, but realistically, that's not going to happen."

"Lenny, I know you're right," Buck said, "but I'm having trouble accepting all this. It doesn't figure. All this because one company is trying to keep another from invading its domain?"

Lenny withdrew her hands from Buck's. She straightened against the back of the booth and looked at him in disbelief. Then she frowned, shaking her head slowly.

"Oh, Buck! Originally, we were only talking about potential profits of *millions! Lots* of people would kill for that." Fiery eyes and the exasperation on her face drove the point home. "Now, on top of that, they'll be facing large fines and jail sentences. Buck, I'm sorry, but sometimes, I'm not sure if you're just naive or being stubborn. You *will* keep your promise?"

"Sure. I'll keep the promise—if I can."

"Thank—*you!*" she said solemnly. "You'll have to condition your mind till it becomes instinct—run first, fight last. Buck, you're a brave man, but you don't have to prove it. Not to me, yourself, or anyone. Now, just a couple more suggestions. Leave the bad guys, at least the ones we know of, to us. I suggest that you just concentrate on the ship and the crew. Okay?"

"I'd already reached that conclusion. I'm running out of time anyway," he said, staring at his Margarita glass as he rotated it slowly on the table top. "Was that one suggestion or two?"

Lenny smiled. "Really was two, wasn't it? Can I have another?"

"*You*," Buck said, returning the smile, "get as many as you want. What else?"

"Security for your family," she replied. "You ought to get them away some place until we get this thing under control. As soon as we nail these guys, they'll be looking for bargaining chips. Who's going to testify when someone in his family has mysteriously dropped out of sight?"

"Oh, my God. I did it *again!*" He thought of the kids. He slumped down on the bench seat, angry, confused, embarrassed, and discouraged. "What in the hell have I done? This thing just keeps getting deeper and dirtier by the minute. I—I never really thought—"

"Easy, Buck," Lenny cautioned, "don't self-destruct now. Since your spy mission the other night, you're in this thing big time. You've got family, company, and law enforcement depending on you. Don't lose your cool now. You'll do fine. I'm sure of it. Now, let's get organized, and everything will be okay."

"*That's* all it takes?" Buck returned. "Get organized? *That's* all it takes?"

"No," Lenny said firmly, "but it's a start. First, you should understand a few things. Since Tuesday, we've been watching Osmundson Transport from every angle. We even sent a truck driver in to apply for a job they'd advertised. We're convinced that this is a big bucks operation. But we also know they're not big in personnel. As far as we can tell, they only have the two enforcers, Amato and Murrell. Now those two can't be everywhere, do everything. So, there's no reason for panic. You still with me?" she asked, looking directly into his eyes.

Buck was surprised, impressed, and somewhat calmed by her explanation—not only the words, but also the strength that came through with them. "Yeah, still here."

"Okay, good. Now, remember this. Those people are probably edgy right now because of your intrusion the other night. But they don't know what's coming down Friday. They're not about to place themselves in real jeopardy until their situation is desperate, and they don't yet know it's desperate. That's why they didn't take you out right at the beginning, tried to scare you out instead. They still do their hits, but not as often or casually as they used to."

"You think I'm not too late for my family?" Buck asked.

"I'm sure they're fine for the moment. Do you think your boss—what's his name?"

"Peter, Peter Hamlin."

"Do you think Hamlin would put up some extra expense money?"

"Under the circumstances? Can't believe he wouldn't."

"Good. Then here's what I think you ought to do—mainly for peace of mind." Lenny rattled off a litany of actions, rapidly but orderly, almost as though she were reading them.

Buck listened intently, absorbing each step, occasionally asking a question. He regained composure with each word she spoke. He knew he was back in control when he found himself focusing on Lenny's tempting lips as she talked. Man, he thought, what strength, what cool, gentle strength.

Fifteen minutes later, Buck had gone to the pay phone, made a series of short calls and was sliding back into the booth. Lenny's watchful eyes followed him. They twinkled slightly. Buck wondered briefly about the look. It seemed to show pride, rather like motherly pride. The thought made him fidget a little, but he liked the twinkle.

"Everything okay?" Lenny asked.

The slender, young waiter appeared with their food. "I held these in the warmer while you were on the phone," he said. "Was that all right?"

"Wonderful, good thinking," Buck replied. "Thanks." When the young man was gone, Buck turned to Lenny. "Everything's fine, all set—a huge load lifted off my shoulders."

"Well?"

"Called Peter. He knows a Laguna Hills hotel manager who will be discreet *and* helpful. Peter will make the arrangements for the kids and Timmy Lee. Peter and Diana will stay at a different one so they're not all in one place. He'll explain to the rest of the staff Friday, without divulging any locations, *after* you call to confirm that the raid took place. Like you said, I stressed the *after*."

"Sounds good," Lenny said. "The family?"

"I caught Bob and Sunny at their apartments. I emphasized the seriousness of it without giving much detail. Sunny, of course, was ready to go right then. And Bob surprised me. I expected some flak from him. Didn't get it. He asked if this was really heavy stuff. I told him it was. He asked if there was reason to be worried for his mom, Roberta. I didn't think so, but he ought to give her a warning."

"He said, 'Dad, I'll take care of Jennifer and Tim. You take care of yourself, you hear?' Then he repeated the instructions, 'We'll each make one call—from home—to our jobs. We'll all use the same excuse. We have to make a trip to the Midwest for a family emergency. Keep the call short so it sounds like an emergency and so they won't have a chance to ask for a phone number back there. After that, phone calls only to you, Peter, Detective Bercovich, or Bercovich's partner.'" Buck smiled. "Then he said, 'Dad? Do I sound scared?'"

"No, son," I said. "You certainly don't sound scared."

"Tell me about your family," Lenny said. "Your kids fascinate me."

"It's just your regular, ordinary, everyday All-American family," Buck began, but in no time he had regressed twenty-two years and was sketching his way back to the present.

"Jennifer—I call her Sunny—is something else! You'd really like her. She's. . . ." His enthusiasm mounted; his pace quickened; and his love was apparent as he rambled on about the brightest star in his sky.

"She does sound like my kind of person," Lenny said. "But I hear a different voice when you talk about Bob. Troubles?"

"Uh huh. Not sure just what they are. Could be he's just four years behind schedule in the rebellion process. When it didn't happen, I convinced myself it wouldn't happen."

"And now it is?"

"Something is. I'm not even sure what it is. But I *think* that, for some reason, he blames me for the family break-up." Buck went on to explain their recent confrontation. "Now, let's have *your* story," Buck said, recalling from their first meeting that she had said, "graduated and married at twenty-two, mother at twenty-three, and divorced at twenty-four."

"After the boring life you've led over the past two weeks," Lenny said with a laugh, "my story will knock your socks off!" Her turned-up, little nose crinkled again as she laughed, and then she went on to capsulize her life.

She was an only child. Her father was a mid-level manager for an electronics company, and her mother was an interior designer. For her first twelve years they had lived in an old, established neighborhood on the edge of a Los Angeles ghetto. Then, her parents, fearful of the potentials, had moved to a middle-class suburb.

"I was a good student through high school and college, not great, just good. I never did drugs, never drank much, but I did have fun. School, the extra activities, and the social life that went with them, just one long, happy party to me."

"Why'd you choose law enforcement?"

"I could say the early years in that neighborhood made their mark, but I really don't think so. And it isn't that I'm attracted to the violence or that I'm driven to leave my stamp on the world. My dad tried to divert me to several other possibilities, but he was gentle about it. Once I firmly declared my intentions, he was as supportive as any father could be. Mom says I just wanted to be different, the pretty girl doing the rough, tough man's job. Could be," she laughed, "but I don't think so. I do like it—and, more important, I believe in it. The challenges are always different."

"You have a what, a son?" Buck took another bite of his stuffed pork chop and then realized he had tasted nothing up to that point.

"Yes. James is almost twelve. We have a good partnership. And James is going to make it. He's going to be all right, in spite of me."

"James? Why not Jamie, or Jim?"

"I've always called him James. That might be my insecurities showing. I guess, from the time he first recognized his own name, I wanted him to feel like he really *was* somebody, somebody to be taken seriously. Does that sound kind of sick?"

"Not at all. I happen to believe the name parents hang on a kid is important, very important."

"Why do *you* think so?

"Oh, for the same reasons."

"How did you feel about your parents naming you Buck?"

"They didn't— Oh, fine. What happened to your marriage? None of my business, of course."

"No trouble with that, not after all these years. It was that old song about being dumped for someone else."

"He dumped *you* for another woman? He's crazy, sick, stupid, out of his mind. He's *pathetic!*" Too late, Buck realized the emotion that had poured out with the opinions.

She smiled. "Some of the words that came to *my* mind at the time. But in retrospect, it was going to happen sooner or later. Better to get it behind me." Their eyes met and held. Buck felt the electricity flowing between them. "Are you going to talk with Bob?" she asked.

"What? Oh, Bob. . . . He was supposed to come over tomorrow. Looks now like it might have to wait until after the burn."

"I'd suggest you talk to him as soon as possible. These things shouldn't wait."

"You're probably right. Maybe we can arrange a lunch together before I leave."

The conversation went back to her son, James, and her hopes for his future. The exchanges flowed naturally, easily. They drifted from one subject to another, and Buck marveled at how easy it was, how relaxed Lenny made him feel. He wanted to learn everything there was to know about her. Yet, he had the feeling that he had known her forever. Suddenly, the reverie was threatened.

"You know," she said, "if we stay here any longer, Dante will charge rent—for *both* booths. You did realize that it's no accident the other booth is always empty?"

"Until tonight," Buck said, "I hadn't figured that out. But I do know that you're one beautiful, perceptive, and captivating woman. And you are causing me serious, ahh—"

"I know. For me, too. Buck—would you like to come over to my place for coffee?"

Buck was astounded. The thought had crossed his mind more than once since he met Lenny. But now she was inviting him, with no hesitancy or embarrassment, right up front inviting him!

"I'd really like that," he said, surprised at how quickly the words had formed.

"I have to stop for a few minutes at my parents' house. James is there with them. Here's my address." She scribbled the Torrance address on a piece of paper and slid it across to Buck. "Give me about forty minutes, and I'll be there." She slid from the booth. He moved to follow. "Uh, uh," she said, gently pressing her fingertips against his chest, "you wait till I've gone, remember?" She flashed her infectious grin at him and disappeared around the corner.

Buck managed to restrain himself for a full two minutes before he left the tip and headed up front to pay the bill. He glanced at his watch twice while he waited for Dante to make his change. He reached to take the bills from Dante, but it was as though they were stuck to Dante's fingertips. Buck tugged again. Then he looked up into Dante's eyes.

"You're half blind, my friend," said Dante. "No shape to be out and about in the big, bad world." With that, he released the bills.

Chapter 23

Buck stepped out into the dim light of the parking lot and paused. A strong breeze, almost a wind, blew in from the ocean, clearing out the smog and adding a fresh and frisky buoyancy to his mood. The stars penetrated the halo of city lights with unusual clarity, and the sounds of the early evening city traffic seemed distant. It was one of those magic moments when some supreme power lifted man's dirty world out of itself and placed it into a new and pure setting.

The scrap of paper in his pocket found his fingertips. Maybe I shouldn't do that, he thought. Maybe I should just go home. But the benign paper projected a magnetism that was not easily repelled. It pulled at Buck's impulsiveness, the quality that had so often led to difficulties. Earlier in the day, he'd have been anxious to get Lenny into bed. But this was deeper, stronger now. Just to be with her, he thought, is what I need. She makes me feel good about myself, even when she disagrees with me.

If I go home and look in the mirror, I see all of the things that are wrong with me. Yet, Lenny's like a mirror, only she reflects an entirely different image. She helps me see things I can't see. She opens the door to my cage, gives me freedom. Aha, gives, gives, gives. She gives, and I take. What have I given to her? Maybe this is my chance, my chance to find something *I* can do for *her*. Does that mean, his conscience asked, that you'd even spend the evening with her without trying to hustle her? Yes—well—yes! Yes, I'll *do* that.

Buck's brisk steps took him toward the back row of vehicles. He stopped and searched for the red pickup. It wasn't there. Oh, Buck, you dummy, he thought. He laughed to himself and angled toward the Camaro which, along with its companions, was nosed up against the far wall.

Then, something caught his eye. One car, only one, was backed in among the lineup. The black Cadillac, two stalls away from his Camaro, seemed out of place, defying the rules of order. Black Caddy? Buck scanned the area. Seeing nobody in the auto, he slowly approached it. Even before he was close enough to read it, he knew what the license

189

---

plate would say. Sure enough—DCOBRA. He's *here*, somewhere close by! He shuddered, then felt a burst of adrenalin sharpen his senses. This was his chance. This time he could catch Amato off guard. He eased quietly into the narrow space between the black car and its neighbor.

"Lookin' for somethin' Barnum?" The voice from behind surprised him, but somehow the nasal twang didn't. Buck turned toward the front of the confining space. It was Amato. His face was partially shadowed by the brim of his old-style fedora. He was even smaller than Buck had remembered. He stood there in a cocky Napoleonic pose, his arms folded across his tiny chest.

"You little son of a bitch," Buck said, his disgust driving him toward Amato.

"Uh—uh! Don't do nothin' yu'll be sorry for," Amato said, pointing at Buck with one hand. Buck stopped when he saw it—the glint of light from the long, slender knife blade. "Pain in the ass 'bout long enough, Barnum. So I'm gonna do a li'l surgery."

Buck froze. The voice went on, but the words were just sounds to him. Electricity sizzled up his spine. His eyes locked on the blade. He tried to move his hands, his feet, but they were somewhere else. Even his attempts to free his brain from the paralysis brought only a repetition of three ludicrous thoughts: My hair *is* standing on end! This *is* lasting a lifetime! But I don't see my life flashing before my eyes—I see a *knife*! My hair *is* standing on end! This *is* lasting. . . . Buck had no count of the cycles. They whirled through him with a frequency that could only come from some distant place in the universe.

Then, just as suddenly as it had imprisoned him, the spell was broken—by Amato's voice.

"Just too smart for yer own good, Barnum. It's time the ol' Cobra taught you a lesson."

Buck had no time to account for the newfound gifts of mind and body, but somehow they were back, alert and angry. He measured the situation. Amato stood, perhaps five feet from him, blocking any escape toward the front. Buck glanced behind him. He didn't see anyone, but a rustling noise told him he was blocked in. "Run," Lenny had said, but where? Straight ahead was best, he thought, but he didn't want that knife in his belly.

He sprang up and forward, placing his hands on the vehicles that flanked him, and with a vaulting motion he swung his feet at Amato's chest. Just as a hot, searing sensation struck his left leg, his feet connected full force. The little man went over backward, and Buck's momentum carried him stumbling over Amato and out from between the cars. Without stopping, he raced across the driveway to the next row of vehicles, bent on making it to Dante's back door. He heard footsteps close behind. But there was something wrong with his stride! His left leg wasn't doing its share—*Whump!*

Buck saw no flashing lights like those occasionally experienced in his football days. His last perception was the bitter taste of asphalt and blood. He didn't know about the club that had caught him behind his right ear and had added several more hard-driven blows to his arms, back, and ribs.

Even the shots that Dante fired into the air, the scurrying as his assailants ran to the black car, and the screeching of rubber against blacktop were in another time, another place. His body became lighter and lighter until he felt it lift gently from the hard surface, leaving the threats and his pain beneath. He floated effortlessly into the black night, carrying with him only one remnant of his existence—the bitter taste of asphalt and blood.

*   *   *

A nice place to work, he thought, such a nice office. On one wall was a huge photograph of an unusual white ship. It looked familiar, but more, it felt familiar, like it was somehow a part of his life. A sour-faced secretary, probably in her late fifties, entered the reception area. She peered over half-moon glasses at the fat lady in the next chair and said, "Ms. Barnum? Ms. Beverly Barnum?"

I know her, he thought. Yes, I know her. That's—that's Viola Erichs! He followed her down a long hallway into a decrepit office where a man sat at an old, scratched and dented metal desk. The stranger's head was tilted down, intent on the work before him. He was impeccably dressed, and he had an attractive head of wavy, strawberry blond hair.

The man looked up, and his red face broke into a wide smile as he reached to shake hands. Ed—Ed Roland!

As Buck shook his hand, he saw the telltale bulge in Ed's cheek. Then, the bulge disappeared, Ed's complexion changed from red to tan, and he began to grow taller. The grip became stronger. Buck looked down at the muscular hand that squeezed his. When he looked up again, he found himself staring at a casual smile on a slender but ruggedly handsome face.

The dark eyes beneath the neatly combed black hair seemed to say, "Welcome back. Welcome back."

"Peter! Damn, if isn't Peter! Where have you been? Haven't seen you in—"

His old friend evaporated, as though whisked away by a magician's wand. But in his place was another familiar figure.

"You didn't do anything particularly wrong. I just found a man and a life I love more," Roberta said.

How'd she get here on the ship? Did she come all the way out here to rub it in?

"I'm too busy for that donkey dew, and I have a headache that doesn't need you."

Without answering, she turned her back on him.

A different figure turned back to face him. A young man with angry blue eyes said, "Mom was right about you." Then his voice softened and he said, "I'll look after them, Dad. You just take care of yourself."

"Bob? You okay, Bob?" Buck asked.

"We'll be fine, Dad," a zippy female voice said. "We're staying close to the hotel. When we have to go out for something, I drive. Bobby rides shotgun, watches for the bad guys."

"Sunny? Sunny? Where are you, Sunny? I can't see you. God, my head hurts."

"I'm right here, Dad. Of course you can't see me. Your eyes are closed. Didn't anyone ever teach you about that?"

"Where'd you go, Bob?"

"C'mon, Dad. Be alert. They're going to kick us out in a few seconds," came Bob's voice again.

"Peter has to get us back to the hotel before noon. He insisted on driving us, so we don't have any choice. Can't you at least say goodbye?"

"What? Oh—bye."

Damn, my head hurts, he thought. What's *that*? Feels like hair against my face. Kissing my cheek? Smells so much like, like Sunny. What—raining? Thought I felt a drop. And what's *that*? On my forehead? A kiss? Bobby? No, not Bobby.

He heard the roar of a huge engine. He turned his head to the left and saw a large, black truck, so close he could touch it, then the bottom of a deep ditch coming at him. Suddenly, charging toward him from out of the ditch, an immense, blue truck with a silver-framed radiator. He turned to the right to miss it. Damn, can't drive with this headache! Turn harder! Stop! Gotta stop! People in the way—just standing there. Look, that big woman—that's Railsback! The tall, blond young man, Murrell? The puffy, grease-stained face with the sneer, Runkle, that ornery bastard. The man with the graying crewcut, that's Hudson. What are they doing? They're—pointing at *me*, pointing at me and laughing! He turned the wheel to the left, away from his tormentors.

Damn! People there, too! People? That's—that's Lenny—and Amato! And they're pointing and laughing—together—laughing at *me*!

"Guess the ol' Cobra taught *you* a lesson," Amato said, his steely eyes peering between squinting eyelids, "and now for some fun with your girlfriend."

"You little—!" Buck shouted. He lurched to a sitting position. His eyes popped open. Amato was gone, and nothing Buck saw made any sense.

"Hey, hey, hey! Easy now," a soothing, warm voice with the texture of velour said. "That's no way to talk to your favorite detective." Gentle hands pushed him back to his pillow and then stroked his face. "They said you were awake earlier. You back to stay this time, Buck?" the familiar voice said. "Can you look at me, Buck?"

"No."

"No? Why not?"

"Every—time—look at someone—they disappear." He closed his eyes again.

"That must have been *some* dream. But I'm real. Here. . . ."

Still holding his face in her hands, she bent over and kissed him. Her moist lips parted, pressed, and moved lightly against his. A mysterious, captivating taste blended with her fresh breath to draw Buck back to the present. This was a new kiss, unfamiliar, yet somehow exactly the kiss in his fantasies.

Without opening his eyes he knew it was Lenny. But his head throbbed harder as though challenging his pleasures for possession of his soul. He reached up and clasped her head in his hands, his fingertips tingling at the touch of her delicate, soft hair. He tried not to think, to lose himself completely to the taste, smell, touch, and movement. But with each heavy throb and lightning jab of pain, his mind reconnected. He moved his arm down to Lenny's waist to pull her closer to him. A sharp pain from his rib cage caused his arm to drop involuntarily.

"Oof!" he grunted as he flinched.

Lenny looked into his eyes. "I'm so sorry," she said. "I'm hurting you."

"Never—anything hurt so bad—feel so good."

"I didn't want to do *that* to you. I just. . . . "

She pulled away and raised up. Buck looked up at her. Damn, she's beautiful! he thought. He had to kiss her again. But when he attempted to lift his head from the pillow, another jolt from his ribs killed the effort. He looked into her brown eyes. They said what he wanted to say, but as he watched, they welled up with tears. A large drop tumbled from each eye and rolled slowly down her face, trailing the contours of her delicate little nose.

"What's this?" he said softly. "Something I did?" The throbbing in his head increased, as though it sensed that victory was near.

"I— I really care for you, Buck," Lenny said with soft intensity. "I know I shouldn't. It's too soon. But I really do." She leaned over him again.

"I love—"

"No," she cut in. "I don't want to hear that from you until I know you're sure. Now, just shut up and let me babble." The first of the tears dripped from her chin, landing on Buck's throat. "I don't know where we go from here, Buck. I don't want to lose you. But the way I see it,

I've got years of your history standing between me and a future with you. Pretty bad odds. If I can't have you forever, I may have to settle for a hundred nights—or ten nights—or *one* night. If one is all I get, Buck, I have to know it's the *real* you. Whatever time I get with you, I want it to be with you alone, no sharing with family, pain, people, ships, crooks, or anything. Just you."

I could look at her forever, he thought, and never get tired of it—if only this headache would go away. The leg, I can stand. The ribs, I can stand, at least until I move. But this headache! He looked up at Lenny's face. She was dabbing at her eyes with a tissue. Buck hurt deep inside at the sight of her tears. Do something, dummy, he thought.

"Lenny," he said, reaching gingerly for her hand and squeezing the love he felt into it, "I'm handling this badly. I want that time with you. But right now, this damned headache—can't talk, can't even *think* straight."

"Rather stupid of me, Buck," she said, straightening up and squeezing his hand reassuringly. "I didn't even ask how you felt. I'm sorry. I had made my decision last night. I was ready to see what would happen when we got together, away from our work, all this bad stuff. Then, when you didn't show up, I was crazy with disappointment. After Dante called, I bounced back the other way. I couldn't wait to see you. I walked in here, saw you, and my heart threw my brain right out the window."

"And I'm—ouch! So *glad* you walked in here," Buck said. "If you'll excuse me from answering, I'd love to have you stay right here and talk to me. Makes me feel good inside, and I think the headache is letting up a little—if I can stay calm. *You*—are good medicine."

Lenny bent over and kissed him tenderly. Then, but inches from his face, she said, "I wish I *could* stay with you, but with everything going down tomorrow morning, I had to go on duty early today." She glanced at her watch. "My partner, Ramon, is waiting for me down front."

"On duty? Partner?"

"Yes, with the big raid about to come off—"

"Raid?"

"Buck, don't you remember?" A tone of near panic displaced Lenny's reassuring, velvety voice.

"The only thing I'm sure of right now is you," he replied. He raised the palm of one hand and looked at it. "Seems like all the rest is right there, but I can't seem to find it."

"Maybe you're doing it the hard way. Let's try something else," she said. "Let *me* tell *your* story the best I can. That might put things in the proper order and perspective."

She began with their first meeting at Dante's café, Buck's task, and she proceeded from there. She described the ship. He recalled the picture on the wall. When she mentioned the two giant incinerators, he peered through an open service door into the huge combustion chamber. Somehow, he thought, it's familiar, but not quite real. When she related the ditching incident, his pulse increased, and along with it, the throbbing. But he could see the black truck, the ditch, and the rock wall. The creases in his forehead deepened.

"You're hurting more? Want me to stop?" she asked, squeezing his hand.

"Keep going."

"There was the night in the rain, up on the bluff, photographing the dumpers."

Buck visualized trucks, a bulldozer, and dozens of multicolored drums, but there was no order or sequence of action. Strangely, he could feel the rain. Lenny reconstructed the chase across the hilltop and down the gulley. His legs felt rubbery.

"And then," Lenny went on, "they shot at you—with shotguns!"

Powmp! Powmp! Buck felt the sting of the pellets, saw the dark creek bed just before he tumbled face-first into it! He slogged down the creek on tired legs, climbed up the bank, and wobbled on to a Chevy Camaro. Gunning the engine, he swerved around a large truck and raced down the treacherous curving road. Lenny had stopped talking. She stood quietly, holding his hand, and watching him. She seemed to sense what was happening.

Buck closed his eyes as the wild roller coaster gained momentum. The visions appeared and changed quickly, his emotions vaulting to incredible peaks and then plummeting out of control to despairing depths. Not only were the scenes real, vivid, and filled with detail, they were in sequential order. On and on they flashed, from Viola to Ed Roland, to The Rum Barrel and Peter, to Dante's, to the first threatening phone call, to Hudson, Grigsby, and the meetings. The visions rocketed along at a fierce pace. Suddenly, he found himself trapped in a dark parking lot facing Amato and the long, shiny knife blade. His body quivered, then went limp.

"You all right, Buck?" Lenny asked, bending over to kiss him lightly on the forehead.

He opened his eyes, absorbing the love that flowed from her glistening eyes. He took a few deep breaths and finally relaxed.

"It's—it's back, Lenny. Not sure I'm glad, though. Except for you, I could forget the whole damned mess and be better off. I can't believe it! How'd I get into such a bucket of bear brew? I can't be very bright. Ohhhhh, here comes the pounding again."

"Calm down, Buck. Try to relax. I think it's dedication, loyalty, and principle that got you into this. I'm very, very proud of you," she said, stroking his cheek. "You're the best thing that's ever happened to me." Tears reappeared and rolled down her cheeks. She snatched several tissues from the box on the nearby stand and wiped her eyes and face.

"And I'm lucky to have found you, Lenny," he said. "So lucky, I can't be—"

"Uh, uh, Buck, no commitments right now," she said. "The ball's in your court, but you're in no condition to serve it." Lenny paused, made one last dab at her eyes with the tissue, and took a deep breath. "Now, back to official business. What happened after Amato had you trapped between the cars? Tell me about it."

Buck thought for some time. "I—I don't know. I can't seem to find that part. The last thing I remember is being caught there, Amato talking at me and waving that blade. After that—don't know."

"But you're sure it was Amato?"

"Positive, no doubt."

"Any others?" she asked.

"Someone had me blocked in from behind—never got a look at him. But Amato only had the knife, so someone else must have beat on me." He touched his throbbing head and then his right rib area. "Feels like there must have been a hundred of them."

"I have a new respect for your toughness, Buck, to get out of that as well as you did. You must have done *something* right," Lenny said. She glanced at her watch. "Now, couple of other things. The raids come off in the morning. Letting Osmundsons get the day going, get things in full swing before we hit them. We'll get more of them and more evidence that way. We hope to get the big boss, Schutte. But there's a good chance that Amato and Murrell won't be there."

Buck smiled weakly at the thought of the raids, but the smile gave way to a scowl when he realized they might not get Amato and Murrell. "If you get any leads on them—they're *mine*."

"You can forget that. You're the last person I'd tell. I want you around."

She bent over and kissed him tenderly. Then, but inches from his face, she whispered, "I do wish I could stay with you, but I have to go." She glanced again at her watch. "Ramon will be charging in here to rescue me any minute now."

"It prob'ly good idea you go now," said a voice from just inside the door.

Buck and Lenny turned as one toward the source of the words. He vaguely remembered the pretty Filipino nurse, apparently from an earlier visit. A small tray in hand, she approached the side of Buck's bed opposite Lenny. She helped Buck to a sitting position and, in rapid succession, popped a series of pills from tiny paper containers into his mouth. After each, he took a couple of swallows from the water glass she held. Buck was grateful when she announced that the last set of pills was for pain. Finally!

"He not up to all that henky penky," she said, smiling. "Mr. Barnum still sick man."

"You—you were here—in the room?" Lenny stammered.

"I leave 'bout time things get warm. *You* get caught—one thing. *I* get caught *watching*—something else." She smiled coyly. "I know you not his wife," she went on, looking at Lenny. "Sure hope you not his sister."

"But we didn't—!" Lenny stammered.

"Course not," the nurse replied, her black eyes dancing above her coy smile. "Whatever treatmint you give him work better than what *we* do!"

Buck laughed. It hurt, but still he laughed right through the thunder of the bass drum in his head and the stinging sword point in his side. He looked up at Lenny's red face. She glared at the nurse, then turned to Buck. An impish smile appeared, and she began to laugh. "Okay," she managed, "I'm out of here." She bent over, kissed Buck lightly on the lips, straightened again, and pointed menacingly at the petite nurse.

"And you," she said, "you keep your distance. I'm number *two* in line, and you're somewhere, way back there behind me." With a wink at Buck, Lenny said, "I'll check on you later." She turned and strode from the room.

"She pretty lady," the nurse said to Buck. She tossed the sheet back and proceeded to strip the bandage from his leg. "She love you a lot?"

"Ouch! I—I think so," he replied.

"She love you more than wife love you?"

"Definitely, no question about *that*."

"Doctor be in any second. He see leg and check you over. Then maybe send you home," she said as she disposed of the dressing and cleansed the leg.

"You're kidding!" Buck said. Through his painful struggle past the rocky dreams and through the valley of throbs, the prospect of a release hadn't occurred to him.

"No, no kidding," she said, securing the new dressing and gathering her things together. "Don't keep people long these days. Too expensive. You leave, you go your place or hers?" She laughed as she scurried from the room.

The thought of leaving captured Buck's mind. Why not? He could get up and walk. In fact, he thought, they couldn't keep him there against his will. He didn't know about that for sure, but he was ready to test it. The more he thought about the prospect, the more obsessive it became.

He began to move his arms and legs, gently at first. Gradually, he extended the movements. The leg wound seemed to bite no harder with the extended movements than it had with gentle ones. The ribs protested more loudly. The headache was still his chief antagonist. While it had subsided a little, it announced clearly that it was not buying into the movement thing. Buck let his body go limp, but the pounding increased as though to say, "And no, you're not fooling me with that old limp body routine."

Buck heard the door open. He turned his head to see a doctor approaching. He had dealt with very few doctors. He knew he had been lucky. He didn't like doctors. To Buck, they all looked just like this small man with a boyish face, wire-rimmed glasses, and thinning black hair. And they all treated their patients with the same condescension, the "you won't understand a bit of this, so let's get it over with" that Buck saw in the eyes of Dr. Norman.

The doctor moved in fits and jerks through an automated sequence. After peering into Buck's eyes and ears, he skipped a cold stethoscope about his chest and back. Then he pressed on Buck's rib cage until he drew the inevitable flinch. He concluded with a cursory check of the stitching in Buck's leg.

"Mr. Barnum, you came through that quite well. A concussion, one cracked rib, and bruises. I thought the nose might be broken, but it turned out to be an old break from years ago. The incision on the left calf? Fortunately, it didn't go deep enough to do any serious damage. How do you feel?" Before Buck could answer, he went on, "We could keep you another night, or we could—"

"Doc, I have things to do and people to see. If you're giving me a choice, I'm not staying," Buck said. "If you're *not* giving me a choice— I'm leaving."

Chapter 24

Several hours later Buck's wheelchair sat parked under a small portico at one side of the hospital. The young man who had wheeled him to this point seemed restless as they waited for Buck's "friend" to pick him up. Finally, the orderly stepped over behind a large column and lit up.

Come on, Lenny, Buck thought. Where are you? His battered body complained with each movement, but the medication had finally dulled the headache. And the moment his wheelchair had bumped through the doorway into the afternoon sunlight, his spirits lifted markedly. Thoughts of holding Lenny close, smelling her delicate fragrance, kissing her smooth cheek, and—

A dilapidated, rusty and dented Jeep screeched to a curbside halt at Buck's toes. Buck stared at the green mud-caked fenders and then at the driver, resplendent in his black double-breasted suit, white shirt, and black bow tie.

"Ah, Mr. Barnumini! Your limousine awaits," a smiling Dante called as he gunned the noisy engine and motioned for Buck to climb in. Although he considered staying with the safe, comfortable wheelchair, Buck clenched his teeth, endured the pain, and crawled up into the shabby vehicle.

"Dante! You?"

"You expecting someona else?"

"Well, no," Buck said, groping for his seatbelt. "I didn't know *who* would be here. They just told me, 'a friend.' Thanks. You know? That's kind of scary. Anybody could have called in and been here to pick me up, even Amato."

Dante popped the clutch out, nearly dumping Buck to the pavement. He turned right into the street, then cut a crisp one-eighty in the face of oncoming traffic. Buck abandoned his search for the seatbelt, grabbing instead for anything solid. With every shift of gears and every bump in the pavement, the little vehicle jerked him about violently, painfully. This, he thought, is the *other* side of Dante. He's still driving up and down the mountains of Afghanistan! For a moment, Buck considered begging for mercy, but something made him tough it out.

As he drove, Dante shouted over the roaring four-cylinder engine and the accompanying din, recounting the events of the previous evening at the restaurant. He had watched Buck leave, and strictly on a hunch, he had grabbed his pistol from the drawer beneath the register, draped a towel over it and followed.

"At first, I can't find you," Dante bellowed past the rattles and squeaks. "Then I hear noises, and I see these two guys beating on you in the parking lot. I come running. I fire a couple in the air, and they pull out fast. One of my people call for the paramedics."

"I don't remember a thing, except for the taste of your driveway. I was still eating that blacktop when I woke up in the hospital." Buck hesitated. "You know, you really ought to do something about that. Your asphalt is really bad." Dante stopped for a red light. "Dante?"

"Sir?"

"Mind telling me why you didn't shoot *at* them?"

"Lika I tella the policia, I hearda the shotsa, but I don' hava no gun." He chuckled softly. "If I shoota them, then I have to hava gun, a bad reputation, and big trouble coming downa the road from dosa bums. You see?"

The light changed. Buck cringed as his friend once again launched the four-wheeled missile.

"I—see, Dante, thanks again. I owe you more than—"

"You'd have done the same for me or anyone, my good man. That's what decency is about."

A short time later, the Jeep bounced to a stop next to the rented Camaro. Buck took in a long slow breath and then let it escape smoothly, naturally, and for the first time in minutes, painlessly. Dante was more than stubborn when Buck insisted on driving himself home from the Catamaran, but Buck prevailed when he said, "You'd do exactly the same, and you know it."

It was three-thirty in the afternoon when Buck completed the long, painful trip home. Fatigue had set in, but the throbbing, jabbing, and aching had become blessings. They had kept him awake. He pulled into the garage and triggered the garage door closer. He stood in the kitchen for several moments, smelling, feeling, and listening to the quiet, empty house. Finally, something in his memory connected and he recalled the plan to hide the family at the— Oh, no, he thought. He couldn't remember which hotel it was! His frustration mounted as he grappled with the question for several minutes. The solution he found only fed the flame within him.

"Sure," he mused, looking at his watch. "He could call Peter at the office and ask." Angrily, he smacked an open palm against the countertop. "He shouldn't *have* to call Peter!" His memory remained dormant, however, and after a brief call to Peter, he reached the Palm Garden Hotel and had Bob on the phone.

But it was a one-way conversation. Buck's explanations drew no response, and his attempts at banter fell flat. He struggled past his confusion and simply announced that he would be over to see them after he had a shower, a nap, and a bite to eat.

"Well, I guess we'll be here," was Bob's reply.

*   *   *

It was nearly eight o'clock that evening when Buck knocked anxiously on the door to Suite 317. As he waited, he recognized his need for love, approval, or at least acceptance, not unlike the needs of the injured child who is ready to break into tears at the sight of a consoling parent. Bob's response to his phone call, combined with the stress of the last twenty-four hours and the persistent pain, had twisted him into a state of emotional vertigo.

He knew it would be Sunny who opened the door if, indeed, *anyone* did. He knocked again. The door opened slowly to a few inches, and it was Sunny's blue eyes that peeked out over the security chain. The chain rattled, and the door opened.

"Oh, Dad!" Sunny exclaimed as she threw her arms around Buck's neck.

"Ouch!"

She flinched and quickly withdrew from the embrace. "Oh, I'm sorry, Daddy!" I wasn't thinking—wasn't thinking at all!"

"It's okay, Sunny." He kissed her on the cheek. "I'll take that kind of boo-boo any day."

Bob eased over to them, hesitated briefly as though unsure of what to do, then stretched into a high-five gesture. When Buck's hand met his he clasped it firmly and held.

"It's good, Dad, to see you up and around," Bob said.

"Really, really sorry about the scare, the hospital, and all that, guys," Buck said. "I'm still learning the job. Be patient. I'm getting it."

"Yeah, you sure are," said Bob.

He surveyed the suite, decorated in desert tan and mauve as he entered the carpeted living area. To his right and elevated three steps, behind a wrought iron railing, was a kitchen-dining area with a brown tiled floor that extended from the tiny kitchen to an open sliding glass door. Beyond the door was a private balcony.

"Hey-y-y, pretty nice," he said as he followed Sunny up the steps. "Peter did all right for you."

Sunny smiled and snatched two sodas from the refrigerator. She handed one to Buck and popped the tab on the other as she slid into a chair at the round glass table.

"Tell us what happened?" Bob asked as he joined them at the table.

"Do you want the full story or the newspaper version?"

"Full story!" It was Sunny, not Bob, who answered.

Buck began, intent on presenting the whole, uncut tale. But as he got into the parking lot scene, his automatic story laundry came into play. He confessed to some fear as he faced Amato and his knife, and he told of his vaulting kick to escape. But beyond that, he offered few details. Was it that he truly couldn't remember the beating? Or was it his built-in instinct to protect the kids?

"Where's Timmy?" he asked, looking around the suite.

"Oh, he's next door in his own room," Sunny offered. "He didn't want to interfere with our time together."

"Oh, that's silly. He's family," Buck said, "but then that's Timmy. He's a gem, a real gem. Have you guys seen anything or anyone that we should be concerned about?

"No—" Bob began.

"Oh, Bobby has!" Sunny cut in. She smiled at her brother who faked a smile in exchange. "Bob saw this absolutely stunning girl at the pool when we came in this afternoon. He's been trying to invent reasons to go down there ever since, reasons like 'I wonder if the latest newspapers are in yet.' Or 'I need a candy bar.'"

"Speaking of, Dad," Bob said, "we'd like to hear about this woman you're seeing. Who is she? What do you see in her? Is she worth it?"

"I'm . . . not sure I understand what you're talking about ," Buck replied.

"Dad, if what the man said is at all true, it has a lot to do with things," Sunny said.

"Excuse me? The man? What man?"

"We both got phone calls just before we came here to the hotel," Bob said, "calls from some of your mob guys."

"You what!?!"

"Yeah, it's true, Dad," Sunny confirmed.

"What?" Buck was stunned. His aching body went numb; his mind stopped working. But the horrible throbbing in his head suddenly returned in thundering fashion. He looked at Bob and Sunny. A slight nod from each verified Sunny's statement. He slid down in his chair and closed his eyes. He felt a new surge of heat swelling within. He was fully primed to fight, but there was no one to fight. He heard Sunny speaking. He missed some words before he managed to open his eyes and tune her in.

". . . .phoned me," Sunny was saying, "and told me you were messing around with some woman. He said that it was her husband who beat you up in the parking lot. Then a man called Bobby. He said some awful things like, if you don't back out of the boat thing, Bob and his little black friend would be shark bait. Then, he called me. He described my apartment, even the pictures on the walls. He said, if you don't get out right away, he and his friends would be up for a visit, and they'd—give me a treat—like I've never had before. Dad, I'm pretty tough, but Dad—I'm scared."

Sunny's last words triggered it. Buck flooded with rage. He pounded the table with his fist. He jumped up and stomped about the kitchen, out to the balcony and back, around the table a couple of turns, mumbling jumbled epithets that made no more sense to him than they did to the others. The faces of Sunny and Bob became contorted masks of fear. On Buck's second trip around the table, he was met by Sunny. She threw her arms around him and hugged him.

"Oh, Daddy! Please, Daddy!"

It stopped him, and in moments, the inferno began to cool. He wrapped his arms around her shoulders and hugged her. They stood there, slowly rocking their way back to reality.

"Dante was right after all."

"Dante?" Sunny asked.

"A long story. Interesting guy. He saved my life. I'll tell you about him sometime. But he and Lenny also told me that these guys make their own rules. Not quite true. They don't go by any rules. Only now am I learning about some of the things they've done, things that would never have occurred to me."

"*You* think it's hard to understand?" Bob said. "You should be on our side of the fence. We have no idea what's going on, especially when we get those phone calls."

"I'm really sorry about that, kids." Buck thought for a moment. "I may have held back on some stuff. I didn't want to cause you unnecessary stress. But you *can* help yourselves. Believe *nothing* these hoods tell you. *Nothing!* You're playing right into their hands."

"Then the woman story isn't true?" Bob asked.

"Only a very small part of it is true," Buck replied. "There is a woman involved in all of this, Detective Bercovich. She goes by Lenny."

"And she's *very* special!" chimed in Sunny.

"And what makes you say that?" Buck asked.

"Because, in three short sentences your expression changed and your pitch went up three steps," Sunny returned.

"Perceptive as always, aren't you, Sunny?" Buck smiled and went on to describe Lenny, her background and career, her son, and the immense help and reassurance she had provided throughout the episode. "And yes, she's beautiful with a personality to match."

The kids said nothing. They simply sat there looking at Buck with noncommittal expressions.

"And yes, I have very strong feelings for her. And no, nothing's happened yet. Any more questions?"

"Mom always said you'd marry a younger woman," Bob said. "How old is she?"

"I'm not sure— I think she's about thirty-five. Yes, Bob, she *is* a younger woman, *six years* younger. And no, there is no marriage in our minds at this time. I'm a long ways from trusting any woman that much again." Buck noted that during the discussion, Bob seemed superserious, while Sunny just sat there and smiled, occasionally nodding her head as though in approval.

"Now, back to the main subject?" Buck asked.

"Dad," said Bob, "you could stop all this garbage by just quitting the job."

Buck thought for a moment. "No, Bobby," he said, turning to his son. "I could have, earlier. Now, I'm caught in a war. I've got to focus on it totally. Not only that, I have to *win*. Only chance, because the snake won't *let* me quit now. And since they've dragged you guys into it, there is no backing down. At this point we have no choice. We have to outsmart them and outfight them." He reached over and gave Bob's shoulder a squeeze. "You follow me?"

"Well, yeah, I guess so," Bob replied softly.

"Okay, kids," Buck said, injecting a lift in his voice, "I've got to cut out. I'm dead-tired and I'm really hurting. I need a good night's sleep. My gear's in the car. I'm moving aboard the ship tonight. Be there for the duration. Here's how you can reach me." He tossed a slip of note paper on the table. "My cell will work for now, but I don't know if you can reach me out at sea. Then use the ship-to-shore number. Now, listen up. This is serious. Okay?"

"Sure, Dad," Bob replied, his handsome young face warming slightly.

"Of course, Dad," added Sunny. "Chalk talk?"

"You got it. I want you to be very, very careful." He pointed to the bruises on his face and opened up his shirt to show the taped ribs. Then he slid the trouser leg up to expose the bandage. "These guys are *bad*—and so far, they've shown no sign of being stupid." He reached into his shirt pocket and pulled out the photo of Murrell and Amato. "There may be other hoods involved, but if you come across these two, make sure you spot them *before* they see you. And here's an extra print that you can leave with the hotel manager. You must understand that when guys like this get caught, the first thing they look for is a chance to kidnap a witness's relative. Then they have a powerful bargaining chip.

"I want you to stay in this hotel and look out for each other. Find some new ways to pass the time. I'll be in constant touch with Lenny. Since you've been threatened, we might qualify to get you some protection. There is some chance, I repeat, some chance that this will be finished in the next day or two. Now, even if you go down to the lobby, you always have a partner and you have eyes that don't stop, eyes that miss *nothing. Nothing!*" he repeated. "You *understand?*"

They nodded as one, and their faces told Buck he had reached them. As he moved toward the door, a lump formed in his throat, and his eyes became moist. He wrapped an arm around each of them.

"Thank you both," Buck said, "for being who you are. I'm very proud of you. And I'm *very* grateful. I love you."

"We love you, Dad," Sunny said softly, squeezing Buck's arm.

"Team's got problems, but we're still a team, Dad," Bob added.

Buck smiled at them. "Okay, Team," he said. "One last order. Remember, *no one* can make you safe if those hoods find you. Stay away from the *pool*, and stay away from that *balcony*. Oh, and if anyone, other than Peter, Detective Bercovich, or me, calls here, do *not* acknowledge who you are or give them even a first name. Watch it. They're really tricky, so be on your toes if the phone rings." He kissed each of them on the cheek, turned, and headed for the elevator.

Chapter 25

The gentle throbbing in his head combined with the jabbing rib and tender leg to wrench him from his trance. His watch told him it was eleven o'clock Thursday evening. He had pondered for nearly an hour, staring at the yellowed pages that were taped to the grungy office wall. But each time he renewed the quest, he was reminded that he faced not one issue, but three—Lenny, the *Ark II* project, and the very real threats of Lester Amato and the Osmundson people. And each time he ventured into the dilemma, the lines that separated the issues became hazy and he had found himself drifting off again into the nonproductive fog.

He shook his head and gulped cold coffee from his mug. Man, he thought, when you started this thing with Peter, you had one real concern, money. Now you have three, and the longer you stay with this project, the longer the list gets. Could you take Bob's suggestion and quit? After all, at sea incineration still faces political challenges, even if the test is successful. The program might fail regardless of what you manage to accomplish.

Would quitting affect your relationship with Lenny? No, in fact, Lenny isn't really an issue. She might be a solution. If you quit, no more troubles with Runkle, Captain Portner, Hudson, Grigsby, or the green groups. Would it get the Cobra and his gang off your back? The exposure of their dumping system is going to really hurt their operation.

"Turn your back on them?" he asked aloud. "Who you kidding, Barnum? After everything they've done? They've already beaten the crap out of you once, and they've threatened the kids big time." He shuddered at the thought of Amato and Murrell getting their hands on Sunny or Bob. "You've played too much detective, and Lenny said it, 'You've got a cobra by the tail. You want to try letting go?'" Barnum, he thought, you're wasting time again.

He got up and moved over to Ed Roland's large leather chair behind the desk. He had been tempted to try the chair before, but each time he had decided it was out-of-bounds. He settled into the comfortable

chair, tilted back, and closed his eyes. It felt good. He let go of his painful body and dozed off.

When his eyes opened again, he was looking at the gold-framed bi-
fold picture on the desk. The three faces smiled at him. On the left, Ed
Roland and his wife Sherrie sat holding hands. Her black hair, brown
eyes, and slender deeply-tanned face contrasted with the strawberry-
blond hair and the rosy, smiling face that was Ed. In the other frame
was their daughter. What was it—Allie? She was probably Sunny's age,
a little on the chubby side, with her mother's coloring on Ed's face.
Her hair was one of those intentionally entangled messes that defied
hair brushes. And she was, according to Peter, causing the Rolands
some concern. Buck wondered what her troubles were. Boys? Booze?
Drugs?

"Welcome to the club, Ed," he said aloud. "Wish I could help
you—myself—*somebody.* That's it—I'm just sitting here *wishing*!"

He pounded a fist on the desktop. Then he leaned forward. The
blinding fog began to clear from his mind, and courses of action began
to fill the void, settling, as if by magic, into priority order. "Okay,
Barnum," he said, "third quarter and you're behind. You can't walk off
the field, even if you *want* to, so get going. First thing, go aboard ship,
get settled in, and get what sleep is left tonight."

Minutes later, Buck stepped onto the boat deck of *Ark II.* He
hesitated. The ship was only partially lighted and the fore and aft
superstructures combined with the masts and deck full of plumbing
paraphernalia to cast hundreds of strange shadows. Anyone on deck
could be well-hidden in the shadows.

Unsure of where he should bunk, he decided to query the most
logical source. His ribs gave him a sharp jolt as he hoisted his two bags
from the deck and headed for the staircase that led down to the galley.
He hoped Indian Joe would still be there.

"Hi there, Buck White Earth! You tryin' to beat the crowd?"

"You still working this late?" Buck asked.

"Jus' finished. Full crew fer breakfast in the mornin'."

"Joe, I need your help on two things," Buck said. "I'm hungry, and
I need a place to sleep."

"No big deal 'tall. Jus' dump yer things in the corner there, an' Joe'll get a frozen dinner up." Joe stepped across into the galley, calling back over his shoulder, "The other thing—where's yer bunk?"

"Right," Buck called. "I'm a night early, and nobody's told me."

Buck heard the loud *thump* of the walk-in freezer door closing. He ran a half-cup of bitter coffee and sipped it while he waited for the hefty cook to return. After a series of rustling noises, the softer bump of the microwave door, and the start of the oven's faint hum, he knew the wait would be short.

"Get yer tools up at the counter," Joe called. "Be just a minute, now."

Buck's nose had just caught the appealing aroma when another flurry of activity signaled Joe's return.

"Here 'tis," he said, plunking a divided plate for each of them on the table. "These ain't yer ord'nary TV dinners, you know." The tray was considerably larger than the standard supermarket fare. The roast beef, mashed potatoes, gravy, and vegetables looked and smelled better, too.

"Ummm, best thing that's happened to me today," Buck said.

"Best thing in *two* days, judgin' from them scabs on yer face," Joe said, his dark eyes fixed on Buck as he shoved a large gob of mashed potatoes into his mouth.

"Oh, you had to remind me, didn't you?"

"Runkle again?" Joe mumbled past his mouthful of potatoes.

"No, but they were a little like him."

"They? How many'd it take?"

"Well, two that I know of—maybe three."

"Three? Yer some shittin' tough dude. That all they done to you?"

"Wish it was. One had a knife."

"Shit, man! That part of yer job?"

"Uh—no. I just got caught in the wrong place at the right time," Buck said. He had almost slipped. He was tempted to tell Indian Joe about the episode, about everything. After all, his suspicions of the friendly cook really had no foundation, and the gregarious human journal of activities aboard ship could be useful. Better wait, he thought, wait a little longer.

"Joe, any idea where I can bunk, at least for tonight?"

"Yer all set up. They moved a double inta the first mate's hole. Gotta make yer own bunk up, though. Kin you do that?" the amiable Indian chuckled.

"Oh, sure. How'd I end up with Hobbs?"

"Joe heard 'em talkin' 'bout it yesterday, what to do with Barnum. First officer offered."

"Good. I like Hobbs. Do you?"

"He's okay. Don't like Indians, though. Looks at me like I'm a Chink."

"Oh, sorry about that."

"It's okay. You see all the shit on the dock? All the hoses an' stuff?"

"Had trouble getting to the ladder. Getting ready to load?"

"Early in the mornin'. Place'll be crawlin' with chiefs tomorrow. Bet the *big* one'll even be here," he said, arching his arms and scratching his ribs in an apelike fashion. "Bi-i-i-g chief."

Buck laughed, as much at Indian Joe's bleating as at his mime of Hudson. "Gonna load 'roun' the clock an' ship out 'bout dawn Sunday."

"Joe, is there anything about this operation that you *don't* know?"

The smiling face sobered, and Joe raised two fingers. "Joe don't know if we're gonna make it, an' Joe don't know if it's gonna work."

"You really *want* us to make it—make it work?"

"Shit yes!" Joe said, the broad smile returning. "Best shittin' job Joe ever had."

Buck searched Indian Joe's face. There was something behind the mask of the portly chameleon that lent credibility to the statement.

"How about it, Joe. If you should happen to pick up on anything I should know, pass it along, will you?"

"Didn't need to ask."

Buck got up to dispose of his utensils. As he picked up his bags, Joe said, "You oughta know, Buck White Earth, yer good friend has the first watch tonight. Jus' five of us on board. All the rest here in the mornin'."

"Thanks, Joe. I'll be careful. Good to know that."

Buck wound his way up the interior staircase to B-deck. He was glad that the forehouse was lighted. But he was also aware that Runkle's cabin was just down the passageway from his own. He made it to the first officer's cabin and closed the door quickly behind him.

When he had hung his extra jeans and shirts in the tiny wardrobe, he looked at the upper berth. Surely, that's where Hobbs would expect him to bunk. Making up the bunk was an extremely awkward and painful endeavor. Buck's back and ribs hurt as he stretched this way and that. While the finished product would fail even the most casual examination, it would have to do. He would sleep.

He retrieved the rest of his personal items from the large athletic bag and found places for them, consciously avoiding any flagrant intrusion into an area that might be Dick Hobbs' domain. Slowly, he pulled the last item from the bag, the holstered .38 revolver. He had exchanged an ordinary belt for the cartridge belt to reduce the bulk.

Slipping the belt over his head, he adjusted it until the weapon hung beneath his left armpit. It was uncomfortable, but it would have to do. Donning his nylon jacket and closing the snaps, he jockeyed for position before the small mirror. He hoped the weather would be cool. He'd have to close all but the top snap to cover this gun. If it turned hot, he was going to look silly—and obvious.

Speaking of obvious—this large rear window with its view of everything aft will also tell Runkle that somebody's here. He quickly flipped off the light and then stood at the window. Runkle is probably down there in one of the shadows, he thought. Buck considered going up to the bridge where the view would be even better. No, he decided, if Runkle is watching over the ship, he might make the same choice. Buck decided to abandon the vigil.

Locking the door, he stripped to his shorts, tucked the revolver under his pillow, and climbed painfully up into the upper berth. Tired as he was, the strange surroundings and circumstances, along with the musty smell of the woolen blanket, brought back a memory that stimulated his pulse and his senses, blocking his sleep. He tried, without success, to sneak around the vivid picture and the tension it brought. But despite his resistance, he was drawn back in time, into the picture of a youthful Buck Barnum who had, on a dare, camped overnight alone in a cemetery.

Chapter 26

Bam! Bam! Buck's body flinched with the blows. The club struck again. *Bam! Bam!* Would they *never* stop? The blows didn't seem to hurt any more, but the frightening sound, the helplessness, and the strange, bitter taste of asphalt. *Bam! Bam! Bam!*

"Buck! Are you in there? Open up, Buck!"

When his eyes finally opened, Buck found himself sitting upright, his head brushing the ceiling in the strange, tiny cabin. By the time the next series of loud thumps on the door subsided, Buck had located himself. He slid quickly off the upper bunk to the floor. The hot, jabbing pains in his back and ribs jolted him into reality. He shuffled to the door and unlatched it.

"Hot damn!" said the freckle-faced Hobbs as he burst into the stateroom. "Man, when you sleep, you really sleep! You snore, too?" He tossed his duffle onto the lower bunk and turned to Buck, a broad smile on his face and his hand extended.

"Sorry," Buck said, shaking the first mate's hand. The flaming red afro brought a slight grin to Buck's face. He had remembered Dick Hobbs for his friendly humor, but he had forgotten the permanent and the freckles. "Sorry," he repeated, "that's the first good night's sleep in a long time."

"Damn! You did get worked over, didn't you?" Hobbs stepped back, looking first at Buck's bandaged leg and then working his way up to the taped ribs and bruised face. "You okay?"

"I—I am now," Buck said, stretching carefully, realizing that he did indeed feel much better. The slanting rays of the early morning sun beamed through the rear window. While Hobbs rummaged through his bag to locate his cap, Buck strolled over and looked out on the main deck below. There were clusters of crewmen standing about, gesturing as they talked. Their attention seemed to be focused toward the buildings on the port side.

"You hear anything during the night?" Hobbs asked.

"You've got to be kidding."

"Just wondered. We've got some excitement this morning. Must

214

have been a hundred picketers outside the gate when I came in. Didn't really know what to do, so I just kept driving, real slow, and came on in. When they saw I wasn't stopping, they let me through."

"Ah, picket poop!" Buck snorted.

"It's not all *that* bad. Kind of nice to be noticed," Hobbs laughed. "Gotta go. Load at 0700 hours. Oh, and no more pictures outside of the forehouse. Can't chance sparks, you know."

By the time the door closed behind Hobbs, Buck had his trousers on and was digging for a clean shirt. He would grab a quick breakfast and go ashore to assess the situation and get pictures. Pulling the .38 from beneath the pillow, he checked it and slung the belt over his head so that the weapon nestled between his left arm and his ribs. He was glad his sore ribs were on the other side. He slipped the jacket on, snapped it, and checked himself in the mirror. The uncomfortable bulge did not show. Slipping his camera strap over his head, he set out.

Buck was the last one through the line in the officers' mess. He wolfed down the bacon, eggs, and toast. While sipping his coffee, he wondered about the picket lines. Would *this* be the opponents' last stand? Perhaps it's just the real *beginning*. The real beginning—he was reminded that the raids on the Osmundson warehouse and pits would begin soon. He sure hoped—

"Barnum! Buck Barnum! Grab your camera, and come with me!"

Buck turned. At first, the figure in the dark trousers, white shirt and tie, didn't register, didn't connect with the ship. He glanced at the white hardhat. It was Hudson!

"Huh? Oh, sure. Be right there, as soon as I take care of my dishes."

"Leave them!" The CEO was gone. Buck hurried to catch up. Hudson led him down the springy steps to the pier where they were joined by Peter, Ed, and Dale Craws. Buck thought they were headed for the gate, where the picketers were gathered. But instead, Hudson moved on down the pier to a point close behind the ship. There, they descended another narrow stair assembly to a thirty-foot white cabin cruiser. Almost immediately, the boat took off to the right, pulling out on the channel side of *Ark II*. Just as Buck regained his balance after the sudden acceleration, the pilot chopped the throttle, and the forces reversed themselves. What? Buck wondered, what's going on?

The others were turned, looking at the ship as they idled slowly alongside it. Buck's attention followed their lead and *there* was the explanation for the extemporaneous expedition. He reached for the camera.

In large red letters on the ship's white side had been spray-painted the phrase: DON'T POISON THE OCEAN! Directly before and after it were large skull-and-crossed-bones emblems. The cruiser eased along. Its throbbing engine was the sole speaker, joined only by Buck's camera. *Click— Click— Click— Click—* The boat pilot swung around to retrace his course. Still nobody spoke. When they were even with the stern of *Ark II*, it was Hudson who broke the spell of the rumbling engine.

"Okay, take us in," he said to the pilot. "Craws, you've got twenty-four hours to cover that shit. Peter, tell Captain Portner I want no less than two men on night watch—I do mean *watch*—from now on. Barnum, get out to the gate. I want pictures of every God-damned picketer, and if you see anything that even smacks of threats, danger, or illegality, get that, too. Who had the night watch?" Hudson asked, looking to Buck for the answer. Buck felt himself tense up.

"First Engineer Runkle and Seaman Evans," said Peter. Hudson glanced at Peter and then turned his angry glare back toward Buck. The lines near the corners of the squinting eyes relaxed a little, and there was a barely perceptible nod of his head.

"Okay, get to it, everybody! Departure is still 0600 hours, Sunday."

Buck returned quickly to his cabin and grabbed the mini-recorder. He headed toward the front gate. As he moved between the buildings the distant mix of human voices became more defined.

"Profits in their pockets! Poison on our plates! Profits in their pockets! Poison on our plates!" He rounded a corner of the office building and started down the drive toward the gate. A group of approximately fifty protesters slowly walked, single-file, forming an elliptical pattern that blocked the entrance. There were men and women of all ages, even two young mothers who carried infants in papoose pouches slung on their backs. Another group of perhaps a hundred people stood across the road from the entrance.

Many of the participants carried signs identifying support groups, such as: FISHERMEN'S ASSOCIATION; GREATER LOS ANGELES ENVIRONMENTALISTS; GROUNDSWELL; and ALLIANCE TO SAVE THE HARBOR. Still others had crude, homemade banners with slogans: CARE FOR THE PLANET – WE DON'T HAVE ANY SPARES; NOT IN MY BACK YARD; BAN THE BURNER; ANOTHER LIE, ANOTHER DOLLAR; and NOAH WOULD TURN OVER. The chant rolled on relentlessly, and on the words, "Profits," and "Poison," the demonstrators rhythmically thrust their signs skyward.

The gates were closed, and Buck saw the regular guard on the phone in the guardhouse, his back to the disturbance. Three additional guards armed with clubs had been brought in, and they stood at ten-foot intervals just inside the gate. Buck knew at a glance that, from a photographic standpoint, he faced a dilemma. Pictures taken through the chain-link fence would present the fence as the primary subject. The protestors beyond would become secondary, almost featureless figures. Further, it would appear that the protestors were indeed the victims, peering as they would from behind the fence.

He tried stepping up, close to the fence, so as to aim the camera through an opening. Each time he tried, he was greeted by a chorus of jeers, and someone would thrust a sign in front of his lens. He leaned in through the guardhouse doorway.

"Don't suppose you'd open up and let me out there?" he asked.

"No way!" said the chubby guard, his eyes wide and beads of per-spiration gathering on his forehead. "They'd have your camera before you could get two shots."

Buck looked about for a solution. Something high? Some position to shoot *over* the fence? Nothing available. He began moving about, catching as many of the people as he could through the fence. There was Juanita Railsback. *Click*— Pankonen and the attorney. *Click*— And there, across the road, watching and talking between themselves—

Murrell and Amato! *Click— Click—* As he snapped the shots, he saw Amato point toward him and say something to Murrell.

Suddenly, something else clicked in Buck's mind. The morning raid! They won't get them! They're here! Murrell and Amato are *here*! He hurried into the guardhouse, digging in his wallet for Lenny Bercovich's card. He called her apartment. No answer. He called the department number.

Nobody there seemed to know what he was talking about. After several tries, he simply left an urgent message for Detective Bercovich and gave up.

When he returned to the gate, Amato and Murrell had vanished. Discouraged, Buck decided that the shots he had taken were as good as he would get. He returned to the ship and paused for a few minutes on the forecastle deck. A strange array of large hoses, supported by booms, were connected to the loading manifolds on the port side of the ship. Parked close to the pier, a large tractor-trailer tank truck fed its liquids to the pumps, and off to one side were two more trucks waiting to unload.

Buck saw Chief Johnson and several others standing near the rail over on the starboard side. They appeared to be looking down at something in the channel. He crossed over to join them. Twenty feet below were five small day cruisers displaying GROUNDSWELL banners. He recognized two of the banners that he had seen during his visit to Jim Reicher's headquarters. Reicher? Sure enough, there he was, at the wheel of the closest boat. Buck leaned over the rail and caught a good shot of him.

Reicher spotted Buck. He held out his cupped hands, as though holding a container, and shouted, "Hey, Barnum! Throw some more money!" Buck felt the heat creeping up his neck. He snapped off another shot, being sure to catch Reicher in his money routine. Peter's advice to stay away from him was pretty solid, Buck thought. He probably knew who I was right from the very beginning. The boats eased slowly past in single file, coming closer to the ship with each pass.

Buck was surprised at how quiet the group was. Perhaps their message was, "We don't shout slogans—we take action."

"Can we, Chief? How 'bout it?" one of the crewmen asked.

"Oh, what the hell—okay, just this one time. Then we've got to get back to work," the chief said.

The four men stepped up on the bottom rail, leaning their thighs against the upper rails for balance. Then, as though it had been choreographed and rehearsed, they unzipped their trousers. Soon, four streams of water sprayed the occupants of the boat beneath them. They finished their show with a rousing cheer, a dramatic rezip, and a coordinated dismount from the rail.

"Think they got the message?"

"They may be stupid, but they're not blind."

"That one guy is. I got him good!"

"All right. Let's get back to work," the chief said.

Buck ambled down to the mess for a cup of coffee. The hectic morning was rolling past. It was time to stop and get organized. He chose a seat near Gantsky and one of Dr. Keene's technicians.

"Hi, Mr. Barn—uhhh, Buck," the friendly Gantsky greeted. "Hear you got into another one, huh?" Gantsky smiled sympathetically. "Didn't come out quite so good this time?"

"You should see the other guys," Buck said, glancing about the mess to see who else might be sharing their conversation. At the third small table, he spotted Runkle. The first engineer sat there, nursing a bowl of soup and looking directly at Buck. Runkle said nothing, but the anger in his eyes was unmistakable.

Gantsky and the technician resumed their discussion of computers. Buck deliberately looked away from Runkle. He pondered the unspoken message from Charles Hudson. Coincidence that the graffiti job was done while Runkle had the watch? Buck found himself reexamining his information. He really had nothing on Runkle yet. He would like to watch, wait, and catch Runkle at something. But it might be better for the project to let Runkle know that he is under suspicion. Knowing that he was being watched, the first might be reluctant to take any further chances. Runkle drained the last of his soup, got up, and disposed of his bowl. He started toward the door. He would have to pass right past Buck. As he approached, Buck put a hand out.

"Hey, Runkle. Did you help paint the town red last night? Or maybe you just got a good night's sleep."

"Why, you cockthucker," the sturdy engineer spit, obviously struggling with a swollen tongue. He reached down, grabbed Buck's jacket in his powerful fists, and pulled. Buck went willingly to his feet. He didn't want to be caught helplessly in his chair. Everything else in the mess stopped. Nobody spoke. Nobody breathed. "I thould beat the thit out o' you right here," the menacing first engineer said.

"Think you'll have any better luck the thecond time?" Buck asked, thrusting his forearms between Runkle's and wrenching free of his grip. Instinct tightened his right fist behind him..

Runkle looked around, scanning the group quickly, scowling his threat at any who might be inclined to laugh. Nobody laughed. Then, he grabbed again for Buck's jacket. His hand caught the bulge under Buck's left arm. He squeezed it, as though grappling for recognition.

"Jethuth Chrith, now thith yellow bathard hath a gun!" He released his grip, looked around at his audience, and added, "I geth thath all we need t'know 'bout *him*." Giving Buck a hard bump, he brushed past, and strode from the mess.

Buck simply stood there, locked in embarrassment. Five sets of eyes looked at him. Gantsky, with whom he had developed such a good relationship, looked down at the table, slowly shaking his head. Confused, Buck put his cup on the tray and left. As he reached the level above, First Mate Hobbs came rushing down the steps toward him.

"Damn, Buck, I don't know what it is *this* time, but the old man wants you in his quarters—*right now!*"

Buck felt himself sliding from humiliation to anger as he climbed the remaining steps and headed along the narrow passageway. It seemed he had taken another shot to the head, for the all-too familiar pain threatened another full scale invasion. Runkle must have gone right upstairs, he thought. Now I have to deal with the robot. Give me a break! His frustration took on a familiar bitterness that carried him back to a fourth grade episode.

An older, bigger kid had been picking on him after lunch. For the first time, Buck had fought back, even won the fight. But afterward, he had been called to the principal's office. He had sensed then, as he did now, that he was in trouble, but for what? Was it really the business of anyone here on the ship that he had no permit for the revolver? After all, it was in their interest that he had carried the weapon.

Captain Portner greeted Buck with silence. He sat there at his desk—didn't even look up—just held out his hand. Buck started to object, but the captain simply wiggled his fingers. It was as though the teacher had caught him shooting spit-wads. He pulled the revolver from the holster and handed it to Portner. The captain rose from his chair, moved across the dayroom, opened the safe, and deposited the weapon, all without a word.

Then, he turned and faced Buck. "When you leave the ship, you can claim it. But, make no mistake about my tolerance. It's Captain Hudson's order that I cooperate with you as best I can. Up to me, you'd be history. If you want to play Rambo on shore, that's *your* business. But on this ship, it's *my* business." As before, the conference ended with a wave of the captain's hand, and that wave seemed to fully open the door to the excruciating headache.

What now? Buck wondered. Just chuck the whole damned thing and walk out? No, that's no longer an option. Get the hell off this damned ship for a while? No, he was all done retreating. He would hang around and mix with the crew as though nothing had happened. Might salvage at least a little respect from the others, he thought. If nothing else, he can show them what he's made of, show them he's undaunted—and still employed. He roamed the ship for a time, singling out and chatting with those who had been most accepting of him.

After lunch, he attempted to renew his meandering, striving to be upbeat, humorous, and confident. But despite the pretense, his mind focused on only two things—the raids and the sharp, penetrating headache. Surely the raids must be wrapped up by now. Did they get enough of the participants and the evidence to shut the Osmundson operation down? What if the company had a spy somewhere in the police agencies? Possible. Their dumping operation certainly had to have been lucrative enough to afford money spent on bribery of officials. With an insider's tip, they could have sterilized their office and warehouse. They could have gotten away. *But,* Buck thought, there's no way they could clean up that dumpsite.

He tried a call to Lenny, but she was out of the office. But did he really care? By three o'clock, he could stand the pain no longer. He headed for his new home, two pain pills, and his bunk. He could do nothing more for this terrible day but try to end it and hope for a better tomorrow.

Chapter 27

Buck strode into the mess at five o'clock Saturday morning. Even at such an ugly hour, his body felt remarkably better, his headache was gone, and his mind seemed clearer. Really, Buck thought, I haven't handled things too badly. My worst mistakes? Other than the gun boo-boo, I've been stopping after each incident and letting the tide of confusion swallow me up. End result? The pitching roller coaster. No more. I'm going to get back on this new track, more like Peter's game plan, keep moving. Can't stop thinking. That would be a disaster. But I can control the thinking, make it productive.

"Hi, Buck White Earth! Yer up early. 'Spectin' trouble?" Indian Joe asked as he sat down across from Buck.

"No trouble today, Joe. Just getting an early start."

"Don' worry none 'bout the crew. Joe fixed that all up."

"What are you talking about, Joe?"

"The crew—the gun thing yeste'day—Joe fixed it."

"Now, how is Joe going to fix *that*?"

"Joe put out the word. By 0700, ever'thin' gonna be okay."

"The word?"

"Shit, man, you know—the fight? Joe told 'em 'bout how that big gang o' Mexes tried to rob you in a parkin' lot, how you whupped 'em good, how they said they'd get even, 'an how you jus' fergot to stash the piece when you came on board yeste'day." Joe's dark eyes flashed, and his round face broke into a grin.

"Damn, Joe! That's about the craziest thing I ever—"

"Ever'body thinks Joe knows ever'thin' that happens roun' here, so when Joe talks, people listen. Comes in shittin' handy sometimes, dontcha think?"

"Indian Joe, I think you're the eighth wonder of the world! I don't know how you dreamed up that story, but that's *exactly* what happened!"

Buck paused, recalling their last conversation. Sure seems like he's with me.

"Joe," Buck continued, "I have the feeling, the feeling that there's a

223

big fish, a big, bad old northern hanging around here. You know, one of those sneaky vicious ones that can really bite hard. Any ideas?"

Two officers entered the mess.

"Big cool front come through," Joe said loudly. "I hear the fishin's been slow." Then he lowered his voice. "Joe ain't seen him yet. But there's a big one down there all right. Yer gonna have to use the right bait, go slow, an' keep yer finger on the line to feel him pick it up. But don't go too deep. I 'spect he's workin' shallow, not all that far from you." Just as suddenly as the affable Indian had appeared, he was gone.

After breakfast, Buck spent a couple of hours moving about the ship, watching and listening. Strangely, instead of inducing lethargy, the drone of the steadily humming pumps seemed to say, "This is it. We're loading up. Now it's for real." As they brought the toxic chemicals aboard *Ark II*, they also seemed to pump enthusiasm into the crew.

At eight-thirty, he headed for the office. When he walked in, Buck noticed that Ed looked a little brighter, but he still hadn't recovered his positive persona. His red face was rigid, and his laugh was only a weak smile. Finally, Buck could stand it no longer.

"Come on, Ed, out with it," he said. "You act like a shark's got a hold of your dinghy."

Ed sat at his desk with one elbow propped on the desktop, his chin resting in that hand. His gaze was fixed on the opposite wall. "I—I guess I can talk to you, Buck. You're right. I've got some real difficulties, and they're getting to me."

"Boy, can I understand *that*!"

"I think probably you can."

"Well, let's get on with it," Buck said. "What's the first one?" He smiled at his switchover to the role of counselor.

"First one? My car's broken down. It's in the shop."

"That's easy. Here," Buck said, tossing his Camaro key on the desk. "I need the car at lunchtime today. Otherwise, it's yours until we get back from the burn. What's next?" Buck expected to hear something about Ed's daughter and her issues back east.

"Peter called," Ed offered. "He said the raids went very well. He's picking up a paper. Should be here soon. But Buck, I—I'm really bothered by the raids and the publicity. You did a great job, Buck, and some of the benefits are already to be seen outside the gate."

"Oh, you mean the picketers backing off?" Buck asked, a smile crossing his face.

"Uh, huh. Only three or four out there today. I guess the rest of them must have read the paper."

"Great, isn't it! Most of them are probably pissed to think they got sucked into backing the hoods." Buck glanced at the somber expression on Ed's face. "It isn't? So why not?"

"I—well, I'm afraid you just riled them up. That Osmundson outfit, with their ties to the syndicate. If you've burned them badly, I don't think they'll just take it, not without some serious retaliation. Buck, we've all got *families*—*you've* got a family to be concerned about. From what I've heard, those people will stop at nothing."

"But, Ed, we've all got our families hidden away in hotels. Has something happened?"

"Do you think *that* fixes everything? Just hide in a hotel? For how long? An hour? A week? A year?" Ed replied, the series of questions escalating in a crescendo. His face suddenly became a vivid red.

Buck would never have believed the man was capable of the anger that showed in his eyes. Even the evening that old Razorback short-circuited his presentation—nothing like this!

"Do you think—do you *ever* think? Do you think these people are going to pay their fines, serve their time, shrug, and walk away from it? Do you *really* believe that?"

"Well, yes. I guess I do. We've identified them. They know the police will be watching them."

"Watching? Watching them? Who is *them*? Have you identified *all* of them? Any idea just how big and powerful they are?"

Ed's question, "Who is *them*?" Dante's words, and Buck had allowed himself to forget. The fear that he had placed others in danger swelled in his gut and brought a lump to his throat. But Ed's anger was beginning to get to him.

"You had no right, Buck, no right to do that to all of us!"

"Ed! Calm down! I was just doing my job. Look, damn it!" Buck twisted his head around and pointed to the two red welts on his neck.

He pulled up a trouser leg and showed the bandage. He opened his shirt to show the taped ribs. "Now, damn it, I've taken my lumps, too. In my judgment, it was the thing to do—clear and simple. Besides, I've been the guy out there in the trenches!"

"I'm impressed with your bravery, Buck! But I'm no mercenary. I'm just a public relations man. What do I do now? Leave the country and try to get on welfare in Siberia?"

Buck's temper was on the edge. Enough, he thought, enough!

"I think you'd better have a long, frank discussion with Peter," Buck went on. "He's the one who should be hearing this."

Buck turned to leave. Ed tossed the car key toward Buck. Buck slid it back.

"No, Ed," he said, "I meant that offer, sincerely. It still stands. Use it if you need it."

Buck needed to cool down. He left the office and went outside to the parking lot where he stood, breathing deeply and trying to relax. Elephant eggs! he thought. No matter what you do around here, there's always someone to bitch about it. Well, that's tough, Ed Roland. I did what I thought was right, and that's what I'll continue doing—you'd better get used to it.

Buck leaned against the building and looked out toward the gate. Apparently the word *had* spread. There were no ASH signs, only three protesters carrying GROUNDSWELL signs.

"Look at that, Ed," he said aloud. "They've lost faith in their leadership. That's what *doubt* can do."

He felt a tug on his arm. Turning, he faced a smiling Peter.

"Come on," Peter said, waving the morning edition of the *Sun*. "Let's go into your lavish office.

Peter and Buck pulled chairs up to Ed's desk.

"I'll take first dibs," said Peter with a smirk, "since I bought the paper."

He spread the paper out before him. Buck tried to read what he could from the distant angle, but the headlines were about the best he could do. But clearly, the raids had made the front page, top slot! Peter smiled broadly as he read. Buck couldn't remember having seen a smile quite like that on Peter's face.

"Good—right—good—*all ri-i-ight*! Good shot, Buck," Peter muttered as he read. "I'd say you blitzed them, really blitzed them!" he concluded.

A warmth spread through Buck, an old familiar warmth that he had missed for a long time. The feeling of accomplishment—combined with such an excited reaction from Peter—it was as though Buck held a Super Bowl trophy in his hands. Even more than that, now he truly *belonged.* He had earned his keep. But, turning to Ed for further reinforcement—he drew a blank.

Ed was now engrossed in the article, but his reactions tarnished Buck's trophy. As he read, he shook his head slowly, groaning as much as speaking when he uttered an occasional, "Brother . . . Ohhh, brother." When he had finished the article, he methodically refolded the section and handed it to Buck. The look on Ed's face was nothing Buck had seen. Anger? Confusion? Fear, perhaps?

Buck stretched the paper out before him. Apparently the police had granted Dick Ballenger an exclusive on the story. How could they do anything else? Buck thought. Without his information, they'd have been nowhere.

STRIKE TEAM RAID NETS ILLEGAL DUMPERS

Strike teams from Los Angeles and Orange Counties snared what they allege is a major participant in the illegal transporting and dumping of hazardous wastes in Southern California. In coordinated moves, the agencies investigated and closed the Osmundson Transport Company and the M & S Sand and Gravel Company, both located at 3220 Seventh Street in Long Beach. Simultaneously, another team investigated and closed an alleged illegal dumpsite along the Ortega Highway in the foothills east of San Juan Capistrano.

Michael L. Schutte, 58, manager of Osmundson and owner of M & S, has been arrested on thirteen counts of conspiracy to violate Department of Transportation and Department of Health regulations.

Authorities have indicated that additional charges will be brought by federal agencies.

The results of a documented private investigation that were turned over to authorities and the *Sun* last week prompted the raids. Preliminary estimates indicate that 20,000-50,000 tons of toxic chemicals may have been buried illegally in the Ortega dumpsite.

"A classic case of abuse of the DOT's cradle-to-grave manifest regulations," said DOT spokesman Henry Alton. "They ship, with falsified documentation, a small percentage of the wastes to federally licensed dumpsites out of state. The rest, they bury in secret locations nearby. We expect to find gross misrepresentations in their shipping manifests. The illegal burial site we've uncovered speaks for itself."

Several employees of the two companies also face charges, and two Osmundson employees, Donald Murrell and Lester Amato, have yet to be apprehended. The men allegedly have ties to organized crime in New Jersey, and Amato is currently wanted on assault charges in Long Beach and New Jersey.

A smaller, crisp, bold headline in the next column caught Buck's eye.

DUMPING VIOLATORS LINKED TO ASH

An investigation by the *Sun* has revealed that the environmental group known as The Alliance to Save the Harbor (ASH) has accepted a $10,000 contribution from the Kersting Foundation, a nonprofit organization alleged to be established and funded by the Osmundson Transport Company. The Osmundson company is a competitor of Southern California Boatbuilding Company, parent of Sea-Going Incineration, Inc.

Government strike teams in a morning raid

have turned up substantial evidence alleging that the Osmundson Company and M & S Sand and Gravel have been involved in a massive toxic waste dumping scheme.

At a recent ASH meeting, Don Murrell, Executive Director of the Kersting Foundation, and also an employee of Osmundson Transport Company, presented a check to the ASH group to aid them in their opposition to *Ark II*, the seagoing incineration ship soon to be tested by Southern California Boatbuilding Company.

When queried about the donation, Juanita Railsback, President of ASH, said, "We accepted the money in good faith from an independent foundation." Asked if the ASH leadership had investigated the Kersting Foundation prior to accepting the money, Railsback said, "Public service organizations such as ours don't have the resources. We simply can't investigate everyone who wishes to contribute to our vital and worthy cause."

"Wow!" Buck said. "Nothing ol' Razorback says can whitewash this! She got her ASH kicked, Ed, just like you promised."

"Certainly takes the wind out of the ASH sails, doesn't it?" Peter added.

Ed was silent.

"What's the matter, Ed? Don't you feel well?" Buck asked.

"No, as a matter of fact, I don't. Think I'll go home and try to shake it off."

Buck and Peter watched silently as Ed Roland struggled from his chair, slipped into his sportcoat, and aimlessly drifted out into the hallway.

"You know, there have been times I was ready to walk out like that—permanently," Buck said.

"I couldn't blame you if you had," Peter said, "but for the right reasons?"

"Meaning?"

"Meaning, you've taken some hits, some really cheap shots, since you came on here, any one of which might justify throwing it in. But, yesterday's episode, the gun aboard ship? Not too bright. Only the captain can do that. And on a ship loaded with flammables?"

Buck dropped into Ed's chair. Suddenly, the reactions of the crew—even Captain Portner—made sense. Peter leaned back in his chair and looked quietly, solemnly at Buck.

"Really stupid, huh?" Buck asked.

"No. I'd call it landlubber's logic, but not the end of the world. And Buck, for what it's worth, I understand. If I'd been in your shoes for the last couple of weeks, I'd have done the same thing."

"Really, really stupid. Ignorance. Just wasn't thinking. There's been so much coming at me from all directions," Buck said. "Kind of feeling my way along, with my eyes closed at times."

Peter nodded. "Seems to me you've felt your way along quite well," Peter said, motioning to the newspaper. "Buck, look at the results you've gotten, far, far beyond our wildest expectations."

"Thanks."

Buck went on to share Indian Joe's explanation on the gun incident and his own decision to let the story stand. Peter's hearty laugh pasted the seal of success to the tale.

"You know, I think you might be right on that kid," Peter said. "He's really a lot sharper than I'd have guessed."

"But Peter?" Buck quizzed, "You've lived in this political tornado for years. I can't imagine spending my life in this perpetual storm. How do you *manage* it?"

"About the same way you're doing it. Tackle the biggest concern, whip it, and go on to the next. One difference though, I don't stop to think after each battle, hoping that it's all over. I keep moving. They have to catch me before they can hurt me."

"You *are* a scrambler after all, aren't you?"

"But I'm slowing with age, too."

"I saw the kids Thursday night," Buck said. "I suppose you knew that the hoods had been calling them with threats? Peter, I couldn't quit now if I wanted to."

"The kids—you've got two great ones there, Buck. I hope you know how lucky you are," Peter said wistfully, directing his gaze to the dirty ceiling. "I've thought about you and those kids so many times through the years. You know, Buck, when I die it's the end of my branch of the Hamlins, nothing left but a birth certificate, a small estate, and a death certificate."

Buck was stunned. Only a few negative words from the most positive person he'd ever known—but they weighed a ton. A damp, awkward silence invaded the room. He searched for that simple response, the response of a good friend, but he couldn't find it. And his failure embarrassed him. Peter continued to stare at the ceiling, and Buck stared at Peter.

"Anyway," Buck finally managed, "it's Saturday. We ship out tomorrow morning. Not much time. I've done about all I can on the outside enemies. Still have at least one on the inside, Runkle, but I can't prove it," Buck rattled on. "We're already loading, and I'm no closer to our inside enemy than when I started. Peter, doesn't that make you a little nervous?"

Peter slowly released his lock on the ceiling and turned to Buck. His face was still serious, but the rare expression of sadness had been replaced by cold dark eyes peering through a stone mask.

"Buck, your unflappable friend here finds that *very* disturbing. In fact—it scares the hell out of me."

Chapter 28

Buck returned to the ship. As he roamed, it struck him—Indian Joe was apparently right about having repaired the attitudes of the crew. Gantsky, the chief, and the others were friendly, and their respect for him seemed to have returned. If anything, his stock seemed to have gone up twenty points.

Just before noon, he showered, changed clothes, and headed for The Rum Barrel and lunch with Bob and Sunny. As he drove, he wrestled with a mixture of emotions. He was excited at the prospect of seeing the kids, especially since they had set up the meeting. But the strain and upheaval the kids were experiencing draped the excitement with an cloud of sadness.

At the top of his concerns was his fear for the kids' safety. When Bob had phoned and insisted on meeting for lunch, Buck vetoed the proposal immediately. Now, as he recalled the conversation, a lump of pride melted some of the fear. Bob had said, "Sunny and I will be very, very careful. You know, we didn't just get off the bus. We'll make it just fine. So, Dad, we're *going* to be there. You coming?"

Damn kid! Buck smiled. He's going to turn out all right. But Buck knew that it was time to cut away from Sunny just a little and give more to Bob. Shouldn't be too difficult, he thought. Sunny will catch on quickly—even help. Somehow, the troubles with Bob didn't seem so serious now. He just wanted to be with him, to be his father. Funny, he mused, it doesn't take anything but a few seconds of ecstasy to become a father. Almost anyone can do it. But it takes a different kind of effort than he'd made to be a parent, a *real* parent. Didn't always use his head. Fourth quarter now, and he was behind.

He almost missed them on his first scan of the inside dining room. Then, the attractive couple seated at a table near the harbor side window caught his eye. The handsome, young man wore sharply creased, gray trousers and a navy blazer over a striped shirt and colorful tie. His partner's deep tan contrasted with her blond hair and yellow calf-length shirtdress. Striking—both of them! A sculptor's chisel couldn't have removed the smile from Buck's face as the two jumped up and hurried to meet him.

"Dad—" Bob's voice choked as they joined in a three-way embrace.

"Oh, Daddy, it's *so* good to see you!" Sunny added, hopping lightly on her toes as she had done in particularly joyous times since she was a little girl.

Buck felt a warmth swell within him. As he gave Bob's shoulders a second squeeze, he saw that his own eyes were not the only watery ones. In times past, he would have felt embarrassed by such a display in public. Finally, they separated, and the kids led the way to their table. Buck looked down at his polo shirt and jeans. He laughed.

"Normally, Bob, I'd be on your case for sloppy dress. Now look at us."

"Gotcha this time, Dad."

"What a pleasant putdown," Buck laughed. "I love it!"

Bob ordered wine, and the threesome sat for a moment, quietly smiling at one another.

"How's your mother doing?" Buck asked.

"Oh, Mom's doing okay. I thought she ought to know what's going on, just in case the hoods decide to reach out and touch someone," Bob's voice trailed off.

"How'd she take it?" Buck asked.

"Surprisingly well," Bob said. "Oh, she had to make the expected remarks about your 'childish, physical approach to things. Her Howard was man enough that he wouldn't need to resort to such nonsense.'"

"Too bad her manly Howard wasn't in that parking lot the other night," Buck replied. "I could have used his help."

"But, you know what?" Bob went on. "I picked up the feeling that, despite what she was saying, Mom felt real respect for you."

"That's—surprising, but good, I guess. Any sign of Amato or Murrell?"

"No," they said in unison.

"Are you being careful? Watching the rear view mirror?"

"*Watching* it!" Bob said. "Jennifer was so busy watching it she drove right through a red light in downtown Long Beach."

The familiar blond waitress served their wine. She directed a long smile at Bob, winked at Buck, and hurried off. Sunny's twinkling eyes met Buck's. Bob blushed and looked away.

"To family," Buck toasted, "and to the two finest kids any man ever had." Six eyes threatened to fill once again. Sunny sidetracked the emotions.

"We read all about the raids and how you kicked ASH," she said, grinning devilishly. "It looks like you finished *that* group off, Dad."

"Really," Buck hesitated. "I hope not."

"You *what*?" Bob asked.

"Seriously, we need groups like that. They're an example of democracy in action at the grass roots level, of people who rise up and take action instead of just sitting around bitching." Buck sipped his wine, then continued, "They're fine, they're necessary . . . until they lose their objectivity. Then they become part of the problem instead of the solution."

"That's my father talking?" Bob asked with a smile and a quick glance in Sunny's direction. Her dimpled smile was her reply.

"Our contamination threat, along with some others," Buck went on, "has been compounded by the contamination of our political system. The little people take on these causes with *no* thought to compromise, and our political leaders dilute the solutions because they're *too* willing to compromise.

In between are the greedy people who take advantage of the situation to make a buck."

"Can I quote you?" Sunny asked. "I have a professor who would be impressed with that speech." The waitress served their sandwiches and cast another admiring look at Bob. Sunny laughed, and Bob blushed again.

"How are things going at the ship?" Bob asked.

Buck gave a brief account of the previous day, including his blunder with the weapon. "It's too early to measure the indirect benefits from the newspaper articles," he said. "But they certainly dissolved the picket lines."

They ate in silence for several minutes. Buck was deep in thought.

It was time to face the big hurdle, and he was searching for words he had seldom used.

"Kids, I apologize for getting you involved in this stinking mess," Buck said, "and I apologize for not doing a better job as a father, especially for you, Bob."

"Oh, Dad, you've got it wrong—" Sunny said.

"No, I mean it. I've really botched up a lot of things. The only thing I can say in my defense, I did the best I could with what I knew at the time."

"Isn't that really what we *all* do?" Bob said, looking directly at Buck.

"If you mean *everybody*, no, but I think *we* do," Buck replied.

They chatted for some time as they ate. Then, Bob brought up the subject of Lenny.

"I'm just wondering if you should be thinking of *any* woman at a time like this, a time when you're up against so much, and getting beat on and everything."

"Kids," Buck said, determination bouncing from each syllable, "Lenny is a fine woman. And I admit, I have strong feelings for her. But if anything, she's a result of the crises—not a cause. And nothing's happened."

"Bobby," said Sunny, "I think this would be a good time, the best time, don't you?"

"Time for what?" quizzed Buck.

"Time to tell you something that's about three years overdue," Sunny replied.

Buck turned to Bob and waited. His son's face showed that he was flustered, perhaps embarrassed.

"Well, Dad," Bob began slowly, "I could take all day dressing this up until I think it's just right. The truth of the matter is, *I* owe *you* the apology."

"What in the world for?" Buck asked.

"Back when you and Mom split up, I made some mistakes. I was really upset, scared, and confused. I guess I read some of my own thoughts into the situation, and I've been trying ever since to make them true—just so I'd be right. Jennifer and I have discussed—"

"Argued, Bobby," cut in Sunny.

"Yeah, argued," corrected Bob. "I had made up my mind that you were the one who caused the divorce, that you forced Mom out. Mom never really said anything like that, but I guess it's what I wanted her to say or thought she should say." He tilted his head back and stared at the ceiling for some time before continuing, "I apologize, Dad. I've tried to resist being judgmental, but I admit, my mind was made up. Sorry."

The look on Bob's face was enough. Buck wouldn't have needed the apology.

"Is *that* what our stand-off has been, Bob?" Buck asked.

Bob looked down and slowly nodded his head.

"It's okay, Son. I'm really impressed with the fact that you could deal with that, especially now, of all times. We've got so much water going over the dam right now, it's hard to catch just a cupful. How about you, Sunny, you okay with that?"

"Oh, Dad," Sunny replied, her blue eyes flashing above the dimpled smile. "I never had any trouble with it. If I ever sounded like it, I was just fishing. Anyway, this Lenny sounds absolutely fascinating. Just think, a real, live, beautiful female detective—"

"Who said she was beautiful?" Buck cut in. "I didn't say that."

"Oh, but you did, Dad, you did," Sunny replied coyly, reaching across the table to squeeze Buck's hand. "I'd like to meet her sometime. A female detective—cool."

"Now, Bob," Buck said, "you also have to be careful not to focus this blame stuff on your mom. There's no need for her to go through all the examination and self-doubt that I've been dealing with. With all of my introspective searching, all of my questions over these last three years I've only managed to come up with yet two more questions: What did I do that made her want to leave? And will I ever be able to trust another woman?"

"Any answers?" Bob asked.

"First question, I think I've finally accepted a few things. The marriage was not the right match in the first place. It was doomed from day one, only I had blinders on for almost twenty years. If she needed to get out to be happy, then it's all for the best. And just look at the fabulous two kids we produced. *This* glass is *far* more than half-full!"

"And the second question, Dad?" said Sunny. Her eyes narrowed.

"I'm not over the finish line yet, but I really think I'm making big strides on that one."

"Lenny?"

Buck smiled. Then he checked his watch. "Look, kids, I've got to get back. But I want you to know I'm very, very proud of you, both of you, for the way you're handling all this."

"Uh, Dad," Bob began, "can you sit long enough for a couple more questions?"

"Why—sure," Buck replied.

"The raids were successful, but that wasn't the end, was it, Daddy?" Sunny asked.

"I think it was—" He paused. "No, I don't think that was the end."

"You expect trouble on the ship?" she asked.

"Yes . . . I expect trouble of some kind. I won't lie to you. We know there's a spy in our operation, but I haven't dug him out."

"Have you thought of calling in sick?" Bob asked. Buck smiled.

"That was a joke," Bob said. He looked Buck in the eye and smiled timidly.

"I know that, Bob. Were you in my place, we know *you'd* never call in sick. No, I'd say that was thoughtful," Buck said, "and yes, I've thought of it. Now, I really don't want to leave you guys, but I do have to get back. More than that, I'm very nervous about you two being out and around, out in the open, especially in *this* neighborhood."

With a quick swipe, Sunny snatched up the check. Pointing a finger at Buck, she silently quashed his protest. Then, while Buck watched with amusement, she wiggled her fingers at Bob, and the siblings pooled their resources. When Sunny headed for the register, Bob discreetly added two dollars to the tip.

"Promise me," Buck said as the threesome headed across the street to the parking lot, "that you'll be careful, be *sure* you're not being followed?"

"Relax, Dad," Bob said. "We know every street and alley between here and Laguna Hills. We're on our home court. We can bury those punks from New Jersey in traffic so thick they'll wish they were back in Hackensack."

Buck conceded that Bob was probably right, but the prospect raised the ugly specter of risk in his mind. He kissed them both and watched as they confidently drove off with Sunny behind the wheel. As they made a turn toward the parking lot exit, a black car fell in behind them. Buck froze momentarily.

"Oh, no!" he said under his breath, breaking into a run for the Camaro. As he triggered the remote to unlock the door, the two cars had cleared the parking lot and were coming down the street past his position. He stretched for a clear view over the parked cars and through the chain-link fence, straining for a glimpse of the occupants of the black car. The driver, a young woman about Sunny's age, was alone in the auto. On his return trip to the shipyard, Buck scrutinized every black automobile he saw.

* * *

Buck met Peter in Peter's office Saturday afternoon for a last conference on what he called, *The State of the Ark.* They poured over all aspects of the operation, political and operational. With most of the heavy stuff covered, Peter asked about the kids.

"Yeah, Peter, they called to let me know they got back to the hotel okay. Couple of wise guys, but they are smart. Just a little too gutsy for their own good," Buck replied.

"Wonder where they picked *that* up," Peter said with his trademark smirk.

"I only hope they won't leave the hotel again while I'm gone."

"You can just about bet they will. But tell you what, I'll check with them a couple of times a day. Maybe a couple daily doses of fear will help keep them off the streets. Anything from your detective *friend* on Amato and Murrell?" Peter asked.

"Going to call her as soon as we're done here," Buck replied. "She said she'd leave word on my voice mail yesterday, but nothing yet." Buck got up to leave. "I'm glad we had this last little meeting, Peter. And I can't tell you how glad I am that you canceled your Belgium trip.

It's good to know you'll be here to handle whatever comes up at this end. I'd have felt pretty lonely out there on that floating bomb with you seven thousand miles away. Thanks, ol' bud."

"The least I can do. I'll keep my cell handy, even take it to bed with me," Peter said, rounding the desk and giving Buck a light high-five. "Good luck."

Back in his dingy office, Buck called Lenny.

"Hello."

"Hi, Lenny, it's Buck. I've tried to call you a couple of times, but you were out carousing or something."

"I can assure you, it was the 'something,' not the 'carousing,'" she said coolly. Buck waited—nothing more. "Are you okay?" he finally asked.

"I'm fine, thank you."

"Good. I was wondering, if you don't have to go on duty this afternoon, I'd like to see you," he said.

"No, not a good idea."

"Does that mean you have something else planned, or it's not a good idea?"

"Both."

Buck was stymied. He groped for his next words, afraid that any he tried would come out wrong. He'd never encountered *this* Lenny.

"Okay—something's wrong. What is it?" he demanded.

"Buck, if you have to ask, you wouldn't understand the answer," she replied.

"Look, I called because—I've missed you. I needed to hear your voice. But the one I'm hearing is somebody else. I may be mistaken, but I really think I deserve better, so why not try me?"

"Oh, Buck," she began, her voice softening, "I—I'm embarrassed, embarrassed to death by that big show I put on in the hospital, and in front of that nurse!"

"Did my 'I've got a headache' routine embarrass you?" he asked.

"No, you big dummy. I just lost it! Of all the times and places, I picked *that* one to let my feelings put my brain on hold. The things I did, the things I said. I meant all of them, but what lousy timing. I've never been such a klutz in my whole life. I just *lost* it!"

"Thank you," Buck said, "thank you for the explanation. Now let me tell you something. I've never been so flattered, felt so honored in *my* whole life. If I hadn't been in such God awful pain, you and I would still be in that hospital bed, even with the whole staff watching. I thought I'd made it to heaven, and then the gates slammed shut. Now, I want to see you in an hour. Where you going to be? If you say, 'Moscow,' I'll be there."

"Buck—it's still not a good idea, not with things the way they are." Lenny's voice had recovered the soft alto quality that held Buck like a magnet clutching a paper clip. "Do you remember anything I said Thursday night? Nothing's changed. I have to wait. You know what's going to happen if we get together. I just can't let a physical bond cloud our thinking. And it will, Buck. It will."

"But Lenny, I'm getting tired of being so damned noble. All I seem to get for it is another kick in the butt. Now I'm getting kicked from two directions." Buck's warm, loving feelings were sliding into the realm of frustration.

"I think I understand how you feel, Buck. But you're not getting kicked by me. I'm frustrated, too. After all, I have terribly strong feelings for you, but I have to be sure of *you*. This isn't like most love triangles, but with those doubts you have, left over from your marriage, it's still a triangle. No, I'm not going to let myself get drawn into another one. Remember, the last triangle I got tangled up in? I lost."

"Part of my mind follows you clearly," Buck said, "but the rest of me doesn't buy it."

"I understand that, too. Now, listen to me carefully. You mean an awfully lot to me, Buck. That's *my* problem. You have to get past your bad marriage. That's *yours*. You concentrate on solving yours. If you can't do that, I'm history, and we'll both be glad we didn't go any farther than we did. If it turns out that your bad marriage baggage is finally gone, then my problem will be taken care of. In the meantime, we're back to a professional relationship—strictly professional."

"But I—"

"And Buck, I think I know you. You'll handle this."

Buck knew he'd gotten the last word. He hated the word, but he had even greater respect for the speaker. He wanted to see her. He ached to see her. He was tempted to hang up and hit the road for Lenny's place, to tell her he loved her, to show her he loved her. But along with the heavy aching in his heart, there was a prickly buzzing in his mind. When he sifted through the buzzing, the message came clear. She's right. Do it right.

"Okay, Lenny, I'm going to try. I don't know what the future's going to bring, and I sure don't know what might happen in the next ten days. So I want you to know, I *do* love you." He felt his eyes water at the words. "Yes, I really do mean that."

Seconds passed. "Okay, Buck, let's check things." Her business voice began to crack. "You leave early in the morning. Anything yet on your spy?"

"Blank—zippo! It's going to be play-it-by-ear."

"You'll handle it. Remember what you've learned. Okay, I have Peter Hamlin's numbers, the ship's COM-SAT number, and the hotel where your family's staying. Anything else?"

"You have someone checking on the families?"

"Of course. I've not gotten a full-time guard, yet, but I'll make sure someone's in frequent contact with your kids. And no, Buck, no word on Amato and Murrell yet. But they'll turn up," she assured him.

"Oh, I *know* that."

Chapter 29

Buck reached again for his coffee. He was short on sleep, but the way he felt that morning, he really didn't need the coffee for a fix. The early predawn darkness had found a rush of activities aboard *Ark II*. Although routine to the sailors aboard, each task had added new impulses to the mounting electricity. *Ark II* is going to sea, Buck mused. *I'm* going to sea!

Over bacon, eggs, and cakes, he reflected on the events of the previous day. Basking in the warmth of the love Bob and Sunny had shown, he smiled. Never had he been more proud of them. Bob had broken out of the side-choosing mode. Now they were both supportive toward both parents. What more could be asked?

After the meeting with Peter came his heart-wrenching talk with Lenny. He had grappled with the matter well into the night. Many times, he'd tried to convince himself that he had simply been trying to get her into bed. It would be easier then to say, "Okay, no big deal, didn't get it done." But he hadn't convinced himself, however, and sometime between ten and midnight he had accepted the truth. Lenny was beautiful, certainly desirable, but it was her spirit, along with her tender warmth, that had derailed him. Finally, after too much contemplation, he had popped a couple of Tylenols, told himself repeatedly to focus only on the job at hand, and drifted off to a welcome sleep.

On his tour of the deck before breakfast, he had watched the crew members disconnect the massive hoses and swing the vertical booms, from which the hoses dangled like gigantic snakes, back to shore. He had felt the sudden surge of vibrations in his feet as the two monstrous two-thousand-horsepower Caterpillar diesels revved up several times. It seemed they were preparing for a drag race. Then they settled back to the almost imperceptible hum that was felt as much as heard.

And while the crew had gone about their duties with professionalism, Buck had detected yet another boost in their enthusiasm. It was time to face their calling, to take this expensive experiment out into the huge Pacific, shepherd her through her duties, and bring her back again.

Alone at his table, Buck became absorbed in the familiarity of the officers' mess. It was more than an eating place. It was the gathering place. At the third table, Dr. Keene was carrying on what seemed to be a rather strained, almost too polite conversation with the three observers from the EPA. The youthful genius had to be feeling immense pressure.

Buck wondered if the observers even knew what they were here for. In earlier discussions among company officials, he had picked up disturbing condemnations of EPA representatives, implications that at least some of them didn't even comprehend the working vocabulary of their profession. Man, he thought, that's like sending officials who had never seen a game onto an NFL football field. Seems to me the agency would send the best they have on a test burn such as this.

He strained to pick up the conversation, but the occasional bits and pieces made no sense. Perhaps Dr. Keene was sounding them out to determine the extent that politics might play in their evaluation. Peter had laid out the possibilities. The observers might come aboard with instructions to recommend approval, no matter what; to recommend disapproval, no matter what; or to perform a completely objective evaluation. The EPA's abrupt abandonment of the previous sea-going incineration project was etched indelibly in all of the minds at Essee Beecee.

The Sunday morning sun had just exposed a sliver of itself in the east as Buck went topside. During his earlier expedition, he had checked the small picket boats off the starboard side. They had been drifting quietly, about fifty feet away. He decided to have another look. As he reached the boat deck on the starboard side, he saw Gantsky on the small, steel-grated platform amidship. The second was waving frantically at Buck and then pointing over the side.

What's he trying to say? Gantsky's shouts were swallowed up by the sounds from the ship and the pier. Buck leaned over the rail and looked toward Gantsky's position. Suddenly he understood. A grappling hook had snared the rail, and suspended from the hook was a knotted rope. Half-way up the rope was a man climbing with surprising agility toward the rail. Gantsky was once again waving, gesturing something to Buck. He had something in one hand. What was it? His other hand pointed, jabbed toward Buck. Buck was confused again. What is he trying to say?

"Behind you, Barnum! Behind you!" came a voice from high on the bridge wing above Buck. He looked up. It was Captain Portner. Buck glanced again at Gantsky. His back was turned, and he seemed to be doing something with the rope. One arm moved in a sawing motion. Buck turned and looked behind him. "Over here!" the captain shouted again, pointing to an area near Buck. It was then that Buck spotted it, another grappling hook about five feet away. Buck leaned over. Sure enough, there was someone on the rope, just clearing the small boat below. Buck tugged at the hook, but with the weight of the climber, he couldn't budge it.

"Over to your right!" the captain's voice said. "There, in the corner! By the lifeboat!"

Following the captain's directions, Buck moved to the bow of the lifeboat. There, on the deck next to the lifeboat stanchion, lay a hacksaw. Suddenly it all made sense! He snatched up the hacksaw and ran back to the hook. His man was but ten feet from the bottom rail. Buck attacked the one-inch hemp rope. He was surprised at how fast the blade melted its way through the sturdy fibers. A few more strokes—he was going to make it! He glanced down at the invader.

The man understood his predicament. He had stopped climbing. His feet had slipped from the side of the ship, and he dangled there, swaying from side to side. Buck hesitated. Below him was a face warped with fear, its two huge, round eyes pleading.

Buck looked over toward Gantsky's position in time to see the rope part and the climber, his arms flailing wildly, fall toward the boat from which he'd come. *Thud!* He bounced off the boat's gunwhale and splashed into the channel. Ouch! Buck thought. Could have killed him. He returned his attention to his own climber.

"Move the boat!" the man screamed to his cohorts below. "Move the boat!"

"He's right!" Buck shouted. "Move the boat. He's coming down!"

Having seen the fall of the first climber, those in the boat below pushed themselves away from the hull of *Ark II*. He looked one last time into the helpless face of the boarder, and with three decisive thrusts, he finished the cut. His victim dropped over backwards and plummeted like a rigid mannequin, still holding the rope in both hands, to the water below. *Smack!* Though the raider landed flat on his back, it reminded Buck of the worst belly flop he had ever seen.

A cheer went the length of the ship, and when Buck looked up, he realized that he and Gantsky had been joined by more than a dozen of the crew. They had stationed themselves at intervals the length of the ship and were armed with knives, saws, and clippers, ready for any more boarding attempts.

The fallen intruders were retrieved by their respective boatmen. The boat beneath Buck eased off to a safe distance, while the one beneath Gantsky accelerated rapidly toward the back channel with its seriously injured mate. Buck removed the grappling hook from the rail.

"Nice souvenir, don't you think?" he said to Dick Hobbs.

Gantsky, however, leaned back and hurled his hook toward one of the remaining boats. It punched a hole in the windshield before glancing off into the water. He turned toward Buck, clasped his hands above his head, and laughed, joined by more cheers from his mates.

"Dick, is this standard procedure? I mean, do we always keep hacksaws scattered about the deck?"

"Damn, you think we're a bunch of cut-ups?" A wide grin split the freckled face from ear to ear. "That was the chief's idea. He thought those crazies might try to board us."

"What's that?" Buck asked, aware of a new vibration.

"Starting up the bowthruster. Gonna get the hell out of here before those fruitcakes try something else," Hobbs said. "You can hear and feel it more than the two drive engines because it's up here in the bow. Looks like we're about set." He disappeared into the forehouse.

Buck moved over to the port side, the grappling hook still in his hand. There on the pier were Hudson, Peter, Craws, and Roland, along with the entire shop crew. He waved the grappling hook in the air.

"Finally got a souvenir that doesn't bleed!" he shouted, holding up the three-pronged piece. They smiled and looked at him quizzically. Buck realized then that, because of their port side vantage point, they were unaware of the starboard side encounter with the radical invaders. And he'd gotten *no* photos!

"Stand by your lines," the loudspeaker from the bridge blared. Buck felt his throat tighten. Damn, we're really on our way, he thought. With the loading completed and the tanks sealed, he'd been given clearance to take a few photos. He checked the Canon and began to shoot. The group on the pier, with the three large buildings in the background. The tall booms with their lethargic, dangling snakes. The men aboard and on the pier, ready at their lines.

"Let go number one! Take in number one!"

The deck vibrated slightly, a slow, rhythmic vibration, as the main propellers began to churn the water. Ever so slowly, *Ark II* inched backwards. Then Buck heard the bowthruster engine increase its speed. Like magic, the bow began to move to the right, away from the dock.

"Let go number four! Take in number four!"

Buck snapped a shot of the two seamen retrieving the thick, heavy stern line. We're on our way, he thought. A few crewmen waved and exchanged last minute shouts with shop men on the pier. As they moved out into the channel, the executives were watching and talking among themselves. Peter gave one last wave, and Buck responded.

He stayed on the port side forecastle deck while *Ark II* traveled the quarter-mile to the intersection with the main channel. As they passed the container terminal there were people standing on the pier watching. A few waved, a neighborly gesture, Buck thought. The unusual ship must have been the subject of many conversations around the harbor over recent months.

He watched the parade of shapes drifting past. He could smell the salt air, feel the hum of the engines and the pulsing throb of the propellers, and he could hear the swishing of the water as it gave way to *Ark II*. Using the bowthruster once again, they brought the ship through a hard left turn and headed south, down the main channel toward the outer harbor. Buck crossed over to the starboard side and moved farther forward. Trailing banners, two of the remaining small boats had moved up ahead, and the other two had chosen spots along the port and starboard sides, cruising just outside of the bigger ship's wake. Buck couldn't make out the printing on their banners, but he recalled his session with Reicher. He knew he'd seen those very banners.

Ahead, on the starboard side, they were about to pass two huge cruise ships at their moorings. Still farther up, Buck could see the white, rectangular box that was the Los Angeles Maritime Museum, and beyond that were the many shops of Ports O' Call. Far ahead in the outer harbor, a freighter, its decks stacked high with containers headed toward them.

A pair of large brown herons clambered clumsily up from the water, reluctant to challenge *Ark II*. Buck watched them struggle upward to about thirty feet, glide gracefully off toward the museum, and touch down near the sea wall. There was a small group of people standing near the museum. They were waving. Buck waved back, and as he did, the intensity of their gestures caused him to look more closely.

Why that's—Sunny! Sunny and Bob, and Tim! He felt his eyes filling. He glanced around. Nobody close by. Good. All that encouragement from the kids was fresh in his mind. He waved again and gave them the thumbs up sign.

As the interval between them swelled, about to break the bond, Buck noticed someone else returning the thumbs up. Standing to his family's right and some distance behind them was an attractive woman with short brown hair. She didn't seem to be smiling, but she held her thumb high in the air. He gave one last response, with extra emphasis. She turned quickly and melted into the crowd.

Walking briskly across to the port side, Buck reached for his handkerchief. A numb hollow feeling settled in his gut, and he felt himself choking up. Damn! he thought. I'm about to start bawling like a baby. He leaned on the port railing, drew several deep breaths, and gradually rejected the demon. Then he turned, stepped into the forehouse, and hurried up the steps to the bridge. He'd duck the whole thing. Escape!

"Right, five degrees rudder," the harbor pilot directed, as Buck entered the bridge.

"Right, five degrees rudder, sir," the helmsman repeated, adjusting their course.

"Like to leave a little more space between us and that incoming freighter," the pilot explained.

Buck looked ahead. The incoming container ship was several hundred yards ahead and to the port side. She was beginning to angle towards them, aiming for the mouth of the main channel. It appeared they would meet just at the point where the main channel opened wide into the outer harbor.

A feather-light vibration tingled through Buck's feet. He felt his body lean slightly to the right.

"Who ordered the bowthruster?" Captain Portner demanded.

"Nobody, sir. It's not—"

"It sure as hell is! Shut it down!" the captain barked.

"Yes, sir—bowthruster off. Sir! It won't shut down. It's not responding!"

Buck looked ahead. The bow was easing slightly to the left, gaining momentum with each second. If the move wasn't corrected, it would pull them directly into the path of the oncoming freighter! The captain whipped his walkie-talkie from his belt.

"Chief! Chief! Where are you?" A burst of static was followed by a garbled reply that Buck couldn't make out. "Chief, get up forward on the double! Get that bowthruster shut down! It's not responding to the bridge!"

"Aye—" *crackle* "—Cap'n."

The harbor pilot stepped to one side, tacitly returning command of the ship to Captain Portner. The immediate threat they faced pertained to *his* ship and were out of the pilot's domain.

"Try full starboard on the thruster!" the captain ordered.

"Nothing, sir. No response."

The bow of *Ark II* had come around ten degrees to port.

The freighter continued toward them, perhaps a hundred yards away, and as she closed she grew larger. She was already too close to the entrance of the main channel to attempt a turn to her right. Her captain was faced with two options. Try to stop—unlikely. Turn to her left—very risky, since he had no way of predicting the eventual position of *Ark II* and would place the burden of liability on his ship. Another couple of minutes, and *Ark II* would be set up for a broadside collision!

Buck stood there in a strange new world, helpless. The threat was beyond his domain. But the oncoming disaster certainly involved him. Wait a minute, he thought. The bowthruster circuit box, down at second deck level near the machinery rooms, where Callin had been checking it—

"Right, full rudder! All engines back full!" Captain Portner directed.

The helmsman responded.

"Callin!" Buck shouted. "It's Callin!" He ran for the interior stairs and plunged down the winding encasement, his hands sliding on the rails for balance and his feet but touching occasional steps. As he descended, the sound of the powerful bowthruster engine became louder. He reached forecastle level and gripped the railing hard to swing himself around the turn.

"Umph!" A pile-driving fist smashed Buck in the midsection. The impact closed his eyes and sent him sucking for air to the tiled floor in the passageway. Get up! Get up! he told himself. As he rolled over to his hands and knees, he saw a figure dart through the opening to the starboard forecastle deck. Callin? It might have been Callin. Drawing on determination, Buck struggled to his feet and headed for the outer deck. Nothing he could do to help the chief. But if that was Callin—Buck burst through the doorway and onto the focusle deck. "Ho–ly—!"

He froze momentarily, as though some force had bonded his feet to the deck. Fifty yards away was the rusty-black freighter towering far above him. It had slowed considerably, but still it came, mushing the water with its gigantic, ugly bow—directly toward him! But the motion of *Ark II* had changed—it felt different. The bow had nearly completed a one-eighty degree turn, and it was still swinging to the left. But the general movement of the ship was no longer to the front and left. She was now moving backward and to the right.

Something near the lifeboat caught Buck's attention. He started slowly back, moving cautiously to the inboard side of the lifeboat. No sign of anyone. Passing the front stanchion, he started to bend for a look under the boat.

A pair of hands flashed out from beneath the lifeboat and grabbed his ankles. They jerked hard, and Buck's feet went out from under him. He landed on his back, his hardhat clunking against the steel deck and then tumbling off to the side. A wiry figure scrambled spiderlike over him and ran toward the bow.

"Callin!"

Buck sprang to his feet and raced forward after the sailor. He caught him at the starboard rail as Callin was hoisting himself, preparing to jump. Buck could feel the smaller man's strength as they fell to the deck. The little seaman was surprisingly strong, and he was quick. They rolled about, struggling for control. Buck's left hand had a grip on Callin's jacket, and he clutched it tightly. Callin grabbed Buck's hair with one hand. His other fist flailed against Buck's chest and face. But they were so close the seaman had no damaging leverage behind his blows. Rolling to one side, Buck found a point of balance where he had the advantage. He struggled to his feet and straightened up, pulling Callin up with him. Callin managed a couple of glancing blows to Buck's cheeks. Still holding Callin with his left hand, Buck smashed a hard right to his face. As the lighter man fell backward, Buck released his grip, and Callin went sprawling to the center of the forecastle deck.

Confident that he had control of the situation, Buck relaxed slightly and took a deep breath.

Too late, he realized his mistake. Spencer Callin had hit the deck, stunned for a second. But when Buck failed to follow up, the seaman rolled over and jumped to his feet like a cat. He sprang toward the portside gunwhale, and before Buck could catch him, he disappeared head first over the side.

Buck reached the gunwhale in time to see a pair of blue jean-clad legs swallowed up by the turbulent, murky water. As Buck waited, watching for his adversary to surface, a monstrous dark shape glided slowly past on his right. The freighter! It was perhaps twenty feet away, and the enormous hull was nearly parallel to *Ark II*. He could hear the engines of the freighter rumbling, the props straining in reverse to stop the behemoth. *Ark II* was now moving ever so slightly left—and backward!

Buck watched the swirling water off the port bow. No sign of Callin yet. Yet? There *had* to be. He had to be back up! Then came the sound of shouts from the deck of the freighter. Buck looked up. Two seamen were shouting something in Japanese and pointing to the water between the ships. Buck crossed over to starboard and looked down. It was like an immense cauldron. Huge, boiling bubbles from the exhaust side of the bowthruster propeller broke the surface, churning the dark channel waters like a giant mixer.

His eyes followed the gestures of the two crewmen. There! An arm broke the surface. There he is! Buck thought. But something else caught his eye, something in the water about twenty feet from Callin—a foot—a leg! It took a moment before the puzzle registered, and when it did, it went straight to Buck's stomach. Just as he leaned over the gunwhale and heaved his bitterness to the water below, the bowthruster engine groaned to a stop.

Chapter 30

Ark II rode low in the water, anchored in the outer harbor away from the shipping lanes. Buck sat alone on the rear upper deck just aft of the incinerator stacks. His feet dangled over the edge, high above the stern deck. To his left was the high hill of San Pedro. Sweeping the panorama from left to right, he scanned the Vincent Thomas bridge, the old Long Beach Naval Shipyard, the Long Beach skyline, the tourist attraction *Queen Mary*, the water inlet to the Naples Plaza area, and far down the Orange County coast to the south. From his vantage point, he could see forever, but try as he might he couldn't see the future.

The gentle sea breezes dropped out of a beautiful afternoon sky and brushed his skin like invisible feathers drifting across the deck. The sun had reached its zenith and was beginning its long descent to the Far East. Under other circumstances, it would have been a truly seductive way to spend a gorgeous, peaceful afternoon. Instead, as he sat there in the lazy sun, Buck teetered on the edge of another confusing self-analysis.

Despite his attempts to control his thoughts, some mysterious force seemed to perpetuate replays of the day's bizarre events. A man was killed, chopped into pieces. Yes, Buck thought, Callin had asked for it. He wasn't exactly setting off ladyfingers on the Fourth of July. He could have killed a lot of people with that bowthruster trick. What if we'd collided with that big ship and blown up? Every way Buck examined the experience, it came down to one simple fact—Callin had jumped. Sure, I might have done things differently. But the fact remains, Callin jumped—his mistake—but he jumped.

The coast guard had boarded *Ark II* hours before, and their investigation was well underway. The container ship had been directed to continue on to its pier. Presumably, its records, officers, and crew were being subjected to the same scrutiny applied to all ships involved in accidents or near misses.

The investigators were pouring over *Ark II's* records, the log, radio communications records, course recorder, fathometer recordings, piloting charts, and audio/video tapes of activities on the bridge during the emergency. In addition, they had begun interviews with crew members who had any information to contribute. If the coast guard was satisfied with what they learned, *Ark II* might be free to resume the voyage sometime Monday morning.

Buck had to hand it to Captain Portner for dodging that collision the way he did. That was a masterpiece. He flopped back on the deck and propped his hardhat over his face. The pungent odor of sweat within the helmet somehow brought to mind floating arms and legs.

"Shut it off, damn it, shut it off," he mumbled.

"You talking to me?" a voice said.

Buck flipped the hat off with an index finger, blinked against the bright sun, and finally focused on Peter.

"How'd you get here?"

"Company boat. They told me you were back here somewhere. Tough time?"

"Uh, huh. But I'm *winning* this one."

"You know, Buck, there's absolutely nothing in any of the statements to the Coast guard that incriminates or blames you in any way," Peter said, sitting down beside Buck. "You didn't throw him overboard." The breeze blew Peter's tie up in his face. He grabbed it and tucked into his shirt.

Buck lay there, silent for some time. "Something else really bothering me," he said. "How did he screw up the bowthruster so they couldn't control it from the bridge?"

"The chief says Callin had it all rigged in advance, an override switch. He could flip the switch, and it simply cut the circuit from the bridge control. When the time came, he opened the circuit box, flipped the override switch, started up the bowthruster, set the pitch control to port, and revved it up. Then he shut the box and locked it with a bicycle chain and padlock."

"Yeah, that's kind of what I figured. That's what he was doing when I surprised him down there. He told me he was just checking it—and I bought it. I really blew *that* one."

"You going to blame yourself for that, too?" Peter looked at Buck sternly.

Buck tilted his head up toward Peter and grinned. "No question

Roger A. Naylor

about it. But I get your point. You're right." Then he jerked to a sitting position, grabbed his hardhat, and banged it on the deck. "Hamlinio, how'd you get so smart?"

"Not smart, just a little different angle on things. You okay?"

"I'm okay—all done kicking myself in the butt every time something goes wrong."

"Good. That's settled. Now, I have to lay something else on you."

"I don't think I want to hear this."

"I'm sure you *don't* want to hear this." Peter hesitated for a moment. "Ed cracked this morning."

"I thought he might. I told him he'd better talk to you. What did he do, tell you off?"

"More than that."

"He didn't quit, did he?"

"No. He got fired."

"He wha-a-at?" Buck looked at Peter, expecting to see the familiar smirk, but Peter's long, rugged face was nothing but serious, very serious.

"He came in this morning, in sheer panic," Peter went on.

"About what the Osmundson people might do?"

"Uh huh. But he went crazy, really crazy. I got a little tough with him, and out it came."

"Out *what* came?"

"The whole story. It amounted to a confession." Peter looked off into the distance as though he were studying something. "Ed is our spy. He's been working for the organized crime group. He's been feeding them information about the ship—and about you. He gave them a complete set of the ship's drawings and specs, and he kept them informed about what you were up to."

"That's impossible! He'd nev—" Buck choked on the word. "Why, that phony son of a bitch! You mean, he set me up so they could work me over?"

"Not with that intent, but yes. That's how they caught up with you before you were even out of the starting gate."

Buck's anger shot to the top. Raw angry heat radiated from his face.

But strangely, something blanketed the anger, kept it from exploding. Confused, he shook his head.

"Damn! Next to you, he's the *last* person I'd have suspected. But why? Money?"

"Believe it or not, there are two good things about this. One, it wasn't money. In fact, he claims he received no money at all. It was a different kind of extortion."

"Extortion?"

"It seems that his daughter's troubles out east were much bigger than he let on. Apparently she got in with the wrong crowd, got hooked on their drugs, and disappeared. Ed tried to write her, tried to phone her. No luck. He even went to New York once to try to find her. Nothing. The police didn't have a clue. When he got back, he got a call. The caller claimed to know where she was, said he had complete control over her. Finding himself cornered, Ed complied with a couple of their demands. And—"

"And once he got in, he couldn't get out," Buck finished. "But the police raids were successful. How could that happen? Schutte's people should have been long gone."

"That's the other *good* thing. Apparently, that's where Ed drew the line. He *didn't* tip them. Are—you bitter," Peter asked, "about the grief he caused you?"

Buck drew a deep breath and slowly exhaled.

"No, not now. Not after hearing the rest. No, Peter, I feel sorry for him. At least my little gang was right here where we could investigate and get somewhere. Wouldn't stand a chance against unknown hoods three thousand miles away." Buck plunked his hardhat onto his head and got to his feet. "So what happens now? You pressing charges?" Buck looked directly into Peter's dark eyes.

"No. We have a tentative deal. He says he'll cooperate with us and testify. If he does, no charges. And I'll do what I can to help him get another job. I think he can really help us." Peter said.

"That's awfully generous," Buck said, unsure of how he really felt about the proposition. "What's tentative about it?"

"I told him it's subject to *your* approval," Peter said softly. "You're the one who got his bell rung. It's your call, Buck. I have to tell you, if we charge him along with the rest, there's still a good chance we'd get some good testimony from him at trial."

"You're serious?" Buck asked.

"Never more."

"What about his missing daughter? As soon as they find out Ed's been exposed, she's a gone goose, isn't she?"

"Possibly. I've talked with Dante. He has good contacts in the Jersey area, people like himself who know what goes on. He says there's a chance she's already dead, a chance they'll kill her, but also a chance they'll just dump her out somewhere, especially if she's been strung out on drugs for some time, no real threat to them. He says they don't wipe people out for every little reason like they did years ago. That's why you're still here. The night they finally decided to take you out, you fought back—and got lucky." Peter looked directly at Buck. "You need some time to decide?"

"Yeah," Buck replied, "I really do—no—I don't. If Dante thinks Ed's daughter has a chance, and if Ed's willing to risk it, I say let him off the hook—get his cooperation."

Buck caught the smile breaking on Peter's lips.

"You knew that's what I'd say, didn't you, Sneaky Pete?"

"I thought you would," Peter said, the smile breaking into a full grin, "but I was prepared to go with your decision either way. Now, one more thing, Buck. I hope you'll back me on this. Captain Portner knows about Ed. You know about Ed. Nobody else on this ship knows. I'd like to keep it that way till the burn is finished."

"Afraid of a mutiny?" Buck asked

"Something like that," Peter said, "but these days they call it mass resignation. You have any difficulty with that?"

"No, guess not. But really, the crew got a good taste of what the bad guys can do this morning. If they stay on after a warning like that, I think they understand the risks."

Buck paused to watch a gleaming white cruise ship cross about five hundred yards astern, headed for the Angel's Gate opening in the sea wall. Just hours earlier, he had stood proudly on deck as they headed for the Gate and the open sea beyond.

"You know, Peter? This whole thing has turned into one great big bucket of lion lumps!"

"Your words for it are better than any I could think of. Now, come on. The captain wants to see us."

"Oh, good. He's *just* what I need today."

They found Captain Portner in his dayroom.

"You both know I'm not one to waste a lot of time in meetings. I want to tell you, Barnum, that I have a newfound respect for you. You did a hell of a job today. Peter told me you'd be upset over Callin's death. I want you to know that none of us, including the Coast guard, sees it as your fault in any way. If Callin were alive, he'd be facing eight to ten extremely serious counts, including attempted murder.."

"I have to admit," Captain Portner continued, "I questioned the stories of your shore-based adventures. Then, even when *they*," he nodded at Peter, "convinced me that those things were indeed happening, I still didn't think they'd follow onto the ship. Obviously, I was wrong. Now, was that *it*? Going to be more?"

Buck gestured palms up and shrugged.

"Any other leads?"

"No, but I'm still wondering about Runkle."

"Okay, we'd better watch him."

"Captain, if I may ask, *we*?"

Buck's question brought a smile to Peter's face.

"Well, it's obvious that, whether I like it or not, we can't simply sail our little boat happily around the big pond and leave you to protect our asses all by yourself. From now on, we work as a committee. You can expect full cooperation from First Mate Hobbs, Chief Johnson, and me. There may be others we can trust, but I *know* Hobbs and Johnson are trustworthy."

"Good. You might tell the others that, while I haven't shared much information with him, I do listen to the cook, Joe Morse."

"The Indian?"

"Nothing gets past him. And I think he wants this to succeed as much as we do."

The captain looked at Peter. Peter smiled and shrugged. "Oh, one last thing," the captain said. "If you come to a situation where it's needed, I will release your weapon."

Buck laughed. "Captain, if I come to that situation, I won't have time to fill out a requisition in triplicate."

Peter smiled again.

"Okay, tell you what. It goes against all the rules, but I need you and I'll just have to trust you to use good judgment." He went to the safe, opened it, and retrieved Buck's .38. "I don't know how you're going to handle this, but *please* don't carry it unless you have reason. You *cannot* forget the cargo we're carrying. If you feel you must pull this weapon out and aim at someone, you must, you absolutely *must* consider where the bullets will go if you miss. One spark in the wrong place. . . ."

"That—could be tough, Captain. But I'll be very, very careful," Buck said, stuffing the .38 into his waist band and pulling his shirt out to cover it. "I'll start pounding that into my brain, trying to develop a conditioned reflex. Oh, as far as those outside of our—committee—are concerned, you still have the weapon in your safe."

"Agreed," the captain said. "Peter, I think we'll have coast guard's clearance sometime tomorrow. Can you have a replacement for Callin out here in the morning?"

"I'll have to fight the union on that. This time, it *has* to be someone we know. I'll get on it as soon as I get back. I'll call you with the candidates." Peter turned to leave with Buck following.

"And Buck," the captain called. Buck stopped and turned. "Thanks again." The captain smiled. Buck was touched. He had never seen a robot smile.

When they approached the ladder that led down to the company cruiser, Buck pulled Peter off to one side. "I need to know, ol' bud, did Ed tell you who his contact person was?"

"Plural, Buck. Amato and Murrell."

"Thought so. And was Callin *their* man?" Buck asked.

"Ed wasn't in close enough to know for sure, but he didn't think Callin connected with the hoods."

"Oh, that's just wonderful," Buck said, raising one eyebrow. "If that's true it means we haven't heard from the *big* boys yet."

Chapter 31

Buck carried a mixed bag of feelings down the steps the next morning. He had recovered some of his excitement toward the forthcoming adventure. But he hadn't slept well. Each time he had drifted off, he ran head-on into one of two visions and awakened immediately. They weren't the kind of dreams that begin with something and end with something. They were singular visions. If it wasn't Callin's body disappearing into the murky waters, it was an arm and a leg struggling in the turbulence to reconnect, to establish some sense, some order.

He was surprisingly free of stiffness, considering that he had been through yet another fight, even before the effects of the previous one had faded. He had two new bruises on his face, and his leg itched. In the rush of things, he had forgotten about the stitches. Man, how they itch, he thought. They should have been removed? Probably too soon. Now, it would be another eight to ten days. Probably too late. He might have to pull the pesky little pricklies himself. He was glad they hadn't used staples.

When he reached the forecastle level, he stepped out on deck. The thick morning fog had erased the world, obscuring even the tops of the incinerator stacks. But the fascinating fog was unlike any Buck had experienced ashore. Here, it wafted along, slowly rolling, tumbling, twisting, and turning. Not simply an atmospheric condition, it was something alive, given voice by occasional deep-throated blasts from other ships.

He stepped back inside and headed down to the mess. As he approached the crew's mess, he picked up an excited youthful voice.

"Man, did you see it? I did! He just picked him up with one hand and beat the shit out of him with the other! He's one tough dude, and—"

Buck hesitated at the doorway. The animated young seaman spotted Buck, lowered his eyes, and quickly attacked his scrambled eggs. Buck smiled and continued on to the officers' mess. Good, he thought, Runkle's not here.

He dished up a hefty helping of cakes and eggs, anointed them appropriately, and turned to find a place. Captain Portner sat with Chief Johnson and the radio officer at the first table. Dr. Keene and two of the EPA observers occupied the third table. First Mate Hobbs was alone at the remaining table, so Buck headed that way. He paused near Hobbs, bent over, and cocked his head.

"Got a bad back?" Hobbs asked without looking up.

"No, just checking to see if you were still snoring," Buck said, sliding into a vacant chair.

"*You're* accusing *me?*"

"Of course not," Buck snapped back, "you don't snore. But if we move out in this fog, the captain should tie you to the forward mast. Won't need a foghorn. They'll be able to hear us in Honolulu."

The amiable first mate's grin widened to a full smile as the others roared their approval. Wow, Buck thought, glancing over his shoulder toward the captain. The robot even laughs.

"Hot damn," the speckled face said with a grin, "with my gorgeous red hair and wonderful, warm personality, it won't matter if they can't hear us. I'll just melt away the fog."

"What I want to know, Dick," Chief Johnson called over, "is what were those other loud explosions coming from your room all night?"

In one motion, Hobbs leaned to one side, raising the other cheek up off the chair, and pointed a finger at Buck. Buck joined in the laughter. It was good. He felt accepted, really a part of things. As they ate, Buck and Hobbs drifted into a chat about their families. While Buck slid through his own family upheavals leaving only a modest sketch of the All-American family, Hobbs, on the other hand, held nothing back.

"Uh, huh, divorced two years ago. Damn, the smartest thing I ever did! Never had a single regret."

"Must have been a hellish situation," Buck said.

"No, not really."

"I—don't understand. Of course, it's none of my business," Buck said.

"Nah. It was a marriage of convenience. We used each other. She used me to provide the income for a nice life style, and I used her for the comforts of home. One day, I asked her if she didn't think our marriage was missing something. She just looked at me blankly and said, 'No.' That weekend, I moved out."

Throughout the morning, Buck walked into conversations around the ship. The common subjects were the near miss with the freighter and Spencer Callin's sabotage. Buck realized quickly that they were dancing lightly around Callin's death, at least in his presence. But they let him know, in various ways, that they respected him and were grateful to have him aboard. A few could articulate it in those words. Others took to comments like, "We've got Noah aboard. He'll take care of us."

The general feeling aboard the ship was that the threat was over. They were anxious to sail, to prove the worth of the wondrous ship. Buck wished he could be as confident. With the thick fog, they could not see any Groundswell boats anchored nearby, but Buck felt they were still out there.

By 1100 hours, the fog had begun to lift. They had been cleared to resume the voyage, and the company boat had brought a replacement for Callin. The substitute was an older retired coast guard seaman who had served under Captain Portner. He seemed a safe enough choice. Buck wondered how Peter had managed to get around the union's priority card system.

The twin Caterpillars came to life, followed by the rhythmic thumping of the huge anchor chain, as it wound its way into the bow of *Ark II*. At 1200 hours, they had cleared Angels' Gate and the seawall that protected the harbor from the recalcitrant moods of the powerful Pacific. Buck felt relieved when the Groundswell boats backed off and headed for home, but on the other hand, he almost wished they'd tried to follow *Ark II* far out to sea in their tiny boats.

Ark II headed due west, and when a sufficient margin separated her from the point of San Pedro, Captain Portner set a northwest heading. The established burn site was over two hundred miles out, at a point nearly equal distance from Los Angeles and San Francisco and comfortably between the shipping lanes that led to the two cities.

Buck stood for a while on the starboard boat deck, protected from the chilling southwest breeze by the forehouse. With more than a million gallons of chemicals aboard, the gleaming white wonder ship rode low in the water, her bow effortlessly crushing the gentle three-foot swells. But there was a noticeable lateral rolling motion. Peter had warned Buck. It had something to do with the liquid cargo amplifying the rolls induced by the waves. Not bad, though, Buck thought. He could handle this. He stayed with his chosen spot a few extra minutes, absorbing the adventure and watching the details of the coastline fade. High overhead, a recent departure from LAX banked and began its trip eastward.

He was about to step inside when he heard the loudspeaker. "Clear the afterdeck! Incinerators firing up! Clear the afterdeck! Incinerators firing up! Afterdeck quarantine in effect! Afterdeck quarantine in effect!"

He moved to a position near a lifeboat. A light chill pulsed through him. It was where the encounter with Callin had begun. Holding the inboard rail, Buck watched the twin stacks and waited. He was surprised by the pounding in his chest, the increased pulse that he felt. This was it! This was what the emotional strain, the conflicts, the detective work, and the fights were all about.

But the feeling of impending victory was tempered by something else. Would it work? He felt like he was holding a bomb in his hand, the lighted fuse rapidly growing shorter and shorter. He wanted to throw the bomb, to get rid of it, but it was stuck to his hand. Would the whole thing blow up?

Bump! The sound was light, almost inaudible. A puff of dark smoke popped from the port incinerator stack and quickly dissipated in the breeze. In seconds, the puff had been replaced by the subtle but unmistakable waves of heat that quivered up to two feet above the stack. He waited and watched. *Bump!* The process was duplicated by the starboard stack. A low-pitched rumbling reached Buck, a rumbling not unlike that of a distant freight train.

He relaxed. The million-gallon bomb had not blown up. But he felt a letdown, too. While he had had no real expectations, no idea of how the event would transpire, it had somehow left him flat. Then he remembered Dr. Keene's explanation. The burners had to be started nearly two days before the actual burn. They were simply initiating the warm-up process by burning fuel oil from the ship's regular fuel tanks.

Ever so gradually, the fuel flow and temperature would be increased so as not to damage the firebrick linings of the incinerators through sudden extreme temperature changes. When the burners had been advanced to twenty-three hundred degrees Fahrenheit, they would be ready to begin the elimination of the toxic cargo.

Hungry and chilled, he popped inside and made his way down to the mess. As he rounded the turn in the passageway, the aroma of hot pizza caught him by surprise. He went through the line and took a place with Chief Johnson.

"Couldn't miss it, could you?" the chief asked with a smile. "I knew your curiosity would have you out on deck."

"Fascinating—but I guess I expected more," Buck said.

"Wait till tonight. They'll have them cranked up to about thirty per cent. You'll know they're cookin' then."

"Chief," Buck said, lowering his voice and glancing about, "from your point of view, with the responsibility of keeping the ship running. . . ." Buck hesitated and leaned forward. "If you wanted to sabotage *Ark II*, make trouble for us at sea, what would *you* do?"

Buck watched the chief. The big, friendly bear typically assuaged his fearsome impact with eyes that smiled perpetually beneath the bushy brows. Those eyes narrowed, and leaning forward, the chief mirrored Buck's scrutiny of their neighbors.

"Well, I guess," he began softly and slowly, "the most critical things are the fuel supply, engines, rudders, ballast system, and the electronics—the navigation system. It would depend on how serious I was. If I was a devious son of a bitch, I guess I could screw up any of those things, at least enough to temporarily disable us."

"Okay, let's assume that you have the knowledge of electronics that Callin used on the bowthruster, could you seriously mess up the navigation gear?"

"I could, if I had enough time up there to do it. Not the best choice, though."

"Why not?"

"Like I said, I'd need a lot of time to rig something, and the odds are that someone on the bridge would catch it right away. Too many backup systems up there anyway."

"Good. What about the ballast system?"

"You know how low we're riding with this load on. I could take on a full ballast. It could sink us. At least, we'd be in tough shape in rough seas."

"Good possibility?"

"No, don't think so. Most of us oldtimers would feel the difference even before we could see it—and that wouldn't take long."

"Scratch?"

"Scratch. The steering system? I could rig an override, I suppose, like he did with the bowthruster. Too many things wrong with that."

"Like?"

"Well, for one thing, there's nobody out here to run into," the chief laughed. "And we have a manual hydraulic power assist backup in the steering room. It's God-damned hard work, and it's clumsy, but it'll do the job."

"Scratch it?"

The chief tipped his coffee mug high and drained it. He wiped his sleeve across his mouth. "Only get serious if we hit bad weather. No weather where we're headed."

Buck sensed a dead end approaching. "Chief, you believe in this tub of technology, don't you? But do you *really* think we're indestructible?"

"Of course," Chief Johnson went on as if he hadn't heard Buck's question, " if I just wanted another incident to make the old *Ark look* unreliable. . . ."

"Guess we have to think that way, too. The engines?"

"Well, if I really wanted to make trouble, that's where I'd probably do it. Again, with no weather, no special danger, but the bad publicity—this high tech piece of magic drifting at sea for several days—sure wouldn't look too good."

"Best ways?"

"I sure couldn't tear the engines down while they're running and not get caught. I could doctor the fuel, add something to it to burn 'em up. But, that would take a lot of something. Not sure how I'd get it aboard and into the tanks. I could screw up the fuel pumps so they won't feed. Probably the best way."

"And who's directly responsible for the engines?" Buck asked.

The chief's eyes narrowed. "Runkle. You're not starting *that* again, are you?"

"Not accusing anyone. I'm just trying to anticipate their next move, that's all."

"You *really* think they're still after us?"

"Don't know, but I *do* know this. The organized crime guys are making a bundle, tax free, with their illegal dumping operations. They stand to lose millions if this process catches on. And they've committed everything but murder so far to stop us. Can you give me one reason to believe they've run out of tricks?"

The chief's eyes lost their glint for a moment. He simply stared across the room.

"Do you mind if I join you?" Buck looked up into the slender smiling face of Dr. Keene. The chief motioned to the empty chair, and the skinny figure carefully placed his tray on the table and sat down. He removed his orange hardhat and slid it under his chair. "Does the cook have any limits on how much of this we can eat?" he asked, following his question with an enormous bite of pizza.

"God, Doc, I've watched you eat. How the hell do you stay so skinny?" Chief Johnson asked, the crinkles returning to the corners of his eyes.

"Hard work," Keene mumbled.

"You know, Buck," the chief began, motioning toward the recent arrival, "*there's* an area I'd be concerned about."

Buck nodded, turning toward Dr. Keene.

"Tell you what, Buck," the chief interrupted, "I don't really think we have to worry, you know, those things we talked about. But just the same, I'll make it a point to check them all—often. Okay?"

"Thanks, Chief. I'll feel much better."

The chief got to his feet, picked up his tray, and then bent over toward Buck. "The thing *I'm* most worried about is the kid there over-eating and getting sick. See you later."

Buck posed the big question to his young tablemate. Dr. Keene looked at him, startled, and stopped chewing, a large bulge showing in one cheek. His face distorted with indignation, and his eyes burned fiercely.

"Let me get this straight," he said. "You are asking if *I,* or one of my *assistants,* has subversive intentions?"

"Of course not, Doc. I'm asking, if someone wanted to sabotage the incinerators, how might *they* go about it?"

The scientist seemed to relax somewhat. He resumed his chewing.

"It's a moot point," he said, "since the burners are already working, and at least one of us will be on duty around the clock until shutdown. It would be impossible."

Buck sighed. He was not handling this very well, and Dr. Keene was showing an unexpected side of his personality. "Doc, what I'm asking is, theoretically—theoretically now, what could have been done back there? Or, what could be done to really mess things up, or at the least, slow you down?"

Dr. Keene looked sternly at Buck. "I suppose, someone could have damaged one of the sensors, messed up the pumps, played games with the burners, stolen the computer chip, or laid limburger cheese on the edges of the stacks. They didn't. Everything is checking out fine, and the only cheese I've smelled is in the pizza."

"Okay, okay. Thanks, Doc," Buck said. "I didn't mean to offend you or spoil your lunch. After all, we've got to fatten you up, don't we?"

The tense slender face relaxed and worked its way into a boyish smile. Buck started up to leave. Then, as an afterthought he asked, "Say, Doc, can I come back during the burn?"

"Why, yes, I suppose so. The captain has cleared you to breach the quarantine." Dr. Keene warmed to a full smile and added, "Yes, yes of course, be glad to have you."

"Will I be able to get any pictures back there?"

"Only in the control room. Above all, nowhere near the pump room."

Once again, the proud young man was in charge.

"Thanks, I appreciate it. Tell you what, I'll get some good shots of you and your staff. We'll have some nice prints blown up for you."

"That would be nice, Buck. Thank you."

Buck got up, stashed his dishes, and headed topside. He hadn't gotten get the answer he'd hoped for, but it helped to formulate a list of possibilities in his mind, and he did get to know something about their supergenius. He hoped he wouldn't have to pull Dr. Keene's head out of the sand. Maybe, maybe he *had* answered the question. After all, nobody knows that setup back there like he does. If he's that confident that everything's working right, it probably is. When it comes to his baby, he's a doting mother.

As Buck stepped out onto the port boat deck, it seemed the deep rumble of the incinerators had increased. It could just be a change in the wind, he mused. The pulsing heat waves looked about the same.

He moved out past the bow of the lifeboat to the rail and looked astern. A large off-white cruiser was overtaking them, about fifty yards off to port and a hundred yards astern. It was perhaps a forty-footer, and it stayed just inside the spreading, rolling wake of *Ark II*. That must be the company boat, he thought. No, it doesn't look the same. It's a duller white, and it seems smaller than the company boat. Nah, *must* be the company boat. I've never seen it from a distance before. Wonder if Peter's on it?

Buck studied the recent arrival. Two men emerged through a hatch on its foredeck. They took positions on their knees, apparently for balance, as the craft bounced through the swells. Although they were too far away to be seen clearly, Buck could see that they were looking at the bigger ship. They've probably never seen anything like this, he thought with a chuckle. But that's a precarious place to watch from, rather strange. Strange?

The word snapped at Buck like a giant rubber band. After recent events anything strange had to be bad. He ducked back into the fore-house and ran up the steps to B-deck as fast as he could. Bursting into his cabin, he grabbed the Canon and slipped the strap over his neck. In another minute, he was back on the portside boat deck, struggling to catch his breath while setting the camera for action.

The white craft had moved up and was just off the stern of *Ark II*. Even before he raised the camera to his eye, Buck could tell that the two men on the cruiser's deck also had cameras—video cameras. Drawing the strange boat up close with his telephoto lens, he had snapped two shots before he noticed. One was a husky, baldheaded man with a goatee and glasses. Reicher? It's Reicher! he thought. Buck took two more shots for insurance.

Then he simply used his powerful lens as a telescope. From his vantage point, he could find no identification, no flags flying. And the men didn't seem to be panning *Ark II* with their videocams. They seemed only to be interested in the stern of the ship. Buck looked aft. There was a trail of black smoke rising from behind the incinerator section, rising to stack height and then trailing off behind. Even as he watched, the smoke became thicker.

"Ohhh, have we got *trouble!*" Buck moaned. For a moment, while his eyes took in the frightening scene, his brain went into meltdown. Suddenly, the pulsing of twin screws slowed to almost nothing.

An alarm sounded, and the loudspeaker crackled, "First! First! Get back there and check that out! All hands to fire stations! All hands to fire stations!"

Chapter 32

It's happening, Buck thought. It's happening! No, no, no—not going to *let* it!" He placed the camera in a safe corner, leaped down the four steps to the catwalk, and took off running toward the stern. Aware of other feet bonging on the steel grating, he glanced over his shoulder. Some distance behind him came Runkle. Buck reached the incinerator area and started up the first set of steps. He slowed as he reached the top. The next level up would take him past the engine stack, and if he continued aft, he'd have to go right between the incinerator stacks. Already, the roaring stacks were shouting their warnings. How close can we get? he wondered.

"Hurry up! Get going!" Runkle shouted from behind, giving him a shove.

Buck gauged the incredible heat against his face as he scampered up the final flight. With Runkle pushing, he ran to his left, around the engine stack, and headed into the narrow corridor between the giants. The stifling, fervid waves blanketed him like an invisible predator, but the throaty rumbling threatened even more. Instinctively, he ducked his head as he passed between the bellowing monsters.

Reaching the rear edge of the upper deck, the place where he and Peter had chatted, he hesitated. The thick black smoke billowed up from the deck below them. The afterdeck alarm screamed at him like a banshee. The steps down to that level? He couldn't remember. Right? Left? He had only been down there once.

An elbow jarred his tender ribs as Runkle charged past and turned to the right. Buck followed, down the steps and toward the door to the steering room, the source of the smoke. The door was cracked partially open. Runkle jerked the door fully open. The concentrated collection of smoke burst out and upward in a gigantic puff and then formed into a thick, dark column. For a moment, Buck stood there helplessly. But Runkle had somehow located a long, white nylon rope. He tied a loop around his waist and handed the coil to Buck.

"Going down!" he shouted over the thundering stacks and shrieking alarms. "If that rope stopth moving, ge- me out of there—you *hear*?" Buck nodded. Runkle bent low and plunged into the smoke.

Buck crouched a few feet back, playing out the rope and wondering how he would get the first out of there if the rope *did* stop moving. When the coil stopped unwinding, Buck dropped to his belly and edged closer to the doorway. The rising smoke left a small, clearer slot near the deck. His eyes smarted as he strained to see beneath the angry black smoke. He listened for some indication of what might be happening below. But the thunderous stacks combined with the counterpoint played by the wailing banshee to bury any sounds from the steering room.

Holding the rope in his fingertips, he increased the tension slightly. He could feel an occasional tug on the rope, not unlike the first bites of a large walleye in the deep blue waters of Big Sand Lake.

"Keep biting. Don't stop," he whispered to himself. A rebellious puff of emerging smoke swirled downward, stinging Buck's eyes. He rolled to one side to escape it. Holding the rope with one hand, he wiped at the burning tears with the other.

As his vision cleared, he caught a glimpse of the mysterious boat. It had moved closer, just off the port stern, and the two men had their cameras aimed at him. Suddenly, a violent jerk on the rope nearly tore it from Buck's grasp. In the same instant, the smoke began to change from deep black to gray. He felt a hand on his back.

"Who's down there?" a voice bellowed close to Buck's ear. He rolled slightly and looked up. It was Gantsky.

"Runkle!" Buck shouted. Pointing to the smoke, which had become silver-gray in color, Buck asked, "What's that? What's happening?"

"Probably fire extinguisher! He's whipping it! Still moving?" The second leaned over Buck to feel the rope. "Not moving! How long?"

"Just happened! Moving when you got here!"

"Gotta get him out! Pull!"

Together they tugged on the rope. Working from their prone positions, they were barely able to move the heavy resistance at the other end. Quickly, Buck got to his feet, dragging Gantsky up with him. They backed away from the escaping column of smoke and pulled furiously on the white rope. Buck could visualize Runkle's heavy body sliding across the deck of the steering room. Then, the movement stopped. Their combined effort accomplished nothing. It was as though they were pulling against the ship itself.

"Caught on something, or he's at the steps!" Gantsky shouted. "Come on, gotta go in after him!"

Following the rope, the second plunged through the opening and down the steps. Buck grabbed Gantsky's belt and followed him blindly, bending as low as he could to stay beneath the thickest of the smoke. They ran, stumbled, and skidded down the steep metal steps, landing in a heap at the bottom atop the motionless body of the first engineer. Gantsky scrambled to one side and Buck rolled off to the other. He pressed his face against the hard steel deck, desperately hoping to find some air. He was surprised when he inhaled. Amid the stinging, choking bitterness, he felt an almost cool sensation. It must be air, he thought. Got to be. He sucked in two deep breaths. Tapping on Gantsky, Buck motioned to the floor. He saw Gantsky emulate his breathing posture for a few seconds.

"You okay?" he asked Gantsky.

"Uh, huh."

"Grab that arm. On *three*—we go!" Buck shouted. "One—two—*three!*" Buck sucked in a deep breath, crooked an elbow under Runkle's right arm, and lurched to his feet. While Buck charged up the right side of the narrow staircase, Gantsky was forced to follow on the left and two steps lower. Because of the dead weight of the engineer and the restrictive narrow staircase, their uncoordinated jerking and tugging pitted one rescuer against the other. Buck kept his burning eyes closed. He could see nothing with them open. He drove upward, pushing his feet against anything they found, hoping he could hold his breath until he made the top. He could feel the thumping as Runkle's feet dragged over each step.

Midway up, Gantsky tripped, threatening to pull the entire effort back to the bottom. Buck held, and his teammate quickly recovered. But after three more steps, Buck knew he wasn't going to make it. The exertion of dragging the heavy man was too much. He wanted desperately to breathe, but he was afraid to try it. Sheer determination could inject strength into the rubbery legs, but he had to have air. One more step, he told himself, then one more. . . .

The vertigo swept in on him like an onrushing tornado. His balance was going. Must have lost Gantsky, he thought. That's why Runkle's gotten so heavy. Can't do it! Got to breathe! The roar of the tornado became louder and louder. Just as Buck let go, exhaling the force that he could no longer contain, hands grabbed at him, at his arm, his neck, his ear, seemingly at anything they could grasp. His body seemed to float through the succession of tugs, jerks, and bumps that followed. He felt his shins scrape over the foot-high threshhold of the watertight doorway, but he didn't feel the pain.

His head swirled amid the confusing thunder, screaming alarm, and shouting voices. He sensed that he was still there, aboard *Ark II,* yet. . . . He felt the oxygen mask being clamped over his nose and mouth, but it didn't matter. He choked, coughed, and sputtered when the first of the cool oxygen hit his system. Then—it felt so good! A pair of strong fingers pried one eye open. He shook his head violently when the first of the icy drops settled into the inferno. But the other eye opened voluntarily, begging for its share of the relief. The tears that ran down his cheeks had become cool tears, pleasant tears. Still the tornado roared on.

"Boy, you guys have been on one hell of a toot, to have eyes that red," he heard Chief Johnson say. Buck smiled through his tears. His lungs were not up to a laugh, but within a couple of minutes, he felt better.

"You ready to sit up?" the chief asked.

"The others?" Buck asked.

"Right here. About the same shape as you," a voice said.

"The fire?"

"It's over. All taken care of."

Buck tried to focus his eyes, but the watery barrier was too much. He gave it up. He sat up and leaned against the rear wall of the incinerator section. The tornado had settled into the low-pitched rumble that he recognized as the burners. He could feel the vibrations in the steel wall.

Hours later, Buck awakened. He was in his bunk. He had slept the deep sleep that follows sheer exhaustion. His eyes still burned some, and his lungs felt like he had inhaled a box of King Edwards. As he slid from his bunk to the floor, the sharp pains that called him to full alert suggested that someone had done a hatchet job on his shins. And the bad rib pained him sharply with each movement. He splashed cold water on his face. Oh, that feels good, he thought. Everything cold feels *so* good.

He made his way down to the mess. As he turned to enter, his eyes swept over the three tables. Only one person there—Runkle. The first was carefully spooning soup into his mouth and seemed not to have noticed Buck. He had been on a diet of soup, eggs, and ice cream ever since the fight. Buck turned to scan the serving counter. Nothing there. His watch told him it was 1900 hours, long past serving time.

"Jus' find a spot, Buck White Earth," came the voice from the galley. "Joe's gettin' somethin' fer ya now."

Buck poured himself some coffee and started toward a table, the farthest from Runkle's position. He kept his eyes directed away from the first, but he sensed that he was being watched. Brother, he thought, what games we play. Any normal man would want to thank me for helping out, but not Runkle. As Buck pulled his chair out, he glanced in the other man's direction. The red eyes were fixed on Buck, and the sneer was locked in its usual mode.

Buck sat down with his back to it. Don't want to stare at that while I eat, he thought. Suppose he's even capable of expressing gratitude? Second thought, maybe it's not warranted. Have to give him credit. He didn't even hesitate, went right down after that fire. He probably expects that any of us should do the same. Obviously, the episode hasn't changed him at all, but it has changed my opinion of him. It sure takes Runkle off my list. List? He *was* the list.

"Here 'tis, Buck White Earth," Indian Joe said, sliding the oversized TV dinner of turkey, potatoes, and dressing before Buck. "Joe took this outa the box special like, just fer you," he chortled.

"Ah, thanks, Joe. You're a culinary artist."

The smile on the face of the corpulent cook evaporated. He wheeled and retreated to his galley. Buck headed for the side counter for some water, and in the time it took, the first engineer had disposed of his dishes and was gone. Almost eery, Buck thought, the way he slipped out of here.

When Buck was nearly finished eating, Indian Joe reappeared. He sat down across from Buck, his ever present coffee mug in hand. "Seems like yer always in the wrong place at the right time," he said with his sly, questioning grin.

"It's a masochistic trait I need to purge from my system," Buck said, "before it kills me."

"Uh, uh," Joe interrupted, putting up his hands defensively. "If you ain't gonna talk American, Joe ain't gonna listen. Now, you tell Joe what you said an' you get back to talkin' American."

"Sorry, Joe. Do you like to learn new words?"

"Gotta learn one a day, or I ain't gettin' no place."

Buck explained *masochistic* and *trait*. He was surprised at the intensity with which Joe listened. "An' that other one—cul - mo - rary?"

Buck laughed, sorry that he had until he found Joe laughing with him. As he defined *culinary*, Joe beamed.

"You want to learn to spell them, too? To write them?" Buck asked.

"Nah, Joe jist wants to unnerstand 'em."

"Now it's your turn to teach, Joe." Buck got up, disposed of his utensils, put his tray on the stack, and returned to the table. "Tell me about the fire. I was right there, but I still don't know what happened."

"Oh, that. A good news-bad news fire. The good news—it wasn't nothin' serious, couldn't a hurt the ship nohow. Jist a smudge pot. Nothin' in the steerin' room to catch on fire anyway."

"A smudge pot?"

"Uh, huh. He torched some ol' dirty oil in a plastic bucket. When the bucket got hot an' melted, it spread out on the floor. The first used a fire 'stingisher on it. Sure made a lot o' smoke fer them guys to take pitchers, din't it?"

"You noticed, too? And, the bad news—we've still got a big, bad fish on this ship, right?"

"Joe thinks maybe yer still fishin' a little too deep. The big one might be closer'n you think, like hidin' in the weeds right aside you." Indian Joe's round face took on a serious cast. The eyes that usually flashed with humor showed a penetrating glint. "Well," Joe said, getting up from the table, "if Joe don't get his ass in bed, Ol' Buck White Earth ain't gonna get no breakfast in the mornin'." He started for the galley and then stopped. "You colorblind?" He turned and was gone.

Colorblind? Colorblind? Buck puzzled over the question.

Some time later, he stood alone on the boat deck, invigorated by the cool night air. *Ark II* plowed steadily to the northwest, her loaded hull barely affected by the gentle swells. It was dark in the distance, but the main deck was lighted by two floodlights, fore and aft. The orange fire cones had become yellow as the intensity was increased, and the yellow was already showing streaks of blue. Buck was fascinated. He had heard that the transition of the fire cones would ultimately lead to blue, then a bluish-white that would be almost invisible in daylight.

The freight train he had heard earlier had now become a deep rumble. He was awestruck by the energy thundering out of the stacks. As he stood there, adjusting to the wonder, the sheer power, he became aware of an eerie feeling. He was standing on the million-plus gallons of chemicals that would feed that power.

The thought jerked Buck back to the reality of the situation. If someone could sabotage the bowthruster and start a fire in the steering room, what could he do with this load? He could blow us halfway to the moon. He shuddered. Indian Joe's words came back to him. ". . . .closer than you think, hiding in the weeds." In the weeds? That smudge pot fire was all for show, simple but ingenious. It might have been the last act. But then again, it might have been just the overture.

If our bad guy plans a more serious follow-up, what would be the most advantageous time? Buck played with the question for some time, but he always came back to the same answer. Early in the burn, before *Ark II* has a chance to prove herself. He'll gain nothing by waiting. So what can we do about it? We need more eyes—a meeting of the committee. He scampered up the steps to the captain's quarters.

By 2400 hours, a plan for patrolling the ship through the night had been formulated. Captain Portner would stay on duty on the bridge. First Mate Hobbs would stroll the crew's quarters on A, B, and focusle deck levels. The chief would, despite the quarantine, watch over the aft portion of the ship, with frequent trips down to the engine room.

And Buck would patrol the lower bow section and the main deck. He had, after some debate, finally convinced the captain to turn the floodlights off, leaving the main deck in darkness, an invitation to their fish. It would be a long, tedious night. He hoped it would be absolutely boring.

Chapter 33

Buck leaned against the afterhouse wall at the rear port side of the main deck. He had positioned himself behind the white nitrogen reserve tank where he could view the long catwalk and yet be hidden from anyone who might be headed aft. He would see them first. It was an advantageous spot, and he had taken to spending much of his patrol time there.

While the blue-white shimmering glow of the stacks did not illuminate the main deck, it gave the hundreds of shadows a nervous, quivering effect. He looked up at the benign floodlight. One word to the bridge and the main deck would be well-lighted in seconds. It would be a real surprise to someone who doesn't belong out here, he mused. He leaned out to scan the deck once more.

He was exhausted. The six hours he had been on his feet seemed like thirty-six, and each foot demanded that he stand on the other. He backed deeper into the corner and drew some support by pressing his entire backside against the wall. Then he wrapped one forearm around a steel protrusion, using it as a prop.

The cool, salty southwest breeze was broadsiding the ship on the port side, and the six-foot waves seemed to pound in frustration against the side of the heavily laden, low-riding vessel. It was as though they stretched to reach Buck but couldn't quite make it. The swells did, however, force *Ark II* with its fluid cargo into a lateral rolling motion. Buck wedged the long heavy flashlight into one armpit while he fastened the top snap of his nylon jacket. Cumbersome as it was, he rather liked the gigantic flashlight. As a light it boasted enormous power, and as a weapon it was certainly heavy enough to do the job.

He shivered as he regripped the heavy light. Field glasses dangled from his neck. A green walkie-talkie hung from his belt, and his revolver rested in the holster beneath his jacket. My God, he wondered, how did I *get* here? Who *am* I? A few weeks ago, I was a travel writer trying to make a resort piece drip with excitement. Now, I'm a private detective, a sailor on midnight watch, and a soldier of fortune. The walkie-talkie interrupted his thoughts. The voice was low and soft but unmistakable.

"Chief here. Leaving the engine room. Everything's okay back here. Coming over the top after I check the steering room. Where are you, Buck?"

Buck fumbled with the strange device, found the right button, and replied, "At the N-tank. I'll wait here for you."

"Keep an eye on the steps in case I flush something out. Be there in two minutes."

As Buck holstered the device, it spoke again. "Hobbs here. Starting up in crew's quarters again. Okay here."

"Captain speaking. Everything looks good from the bridge."

Buck looked up away from the glow of the stacks. The stars hadn't hung so low or so bright since his last trip into the mountains. It was as though they wanted in on the action, too. He edged toward the rail, leaned against it for balance, and raised the glasses. Slightly off the port stern and two or three miles back he could just make out the running lights of the mystery boat. Still there, he thought, but they're getting a rough ride tonight. He hoped they were miserable. They were certainly determined.

He moved toward the center catwalk, scanning the expansive main deck for any sign of movement. The musical *thunk* of feet on the metal steps jerked his attention upward. He tensed, unable to make out the silhouette in the darkness.

"God-damn, do I need a cigarette!" the chief said as his feet hit the main deck. He turned his back to the wind as he lit up.

"Should you do that?"

"Oh, hell, it's okay. With that breeze, I'm not going to blow us up."

"Chief, I've been thinking. Was I right?"

"Right? About what?"

"The captain wanted to explain the situation to the crew, to get them all watching for anything suspicious. I suggested keeping it as quiet and low-key as possible. Kind of surprised me that the captain went along with me so quickly."

"Ha!" Chief Johnson laughed, "doesn't make any difference. Every man aboard knows what's going on."

"They do?"

"Sure. And if our guy is an officer," the chief went on, tapping his talkie with one hand, "don't you think he's listening in? Nah, all we're doing is a little preventative maintenance."

"Kind of stupid of me?"

"Welcome aboard. None of us ever thought it would come to this, so you were way ahead of the rest of us. But I agree with you. If they're just up to little tricks like the smudge pot, they could pester us the whole damned trip. But, if they've got something really serious in mind, it'll come in the next twenty-four hours."

Buck looked at his watch. It was 0345 hours, almost time for the shift change in the incinerator room. He mentioned it to the chief. "But I really should go check the bow area."

"Don't worry about the shift change back here. The old man'll be watching from up there, and I'll just wait here and have another smoke. See you later."

By 0415 hours, Buck had checked the galley, sneaked a couple of swallows of bitter coffee in the mess, and was checking the bosun's storeroom ahead of the galley. From there, he went down to the auxiliary machinery room and on to the bowthruster engine room. He was about to leave the small compartment, satisfied that everything looked normal, when he stopped. Behind the huge Caterpillar diesel, there was a small space that he hadn't checked. He worked his way around one end of the quiet monster. There, perched beside a section of the *Los Angeles Sun* was a white five-gallon plastic bucket! Shining his light into the container, Buck found it half-filled with dark, dirty motor oil. The acrid odor was unmistakable.

A familiar chill darted from his tailbone to his neck, bringing the tingling hairs to attention. He jerked upright and spun around. Nobody there. He grabbed for the green talkie.

"Chief, this is Buck. I'm in the bowthruster engine room. There's a bucket of old oil and some newspaper down behind the engine. Is that kosher?"

"Sounds to me like another smudge pot, Buck."

"Buck, captain here. Don't touch the handle—fingerprints. Lock it in your quarters, then come up to the bridge. There's a SAT-COM call for you. Dick, Chief, check every corner. You know what you're looking for."

Buck grabbed the wire portion of the handle, scooped up the newspaper, and raced up to B-deck. He locked the simple incendiary device in his cabin and proceeded up to the bridge. Captain Portner motioned him to a phone. Struggling to catch his breath, Buck hesitated before picking it up. Must be Peter, he thought. Trouble for the kids? Damn! Is there no way to get ahead of those bastards? He whipped the plastic piece up to his ear.

"Buck Barnum," he said cautiously.

"Buck, this is Lenny." She spoke slowly, and her soft voice had a somber quality that was new to him. "There's—there's been an accident. No, a tragedy, *not* an accident."

Buck felt himself choke up. His left hand seemed about to crush the telephone. "Who? The kids?"

"Buck, a vehicle was blown up on the Harbor Freeway an hour ago. Obviously, a bomb. Buck—it was *your* rental, the Camaro. I've checked it from the plates. We don't know who the driver was yet. . . ."

Buck heard words, but they were meaningless sounds from some distant universe. They weren't Lenny's. They belonged to no one he knew, and they spoke of things that were beyond his comprehension. He felt the powerful sobs mounting in his chest, rising swiftly to a place behind his eyes.

"Buck? Are you there?"

Just as he was about to break, his body went numb. The surging sobs disappeared in the void. The pounding in his veins stopped. Only the tears that trickled down each side of his nose gave any sign that he was alive, and he really didn't care.

"Buck? Are you all right?"

But Buck was far away. From somewhere in the distance, he heard the *Powmp! Powmp!* of shotgun blasts followed by a peculiar light that reflected off a shiny knife blade. A terrible explosion followed, and he could see Ed Roland struggling frantically to escape the inferno. His eyes swept the strange, foreign place in which he sat. Huge windows everywhere, like giant eyes watching him, mocking him. A strange man in khaki clothes looking at him. All of this, for what—money? For *money?*

Then, as though some giant puppeteer had maliciously jerked his strings, Buck felt a change. The pulsing in his forehead returned, surging to a peak, a boiling, stirring caldron, working itself toward overflow. It was anger and hate swelling into an undeniable craving for vengeance. Yet, from outside of the mounting irrational force came a voice, a voice that he knew and had grown to love, a voice that was crying, pleading, begging.

"Buck! Please, please, Buck. *Talk* to me!"

"Lenny," he heard himself saying, "It was Ed—Ed Roland. I loaned him the Camaro. It was Ed. I never thought they'd—never occurred to me. Guess I really didn't get it, Lenny. Even with the other scares, I guess I didn't believe you and Dante. You were both right—in way over my head."

"You've got to remember something, Buck." Lenny's voice seemed to recapture its assertive quality. "*You* didn't do this to Ed. *They* did! Now, can you think of any reason they might have been after *him?* Isn't it possible they *knew* it was Ed?"

Buck reached out for the glimmer of hope Lenny's question put before him.

"They—they might have." Buck went on to explain the extortion set-up, Ed's reluctant cooperation, and his confession to Peter. "But, they couldn't have known about Ed's talk with Peter, his confession. No, Lenny, it looks like they meant to get old Buck Barnum, the amateur pain-in-the-ass."

"Not true," Lenny replied, "but before you sink too far, remember this. Your escapade exposed the dumping operation. But Ed's testimony would tie them to the criminal actions against you and the company. With things coming unraveled for them, and even if they didn't know about Ed Roland's turning, do you think they'd want to leave him out there on the streets? And another thing, the M.O. fits the little snake, Amato. He seems to favor the knife and plastics. Now, many of us saw you leave aboard that ship. I doubt very much that Murrell and Amato missed that. Don't you suppose Amato knows where *you* are? He *always* knows where you are!"

"What if he finds my family?"

"They're all right. I called Orange County as soon as the report came in. We now have people watching over them. And I called Sunny at the hotel. I told her to keep all of them in their rooms. I'm going out there to talk with her this morning."

"You—"

"It's okay, Buck. She wants to meet with me. I'm calling Peter Hamlin next. Has anything happened out there?"

Buck briefed Lenny on the mystery boat, the smudge pot, his latest discovery, and their efforts to ward off further sabotage.

"Lenny, I wish you were here with us. We could sure use you. We know we've still got a live one on board, but I can't figure out how to catch him."

"You know, for an old jock, you've become a pretty good detective." Lenny's voice took on that reassuring quality that Buck needed to hear. "And, now that you really understand what you're up against, you'll do even better. You going to be okay?"

"Okay? I've gone from sad as hell to mad as hell. At the moment, I'm just damned numb and determined."

"Please be careful. I love you. Bye."

Buck hung up the phone, drew a deep breath, and slumped into his chair. He felt like he was doing a high wire act. To fall to one side, he'd be in hopeless depression. To fall to the other, he'd become so angry that he'd lose control. He *had* to stay on the wire, using the threats of the other two options for balance without succumbing to either.

He explained the phone call to Captain Portner. "I guess it tells us something, doesn't it?"

"I certainly don't like what it tells us, but I'm glad we know," the captain said. "Why don't you toss your gear over there on the chart table. I'll bring in the second mate to cover your watch. I think we can trust him. Grab a cup of coffee and take it easy. I'll get some things going here."

Buck did as directed and took his seat. The coffee did help, and it was fresher than that in the mess. Captain Portner called Hobbs and the chief, mentioning the bombing and cautioning them to expect the worst. Then, he bent over and unlocked a small corner cabinet. When he straightened, Buck saw that he had strapped on a .45 Colt, military model.

"It's time," he said simply. "You have yours?"

Buck patted his jacket at the left shoulder.

The captain directed the radioman to get Peter on the phone. When the connection had been made, Portner explained the events of the last hours. Piecing together the conversation, Buck understood that Peter would get the company cruiser manned and underway as soon as possible. The captain repeated his demand that they come well-armed. At a speed of just under thirty knots, the company boat should catch *Ark II* at about 1300 hours that afternoon. It made Buck feel better to know that they would have more men, more weapons, and another boat to deal with the mysterious follower—as well as provide ready assistance in case the worst happened.

"Why don't you turn in for a couple of hours?" the captain suggested.

"We'll shake you out at 0700 hours."

"Don't think I can sleep, but I'll try it. Thanks."

As he hoisted himself into the upper berth, Buck knew, tired as he was, that sleep was out of the question. The oil in the plastic bucket filled the tiny cabin with its pungent fumes. His mind raced from one thing to another. He wished he had something, just one little thing, to point him toward the saboteur. It would seem that Runkle was no longer a suspect. On the other hand, what if he *did* start the fire? He could rush in, knowing exactly what the fire was and where it was. Not likely. He almost died of smoke inhalation. No man would take that chance simply to remove suspicion—would he?

Chapter 34

C'mon—up, baby!" First Mate Hobbs said as he rolled Buck out at 0700 hours. "You're snoring so hard you're blowing us off course."

"Can't believe I even got to sleep," Buck mumbled, squinting at the freckled face.

"Frankly, I'm surprised, too. But you've been through some pretty tough days. Peter Hamlin got the company boat off a few minutes ago. Should rendezvous by 1300 hours. Grab some chow and take up your old routine. The second mate will spell me for a couple of hours, and then I'll relieve the old man for a couple."

"What about the chief?"

"Don't worry about that old grizzly bear. He'll grab a few minutes stretched on the deck in the engine room and be good as new. Dr. Keene says we'll be heated up ahead of schedule. Should be able to start the real burn about 0900 hours tomorrow."

Almost in one motion, the first mate stripped his shirt and shoes and dropped into the lower berth. "Nigh—nigh," he said, as he turned over, leaving Buck staring at the bundle of flaming red curls.

Buck rinsed his face with cold water and finished dressing. He slung the .38 under his jacket and set out for the mess. Breakfast was uneventful, and before long, Buck had resumed his patrol, a routine which rapidly evolved into a humorous game of peek-a-boo. As he moved about, watching the crew members as surreptitiously as possible, he became aware that they were watching him in the same manner. Given time to think about it, it made sense. Wherever he went, trouble showed up.

Whoever our firebug is, Buck thought, he certainly won't go into action right in front of me. But like the chief said, it's preventative maintenance, more like fire prevention. As he roamed from bowthruster to afterhouse, his mind jumped from one thing to another. Poor Ed—Ed's family—

Buck's own family—Lenny—the rapid and sound decision-making by Captain Portner. And for the first time in days, Buck's mind drifted back to his own career crisis.

Maybe I did blow that decision after all, he thought. Covering high school games was certainly a lot more secure than this. And people treated me well—they wanted me to write nice things about them. I never had anyone try to shoot me, knife me, or blow me up. But that was then.

He chose not to stay long at his post near the nitrogen tank. In the light of day, he was hiding from nobody, simply pointing out his favorite hiding place. And the rumble from the incinerator stacks was wearing on his nerves. He looked up. The emissions were colorless, but the rising heat waves were gaining in intensity. He noticed that those few seaman working about the deck went no farther aft than amidships.

"Buck," Dick's voice came over his walkie-talkie, "we've had another bucket turned in at the bridge. When you get up this way, pick it up, will you?"

"Sure thing," he replied. He looked at his watch, 1140 hours. He turned and started toward the forehouse, smiling to himself, rather surprised at the ease with which he had adapted to the maritime twenty-four-hour clock. And as he strolled slowly along the catwalk, he became aware also of the relative ease with which he walked the deck of a rolling ship, proof of the old practice cliché.

As Buck reached the forehouse, he suddenly remembered the mystery boat. He stepped over to the port rail and looked back. No sign of it. He tried again at the starboard rail, again with no success. That's funny, he thought. Either it's gone, or it's right up close behind us where I can't see it. The thought touched off a spark, and Buck realized just how dopey he had been through the morning. Behind us? *Right* behind us?

He ducked into the forehouse passageway and hurried up the steps. It was almost 1200 hours when he burst into the bridge. Captain Portner, Hobbs, and a helmsman were on watch, and Nelson was in the radio room. Hobbs motioned to the white bucket and pile of rags off in one corner.

Buck glanced at it. Sure enough, a similar bucket of dark putrid oil. Rags instead of paper. Work just as well, just dampen the rags with a little oil, lay them out as a fuse, and light them, he thought.

"Who found this one?"

"Second engineer," said Hobbs, "down in the auxiliary machinery room."

"Good for Gantsky," Buck said.

He raised his glasses and stepped to one side of the bridge in order to improve his line of sight around the afterhouse and the stacks. There it was. The white boat was directly behind them, perhaps two hundred yards. As he watched, it seemed to be closing on *Ark II*.

"Captain, I don't like it," Buck said. "That other boat is coming up fast. The last time, that meant trouble."

The captain moved to Buck's window and spotted the cruiser as it flared slightly to the starboard side.

"You're right." He reached for his talkie. "Chief, be alert. That other boat's pulling up on us. They're up to something. Oh, and watch your step. We're going into a zig-zag." The robot's voice was a near monotone. He turned to the helmsman.

"Start a zig-zag pattern, smooth but firm. Take fifteen degrees to port for ten seconds. Then alternate starboard, port, and so on, five seconds each leg. After one minute, resume course. That should slow them down a little. They'll have their hands full battling our wake. About the time they've climbed out, they'll be back in it again." He flipped on the P.A. system and warned the crew members of the turns.

Buck continued to follow the white boat through his glasses. This time, there were no figures out on the deck, no video cameras to be seen.

"They don't seem to be taking pictures this time, Captain. They must have something else in mind."

He lowered his sightline to the main deck of *Ark II* and adjusted the focus of the glasses. There were three men starting aft on the catwalk.

"Time for the shift change in the incinerator room?" he asked.

"Right on time," Hobbs said.

As Buck watched, the three men paused. Their gestures indicated some kind of friendly discussion. He could see them shift their weight to cope with the abrupt turns. But his mind had drifted to something else, something he had missed or lost. "Where did you say that last bucket was found?"

"Auxiliary machinery room," Hobbs replied.

"Can't be. I checked every inch of that room several times, especially after finding the one in the bowthruster room. It wasn't there. I would have seen it."

"That's where he said he found it."

"The second? Gantsky?"

"Right," Hobbs said.

Buck lowered the glasses and thought for a moment. Words of Indian Joe came back to him, "Joe thinks yer fishin' too deep. That big fish is right there close aside you." He had struggled for an answer, just one answer that would set them on the right path. Suddenly, his mind was alive, not with answers— but with questions! He had been asking himself the wrong questions!

"Captain! Over here, please. Quick!" Buck called. As Captain Portner hurried to the aft window of the bridge, Buck unloaded a salvo of questions.

"Who's one of the most likeable, cooperative men on the ship?"

"*What?*"

"Gantsky?"

"Yes, I guess so."

"When was Gantsky hired on?"

"One of the four replacements, just before you came with us."

"So he's *not* one of the longer-term crewmen? And who's in charge of engine lubrications? Oil changes?"

"Gantsky."

Buck was amazed at himself. The logical sequence of questions came bursting forth like he was reading a script. Always quick with his hands and feet, he had never considered himself a quick thinker, certainly not a Gatling gun with words.

"Captain," he continued, "when we had the fire in the steering room, the alarms sounded. Did the computer do that?"

"No, I did it, manually."

"And did the incinerators automatically shut down like they're supposed to?"

"Yes—no, no they didn't. And the crisis was so short, frankly, I was glad they *hadn't* shut down."

"Shouldn't they?"

"Of course. The manual alarm triggers the computer. I should have caught that."

"Next to Dr. Keene, who's the best computer whiz on the ship?"

"Why, I don't—"

"Gantsky," Hobbs said. "He's an absolute computer freak."

"Captain, down there heading aft," Buck said, "an incinerator tech, an EPA observer, and. . . ."

Buck and Captain Portner raised their field glasses simultaneously.

"Gantsky," they said in unison.

"Does he have clearance to breach the quarantine?" Buck asked, studying Gantsky intently.

"No."

Despite Buck's alarming questions, the captain's voice retained its boring quality.

There was something about Gantsky that wasn't quite right. Same hardhat, same clothes, but something's different, he thought. Wait a minute—that's *it!*

"Take another look, Captain. All the walkie-talkies I've seen aboard ship are green. The one on his hip is black. Can you explain that?"

"That's not one of *our* walkie-talkies—not even sure it *is* a talkie! Could be a radio or some kind of transmit— Jesus H. Christ!" the captain roared. "That could even be some kind of detonator!"

Buck was already on his way through the tiny foyer to the outside steps.

"The chief's out there somewhere. I'll call him!" the captain shouted after Buck.

As Buck pivoted and started down the narrow, threatening steps with the switchbacks at each level, he was oblivious to the height. He was bent on erasing four flights of steps in a time that came out in minus figures. During the first flight, he had no rhythm. He jumped, slid, bumped, and stumbled his way down to B-deck. Swinging around for his second assault, he wanted to look aft for Gantsky, but he didn't dare lose his focus. Go for it, he told himself. From that point on, he concentrated on alternate steps, merely sliding his hands on the rails for balance. Reaching the bottom, he swung around the turn, and leaped the four steps down to catwalk level, shedding the bouncing field glasses as he turned.

Off and running, Buck looked toward the afterhouse for Gantsky. He had disappeared—no, there he was, starting up the last set of steps to the top deck. In no apparent hurry, the second was going over the top, not to the incinerator room. That means, Buck thought, he's going to blow it and jump? God, hope I'm wrong. Don't think he's seen me yet—really gaining fast. Grateful for the traction his running shoes gave him, Buck pounded along on the steel grating. His .38 bumped about under his jacket.

Somewhere along the way his hardhat had flipped off. Better without it, he thought. As he hustled up the two flights to the top deck aft, he felt his legs giving out, and by the time he reached the turn at the top, hot knives were carving into his lungs. He swung around the sharp turn and smacked into an invisible wall of heat. The blood was pumping past his ears so hard, he scarcely noticed the noise of the stacks—but the heat! It told him why his lungs hurt so badly—the smoke he had inhaled the day before! He was no longer the smooth, conditioned athlete, gliding with rhythm and confidence. He faltered, and he was frustrated and angry as he aimed for the narrow space between the stacks.

Damn, he thought, if it hadn't been for that fire yesterday, I'd have him by—from behind the stack housing, a stiff arm swung a flattened hand, knife-like toward his throat. Buck's reflexes jerked his head down slightly. *Crack!* The blow caught him on the jaw, knocking him to his back on the hot steel deck. Football instincts returned. He was down, but conscious. Lucky. Hurt? No time for hurt.

"Up—damn it—up!" he told himself. As he rolled over and raised his head, he saw Gantsky staggering to the steps aft that led down to the stern deck. Buck struggled to his feet. He got smoked yesterday, too, Buck thought, he's hurting, too. More interested in doing his thing and getting away than he is in me. One last chance to stop him. As Gantsky rattled down the last flight of steps, Buck vaulted over the top rail and landed hard on his feet on the next level down.

Never catch him, he thought. He's *still* a level below me. He reached inside his jacket and pulled out the revolver. Cocking it, he looked for his target. Hunched over like an injured animal, Gantsky dragged himself across the deck toward the stern rail. As he moved, he reached to unholster the black device.

Two hundred yards off the stern rode the mystery boat. Up on its foredeck was a man with a life ring attached to a rope. He waved frantically, gesturing for Gantsky to hurry.

Buck spread his stance. The barrel trembled as he raised the .38 in a two-handed grip. He wondered if indeed he *could* shoot. The shaking sight traced its way up Gantsky's legs to his midsection. Buck exhaled and squeezed. The shot offered only a weak popping noise beneath the roaring incinerators. Gantsky's left leg whipped out from under him as if it had been struck by a club. Down he went. The black object flew from his hand and landed several feet away.

The second looked up at Buck in disbelief for a moment. Then he began to bend and slither toward the black plastic appliance. Buck squeezed off another shot, glancing it off the deck a foot from Gantsky's nose. The second looked up and blinked.

"Don't try it again!" Buck shouted. "You guys blew up my friend last night, and I'd like nothing better!"

The second rolled over on his back, stretched his arms out fulllength, and waited. Buck descended the last flight of steps slowly, keeping his aim on the young man. He was surprised—the revolver had stopped shaking.

Chief Johnson came thundering down the steps as Buck walked cautiously toward Gantsky. While Buck held the gun on the wounded second, the chief picked up the black device, removed the batteries, and flipped them over the side. He handed the detonator to Buck. As he took it, Buck looked for the friendly eyes beneath the chief's thick, bushy brows. What he saw there was frightening.

The chief's big, round eyes and contorted face radiated anger—rage like Buck had never seen before. The huge man reached down, grabbed Gantsky by the crotch and the back of his neck, and hoisted him like a rag doll, up off the deck to head height. With a grunt, he threw the man toward the steps. With arms flailing wildly, Gantsky crunched to the deck in a helpless heap.

"Now, you pile of shit, get up and walk!" the chief bellowed. "Move it, you hear me?"

"I—I can't," Gantsky moaned.

"You God-damned well better, or I'll—"

Buck looked for the other boat. It was turning off sharply to starboard.

"Buck!" the chief shouted. "Put a couple of slugs in her while you still can. Leave some marks so we can find 'em!"

Buck emptied his weapon into the port side of the cruiser, just below the deck.

The chief pushed and shoved Gantsky up the steps with Buck following behind. My God, Buck thought, I'd crap my pants if the chief ever got that mad at me. He couldn't help but glance at the back of the prisoner's jeans as the limping Gantsky struggled around the turn at the top of the steps. Well, you sneaky bastard, he thought, that's *one* thing you got right.

Chapter 35

The committee meeting began at 1430 hours, and after an hour it had lasted twice as long as Buck thought was necessary. He sensed that Hobbs, the chief, and the second mate were also wiped out. The small dayroom was enveloped in body odor, and the smoke from the chief's cigarettes kept drifting to Buck. He sympathized with the chief, but after the fire of the previous day, he preferred the body odor.

He felt confident the crisis had passed.

Congratulations had been passed around. Their situation had been reviewed again and again, but the captain would not let it drop. The robot had done a complete reversal, had become nervous and paranoid. He alone seemed convinced that there was yet more to come. *If I weren't so tired,* thought Buck, *it would be amusing.* Still, he felt powerful respect for the man. His reactions under pressure had been quick, effective—superb.

Gantsky had received the best they had in first aid. But his knee had been shattered by Buck's .38 slug. Chained to a berth in the medical treatment room, he had tearfully confessed into Buck's tape recorder. First, he directed them to the plastic explosives just inside the hatch of tank number eleven. Then, he admitted that he had substituted a chip that reprogrammed the computer to override the protective nitrogen, automatic shutdown, and alarm systems.

With witnesses carefully placed, Buck had used his telephoto lens from a distance to photograph the entire procedure as the chief removed the deadly package. Buck zoomed in for several angles. After he had carefully separated the electronics from the deadly plastic, the chief had Buck photograph the dangerous C-four. Then he hurled the explosive as far as he could into the sea. The captain had agreed that keeping that portion of the evidence aboard ship was too risky. There was no doubt that Gantsky's black plastic device was a radio transmitter, set to a frequency to match that of the receiver found connected to the bomb.

Dr. Keene had shut down the computer system, quickly inserted a backup chip, and restarted the incinerators. He was satisfied that there would be no cool-down damage to the burn chambers or the stacks. Although he had run every conceivable check that could be run on the computerized system while it was in operation, the matter really came down to Gantsky's assurance that nothing else had been altered. Helplessly chained to the berth as he was, Gantsky had to know that a disaster on the ship would become very personal.

The second engineer had been recruited by two men, "a tall blond man and a funny-looking little guy." They had somehow arranged his hiring as a crew member and had given him half of what would be enough money to start his own computer store and consulting service. He was to have been picked up by the trailing boat, but he claimed to know nothing of its occupants.

As the mystery boat pulled away, Captain Portner had called Peter who was aboard the company cruiser. Peter had intercepted the white boat and stayed with it until the escort duty was assumed by the coast guard. Peter would soon be joining *Ark II*. Gantsky would be transferred to the company boat and taken ashore.

Still, Captain Portner demanded that his tired committee members search the entire ship once again for any further signs of sabotage. While Hobbs toured the forehouse, bow, and main deck, Buck followed the chief through the afterhouse. They ignored the rules of quarantine, except for two areas, the incinerator room and the forced-draft room beneath the incinerators. To open the sealed door would result in automatic shutdown. At 1600 hours, they reported once again to the captain that the aft section of the ship was clean.

After a shower and a late dinner, Buck retired to his quarters. Hobbs had stripped to his boxer shorts and T-shirt and was already asleep. He would have the midnight watch on the bridge. As Buck undressed, he looked at the carrot-topped first mate and smiled. Sleeping in the fetal position, Hobbs had one hand tucked in his crotch. The other hand was cupped over one ear, and its index finger was jammed into the bush of hair with several strands of the red silk tightly wound around it. An overgrown little boy. Sleep tight, kid, Buck thought. At least I get to sleep all night.

It was 0730 hours when Buck awoke Wednesday morning. He had slept—really slept. No dreams, no nightmares, just deep sleep. And he felt good, except for his sore jaw and the stitches in his leg. On the way down, he stopped in the medical treatment room, where he located scissors, tweezers, alcohol, and some cotton.

A quiet Greg Gantsky watched as Buck gritted his teeth, snipped the stitches one-by-one, and jerked them out. Gantsky's laserlike eyes seemed to have lost their penetration, as if the battery had gone dead. As Buck had turned to leave, he noticed the untouched tray of food and the single tear which was caught in a crevice beneath one of Gantsky's eyes.

Buck was surprised at the compassion he felt for the second engineer. Gantsky was intelligent and talented, and the qualities seemed to have been perfectly packaged. Was it only a persona?

"I don't know who you really are, Gantsky," Buck said. "Maybe *you* don't even know. If you're really the guy who tried to kill us all, I shot too low. If there's any of the great guy I thought I knew, I feel sorry for you, because you *really* blew it."

Buck turned and left. When he reached the mess, he was greeted by the friendly cook.

"Some shittin' fisherman *you* are," Indian Joe said, "hookin' a northern in the fin. That yer best shot? Some shittin' fisherman."

"Important thing is, Joe, I got him. We do what we have to. He did bite me once before I got him in the boat. At least I didn't have to use a *gill net* like some others I know." The cook's bleating laughter once again brought a smile to Buck's face.

"Now, Joe, before you bring me that special victory meal I know you're anxious to fix, I want to thank you for all your help. You know—feeding me the way you have, and the good advice. Like the other day, you asked me if I was colorblind. I was puzzled about that—couldn't figure out what you were driving at. Then, when I saw Gantsky heading aft with a *black* walkie-talkie, I knew."

Indian Joe's face took on a strange look. He grinned nervously and then sobered again.

"Joe don't know nothin' 'bout black walkie-talkies. It was jist—you put yer *yella* tray on the stack o' *gray* ones."

Buck looked at the round, red face and then broke out laughing. In a moment, Indian Joe joined in with his bleating.

"Anyway," Buck said, reaching across to shake Joe's hand, "Thanks, Joe. If I can ever do anything to help you—anything—you just let me know. And I mean that. Now, got anything here to eat?"

"The ole man sent orders down. All meals and coffee breaks at reg'lar times again from now on, no more speshal, a la cartey treatmint."

"Oh, hell, the robot's back to normal."

"But what the robot doesn't know won't hurt him," a familiar voice from behind Buck said.

"You out water-skiing today, Peter?" Buck asked without turning.

"Just got aboard," Peter said as he joined Buck at the table. "Came to get Gantsky. Got to get that leg looked at or we could be liable. Could we have some of your excellent food?" he asked Joe. "It's much better than what we have on shore."

"Joe git right on it. Like you said, what he don't know. . . . "

"Anything new?" Buck asked.

"A few things. They picked up the crew of the other boat. Reicher was the leader all right. He denies being anywhere near the *Ark*. But he's in deep doo-doo. We have your photos of him up on deck and the bullet holes in the hull, plus the fact that the other two on his boat are very, very scared. If he doesn't break, they will. The L.A. police picked up Murrell—still no Amato. It's looking like he's skipped town.

I talked with Lenny Bercovich," Peter continued. Her boss thinks that if Gantsky cooperates, they'll have some hefty criminal charges against Schutte, charges he can't buy his way out of, as he can with most of the environmental violations."

"That's good, but does it mean anything special?"

"It means that we might, just might be getting some help in locating Ed's daughter in New York. And Dante has some connections that might help in the search. He's hard at work on it."

"Too late for Ed, but—"

"I stopped out to see Ed's wife. She's doing as well as anyone could under the circumstances. Her sister is with her, flew in this morning."

"I think we can count on Gantsky," said Buck. "He played with the tantalizing fire and got burned. Right now, he's at rock bottom." Buck paused, took a sip of coffee, and looked at Peter. "I—I really feel sorry for him. I *should* want to kill him—now that it's behind us, I feel sympathy. What a waste! He has the personality, looks, and high-tech skills to go a long way. But that little snake, Amato, I *could* kill *him*."

"For your sake, I hope you don't get the chance."

Indian Joe placed heaping trays before them, grinned, and returned to the galley.

"Interesting character, isn't he?" Peter said, gesturing toward the pudgy cook.

"Very interesting. A good man to have with the cause."

Buck tore into his scrambled eggs, while Peter took a huge bite out of a fresh cinnamon roll. For several minutes, neither appetite allowed time for words.

Finally, Peter sipped his coffee, then said. "Speaking of causes, have you given any thought to the future? You interested in staying with us, or are you, pardon the pun, all shot?"

"All shot," Buck said, adding, "at least right now."

"Understandable. Consider taking Ed's place?"

"No." Buck popped a piece of bacon into his mouth. "You think I could handle it?"

"Certainly, and you've earned—" Peter stopped when Indian Joe approached the table.

Buck was surprised when Joe began to gather up their dishes, but he was amused when he realized how long Joe was taking to do it.

"Give it some thought, will you?" Peter continued. "The company is going to make it. We will survive this, Buck. And there are going to be some dramatic changes made, *very* soon. I'd like to have you stay on with me."

"Changes? What's going on, Peter?"

"Too soon to talk about it. In a couple of days we'll know more." Peter raised his coffee cup to his lips, but he paused, simply holding it there without sipping from it. His devious smile told Buck that his old quarterback was scrambling again, but in complete control of something. Then, Peter's eyes changed to that curious stare that had always baffled Buck. His old friend seemed to be going superserious.

"I am concerned about one thing," Peter said. "Essee Beecee must maintain an image of sophistication if we are to sell a new program to the public. Our credibility might be jeopardized if we're represented by some one with a name like Buck. Maybe you could use your middle name, or your initials? Or both? Like B. blank Barnum?"

I can't believe this—this pompous attitude, thought Buck. After what I've been through? He can't mean it, but he's dead serious.

"Are you telling me," Buck finally managed, "that you wish to be represented," he went on with affected pronunciation, "by Mr. *Swanson* Barnum? Or by Mr. *B.* Swanson Barnum? Forget it."

"Well, maybe using both initials would be the way to—"

"Oh," Buck cut in, "you prefer good, old *B.S.* Barnum. Especially appropriate for a P.R. man, don't you think? How about *Beverly*? That what you want—*Beverly*?" He could feel his face heating up.

Suddenly, the mischievous look was back in Peter's eyes. He broke into a smile and looked at his watch.

"Come on. Let's go up on deck. They're about to start the burn—for real."

"I'm burning for real," Buck said, cuffing Peter on the shoulder as they walked out. "Someday, I'm going to hang you up really good. You'll get yours."

Amid a group of officers and seamen, Buck and Peter stood on the port boat deck, chatting and watching the towering stacks. Nobody knew exactly what to expect, perhaps a change in the sound, or an increase in the intensity of the wavering emissions above the stacks, or possibly the addition of some color to the translucent heat waves. The twin giants simply rumbled on.

"Your attention, please!" came the captain's voice over the speaker above them. "I know you are anxiously waiting for the burn to begin. Unfortunately. . . ."

"Oh, no!" somebody said.

"Now what?"

"Is this ship jinxed, or what?"

Buck looked at Peter. His friend simply shrugged and rolled his eyes. Trouble? Buck was about to head for the bridge when the voice continued.

"Unfortunately, for you who are waiting, Dr. Keene initiated the burn forty-five minutes ago. We have been incinerating our cargo for that period of time, and Dr. Keene reports that everything is working exactly as planned. Congratulations to all of you for getting us here."

Cheers and applause replaced the groans of disappointment. While the ovation proved to be no competition for the thundering burners and the ocean breezes, its meaning was clear. They had brought the magical assortment of technology this far, and the system worked.

A short time later, Buck watched as Gantsky was helped from the bottom of the springy ladder into the lifeboat from the company cruiser.

"You have a nice vacation cruise now, you hear?" Peter shouted up from below. Buck waved, and the small boat set out, rolling over the quartering waves toward the cruiser fifty yards away. For much of the day, Buck's emotions hopped about like a rabbit searching for food. This way—pause, nibble, and enjoy. That way—pause, nibble, and enjoy. But all the time, his eyes were alert and he coped with worries, afraid to believe they really had made it, that the troubles were over.

It was the positive attitudes of the crew that gradually eased him over the hurdle. The men were up, really up, and while they were unaware of the scope of adversarial threats that had been overcome, it was impossible not to absorb their spirit. Even Runkle's sneer was seen to crack into a slight smile on occasion. With each hour, Buck's fears faded more. He began to see it almost like a vacation cruise, albeit a noisy one.

For the rest of the day, he alternated between the bridge and the incinerator control room. On the bridge he learned that, for some of the burn, *Ark II* would be doing a controlled drift to conserve fuel. The main diesels simply idled, and the captain used the bowthruster to keep the ship pointed into the wind.

Dr. Keene enthusiastically explained the activities in the control room. Buck recorded their conversations, preserving such information as the composition of the chemicals currently being consumed, the rate of flow, burn temperatures, and draft settings. As one of the huge tanks was drained, Dr. Keene followed a preset plan in selecting the next tank in order to maintain the ship's stability. The sea water that was taken on as ballast was pumped into the bulkhead spaces between the tank, not into the tanks themselves, an innovation designed to avoid expelling contaminated ballast water back into the ocean.

Because of the burn operation, the crew was restricted from many of the routine maintenance duties normally assigned on a ship at sea. They thoroughly enjoyed the relaxed atmosphere, the time to chat, and more than one was heard to say that he had found his calling. Buck enjoyed the camaraderie, and he frequently dictated short blurbs into his recorder to remind him of sea stories and other anecdotes that might prove useful at some future time. From time to time, word passed around the ship that they had now burned down to ninety-five percent capacity, ninety percent, then eighty-five percent.

By that evening, Buck had collected sufficient data on the burning process, and a day later, he had written two distinctly different accounts of the voyage. The *dirty* version included in detail the efforts of the subversives to stop *Ark II*. The other described only the positive aspects, with no mention of the negative episodes that had occurred. He would leave it to Peter to decide which version to publish, though he strongly suspected that Peter would choose the *clean* story.

"We have a variety of adversaries out there," he could hear Peter saying, "and each will point to the violence and sabotage with which *they* had no connection and say, 'See, these are the kinds of threatening activities that sea-going incineration will attract if we allow it to set up operations here.'"

Friday morning, with his work behind him, Buck staked out what had become his favorite place aboard ship. The top landing of the outside stairs behind the bridge, that high, insecure place that had once tested his nerve had become his private crow's nest. Seated up there on a couple of cushions he had scrounged, he was in full view of everyone on deck. But it offered him, in addition to protection from the wind, the seclusion to think, dictate, or simply watch the marvelous ship, the endless sea, the gorgeous sunsets, and the stars. More than once, he found himself studying the sheer power of the two incinerator stacks, wondering if the designers couldn't channel such force directly aft into the water, thereby utilizing a form of jet propulsion while burning up the earth's toxic garbage.

Far astern, he occasionally caught a glimpse of the lab boat, a smaller cruiser the company had leased. With an EPA supervisor aboard, its crew took regular water samples from several depths and at various distances, as far as miles downwind from the ship. The samples were then tested for their acid content. The process would continue for several days after the burn. It was vital to the success of the project that it be proven the acids discharged were truly neutralized by the salt water and thus had no adverse effect upon marine life.

Saturday morning, the third day of the burn, Buck lolled lazily on his perch high above his new world. It was a gorgeous morning with clear skies, a warm sun, and just enough breeze to drift the emissions back away from *Ark II*. Like many of the crew, Buck had taken to wearing ear plugs to muffle the giants.

For the first time since the Gantsky episode, he found himself delving into his relationship with Lenny, weighing the events of the past and searching for a solid foundation on which to base one of the biggest decisions of his life. He had said that Lenny Bercovich was, if anything, a result of the problem, not a cause. Maybe that wasn't quite true when I said it, he thought. But up here, far away, it was easier to be objective.

Then, at the thought of Lenny, a vision began to form in his mind. It was vague and ethereal at first, gradually became clearer. There sat Lenny across the table from him, the highlights in her short brown hair flickering with the candlelight. Warm, brown eyes glowed from behind a complexion so pure he wanted to kiss it. Her hands enveloped one of his, squeezing it gently. She was talking to him. He couldn't make out the words, but they didn't really matter. Her pleasant satin voice seemed to stroke every nerve in his body. He felt an urgent swelling.

I think this *is* the way I want to go, he thought. Follow through with Lenny and see where it goes. Not only is she so appealing I'm aroused just thinking about her, but she has a good mind. I like the way she thinks. She's independent, but she isn't a loose cannon. And most important, I think she actually loves me. I can't remember the last time a woman other than Sunny showed me real love. If I shut Lenny out, I might be sacrificing what's really best just to serve an unfounded, rather sick principle. And isn't that what I've *been* doing these last three years? Trust no one because. . . . Buck looked upward into the endless blue. Then he closed his eyes for a moment and took a deep breath.

When he opened them, something far astern caught his attention. Probably the lab boat, he thought. He raised the glasses for a better look. It wasn't one boat, but three boats coming up on *Ark II*. They were about a half-mile off and traveling in a V-formation, obviously together, somehow organized. The now-familiar alarm went off within Buck. He jumped up, grabbed his cushions and portable radio and stowed them in the radio room on his way to the bridge where Dick Hobbs had the watch.

"Dick! You see what's coming up behind us?" Buck asked. "Looks like more trouble."

"Oh, it's trouble all right," the freckle-faced first mate replied, "but it's not the kind that you and I can do anything about."

"Don't like the sound of *that.*"

"Peter was on the horn about an hour ago. Late last night, he was on his way back to the office. He saw three boats heading out the main channel streaming anti-burner banners. He managed to drive himself to a spot where he could watch them. He said they went on out through the Gate, so they must have been headed for us," Hobbs explained. "Just about time for them to get here," he added, glancing at his watch.

"Did he speculate on their intentions?"

"As a matter of fact, he did. He thought it was about time for the greenies to get their water scoopers out here. You know, like they did to the European boats? They get right up close and take samples. They hope to get them before the emissions have had time to disperse and neutralize in the water. Can't help but make us look bad. For that matter, they may even doctor their samples."

"Can't we do something?" Buck asked.

"Oh, soon as they stop to go to work, we're gonna do something all right," Hobbs said. He picked up the phone and tapped a button. "Okay, Jonesy, start broadcasting the word. Hit every frequency at least three times. If your CD wears out, I've got a spare for you."

Buck looked back at the boats. Sure enough, about a hundred yards away, they had stopped. He could tell now, they were private fishing boats. On each, he could see several figures moving about the open rear deck. It looked like Hobbs was right on.

Buck was becoming frustrated. "And what are *we* doing?"

"We have taped messages running over the SAT-COM channels and from our external P.A. system. Here, listen in." Hobbs switched on an inside speaker to monitor the P.A. announcement.

"To the nearby sea traffic from U.S. Government Test Vehicle *Ark II:* You are advised that you are encroaching in a restricted zone during government-sanctioned tests. You are jeopardizing the safety of the testing vehicle and you are subjecting yourselves to undesirable airborne emissions. You are directed to leave the area at once. I repeat, You are directed to leave the area at once."

"Whoop-de-doo," groaned Buck. "I'm sure they'll be on their way in seconds."

"Thought you'd like that," Hobbs said.

Chapter 36

Buck felt frustrated and arm weary. He had watched the scooper boats for nearly two hours, helpless to do anything but zoom in for some close-ups of the intruders scooping up their samples. He tried to get a number of shots that included the aft rails of *Ark II* to show relative distance to the boats, how close they actually were. Once done with the Canon, all he could do was watch. And after the first hour, the field glasses became heavier and heavier. Then, when his patience had all but leaked out, Buck saw something that perked him up. The boats were moving again, joining up and heading southeast. He stepped through the vestibule to the bridge to announce the news.

"Wonder how long before they come back," the helmsman said.

"That's probably it," Buck replied, "they got what they came for. The samples won't get any better for their purposes than what they already have. We lost that one." He turned to the rear window of the bridge and raised his glasses for another look. The three boats had settled on a course straight for the coast, their white wakes spreading out and crossing behind them. They didn't appear to be fast boats. He guessed they might have a ten-hour trip ahead of them.

He retreated to his perch and plopped down on his cushions. After a lengthy and fruitless search for a course of action to counter the scoopers, he was ready to accept the final defeat by the scoopers. They would send their biased samples to the EPA, the London Convention, and probably the news media. Nothing anyone could do about it. Without adequate time for the acidic emissions to be neutralized by the salt water, the samples might show contamination. Sure, he thought, we can come back with our explanation, but the damage will already be done. Who will believe us?

On second thought, my photographs should clearly show the boats within a hundred yards, and the photos should be detailed enough to show them collecting their samples. Come on, Buck. That's more like it. Think like *they* do.

Shifting to the opponents' point-of-view, he could already see the headline: INCINERATOR SHIP TAINTS WATER 125 MILES

AWAY. A hundred and twenty-five miles away from *what?* And they'll claim the samples were taken days *after* the burn concluded.

Then he remembered his friend at the *Sun.* Yeah, Ballenger owed him one, and this is pay-back time! No, the scoopers didn't hold all the aces on this one. If they can't be beaten in the media, they could be neutralized. He stood up for a final look at the tiny specks, but a flash of white off to one side caught his eye. Putting the glasses on it, Buck was surprised to discover it was the company boat. Its sleek hull sliced the flat surface like a knife. Really fast, he thought, recalling that the forty-six-foot cruiser, a small yacht to some, had been a special design, built by Essee Beecee in the last year of their pleasure boat construction phase.

Because the ocean was calm, the cruiser pulled directly up to *Ark II,* draped large bumpers over the side, and tied up to the bigger ship. He trotted confidently down the outside steps, dropped his glasses, recorder, and camera off in his cabin, and proceeded down to the boat deck. As he approached the boarding ladder on the port side, he was startled by a chorus of whistles, shouts, and cheers from crew members gathered along the rail. Above the gunwhale, a swishing, blond pony-tail appeared, followed by a slender but shapely young body dressed in white shorts, a yellow shirt, and sneakers.

Obviously flustered, she stopped and looked about. Peter touched her elbow and pointed toward Buck.

"Dad!" Sunny rushed the remaining distance and threw her arms around his neck. The whistles and shouts increased. Buck first shrugged with embarrassment, but then, as he hugged his daughter, he found himself trying to will away tears. Not here, he thought, not now. Still, one sneaked down each cheek as he pushed her to arms-length to look at her.

"Damn! Am I glad to see you! I shouldn't be surprised. If anyone could pull off a stunt like this, it would be my Sunny. Did you stow away?" he asked, noticing that her smile was as lively as ever.

"Oh, Dad, I'm so glad you're all right! Peter says you're a hero, several times over. I'm not surprised at that. But, ohhh, I'm so glad you're okay!" She hugged him again.

Buck spun her around to face the crew. With one arm around her waist, he gestured grandly with the other.

"I'd like all you slobs to meet my wonderful daughter, Jennifer!" Another round of cheers went up. "Eat your hearts out, sailors. I'm not letting one of you within ten feet!" The cheers modulated abruptly to boos and hisses. Sunny blushed and then beamed her best smile at the men as she waved. The cheers escalated again, louder than before.

Buck led Peter and Sunny down to the officers' mess. As he was about to get their coffee and rolls, Indian Joe appeared, his round face one massive grin.

"What the old man don't know. . . ." he said slyly, his eyes never leaving Sunny. With all of the class he could muster, he presented them with silverware, carefully folded cloth napkins, warm cinnamon rolls, and coffee from a tray he carried. In a posh restaurant, his technique would never make it, Buck thought, but for Indian Joe, it was impressive.

"If ya need anythin' else," he concluded, giving Buck a sharp rap on the head, "jis' knock on wood." Obviously reluctant to leave, Joe finally eased away to watch from the galley.

"Oh, smell those rolls—they're terrific!" Sunny exclaimed. "You may have been through hell, Dad, but I know you didn't do it on an empty stomach."

"You know, that's odd," Peter said. "First time I ever heard Joe crack a joke without that nannygoat laugh."

"That's a nervous laugh," Buck said. "Right now," he added, smiling at Sunny, "I think he's too nervous to be nervous. Latest developments, Peter?"

"Gantsky readily confessed to the authorities, told the whole story. We'll want to turn a copy of your tape over to them to see if they missed anything. You knew that Murrell was arrested?"

Buck nodded.

"He's not very talkative. Apparently, he's out here on loan from a New Jersey *family*, so he probably figures that his best life insurance is a closed mouth. But if the police can hang one or two more things on him, he might loosen up."

"What about the mystery boat?"

"Leased to Reicher and the Groundswell people for two weeks. Reicher claims to know nothing of the plot. When he finally admitted to being out here, he said he was just following *Ark II* to take pictures. We know better, of course. But his two helpers don't seem quite so tough. Given a chance to get their heads together, they might come forth with enough of the truth to nail Reicher without implicating themselves too deeply."

"If one of them was a slender, dark-haired guy with dark-rimmed glasses," Buck said, "he's an attorney, kind of a wimp. That might be good. He might be smart enough to weasel out and leave Reicher holding the bag, and chicken enough to want to do it. Still no Amato?"

"Sorry," Peter said, shaking his head slowly. "They do have an APB out on him."

"With that Caddy of his, it shouldn't be too hard to find him," Buck said.

"Sorry again. They found his black Cadillac. Apparently, he made a quick trade for a red Corvette. "I'd bet anything it has stolen plates on it by now. The police think he's skipped town, possibly up to San Francisco." Peter looked reassuringly at Buck.

"No way," Buck said, shaking his head slowly. "He's still in town. I can feel it."

Peter shrugged. "But, it really comes back to Gantsky. He's fingered Murrell, and the prosecutors are confident they can prove that Murrell's money came from Schutte. A good case."

Buck turned to Sunny, "Isn't this *fun*?"

"I think it's exciting! In fact, I'm thinking of changing my major from music to law enforce—"

"Buck," Peter said, glancing at his watch, "it's nine-thirty. We should shove off in fifteen minutes—long trip home—and you still have to pack your gear."

"I *what?*"

"Did you get everything you need for the story?"

"Why, sure. It's all written—two versions. But I—"

"Then I don't see any need for you to ride out the rest of the burn— unless you want to, of course."

Buck looked at Sunny. She smiled and nodded. He looked at Peter. The devilish grin was there. He was serious.

"Sure, I'll—"

"You got fifteen minutes," Peter said. "Start by checking out topside. Get your stuff, and cram in as many goodbyes as you can in that time. Sunny and I'll see Captain Portner for a minute, and I have an announcement to make. Should work out about right. We'll meet you on the boat deck."

Buck jumped to his feet, inhaled the last bite of roll, gulped some coffee down with it, and headed for the bridge. He hurriedly explained to Captain Portner and Dick Hobbs.

Hobbs grinned, ran his fingers through his red afro, and said, "Must be a good sign for *us*. The way trouble finds you, probably a good idea for you to go ashore." He shook Buck's hand.

"Oh, by the way, Dick, I'll leave my .38 under my pillow for you, just in case."

"Are you *sure* you should leave?" the captain asked. "How do we know they're all done with us?"

"Another case of take my word, I guess," Buck replied. "Certainly, they're not all done with us, meaning the project. But we're sixty percent through the burn. We beat them on their *big* efforts. By the time they organize another effort and get back out here, you'll have finished the burn. Most important, I've got to get back to handle our publicity attack on the scoopers." He shook Captain Portner's hand and smiled reassuringly.

"I hope you're right, Buck," the captain said, prolonging the handshake. "Thanks—thanks so much for everything you've done. And I apologize for my earlier disbelief." His face was as blank as ever, but his grip and his voice exuded warmth far beyond any Buck would ever have expected. So much for the robot, Buck thought, as he gave a final wave and started for the outside steps.

Reaching his cabin, he quickly gathered his clothing and gear, stuffing them carelessly into his bag. He slipped the holstered .38 under his pillow and started for the door. He paused and looked back at the tiny compartment. Recalling the tension he had felt that first night when he stood in this strange place and looked out over the ominous shadows of the main deck, he smiled. Had he been able to see in those shadows the surprises and challenges of the days to come, he'd have left the ship right then.

He smiled at the group of men gathered at the boat deck when he got there. That's pretty nice, he thought, touching, all these guys here to see me off. But when he dropped his bags on the deck, he realized that he was not the focal point of their attention. To a man, they stood with necks craned, staring nearly straight up at the bridge.

"There she is," came a hushed voice, "there in the main window, beside the captain. See her?"

"I can't," said another voice, "your God-damned head is in my way. Move!"

Buck scanned the group. They were still unaware of his presence. And over to one side stood Indian Joe, shading his squinting eyes with one hand. Buck realized it was the first time he'd ever seen the cook outside of his domain.

"Your attention please—your attention please!" crackled the P.A. speaker above them. "This is Captain Portner. I wish to report that the burn is now sixty-five percent complete. Everything is working well and we are ahead of schedule." The crew responded with a brief burst of applause. "You are probably aware that Mr. Peter Hamlin and a guest have joined us. You are probably *not* aware that Mr. Hamlin has been appointed the new *CEO* of the company. Listen up, now. He has a few words for you. Mr. Hamlin?"

The new CEO? Buck shouldn't have been surprised. Peter had predicted it days before. But it hadn't occurred to Buck that it might happen even before the burn was completed.

"Thank you, Captain." Peter hesitated and then continued. "We are approaching the end of a most unique scientific test, a test that may bring about a significant change in the industrialized world. Indeed, it is that industrialized world that has made this test so important. It looks, right now, like the burn will be the success we predicted." A cheer went up from the group on deck. As it faded, Peter continued, "And for that success, we have *you* to thank, each and every one of you. You've worked hard. You've done everything asked of you—and more. You've been through some tough times, some frightening times.

Still—you've come through. However, things turn out, you did your jobs, and you did them very well! It's that kind of dedication that produces winners."

Buck glanced at the seamen surrounding him. They were quiet, but their faces showed the pride that swelled within as Peter spoke. In approximately four weeks these men, many of whom had been strangers to one another, had developed that closeness that comes with teamwork through troubled times.

"Speaking for everyone in the company, I wish to thank Captain Portner, First Mate Hobbs, and Chief Johnson for the incredible leadership they provided under extreme duress."

Buck was somewhat surprised at the sincerity apparent in the crew's applause. For the officers? I guess, he thought, that *really* says something.

"We owe tremendous gratitude, however, to one man in particular. Before many of you had even boarded *Ark II*, this man was going through hell, fighting to give *Ark II* her chance. Indeed, several times our mission would have been scrubbed or ultimately destroyed but for the determination of this one man."

The crew had become quiet. Even the incinerators seemed to have backed off a little. Peter's voice had dropped from a speech-making mode to one of warmth and sincerity. Buck glanced around. Most of the eyes were on him. It was then he realized what was happening.

"Since he joined us, I've heard him called different things," Peter went on. The crew laughed. "He's been called *Noah*. He's been called *Troublemaker*. He's been called *Wyatt Earp*." The crew laughed. "I hear that he's gotten over his fear of heights and is known to some as *Big Bird*."

"All right, *Big Bird!*" someone shouted.

"I would call this man—*hero*," Peter said, "and I'm very proud to call Buck Barnum *my friend*." A cheer went up and Buck felt the balloon of pride puff up within him, puff almost to the bursting point. He looked down at the red steel deck, but he felt the slaps on the back and the firm handshakes.

"Thank you all again," Peter said. "When you get back to port, we'll have one hell of a party!"

"All r-i-i-i-ght!" shouted one voice.

"See, Jonesy! I told you—now pay up!"

The clamor was slow to fade. One-by-one, the men came to Buck to thank him, to shake his hand. Few had many words to say. Words did not come easily to men like these at times like this. But he had no trouble understanding their message.

A powerful hand suddenly clamped high and hard on Buck's hand, seizing the advantage of leverage. Quickly it tightened like a vise. He turned and found himself nose-to-nose with Mal Runkle. The sneer was there; the bloodshot eyes glared. Ouch, Buck thought, he's going to break my hand! Clenching his left into a fist, he was ready to swing for the first engineer's jaw. The pain became excruciating, but he returned Runkle's glare, refusing to capitulate in any way. He means it, Buck thought. He's going to break it! Hang on, Buck, he told himself. Give it a three-count and then—

"One—" Runkle showed no sign of letting up. "Two—" Runkle's sneer seemed more deeply set. "Thr—"

Suddenly, the first engineer's grip relaxed. The sneer melted into a devious grin.

"You did good, Barnum. I'd still like to meet you in an alley some-time, but you son of a bitch, you did good."

"I apologize, Runkle," Buck said. "I was wrong about you," he added with a smile. As he unclenched his left hand, he sensed as much as heard a sigh of relief from the crew. "See you in that alley, Runkle."

With a final shake, they separated and Buck turned away just as Peter and Sunny stepped out from the forehouse. To his surprise, the men became silent. A couple of whispers, but nothing more. They parted, leaving a clear aisle to the boarding ladder, an impromptu honor cordon. Buck grabbed his bags and followed Sunny down the springy steps. Standing on the afterdeck of the cruiser as it eased away, he gave those on the deck of *Ark II* a final salute. A major chapter closed. A new chapter was about to open. Buck wished he knew how it read.

Chapter 37

"Strange," he said to Sunny, "I should feel relieved, but this hurts."

Sunny jabbed him lightly in the shoulder. "You just finding out that the tough, old turkey really has a heart?" she asked.

"Not exactly. I've always had my soft spots, but *this* one surprises me."

The streamlined craft smoothly accelerated, easing up on plane. The wind tossed their hair. Buck pointed at Peter and laughed. "Now we'll find out that's just a hairpiece!" he shouted.

"Stay out here if you want! I'm going in!" Peter replied. He moved forward, opened the door to the large cabin, and held it for Sunny and Buck who had decided to follow close behind.

"Wow!" Buck said softly, as he scanned the luxurious cherry-paneled lounge. On the thick, light blue carpet sat two identical clusters of furniture. Each was composed of a round cherry table surrounded by four swivel-style, barrel chairs covered in soft, blue leather. One cluster was up forward on the starboard side, while the other sat just inside the rear door on the port side. Large windows trimmed with blue and gold curtains lined both sides, giving excellent visibility to everyone in the lounge. Built in along each side with its back to the outside was a matching blue leather couch.

Two narrow sets of stairs occupied the center of the front wall of the lounge. The stairs on the right led up six steps to the pilot house, while the others led downward the same distance to what Buck presumed was the sleeping area. To the right of the contrasting stairs was a bar, behind which stood a small refrigerator. Buck was impressed by the quality of the paneling, carpet, and leather.

Peter gestured to chairs around the table on the port side. "Let's sit here. Sun's pretty bright on the other side," he said. As Buck and Sunny sank into the soft comfortable chairs, Peter asked, "What'll it be, Buck? Margarita or beer?"

"Beer's fine, thanks."

"Sunny, Coke or—"

"Scotch on the rocks."

Peter looked up and blinked. Buck and Sunny broke out laughing.

Peter shrugged. "What do I know?"

"If you have a white wine, that would be my choice," Sunny said demurely.

"Not sure I can accommodate you, Sunny. I happen to know you're two months from twenty-one," Peter answered with his mischievous grin.

"Peter! We're not even in the *United States!*"

Peter's hands went up in mock defeat. "Okay, okay—wine it is," he said.

Peter set their drinks before them, along with a large cannister of mixed nuts. He returned to the bar, prepared a Bloody Mary for himself, and joined them at the table.

"To a job well done," said Buck, lifting his beer in the traditional gesture.

They had only sipped their drinks when Sunny raised her glass. "To my dad, Buck—Beat 'Em All to Hell—Barnum."

Buck feigned a blush as they tipped their drinks once more. Then, he looked at Peter expectantly. But Peter sat solemnly, staring at his drink as he stirred it slowly with the celery stick. The drone of the two powerful engines filtered into the lounge from beneath them. Through the rich carpet, Buck could barely feel the friction of the water rushing past the sleek hull. For such a vessel, slashing through the ocean at thirty knots, it was extremely quiet.

Finally, Peter hoisted his glass toward Sunny, and then to Buck. His eyes took on a peculiar look, almost, Buck thought, as though he were looking into some other world. Peter's eyes fixed on Buck.

"To change," he said. Nothing more.

After moments of the frozen silence, Sunny rose and said, "I've got to use the john."

"Out here, Sunny, it's a *head*. Down the steps, on your right, remember?" Peter replied. The glint returned to his eyes; the voice carried his familiar teasing tone.

As Sunny trotted down the steps, Buck smiled at Peter.

"I don't care what you say. That's a *john*." He took a large swallow of beer. "You know, Peter? Feels good! Really good! I've gone from loser to winner in a few weeks."

"And the path was?"

"Damned tough."

"You had *forgotten* that?"

"Of course not," Buck retorted. "Well, maybe I had. Seems like the lower you sink, the more you look for quick fixes, instant remedies. It probably ties to desperation—don't have time to wait for things to get better when you're drowning."

"I'm certainly proud of you, Buck," Peter said. "You did a fantastic job for the project and you fought your way out of that hole. Excuse me a moment." He reached across the table and punched a button on the wall- mounted intercom.

"Yes, Peter," a strong bass voice answered.

"Skids, what's it look like for time?"

"Lookin' good, Peter. She's purrin' like a kitten, and on this skatin' rink we've got out here today we can really move. Hittin' thirty-two knots at cruise. Should make the Angels in about seven hours—fifteen."

"Fine, Skids, but—"

"I know. Don't burn her up. You know I wouldn't do anythin' to hurt *this* baby!"

"I'll be up in a minute. Do you and Larry need a beer?"

"That'd be fine, Peter, just talkin' about that."

"You got it," Peter said, pushing the off button. "Good man," he said, turning his attention back to Buck. "Skids and Larry were in the Navy together—patrol boat in Viet Nam. Got both of them when they retired. What they don't know about making a boat run hasn't been discovered yet. Skids does his job like you do, Buck, a hundred and ten percent."

Buck warmed at the compliment. He had felt a steady glow since Peter arrived on *Ark II,* and while Sunny's presence contributed to it, he recognized that Peter's constant stream of praise was really feeding the flame. Enjoy it, he thought to himself, you earned it. All that stress alone, not to mention the physical dangers. You paid your—

"Buck," Peter said, tilting his head down slightly and peering from just beneath his eyebrows, "I have something you and I need to discuss.

It's rather important," he went on in a serious tone. "But we can hit it later. I promised Sunny she'd have first crack at you." Peter got up and headed for the refrigerator. Pulling two beers, he turned and looked at Buck.

"What is it?" Buck asked. "Might as well discuss it now."

"It can wait," Peter replied. He turned and headed up the six steps to the pilot house.

Buck sat quietly recalling Peter's words but focusing more on the expression his friend's face had shown. That habit of dipping his head, he thought, it always means he's serious, really serious. About what? He got up, walked to the rear of the lounge, opened the door, and stepped out onto the open deck. The thirty-two-knot slipstream sneaked around the corner and ruffled his hair. Ahhh, he thought, he's going to lean on me again to take Ed's job. Should I give in now or make him wait?

Chapter 38

Buck leaned against the outside rear cabin wall and looked back over the cruiser's stern. The white foam wake spread into an ever-widening V. Occasional traces of the light blue exhaust faded into the slipstream above the throaty sounds of the powerful twin engines. Swaying almost imperceptibly above the transom, the white sixteen-foot dinghy that served as taxi and lifeboat hung crosswise between its stanchions. The small boat, with its forty-horsepower Evinrude engine, reminded him of his fishing trips to northern Minnesota. Many happy hours in a rig just about like that, he thought. But his thoughts shifted. He wondered what Peter was up to now. He sensed a movement beside him. It was Sunny.

"What's the matter, Dad? I'd think you'd be doing flips out here," she said. "Thanks to your heroics, things are looking good!"

"Oh yeah, good, I guess. But it's something else I'm thinking about."

"Oh?"

"In there just now, something about what Peter said—or didn't say."

"Brrrr—I'm cold. Not dressed for this," Sunny said. "Can we go back inside, Dad?"

Buck felt the chill, too, but he was less sure of its cause. "Sure," he said, holding the door for Sunny. Once inside, he dropped into a blue leather chair. Sunny busied herself behind the small bar preparing a pot of coffee.

"Dad?" she began as she returned to the table and took her seat, "is it S.C.B.C. that worries you? Or is it Peter?"

"In case you hadn't noticed, they're one and the same."

"You don't trust Peter?"

"Yes—and no."

"Now what kind of an answer is that? Peter's never let you down, has he?"

Buck thought for a moment. "No, he's never really let me down. But he's left me out there on the end of a limb that's being sawed off, sort of like he's saying, 'Go ahead, Buck, fly. And don't worry. If it doesn't work, I'll catch you.' Sunny, have you ever felt like you're a puppet? And someone else is pulling the strings, someone in whom you have about ninety-five percent trust?"

"No, not exactly. But when it comes right down to it, Dad, you're the only person in my life who'd rate higher than ninety-five."

Buck smiled. "Thank you. That's—"

"And *you'd* only get a ninety-eight!" Sunny laughed, reached across the table, and slapped Buck lightly on the chin.

"Okay, okay," Buck said, putting up his hands. "Now, different subject. Back there on *Ark II,* you babbled something about changing your major to law enforcement. You were kidding, of course?"

"No, I'm really quite serious." Sunny got up, crossed over to the bar, and poured two mugs of coffee.

"You've been talking with Lenny Bercovich?"

"Uh-huh." She said seriously. "We've had a couple of long talks. She's really something, isn't she, Dad?" Sunny placed a mug before Buck and then sat down with the other. She folded one leg beneath her on the seat and looked directly at him.

"Yes—yes, she is." He felt his face flush. He hesitated, unsure of what to say next.

"She's beautiful—and sharp, too. And her son, James, he's the *neatest* kid." Sunny's smile intensified slightly.

"What? You've even met her son? How did all this come about?"

"Lenny came out to the hotel to check on us. She and I had coffee and talked, mostly about the dangers and what to do. And she taught us some tricks, like how to mark my apartment door so I could tell if anyone had opened it while I was gone. Then she called about three days later to tell us she thought it was safe to go back home. With all of the others rounded up, she didn't think Amato would stay around to give us any trouble, so we moved out of the hotel.

"Dad, she's a fantastic person. Do you love her?"

"There's that word again," Buck said.

"Do you think you *might* love her?"

"Yes, I think I do. And I don't mind telling you that right this minute she looks *very* good to me. But I think she deserves better—we *both* deserve better—than a relationship built on a rebound. She's long past that temptation, and at my age I've got to *get* past it. Too old for another mistake."

"How many years will that take?" she asked.

"One thing I have to do," Buck said, "is get myself on firm financial footing. Sure glad I have this job, even if it's temporary. I think I've earned my wings with the company, and I think Peter wants me to take Ed's job."

"You certainly deserve it," Sunny said. "He's *got* to offer it to you." After a natural pause, Sunny continued, "You know something, Dad?" For the first time, Sunny laughed, really laughed. "This would be too embarrassing to tell anybody but you. Back when Mom married Howard I found myself thinking about how awful it'd be if I had to introduce that creepy Howard as my *stepfather!*"

"What do you mean? Howard's a handsome man, looks like he's right out of Hollywood," Buck said.

"That's *exactly* what I mean. He's a primped up, dressed up phony, all image. Luckily, despite all that, he's almost a decent guy. Now, Lenny, on the other hand—that might be tough, too. She seems more like a sister. Could I actually call her my *stepmother?*"

Buck laughed. "You said you had a *couple* of talks with Lenny?"

Sunny nodded. "She told me she'd like to get together again. I should call her someday. So I did, and she invited me over to her place. She told me all about her job, and—"

"And, you talked about me?" He looked intently at the serious, young face.

"She told me she thinks she loves you, but that absolutely nothing had happened between you. She said that was your fault, more than hers." Sunny paused and looked down. She watched her index finger, as it lightly traced its way around the rim of her coffee mug. "Daddy, I'm not sure I would have believed any other woman, but I believed her."

"But I *told* you nothing had happened. Didn't you believe me?"

"Yeah—until I saw Lenny."

"Okay, okay. So?"

"Dad, are you all right? Did all that disappointment with Mom, all that hurt make you impotent?"

Buck felt his face flush. "What kind of a question is *that*?"

"A lot better than the answer it got," she replied. "It wouldn't be too surprising after all the trouble you've been through. It happens, you know."

"Correct me if I'm wrong," Buck bristled. "You're saying there had to be a physical problem or I'd have been in her bed?"

"Well, not exactly. But if I were a nice, handsome man like yourself and a woman as beautiful and nice as Lenny had a thing for me, I don't know. . . ."

"I'm disappointed in you," Buck said in mock anger, "and this part of our conversation is over." He grabbed a handful of nuts from the container, tossed them carelessly into his mouth, and crunched down hard. One of the nuts lodged in his throat until he coughed it loose.

Sunny frowned. "I'm sorry, Dad. That was an awfully personal thing to bring up." She sipped her coffee, paused for a moment, and said, "Anyway, Lenny's decided to stay away from you, no phone calls, nothing until you've had time to figure out what you want.

"Anything I can get you two?" a voice behind Buck said. He turned to see Peter at the bar mixing another Bloody Mary.

"We're fine with our coffee," Buck said. "Kind of hungry, though. Do we have anything to eat besides mixed nuts?"

"Sure do," Peter said, checking his watch. "Larry will be down to break out our lunch in a few minutes." When Peter had finished with his drink, he took his seat across from Buck. "Now, *my* turn?" he asked, smiling at Sunny.

"You want me to get lost?" Sunny asked.

"Of course not," Peter said. "You're a part of all this." He paused, then looked straight at Buck. "The fact is, the *Ark II* project is dead—finis—kaput."

Buck stared at Peter. The stifling silence blanketed everything but the humming engines. "Pardon me? Those roaring incinerators have screwed up my hearing," Buck said.

"Buck, the project is a wash-out," Peter replied.

"I—I don't believe what I'm hearing. You sound serious!" Buck replied.

"I've considered everything carefully, and I've determined that we've lost—"

"Oh, *you've* determined?" Buck felt that familiar heat flare up. It was the instant volcano, the fiery reaction ignited by a fist to his face or a kick at his crotch. "*You've* determined? After all I've gone through—all the whole staff and crew have gone through—you sit there like Mr. Cool and tell me it was for *nothing*? Before the burn is even *finished*?"

Buck realized he was on his feet and shouting again. It was all too damned much! Roberta had quit on him—and now *Peter*?

Peter sat there, his handsome face blank. Finally, he said quietly, "Would you like to hear me out—and then blow up? Or would you prefer to blow up first—and then hear me out?"

"Peter! You can't!" Sunny protested in a loud, whisper. She jumped to her feet, her angry face accenting her objection.

Buck struggled to control his rage. He took a deep breath and dropped wearily back into the soft blue leather. Reaching for his coffee, he took a nervous sip. Then he motioned for Sunny to sit down.

"Okay," Buck said, "the kid's got his temper under control. Let's hear your speech. I hope to hell it's more honest than the last one."

"No more honest," said Peter. "I meant every word I said back there on the ship. But you recall, except for the promised party, I said *nothing* about the future."

Buck detected an unusual increase in Peter's intensity, almost like his friend was about to embark on his own rampage.

Looking at Buck he said, "If you're ready to listen, I'll explain."

Buck glared at Peter and pointed a gunlike index finger at him.

"We're forced," Peter began, "to terminate the incineration project as soon as *Ark II* reaches port, for two reasons. Like our predecessors who went down before us, we should be on the same side as the Greenies. But you saw what they will do to discredit us. It would be all of that and worse with each step we take. We've had one murder and another attempted. We've had spies come that close to blowing up the ship and likely killing twenty-five more good people, not to mention all the sabotage and stress."

"Excuse me, Peter," Buck said. "If it's all over, why finish the burn? Why not bring the guys home now?"

"Because we still have three hundred and fifty thousand gallons of toxic chemicals to get rid of."

"I know where you can buy a dumpsite in the mountains—cheap," offered Sunny with a scowl.

"*Dirt* cheap," Peter added with a smirk. "For me, this part of the loss, the failure to win public support, is very difficult. We *know* the program is right, but the people who should make up the support base we need simply aren't ready for it yet. They see us as another commercial venture, and they just *don't* see the need. At-sea incineration would have a better chance if it were taken over by the Lions Club—or the Band Boosters Club. By contrast, you've seen the interest, the dedication our opponents can stir up. I guess the reality is we're ten, twenty, maybe fifty years ahead of our time."

"It's going to take another Love Canal?" Buck asked.

"It's going to take several disasters of much greater magnitude than the Canal before America wakes up," Peter replied.

"You really don't think the right kind of media blitz could do the job?"

"No, but even if PR *could* do it, there's another little difficulty." Peter went tongue-in-cheek after his statement.

Buck was reminded of Ed Roland. It was Ed's way of laughing at his own joke. Damn, he thought, looking down at the tabletop, aware of a knot building in his gut. How long does *this* go on? I really do miss Ed, his sharp mind, his sense of humor, and—and he's *dead*. And for *what?*

He looked over at Sunny. She was watching him, her blue eyes radiating quiet compassion his way.

Buck squirmed with impatience. He was balancing precariously on another major upset, and Peter seemed to be in no hurry to explain.

"Peter, you just shot down the most inspiring project I've ever touched. Now, come on!"

"Sorry. Okay, that little difficulty I mentioned. I received word last night that the London Convention has rejected our petition—*without* a hearing. And to make sure we got the message, they issued a statement.

I quote, '. . . .and while the Convention respects your efforts, we cannot foresee a lifting of the ban anytime in the future,' unquote. That about says it," Peter concluded.

The knot in Buck's stomach tightened. It felt like a huge fist twisting and driving deeper and deeper. Despite Peter's opening announcement, Buck had felt that somehow the conclusion might still be negotiated. That hope had brought him to realize just how much the project really meant to him. And with that realization surfaced a parallel thought he'd repressed. The whole effort, with its verbal conflict, beatings, crashes, shootings, and hidden bombs, had represented a door to the future for Buck. Success in the venture might have opened that door to a career based upon respect as well as challenge. But now. . . .

He looked at Sunny. The tears in her eyes told him she understood his disappointment. She, perhaps more than anyone, *really* understood.

"It's all right, Dad," she said. "Lots of jobs out there. You'll find a good one—I *know* you will."

"But with that attitude, Peter," Buck managed to say, "why did they let us go on with the test? It makes no sense."

"I think—I think there were probably two reasons. One, by allowing the test they reduce the perception that they never gave us a chance, and two: I suspect that, why'll they'll never admit it, they wanted the results of our test on file for future reference. By that I do mean *future.* When the world becomes desperate, they may *have* to reconsider at-sea-incineration. Now, it isn't all so ba—"

"Peter," Sunny snapped, "you knew it could turn out like this. Why'd you bring Dad in? You call *this,* after all he's gone through, a *favor?*"

"You know," Buck injected, "I *could* work at the lumber yard or bag groceries. Be a hell of a lot safer."

"Are you two *finished* now?!!" Peter barked, slapping the table top with his hand.

Sunny flinched.

Buck's head jerked up. He hadn't heard such emotion in Peter's voice since football days. The surprising jolt snapped him back to the present like the crack of a whip.

"Now, before you two start to carve me up, I'll remind you *I've* not yet finished. *May I?*" Peter asked, his question more of a demand. "This thing, the *Ark II* project, was brought to the company by Hudson. In fact, it got him his job. I saw the risks, but I felt it had a good chance. *That's* why I brought you in, Buck. And I still believed it had a chance—until last night. You know, I gave it *my* best shot, too."

Studying his friend Buck thought, Yeah, he's telling the truth. "Okay, go on, Peter."

"I hate to admit it, but we've been used by the politicians again. I saw it coming and I tried to get through it, but. . . ." Peter shrugged. "When the ship's first owner tried at-sea incineration, the EPA backed out on them, left them holding the bag. This time, the government people supported us right up to the end. They lobbied actively to get the ban lifted." Peter hesitated. "I think they knew all along how the story would end, but *this* time, it wouldn't be *their* fault."

"I guess I can buy that," Buck said, taking a swig of cold coffee.

"Hudson was bent on making this work," said Peter. "Now, he's out and I have the challenge of resuscitating S.C.B.C. Garland Grigsby will be working with me, and we have the solid support of four board members. I believe the fifth member will come around in a month or two, when the shock wears off."

"Excuse me, Peter," Buck said. "The board supported *Ark II* by a three to two majority. Now you say you have a four to one majority. Awfully quick turnaround."

"Two reasons. The first is called, 'Save your ass.' Excuse me, Sunny. They can band together, be decisive, move quickly, and try to save what's left, or they can sit back, whimper, and lose everything. The second is called, 'Have a backup plan ready.' Garland and I had already put together a good backup plan, and Buck, it includes *you*. What would you say—"

P - p - p - p - p - p - punk! A rapid series of crisp, sharp sounds came from the pilot house. Buck jerked around. *P - p - p - p - punk*! The second cluster brought with it strange ripping, shredding sounds and they were but a few feet away.

"What the hell!" he exclaimed. He saw an irregular row of holes in the large Plexiglass windows along the forward, starboard side of the lounge. "Those are—bullet holes! Down—quick! Get down!"

As one, they tumbled off their chairs, sprawling on their bellies on the thick carpet. Buck moved to shield Sunny with his body.

P - p - p - p - p - p - punk! The third burst came through the starboard windows opposite them and raked the table area.

When the splintering stopped, Peter jumped up, punched the intercom button, and flopped back on the deck.

"Skids! What have we got out there?" he asked breathlessly.

"A shit pot full of trouble, Peter! Got a thirty-foot cigarette boat, maroon with gold trim, sleek and fast—she has a good twenty or thirty on us, maybe more. Three guys—a driver and two with automatic weapons! Larry's down, and the instrument panel is a mess. Any of you hit?" he asked.

"Okay here," Peter said. "How bad is Larry?"

There was a prolonged silence. Buck could feel convulsive sobs from Sunny's body as though she were gasping for air.

"Peter—Larry's done—took one—right in the head."

Chapter 39

Buck turned toward Peter. His friend lay there on his belly on the plush carpet, his upper body propped up on his elbows, his face in his hands. Buck knew Peter was hurting over this one.

"Skids! It's Buck. Where are they now?"

"You can get up. They're pullin' around for another pass, I think," Skids said, his deep bass voice calm and reassuring.

Buck straightened up for a look around. He spotted the speedboat far off the starboard side, nearing the first-quarter point of a large, looping turn.

"What have you got left?" Buck asked. "Can you control the boat?"

"Got a steering wheel and two engines. Everything else shot to hell—hopin' I still got a radio—not sure yet. If you don't get those weapons out of that front couch and start returnin' some fire, they're gonna pull up close and shred us to bits. All we are is aluminum and plexiglass. Won't stand a chance!"

"Come on, Peter!" Buck ordered, slapping Peter lightly on the shoulder. "Let's go! Need your help!"

To Buck's surprise, when he reached the forward couch his friend was right there with him. Peter flipped up the seat cushion, reached inside and began to pull items frantically, tossing them on the carpet beside the couch. After two large caliber bolt-action hunting rifles with scopes, came spare clips of ammunition, a Browning pump-action shotgun, a handful of shells, and several zip-on life vests.

"Dad!" Sunny shrieked as she scampered over to them. "Why are they doing this? The project is dead!"

Buck looked up into a ghostlike face with huge, fear-filled eyes, a face he had never before seen. "They don't know that, Sunny. But I don't think this is about the project, or even revenge. Probably about Buck Barnum, the principal witness—called *damage control.*"

"What can *I* do, Dad?"

He tossed her two of the Stearns life vests.

"Here, put one on and toss the other up to Skids. Then get below, pull a pad off a bunk, and wrap up in it. And stay on the deck right below the steps where we can find you! Got that?"

"But maybe I can help," she pleaded.

"You'll probably *have* to before this is done. But not if you're dead. Move it!" he bellowed as he zipped up his vest.

"Open the windows!" Peter ordered. "Give us some options. You take those." As they worked their way aft, sliding the large starboard windows open, Skids's voice came over the intercom.

"Here they come! You got about ten seconds. I'll maneuver best I can, but when they get close, I'll be on the deck. It's too damned hot up here. Nothin' but glass."

With the windows opened, Peter met Buck back at the front couch. Motioning for Buck to watch carefully, Peter inserted a clip in his .30-06 rifle. Buck imitated the move. Then Peter showed him the safety latch. On—Off—On.

"We're best right here," Peter said. "They'll shoot right through our hull, but we'll get a little added protection from this couch. On the first pass, put as many as you can into that cockpit. Don't stop to aim. Got to make them dance—keep their distance. We've got plenty of—what are you doing?"

"Just in case," Buck said as he jammed shells into the shotgun. After shoving extra shells into a pocket and laying the shotgun on the deck, Buck rejoined Peter. On their knees on the couch, they faced the open window, resting their rifles on the back of the couch.

The hostile boat rocketed toward them. It was so streamlined, it barely disturbed the surface of the water. With it approaching so fast at a ninety-degree angle, Buck wondered for a moment if the raiders were going to ram them.

"Okay, Buck," he heard Peter say. "It's time. They're in *our* range, but still out of *theirs*."

Sighting through the scope, Buck drew a bead on the windshield, about where he figured the right-side-seated driver should be. The explosions of the two rifles firing almost simultaneously startled him. He froze for a moment, simply knelt there smelling the acrid smoke from the gunpowder. But two rapid shots by Peter, accompanied by the metallic clicking of his bolt action snapped Buck back to reality.

He hurriedly jerked the bolt back and forward and lined up for his second shot.

"Hurry up, Buck! Shoot that thing!" Peter shouted, squeezing off another round. "They haven't gotten the message yet. Don't pick targets! Just shoot!"

"Come on!" came Skids's voice. "Do something! Keep 'em away from us!"

Buck fired, bolted, and fired again, pointing at vague outlines behind the windshield. But he knew he was hurrying too fast. He was jerking the trigger, probably shooting high. The speeding boat was within fifty yards. Suddenly, it slewed to the right, drew even with the cruiser, and slowed. There were two men with weapons standing in the open cockpit facing the cruiser. Buck didn't know weapons, but he knew they had some kind of assault rifles. He sighted on one of the men through the scope.

"Peter, it's Amato!" He steadied his aim, but before he could fire—*P - p - p - p - punk*! *P - p - p - p - p - p - p - p - punk*! The barrage raked back and forth. An unrelenting cacophony of frightening *punks* and *splats* ripped into the cruiser above them, beside them, and beneath them. Buck could hear bullets tearing through the pilot house. Midway between Peter and himself, a hole appeared in the blue back cushion of the couch. He rolled backward off the couch, grabbing Peter by the shirt and pulling him along to the deck.

"They're zeroing in on us. Move back here and spread out!" Buck shouted. A rapid crabwalk took him to the window farthest aft on the starboard side. Peter took up a position two windows away. They hunkered down, reluctant to expose their positions. *P - p - p - p - punk*! *P - p - p -p - p - p - p - punk*! The shots of the raiders tore into every part of the lounge. Buck glanced over his shoulder in time to see the cannister of nuts slam against the far wall, its contents flying wildly, landing in the red remains of Peter's Bloody Mary.

He turned to Peter. "Pure luck they haven't hit us. Every second lowers our odds."

Got to do something, he thought. Maybe a linebacker blitz. . . . He turned and shouted at the intercom, "Skids, pull her hard right if you can, right at them!" *P - p - p - p - punk*!

"You got it!" came the answer. "But you gotta be my eyes. I'm flat on my belly—if I get up, I'm *dead*! Here goes!"

Buck felt the cruiser lean to the right. He raised his head slowly. They were angling sharply toward the raiders, forcing them in turn to veer right. The sudden maneuver threw Amato and his partner off balance. Their firing stopped as they fell to the deck. The turn into their attackers had worked even better than Buck had hoped. For the moment, the quarry had become the hunter. Now's our chance, he thought. Got to hit something this time.

"That's it, Skids!" Buck shouted. "Straighten her out, count to ten, and break left. Okay?"

"How's that? Straight?"

"A little more left . . . there. Start counting!"

Peter reached into a pocket for a fresh clip. Buck raised up and put his scope on the speedboat which was running away from them at a slight angle to the right. He had a clear view of the rectangular cockpit from the rear, and there was Amato! Buck steadied his aim on Amato, but the little man suddenly moved. As Buck followed the movement, he found himself aimed perfectly at the back of the driver. He held his breath and squeezed the trigger. He was so intent on his effort, he hardly heard the shot or felt the recoil of the powerful weapon.

The driver lurched forward and to his right, turning the wheel and apparently jamming the throttles open. The maroon missile swung right and took off like it was airborne. The remaining two gunmen scrambled to regain control of the runaway craft and clear the driver's seat.

Buck felt his knees pressing into the carpeted deck as Skids swerved to the left at the appointed time.

"Skids! Stop this thing as fast as you can!" Buck shouted. He felt the lurch as the engines slowed and the cruiser's momentum suddenly dropped off. The stern came up, and the water made a rushing sound as their wake passed them by.

"Sunny!" he called. "Are you all right?"

"Dad, I'm okay, but I'm—scared!"

"Good, that might save your life," he replied. "Quick, Peter, help me get the little boat down. By the time I figure out how to do it, it'll be too late." Buck grabbed the shotgun and headed aft. "Skids!" Buck shouted. "Can you shove her in reverse? Get her stopped? Come on, Peter."

He stepped through the rear door onto the open deck. He swayed momentarily as the twin diesels revved up in reverse, raising the stern abruptly and killing the last of their forward momentum. Stopping, he turned to look back inside the lounge and froze at what he saw. Peter lay face down on the lounge deck, one side of his shirt showing blood. "Oh, my God—" Buck moaned. Peter's dying—could even be dead.

He started toward Peter, then stopped. Blinking, he shook his head and turned angrily toward their attackers. There, about a mile away, drifted the maroon speedboat. And they'll be back in a minute for the rest of us. With the thought, a bigger part of him, a combination of competitive spirit, anger, and adrenaline rose up, refusing to yield to the tragedy.

"Sunny! Come on out! Need you now!" he called. "Skids! Get down here—fast as you can. I need your help!"

Sunny rushed up from below, saw Peter, and stopped in her tracks. She jerked her hands up to cover her face.

"Is he—dead?"

Then, she lowered her hands slowly, snuffled loudly several times, and bent low over Peter. She looked up through watery eyes.

"Can we help him?"

"Your job, Sunny," Buck replied. "Find the first aid kit and do what you can for him. But when they get close, you get back down in your hole, understand?"

He hurried to the lifeboat and propped the shotgun against one of its bench seats just as Skids emerged from the lounge. Strange, Buck thought, as the tall, slender man, all of six-feet-four inches, dressed in khaki trousers and shirt, hustled toward him. He had never met the man, and there they were, the two of them to determine whether their group lived or died. He looked up into the face, perhaps five years older than his. The set of the lantern jaw and the steel in the eyes told Buck he was paired with a fighter.

"Need the boat down quick!" Buck said. "I'll explain while you do it."

"With you all the way," Skids replied. "If those bastards ever get smart, they'll just blow holes in our bottom till the bilge pumps can't keep up, and we're history. But they're like some of the guys we had in Nam. They're so into shooting people they forget about winning the battle."

He released the mechanism, swung the boat out over the transom of the cruiser, and began lowering it. "You know how to run an outboard?" he asked.

"Here, I'm out of my element," Buck replied. Pointing to the white sixteen-footer as it settled into the water, he said, "There—I'm as good as you are. Gas?"

"Both tanks full, twelve gallons. Won't get you to the coast by a long shot, though."

"Don't expect to go there," Buck said, "but they're after me, not you. I want them to *think* I'm running for the coast."

"Don't know about the radio," Skids said. "Receiver's out. I've sent Mayday several times, but no way to know. . . . " He looked off to starboard, and Buck's eyes followed.

"They're on the move again," Buck said. "Still two of them in a damned fast boat, with awesome firepower, but by splitting up we can even things up a little.

"Skids, you take good care of my daughter till I get back." Buck jumped down onto the diving platform and slipped into the trailing boat. "And look after Peter!" he shouted. For the first time, he noticed the name on the cruiser's stern: *Miss Essee.*

He released the bow line, pulled it in, stepped over two bench seats and settled on the rear seat. Drawing on times past, he automatically released the tilt latch, lowering the outboard shaft into the water. He squeezed the gas line bulb several times to pressurize the tank, pulled out the choke, set the tiller arm throttle, and pulled the starter cord. On the third pull, it started, sending up a cloud of blue smoke.

Simultaneously, the large twin engines of the cruiser belched loudly as they blanketed Buck with fumes. The stern of the cruiser dug in, and the large craft accelerated rapidly, leaving Buck to bob about on its turbulence.

Buck looked for Amato's boat. It was coming fast, perhaps half a mile off to the starboard side. He twisted the throttle grip half open and the small boat came to life. As soon as he dared, he turned left and leaped over the high wake of the cruiser. Then he opened up the throttle and set his course due east. He hoped Amato would buy into his plan. With Skids heading southeast to L.A., if Buck headed straight east those hoods should conclude that he's heading for Santa Barbara and come after him. The wind blew his hair wildly as the small boat skimmed over the nearly calm surface.

He looked over his right shoulder. Buck saw the cruiser come between the maroon boat and himself, breaking his line of sight to the hoods. Unless Amato abandoned the big boat to come after Buck, she was in for another pasting. He knew he'd hear no gunshots over the noisy outboard engine behind him. He swerved slightly from side to side, getting the feel of the boat. It planed nicely with only one occupant. Feels good, he thought. Can't begin to match their speed, but they can't maneuver with me.

With his free hand, he picked up the shotgun, rested it across his tiller arm, experimenting with side-to-side aiming. He could cover the range on the left side and to the rear quite well while operating the outboard. But anything on the right side and behind him was limited or impossible. He let go of the tiller arm momentarily to see if he could use two hands on the weapon. The boat tracked true, but as soon as he released the throttle grip, the engine began to slow. Dead man's throttle, he thought. But he just might have to let go to do anything.

"Come on, Amato! Come on! Here I am!" he shouted.

With the forty-five degree angle set by their respective courses, Buck and the cruiser drew apart rapidly. The distance between them expanded to half a mile. Was it possible? he wondered, could it be that Amato hadn't seen him take off? What could he do now, wave a flag? He angled slightly to the right, to keep the gap from growing too large and to try to regain sight of the speedboat. There was nothing more he could do—simply wait and see. Surely Amato wouldn't pass up this chance to finish him. He wished he had pulled away from the company boat on the right side, the same side Amato was on, so he would have been more visible. But he had thought at the time that he would try to draw Amato as far as possible from the company boat before he was caught. It would buy them some time.

He followed the new course for a minute or two, glancing back and to the right frequently for any sign of Amato's boat. Then, as he looked at *Miss Essee* again, he saw that something had changed. Her attitude in the water was different, almost level, and there was no wake showing behind her. A hideous thought descended on Buck like an ugly, black shadow.

"The cruiser's not moving—dead in the water!" he said aloud. "They're getting shot to pieces, and here I sit, the only one left to shoot back. Here I sit—in *their* lifeboat! I'm not a decoy! I'm a damned runaway coward!"

The anger raged in Buck's gut as he turned toward the cruiser. He was beyond the half-mile point now, and that meant something over a precious minute. Could they last? Could they survive another minute of rapid fire automatics? He twisted the throttle harder, but there was no more there. He forced himself to sidestep the anger and panic by weighing his options. If Amato and his buddy were where he thought they were, sitting off to the starboard side like before, maybe—it was worth a try.

As he drew to within a few hundred yards of *Miss Essee*, he angled the small boat to the right, continuing on behind the cruiser before turning left to cross to its starboard side. Sure enough, there sat the raider boat, its two remaining combatants firing at the cruiser. He could make out Amato standing in the rear of the cockpit, while a bigger man stood behind the wheel.

Buck had reached a critical point in his plan. Both men were occupied with their helpless target. They had missed him before. If they missed him again, he could slip across to the area behind them where he had a chance to surprise them. But if either man happened to turn in his direction in the next few seconds, they'd spot him for sure.

Instinctively, he ducked down to reduce his profile. He was confident they wouldn't hear him. The sounds of their huge engine and their firing weapons would certainly cover his engine noise, at least until he got close to them. Even after he had passed over the imaginary line extending back from the maroon speedboat, he continued on away from the battle. He had to be sure the men wouldn't pick him up with their peripheral vision.

Finally satisfied that he was comfortably behind the standing gunmen, he turned left. At his twenty knots, he closed fast on a forty-five degree angle toward the drifting raiders. With fifty yards to go, he picked up the shotgun with his right hand, switched the safety off, and cradled it in the crook of his left arm.

"Looking good, Buck," he said aloud as the range closed to thirty yards, then twenty yards. He began his sharp right turn, resting the shotgun on his tiller arm. He would do most of his aiming by how he steered the boat. The big man standing behind the wheel turned, spotted him, and spun about. Buck's boat slewed through the turn. He waited until his barrel was lined up on the boat's driver. With but a slight adjustment, he squeezed the trigger.

Powump! The recoil from the blast jerked the long-barreled weapon upward, nearly ripping it from Buck's right hand. The large man had almost brought his automatic rifle around when his face disappeared, replaced in an instant by a massive, red blotch. His huge body straightened up, posed for a moment like a damaged statue, and then coiled downward into the driver's seat like a withering vine.

Now headed directly away from the maroon boat, Buck guessed that his action would bring Amato scurrying to the right side of his boat. He pulled hard on the tiller, cranking the small boat into a sharp left turn, a course that would bring him back across the bow of the raider boat. Just as he completed the turn, Buck saw curious little geysers spurting up from the ocean around him. Amato was all over him! Several slugs penetrated the thin aluminum skin of his craft.

He ducked, ignoring the spouts of water pouring into his boat, turned again sharply to his left, and quickly scooted the remaining twenty yards back to Amato's boat, to the safety of Amato's blind spot. Chopping the throttle, he ground the gearshift into reverse for braking and eased directly under the long bow of the drifting cigarette boat. He shifted into neutral, stood up and grabbed the mooring ring at the bow point of the larger boat. Holding himself closely against its hull, with the wide foredeck overhanging above him, there was no way Amato could sight in on him from the cockpit.

Already, the water had risen to his shoe tops. He knew he'd have to hurry. Careful to stay in under the overhanging deck, he twisted his boat around until it was nestled tightly against the port side of the maroon hull and pointed in the same direction. Quickly, he released his grip on the speedboat, grabbed the Browning, and pumped a fresh shell into the chamber. Bracing himself, he picked a spot at the water line, well back from the sleek point of the bow.

Powump! Click, click. Powump! Tucked in as he was in the concave shape of the speedboat's hull, the twelve-gauge blasts slammed against Buck's ear drums like heavy, wooden planks. A jagged six-inch hole appeared with the first shot; it grew to nearly ten inches with the second. Buck dropped the shotgun against the forward bench seat, pulled the gear shift into forward, and gave the outboard full throttle. Now, he thought, stay directly in front of that big bow as long as you can. That's his blind spot.

The sudden burst of power lifted Buck's bow as he expected. But he hadn't expected fifty gallons of renegade water to rush to the back of the boat. A familiar chill ran up his spine. The boat mushed through the water, its bow high in the air, its rear bench seat barely above the surprising flood that was over half-way up to Buck's knees. The engine labored, but the boat barely moved.

"Damn!" Buck swore. "He'll cut me to pieces!"

Come on, he thought, get control here. Think! Suddenly, the most insignificant piece of trivia that had ever touched Buck's life came to mind—a trick old Swen, a fishing resort owner, had shown him many years before. It was a quick but delicate way to drain water from the bottom of a boat. He bent over and reached down into the water at the base of the transom, groping for the removable drain plug. His fingers located it, released the small lever, and began to wiggle the rubber plug from its hole.

Concentrating on his task, Buck unintentionally turned the boat slightly to the right. The water rolled quickly to that side, tipping the boat and briefly dipping the right gunwhale below the ocean surface, nearly capsizing the boat. He stiffened and quickly corrected with the tiller arm. The water sloshed to the left, nearly rolling him over in the opposite direction.

"Woof!" he exhaled. "Too close that time!" After a series of over-corrections, each of which sent the threatening cascade rolling, he managed to free the plug. If I'm not going fast enough for the venturi effect, I just sank myself, he thought. Expecting to see water rushing in through the drain port, Buck was ecstatic when a small whirlpool developed just inside of it. Incredible, Swen, he thought. It works! Now, if he could just keep the boat right-side-up while he siphoned all the water out— Balancing precariously on the bench seat, he forced his mind beyond the panic once again.

He was now about a hundred yards in front of the larger boat, which had not yet taken up the chase. Why not? he wondered. Probably Amato. He has to get that big guy out of the driver's seat, and then, simple as it is, he's got to figure out how to run that boat. Should see him moving pretty soon. If Buck could squeeze out another minute, he should have his speed and control back. The shotgun would be no help after soaking in that water.

His confidence grew as the bow came steadily down and his speed increased. By the time Amato headed out after him, Buck had a lead of almost three hundred yards. Only a couple of inches of water remained, sloshing about harmlessly in the bottom of the boat. As the speedboat closed the gap, Buck studied its attitude in the water. It looked like a normal planing attitude. He couldn't be sure. But the lateral see-saw motion of the boat told him that Amato had no experience. He was over-controlling like a beginner.

"Come on, Cobra!" Buck found himself yelling. "The playing field's level now. But it's *my* field!"

The moment of moments had arrived—the resolution that ditchings, beatings, and bombs had demanded! He set his plan in motion as Amato drew to within fifty yards. At that range the big bow of the maroon speedboat created a blind spot for its driver. Buck looked back. Sure enough, he could no longer see Amato, and that meant Amato couldn't see him. He turned sharply to the right. Amato reacted in a couple of seconds and turned to cut him off. Buck swiveled hard to the left. Amato continued straight, bouncing across both segments of Buck's wake before he seemed to realize what had happened.

As Amato turned left to follow, Buck focused on the hole he had blasted. It was a little higher than he'd have preferred, but on the sharp left turn it was catching water. He repeated the sequence three times, feint right—turn hard left. Occasionally, on his bluff to the right or his bigger turn to the left, he gave Amato too much of a target, but the little man was too busy managing his big vehicle to shoot with any accuracy. As long as Buck kept the crazy chase working to the left, he was accomplishing two things. In addition to protecting himself from the slashing fire of the assault weapon, he was forcing the damaged port side of the chase boat to scoop more and more water from the sea.

With each successful maneuver, the powerful raider boat rode a little lower in the water and Buck's confidence soared higher. After weeks of reacting to surprises, he was now in complete control, dictating the course of events. Despite all his firepower, Amato was helpless. The sleek boat no longer planed lightly over the surface. It plowed heavily, barely able to keep up with the small, white boat.

I've got a cobra in a tub, Buck thought. Let's play *Tip the Tub*. He repeated his feint to the right, but he maintained that course a little longer than in his previous moves. We'll give him a little time to think. Now—let's see if he was thinking. Buck began his sweeping left turn. As he expected, Amato reacted immediately, slashing viciously to his left to cut Buck off, to keep him on the right side, the driver's side, where he'd be an easy target.

As Amato began his turn, the maroon boat tilted sharply up on its left side as it had before. But instead of holding that position through the turn, the boat continued to roll on over, the left side disappearing until the bottom of the hull became the top. Their propellers slicing air, the engines screamed as the big maroon turtle splashed to a stop. Then the engines quit, and it began sinking stern first.

Buck circled as the maroon and gold bow slipped beneath the oily slick. Was it better, he asked himself, for Amato to drown? Or should he come up and accidentally get run over by Buck's boat? The Cobra never surfaced. Though he had pronounced the snake dead, Buck found himself circling the spot several times. He needed to be certain. The rite of victory gave him a lift, but the assurance that Amato would never again injure or kill anyone took front and center in Buck's mind.

But then, a glance at *Miss Essee* sobered him sharply, indeed refueled

the fears and tension. Sunny—Peter—Skids— Were they alive or—
He wheeled about and headed for the stricken vessel that now drifted
aimlessly a half-mile away. The more he thought of Sunny, the tighter
the vise of fear squeezed. Through the fight, indeed through all the trials of recent weeks he'd felt no fear like *this*.

Shortly, he bumped against the diving platform, grabbed a railing,
and pulled himself up out of the battle-scarred, little boat. He quickly
tied it to the cruiser and, shotgun in hand, climbed up on deck. It was
quiet. It was eery. No engines, no voices. Like a ship of the dead. No,
he thought. No—no—no! He dropped the Browning and ran for the
battered lounge.

Chapter 40

Buck's shout stuck in his throat as he ran for the lounge. He jerked the door open and stopped, petrified by what he saw. The large blood stain at his feet trailed toward a huge pile of furniture in the center of the cabin. He looked to the starboard side where he saw two splintered tables, propped on edge against the outside wall, obviously an improvised cherrywood barrier against the onslaught of the automatic weapons. The entire starboard side, paneling and windows alike, had been shredded.

Bullet holes, what seemed like hundreds of them, spoke silently of death.

He shuffled slowly forward, his energy sapped, his gut churning a nauseous chant. *Nobody* could have lived through that—*nobody!* He stopped and stared hopelessly at the mound of luxurious rubble, his numbed mind locked on one track. I should have *been* here. *I'm* the cause of all this, and I should have *been* here. If she's gone I'm as good as dead—I'm over the side.

"Dad?" a tiny voice whispered. "Is that you, Dad?"

His heart picked up briefly and then sagged. Toughen up, Buck, he thought. You're hearing what you *want* to hear! Drawing closer to the piled furniture, he saw a pattern. The chairs lay on their sides two rows deep, forming a U-shaped barricade with a space in the center. Is it possible? he asked himself.

"Dad, I need you," came the voice again.

The despair drained from him like water through a sieve. He stepped quickly to the barricade. There in the center lay Peter, on his back and bare to his waist but for a heavy bandage wrapped around his midsection. His squinting eyes seemed to be focused on the ceiling. Beside him sat Sunny, cross-legged on the carpet, hunched over with her chin in one hand while the other hand pressed on the thicker portion of the bandage on Peter's side. She looked up. Her face was drawn, her eyes dull, and beneath her right eye was a large, purple patch, the beginning of a real shiner.

"Hurry, Dad! Take my place holding this. If I don't get to the john *right now*—"

Sunny was alive! Peter was alive! But the greeting threw him for a moment, and he hesitated. Then he darted around to the far side, the entrance to the blue barricade. He reached down to pull her to her feet, his only thought—to hug her. Instead, Sunny pulled him down beside her. She took his hand and carefully placed it over her other hand.

"There, right there. Now, spread your fingers between mine. Okay, now very gently, press. Not too hard. There, that feels right."

With that, she jumped up and scurried down the steps. Buck heard the door slam. He looked down at his friend. Peter's dark eyes tilted his way, and a weak smile crossed his lips.

"Good job, Buck," he murmured. His eyes closed.

"You going to make it?" Buck asked, looking at the blood-stained bandage beneath his fingertips.

"Yes." Peter's face was as expressionless as his answer.

"You damned well better," said Buck. "I'd hate to think you'd cop out on me after all this." A thousand questions bubbled toward the overflow point, but he knew he'd have to wait. "Looks like your scrambling didn't work this time. You got sacked big time."

"My blocker—was out—messing around—at the pool. Buck, get us home?"

Buck felt the movement in Peter's side with each word.

"Done," Buck said. "Now you just shut up and lie still."

When Sunny returned, she carried two blankets. She covered Peter and then perched herself on the arm of an overturned chair. Buck reached up with his free hand. She took it and squeezed.

"You okay?" he asked.

"Compared to all the other times I've done this? Yeah—I'm okay," she said dryly, giving his hand another squeeze.

"Is Skids? . . ." Buck couldn't get the word out.

"Not exactly okay," she replied, "but he's far from dead. I don't think they could kill him with a thousand Uzis, or whatever they were. He's in your class, Dad, one tough dude."

"So where—"

"Oh, he's down below trying to fix the engines. Careful, Dad, keep the pressure steady. When the engines quit, he came tearing down those steps. He said he couldn't do any more good up there. I'd swear it didn't take him thirty seconds to drag Peter over here, build this fort around him, rip those tables loose and prop them against the wall. Next thing I knew, he was over there," she said, pointing to one of the tables, "reloading an empty clip."

"And you were here with Peter?" Buck asked.

"Skids put me in the chicken coop with Peter, but somehow I ended up at the other window with a rifle. Dad," she paused, "those big things really *kick,* don't they?"

"That where the black eye came from?"

"Just couldn't seem to get it right." She smiled impishly down at Buck.

"Found out how thick those table tops are, though."

"Who did the job on Peter?"

"Skids did that. Then he showed me how to apply the pressure. I think the bleeding's stopped." She released Buck's hand and jabbed a finger into her side, just below the ribs. "The wound is right about here. Skids says it went in from the front. He thinks it's far enough to the side to miss everything."

"And Skids? He got hit?" Buck asked.

"Twice," she said, "plus a splinter in his cheek. After we saw you sink Amato, he had me pull the splinter and bandage him up. Sure doesn't bleed much. Probably got ice water in him."

"Not a nice thing to say about a warm, compassionate old sailor," came a deep voice.

Buck turned to see the lanky man, clad only in blue boxer shorts, a blood-stained white T-shirt, and once-white deck shoes limp up the steps from the lower level. His left thigh was heavily bandaged. A gauze bandage was wrapped around his head covering one ear. One cheek sported a square bandage, secured by tape crossed in an X. Buck motioned for Sunny to take his place with Peter. He got up to shake Skids's hand. The grip, the look in the man's eyes—Buck felt like he'd known Skids all his life.

"Thanks," he said. "Thanks so very much. If there's ever—"

"No time for speeches right now," Skids cut in. "Still got a long walk home."

"Okay, you're the skipper. What's our situation?"

"I think we'll have power again, ready to go up and try the engines. There was a broken fuel line. I spliced it together. It reeks of fuel oil down there. Don't know if it's from the broken line or if they punched holes in our tanks. No way to tell. Fuel gauges are shot out. So, even if we have power, don't know how far we'll get." Skids shrugged, palms up.

"Something we got to take care of before we get underway. Come on."

Buck followed Skids up to the pilot house. He felt a chill when he looked down at the curled up body of Larry lying on the upper deck. Working together, he and Skids half-dragged, half-carried the body down to a bunk at the lower level, stretched it out respectfully, and covered it with a blanket. As Buck turned to leave, he saw tears trailing down Skid's face. The tall man reached down to touch his friend.

"Don't make sense, Larry," he said. "After all the times we got shot at over there, I got to lose you—like *this?*"

Buck retreated silently up the two flights of steps to the upper level.

Moments later, he heard footsteps, and Skids popped energetically into the pilot house. He started the engines, then rolled his eyes.

"Boy, that's a relief!" he said. "The bilge pumps would have killed the batteries in another hour, and then—" He eased the twin throttles ahead, and the cruiser came to life. "Strange," he said, "they're runnin' fine, but she's not takin' off like she should."

"We're dragging a sea anchor behind us," Buck offered. "The little boat's full of water. Should I go cut it loose?"

"No, we might need it. Have to use your trick again," Skids said. He backed off on the throttles.

"I'll run down and see that it's tracking right-side-up," Buck said.

He hurried down the steps and back to the stern. For the first time, he realized that his shoes squished with each step. He realized his mind was just catching up. The little white boat trailed behind, upright but very low in the water. The gunwhales were barely above sea level. He climbed down on the diving platform, checked the rope, and signaled Skids to increase their speed. In minutes, the small craft had drained enough water to convert from a submarine to a surface vessel once again, and Buck returned to the pilot house.

"The water's down to about six inches," he told Skids.

"Good. We'll drain that in no time." He advanced the throttles to the three-quarter point, and *Miss Essee* went up just short of full-planing. "About the best speed to make headway and save on fuel."

"Okay," Buck said, "what else do I need to know?"

"The good news," the skipper began, "Engines runnin' good. Bilge pumps seem to be keepin' up with what's comin' in through the holes. Peter's bleeding has stopped. And we put out a bunch of Maydays."

"And the bad news?"

"We're about a hundred and fifty miles out. No idea how much fuel we got. Don't know if coast guard heard our calls. Be hittin' heavy fog inside of three hours. Dark in five. And we've got no lights."

Buck picked up on the strength in the sailor's bass voice, but he also caught the tension in his face as he spoke.

"What else can I do?" Buck asked.

"Sometimes, things that ought to be said don't get said, and then it's too late," Skids began. "Now that we're movin', there's a little time to talk."

Buck heard a rustling noise and turned. Sunny had joined them.

"I think Peter's okay. He's sleeping now," she said.

"You know," Skids continued, "you two Barnums saved our bacon today. And this little gal," he nodded Sunny's way, "she's a real fighter. Any more like you two in the family?"

Sunny looked at Buck and grinned, "One more," she said, "and he's the meanest one. Right, Dad?"

Buck smiled and nodded.

"Christ, that must be some family. You all live under the same roof?"

"Sometimes," Buck said with a smirk.

Skids looked at him quizzically. "Well, you guys—your whole family can sail with me anytime. Buck, that was a hell of a show you put on out there. Wish we'd had you over in the Mekong. You're good. You know somethin'? I never believed much in that spooky communication stuff." He paused to make a three hundred-sixty degree scan of the horizon. "But when you pulled away from that boat and almost got swamped—"

"He's down there watching, Dad," Sunny interrupted with a laugh, "and he's yelling, 'Pull the plug, Buck! Pull the plug!' You couldn't have heard him from there, but that's just what you did! Somehow, you heard him?"

"I thought at the time it was old Swen, but—"

Skids and Sunny glanced at each other.

"Uh, Skids?" Buck asked, "how about you? How bad are those?" Buck motioned to the bandaged areas.

"Oh, this one," the lanky sailor said, pointing to his head, "took a little chunk out where the ear hooks on. The thigh? Hit mostly flesh I guess, maybe some muscle. It is—startin' to bite pretty good."

Buck studied the tall man. He was pale, and his movements suggested that he was beginning to feel woozy.

"That daughter of yours, she should go into medicine. Did a *hell* of a job!" Skids said.

"Sure did," Sunny said. "When I looked at his ear, I threw up."

"No doctor," said Buck. "She wants to be a cop." He watched Skids closely.

"Well, she might be all right there, too, as long as they don't hand her a .30-06," Skids snorted. He turned and looked down over his shoulder at Sunny. "You? A cop?"

"I *had* considered it," she said seriously, "but that was a long time ago."

"At the moment," Buck said, with a nod toward Skids, "you are back to playing Nurse Jennifer. This guy's about to go out on us. He needs rest."

"Yeah," Skids agreed, to Buck's surprise, "I think you're right. Here, take over, Buck."

"How do I navigate?" Buck asked.

"Short term, watch your wake. Keep it straight. Long term, watch the sun. See where it is now?"

Buck turned. He looked up and back over his right shoulder.

"Okay, it's sixteen hundred hours right now. Imagine the arc the sun'll follow as it finishes comin' down to the horizon. It's going to take about four hours, and you want to make her splash dead astern. If you only watch the wake, you could make a long, slow turn and not know it. There's a Very pistol in that little cabinet," he added, pointing across the pilot house. "See anything, boat, plane, or mosquito, shoot that sucker off."

"Got it," Buck said. "Now get down there and sack out. You see that he does, Sunny."

Skids started down the steps, stopped, and turned. "Oh, be careful you don't hit any other boats. Grigsby'll take it out of your wages."

When the two had gone below, Buck checked their course by wake and sun several times. Feeling more confidence in his navigation, he began to assess the situation. They were in good hands with Skids, but what if *he* conked out? He was hurting a lot more than he let on. That'd leave everything to Buck. What did he know? How to steer it, change speeds, stop the engines, and find the Very pistol. Didn't even know how to shoot it. What else did Skids say? Buck couldn't remember. Oh yeah, going to hit fog. How did he know *that?*

Buck slid the bullet-punctured starboard window open, leaned over and smelled the cool, fresh air. He thought, *fog?* Not a cloud in the sky, bright sun, no wind. *Fog?* Buck hoped he was wrong on that one. He checked his course frequently. But as the time wore on, his mind circled continually on the things that could go wrong. They run out of fuel—Skids dies—Peter dies—the bilge pumps quit and they sink—they hit the fog and get off course—they have engine trouble—or fire.

From time to time, he dragged himself up and out of the negative quicksand. But each ascent was short-lived. Alternately, he scolded himself for worrying, then acknowledged that he had little else to do, then worried some more. He scanned the pilot house, the bullet holes in the glass and walls, the mangled instrument panel, and the large blotch of dried blood on the deck. As time wore on, Buck settled on the fact that they were at risk—*great* risk.

Just after seventeen hundred hours, Sunny brought him dry clothes and shoes, a sandwich, and a beer. She took the wheel while he changed. He wiped down with a damp towel she had brought along, and he felt refreshed. Then, she stood to his left, scanning the sea and chattering as he ate. While her voice was comforting, it reminded Buck that his precious daughter was indeed there, trapped in a threatening situation in which she didn't belong.

"How's Peter?" he asked.

"Still sleeping, seems okay. His breathing sounds normal."

"Skids?"

"He said he'd go down below and curl up in a bunk, but he came right back up with a blanket and a pillow. Probably because Larry's down there. Skids is stretched out on the lounge floor. Seems to be having bad dreams, though. I keep covering him up, and he keeps kicking the blanket off. I know he said to wake him in an hour, but I just can't do it."

"No need for him yet," Buck said. "Give him some more time. Could be that one that creased his head hit harder than he's letting on. And—he just lost a close friend."

"You're—you're really up tight, aren't you, Dad?" she asked.

"Sunny, you know your dad is always in complete control, confident, and afraid of nothing," Buck replied. He turned and looked into her eyes. "Fact is, I'm so scared the B-Bs in my gourd are rattling."

"I'd really worry about you if you weren't," she said. "But I'm not sure I understand. Back there, you took on Amato and his men. Now, you sit here, high and dry."

"Back there I had some options. I could do something about the situation. Here, it's like holding my breath for six hours waiting for the guillotine to fall. Nothing I can do about anything. I don't like being that helpless, especially when *you're* trapped here, too."

Sunny moved over, put her arms around his shoulders, and hugged him.

"Daddy," she said softly, "I'd never volunteer for a situation like this, but since I'm in it, there's nobody I'd rather have trying to get me out of it."

She leaned around and kissed him on the forehead. "Now, the old cliché, 'Prepare for the worst and hope for the best.' What can I do to help?"

"Damn, maybe you *should* be a cop," Buck said. "Your watch still working?"

"Why, ah, yes. It's five-thirty."

"Okay, here's your assignment. Go down and close all the windows—what's left of them. Even with all those holes in them, it'll help. Cooling off fast, and we don't want to chill our patients. Oh, get some warm clothes on those guys. Then see if you can find any flashlights. Round up all the life jackets. By eighteen hundred hours, by six o'clock, I want everybody in one with a spare handy. Pack as much food as you can, fill everything you can find that will hold water, and put them out on the rear deck. Then, make sure you've all eaten as much as you can."

Buck stopped suddenly, surprised at the orderly sequence that had just poured from his mind. He smiled at Sunny. "When we hit that fog, or when the sun goes down, I want to know we've done everything possible to be ready—for whatever. Beyond that?" He simply shrugged.

"That's a tall order, captain," she said, saluting. "But I can handle it." She turned toward the steps. "By the way, what am I, a sea attendant or a stewardess?"

He heard her skip lightly down the steps. *Real* or *bravado?* he wondered. Did it really matter? But, he thought, that little conference *did* help. Even those limited preparations eliminate a few unknowns, give us some small influence on the outcome. He turned around to check the wake and then the sun. Everything as it should be.

Up ahead, he saw a large, low cloud bank, barely above the horizon, that extended from left to right as far as he could see. Looks like those clouds are about fifty miles ahead, he thought. Could that be the fog Skids talked about? He checked his watch. Nearly 1800 hours. Something over two hours of light left. Okay, Barnum, he mused, you've still got some time. Figure it out.

Assume that *is* the fog. So? He realized that, up to the moment, they'd had only one course in mind, continue on their southeasterly course toward L.A. Now, with that immense, ominous barrier rising before him, Buck found himself contemplating other possibilities.

Option One—Stay on our present course. The pluses are? Shortest distance to home. Minuses? Not the shortest distance to land, going to be hard to stay on course in that fog, and if the coast guard heard Skids and comes looking for us, they won't find us in the fog. He shuddered at the last thought. Options?

Second Option—head due east to the closest land. Pluses? That's it, closest land. Minuses? Still in the fog, trying to hold our course and help coast guard find us.

Third Option—turn right and head south, paralleling the fog bank. Pluses? We're at least heading south, we can see, and coast guard could see us—*if* they're out here. That's a hell of an *if*, he concluded. Minuses? We'd be visible, but we'd actually be moving farther from the coast, betting the last of our fuel that they're out looking for us.

Damn! he thought, those three choices aren't much better than the fourth—do a one-eighty and head for Tokyo. He leaned forward instinctively, as though it would help him to examine the misty adversary. With nothing for reference, the distance was hard to judge, but—

"Oh, my God!" Buck exclaimed as feathery tendrils drifted past the pilot house. "We're *in* it! That wasn't clouds. It's the fog!"

In but seconds, the bow of the cruiser all but disappeared from view. Buck had completely misjudged the distance to the fog bank. He turned the wheel hard to the right. The cruiser leaned over. He heard a thumping sound behind him.

"Where is he, Buck? Where is he?" Skids shouted as he limped past Buck to the cabinet and grabbed the Very pistol. "Take her on around! Get us out of this soup!"

"Where is *who*?"

"You don't *hear* it?"

"Hear *what*?"

"The chopper! I can pick one up five miles away!" Skids shouted. Just as *Miss Essee* retreated from the threatening fog, Skids reached out through the starboard window and fired. Things were happening too fast for Buck's tired mind. Slowly the implications of Skids's behavior began to filter through his private fog. And when Buck picked up the *slap—slap—slap* of the rotor blades, he cut the throttle, heaved a sigh of relief, and slumped back in his seat. As he watched the miniature comet arc through the blue Pacific sky, he felt heavy but comfortable fatigue wash away the tension.

Twenty minutes later, the coast guard helicopter crewmen had in turn hoisted Larry's body, Peter, and Skids aloft. The downdraft from the hovering chopper blew Buck's hair wildly as he watched Sunny ride the cable upward. The crewmen above pulled her in through the large side opening, and she waved at Buck with a thumbs-up gesture that said, "Come on!"

Now, he thought—*now*—I can relax! She's safe. He looked around at the bullet holes, the shattered plexiglass, the wrecked instrument panel, and the stain on the floor. I really got in over my head on this one, and for *what?* I guess I'm back starting over again. One giant thing about it, though. After all this, I think I could be happy pushing a broom—as long as there's nobody riding on it. He smiled as he recalled Sunny's thumbs up gesture. Yeah, I could push a broom, and I'll bet I could be pretty good at it, too.

Epilogue

"We hope you've enjoyed our little afternoon mini-cruise today," Buck Barnum said. "When you take delivery of your *own* new yacht, the good times will *really* begin," he added, returning from the bar with fresh drinks for his two guests. "And I think you can now see," he continued, looking across the luxurious, kidney-shaped marble table at the huge, bald-shaven basketball player, Quintaine Paxby, "why you will pull into any harbor in the world and be extremely proud of your 150-footer."

Turning his attention to the giant's diminutive manager, he added, "And you'll be doubly proud of the fact that you spent a million less than the only man in the harbor with a unit that's in any way comparable to yours. You're never going to regret having made *this* investment!"

As the pasty-looking manager smiled and nodded agreement, the director of marketing for Southern California Boatbuilding Company went on, "Now, the hull will soon be ready, so we need to complete your selections from among your decorating options. These are the things that will mean the most to your wife, your mother, and *other* female guests," he said, tongue in cheek, as he looked across at the dainty gold earring in the giant's ear.

"Nothin' too good for *my* ladies," the massive man said, his smile stretching back almost to the ornament.